Four

FOUR (The Republic 2)
By Archer Kay Leah

Published by Ashborne Stardust Press

Second edition, January 2020
First published by Less Than Three Press, 2016

Cover designed by Natasha Snow Designs;
www.natashasnowdesigns.com

Map designed by Raelynn Marie

Print ISBN 978-1-9992029-9-6

Content Notes, Warnings, and Disclaimers

Four contains some explicit content, all of which is meant for adult readers. The relationship at the heart of the story is an MM romance. There is a minor amount of MF and MMF intimacy included, but this is not an MMF poly romance.

This story contains emotional and physical situations that could bother some readers, including references to and depictions of self-harm, depression, and complex PTSS/PTSD (post-traumatic stress syndrome/disorder). The story also contains mentions of human trafficking, torture in a character's past, gang matters and violence, discussions of an execution by way of stoning, and references to an accident in a character's past that resulted in a loved one being left paralyzed.

Please note the story uses gender-neutral pronouns for certain characters (*vir, they, them, their*). These are not mistakes: they are the chosen pronouns of those characters.

To Victoria. Thanks for being a cheerleader, beta, reader, fan, and all that good stuff. You're amazing and help keep me going! But thanks most for being a friend. <3

Also to Jaymes, aka Spawn. Without you, the Eseldeer seeing stones wouldn't have been a thing. One comment from you in a meeting with the grove filled in the all those details I was stuck on. Thanks, kid, and keep up that wise thinking. It's a true joy to know you!

And for Megan, for supporting these guys and this book all these years. It's meant everything and more, and I hope you'll still love them until the very end. <3

Four

THE REPUBLIC BOOK 2

ARCHER KAY LEAH

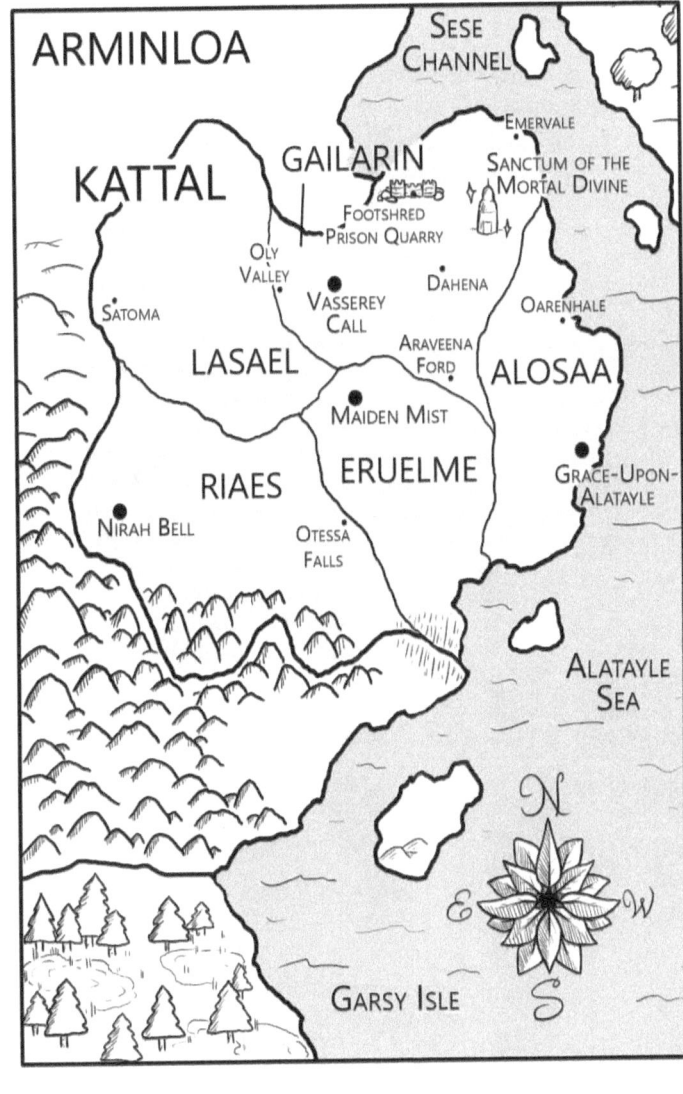

Chapter One

If this was how his afternoon off was going to play out, Mayr was more than ready to drag his sorry ass back to work. At least he could have had both his hands back.

As it was, he was all but forced into being Head of the Guard right then, stuck in the middle of the road between two of the feistiest offenders responsible for the mess they were in. With one of his hands holding tight to each of their foreheads, he kept the men apart as they snapped and snarled, daring to go through him just to get at one another. Onlookers gathered around them, lining the side of the red dirt road and slowly forming a lopsided circle, their whispers almost as irritating as the fading shouts of the commotion.

And just *what* was that stickiness on the younger guy's face? Its dusty grittiness grazed Mayr's palm, but the stench of ale wafted around the man—a strong brew, and one of Orae's finest offerings, imported to her tavern at great cost.

That just aggravated Mayr more, knowing how much Orae spent on the shipments, only to have some whelp barely out of adolescence practically bathe in it and get into a fight nearly thirty feet away from her very door.

Though if they made him miss his meeting with Sarene…

"Would you settle it down already?" Mayr bellowed, squeezing the men's foreheads until they cursed and swatted his arms away. Both stumbled back, glaring at him, no doubt ready to tear into him for stopping their brawl. But as the ale-doused man glanced towards the two women behind Mayr, his sneer slid into a grimace, then a sloppy, apologetic smile before he wiped his wrist across his split lips. He backed away, hands raised as he nodded at Mayr, the messy fringe of his bright orange-gold hair falling into his bloodshot eyes.

"'It's fine, 's fine. Sorry." Staggered steps took the man closer to his friend, another young man with shaggy brown hair and dark eyes who only whispered, "*Quit it, Raine,*" before ducking away from Mayr's gaze—likely to hide the glazed look in his eyes from whatever drug he had used, the rest of which was probably in the back pocket of his too-tight trousers if not in his boot. A good pat down would turn it out.

And absolutely none of it is my bloody responsibility. Mayr gritted his teeth and flicked the loose braid of his black hair back over his shoulder, then swung his attention to the three men to his right. They were older than Raine and his companion to Mayr's left, at least by five years, judging by their features. Though with how red the face had gone of the brawny, curly-haired one who Mayr could only assume was their lead fool, they might as well have all been eighteen and begging for the ass-kicking of their life. *That* he could help them with... if only he had the time, and maybe the interest. And the likes of Stuck and Keyer by his side, ready to haul them to the magistrate by the ear.

Yet all he had was himself, assuming he continued to ignore the few Kattal soldiers in the crowd. They watched, though, and seemed ready to act if given the command despite being off duty and late to the altercation. A quick glimpse of their hands at their swords and knives said all he needed.

Timing. He needed to work on having bad timing.

"Right." Mayr crossed his arms over his chest, the edges of his black leather bracers digging into his forearms just under the turned-up cuffs of his thin black shirt. Ear turned slightly to Tiele and Haddie as they continued to linger behind him, their whispers inaudible but close, he cast his glare to the left then the right. "So you're brawling in public *because*?"

"Handsy," Raine answered, his tan skin reddened with a deepening flush. "Getting handsy. With the ladies." He flicked his chin towards the group to Mayr's right. "Last I checked, *stop* and *leave us alone* meant piss right off. They needed redmindi... redminers... re—" Raine frowned. "We helped," he finished with a shrug and another look at Tiele and Haddie.

"We were bloody well not!" A snarl came from the man Raine had been punching and kicking before Mayr stepped in between them. "And *helped*, my ass, you tit-shriveling bastard—"

The man launched forward, hands out, ready to attack Raine again as one of his friends shouted, "*Dammit, Vedan!*"

One step too many saw Vedan landing face-first on the road, mostly due to Mayr tripping him with a swift kick at the knees.

Groans and gasps sounded from the crowd. They moved back, fingers at their lips, more than one onlooker covering their face and shaking their head.

Yeah, exactly. Mayr eyed Vedan's friends, one brow arched. Both men shrank back with their hands raised, giving him the same frantic head shake. Sweat beaded on their foreheads from the late-summer heat if not from the thought of being thrown into a cell and left for solitary confinement.

Working for the Tract Steward of Gailarin *did* have its advantages.

Except Mayr was supposed to be taking a break from that work—Aeley Dahe's very orders, in fact. Something about Mayr having a life instead of hiding behind the Dahe family's guard and telling life to shove itself into the nearest corner and stop sniveling.

Aeley knew him all too well, especially when he was still suffering from a broken heart.

A confused, hopeful heart that was *supposed* to be preparing for a meeting with Sarene, who had called off their relationship weeks ago, leaving him for some new conquest he never wanted to meet. But Sarene had wanted to talk, and talk meant… something. He had no idea what, but her message to him had sounded optimistic, almost as if she was going to…

Mayr grunted and nudged Vedan's leg with the toe of his boot. "You, up." He was *not* having this today. If he wanted to school headstrong fools about behaving, he would have hauled his newest recruits into an impromptu training session. His only reason for wandering down to the village had been to see Sarene—and maybe to check on Orae and her staff since he visited the tavern enough to consider it a third home.

Meanwhile, Orae was standing in the front entry of the tavern, a thick green towel slung over her one shoulder, the long braid of her snow-white hair twisted over her other shoulder, and her dark brown gaze as prodding as the smirk on her lips. Around her, three of her serving women haunted the doorway, all of them waving at him as they caught his glance.

He hated having an audience.

"We weren't doing a damn thing." Vedan stood and brushed the dirt off his clothes, then tousled the tight, finger-length curls of his disheveled, dusky brown hair. "It's not like we had our cocks out. We kept them tucked." He smiled too sweetly, only to leer at Tiele and Haddie. "They wanted our attention, so we gave it. Not our fault if they couldn't handle us."

Vedan's wink had Mayr just about ready to feed said cocks through Orae's meat grinder.

Mayr stepped directly between the women and Vedan, his hand on the hilt of the short sword strapped to his waist. Grinding his teeth, he turned towards Tiele and Haddie. "Is that what happened?" Mayr asked quietly, meeting their hesitant gazes before noting how tightly they held each other's hands.

Both Tiele and Haddie nodded, though the taller of the two—Haddie—pinned an icy glare of her own on Vedan over Mayr's shoulder. They were barely twenty-five, both of them from families on the outer edges of Dahena Village. With one hand, Haddie kept a tight grip on a green wicker picnic basket, its lid open just enough to reveal beige linens and a stopped bottle. Next to her, Tiele clutched a worn blue book and a bouquet of pale orange flowers, delicate pink blossoms, and fern fronds, all tied with narrow yellow ribbon.

"We were going about our business, minding our own, and now we're everyone's noontime entertainment," Haddie muttered, flicking her plaited black hair over her shoulder, its length almost a match to Mayr's. As the thin fabric of her cream-coloured shawl slipped down her arm, she tugged it up and rolled her shoulders back, her chin lifted. Her gaze met Mayr's as she scowled, her umber-brown eyes almost as dark as her skin. "They weren't welcome to touch, but they did it anyway, even after I told them to fall down a well." She tipped her head towards Vedan, then Raine. "The cocky one landed the first punch. Those guys were trying to get them to stop."

Tiele nodded, the teased fringe of her blonde hair swaying with the movement. With her bottom lip caught between her teeth, she played with the chain link belt around her waist, wrapping the trailing end around her fingers. Her golden-brown complexion looked paler the tighter she coiled the silver chain, and she hugged the flowers to her chest, the depth to her blue-grey gaze similar to that of Mayr's sister.

"Are you all right, Tiele?" Mayr asked softly. When Tiele nodded again and leaned into Haddie, one arm wrapped around Haddie's back, Mayr cast a quick glance over his shoulder. "I'm sending them to Dreca so he can deal with this. What happens now is up to him, being village magistrate, but if you tell him what happened, he'll have a better idea of what to do. If you'd like a charge laid, he'll discuss that with you, or negotiate some form of recompense, or something else—however you'd like to handle this." He offered them a brief smile. "If you'd like, I'll have someone escort you and take the short way around—"

"Yes," both Haddie and Tiele said at the same time, Tiele looking more than a little relieved.

Mayr inclined his head, then turned on his heel, his smile traded for a *don't test me* glower—

Only to lose it the moment he glimpsed Sarene.

Across the road, well behind the crowd, she stood in the yard of the weaver's workshop, a flash of pale purple dress and a radiant, almost metallic blue sash. Her long flaxen-blonde hair was partially pulled back, twisted tight and crisscrossed with bright blue ribbons, their tightly curled ends brushing her shoulders and catching on the slightest shift of air. Standing under a tree in the midst of changing colour to the bright gold and dull orange of autumn, Sarene's dark green gaze caught Mayr by surprise.

Lust played in her eyes, the slow lick across her bottom lip saying more than a single word could have.

As quickly as she had given him up, it seemed she wanted him back.

For a kiss. A taste. A tumble between the sheets.

Goddesses, he was doomed, because that look—that *I want you, now* hanging in the silence, lewd as it was naked… it torched his nerve with memory, a spark catching on every touch, every kiss, every moan they had shared, storming through him with the crushing weight of loss and desire. Moments seared into his existence, hot as the flames he would walk into and back just for another taste of those soft lips…

Fists clenched, nails digging into his palms, Mayr managed a strained smile for Sarene—unless he had missed the mark and grimaced like the fool he was.

A talk. They were supposed to meet for a *talk*, nothing more.

And these bastards are in my damned way—literally.

But by the Four, was Vedan's smirk ever pissing him off.

"You and you—" Mayr spat out, pointing at Raine and Vedan "—here, *now*." When neither of them moved, he snapped his fingers and added a throaty growl. "Means *now, not* tomorrow," Mayr barked. "Quit wasting my time or you're seeing a prison cell."

That had both guys rushing to stand before him, Vedan caught between panic and visibly struggling to bite his tongue. Their friends followed just as quickly, stopping close enough to hear what Mayr said but far enough to stay out of his reach.

When Vedan's gaze strayed to Tiele and Haddie, Mayr got into his face, nearly stepping on Vedan's toes with barely a finger's length between their noses.

"*Me.*" Mayr snarled. "Not them. Eyes here, and only here, or I'm damn well ripping them out."

That threat landed as easily as the first, Vedan's green eyes widening before he lowered his gaze and stepped back.

Better. Mayr surveyed the crowd, on the hunt for… *Rema. Colsin. Paw. And… good. Blythe.* He narrowed his eyes. Dornes was there, too, beside Blythe, almost lost in the crowd. Three republic soldiers and two of Mayr's own guards was more than sufficient.

Making eye contact with each of them and raising one hand to their eye level, he called them forth by flicking two fingers at himself before returning to Raine and Vedan.

"First of all," Mayr said loudly, "quit the ego and keep your hands to yourself. Second, *leave us alone* means *leave us alone.* Third, I don't care who you are, or what you think you're owed, you're Magistrate Dreca's problem now."

Vedan's angry protests drowned out the murmurs of the crowd. Before Vedan could lash out with his fists, he was yanked back by Colsin, one of the highest-ranked soldiers stationed permanently in Dahena.

The moment Vedan hit Colsin, the crowd gasped—only to gawk as Colsin took him down with a leg swipe and a strong hand around the neck, forcing Vedan's head to the ground.

"Right," Colsin muttered, "a lively one." He glanced up at Mayr, one blond brow arched.

Mayr shrugged. "Take them the long way around. Get Raine sobered up—him and his friend both. They didn't start this, but they might just end it. Vedan needs cuffs. Anyone else with the same bright idea gets the same. Blythe, with me."

Blythe obeyed without question, following Mayr as he escorted Haddie and Tiele away. Quiet protests sounded behind them, but at least Vedan kept his mouth shut... for all of the time it took to drag him through the crowd.

Mayr prayed the meeting with Sarene went better than this, not that he expected much, even with her staring at him like she used to. Because the *actual* chance of her saying she wanted to get back together permanently, even if she *did* want him back in her bed...? That was a likelihood he knew better than to entertain, no matter what feeling whispered to him. She had made that painfully obvious the night she broke up with him, sending him out the door with nearly every gift he had given her shoved into a small wooden chest for him to take home—save the most expensive gifts, which she insisted were too precious to give back.

"They're sentimental," she had choked out with plenty of tears, a bracelet of tiny ice-blue pearls and white crystals in her fist, his gift to her on her last birthday; a piece he had purchased during

one of his trips with Aeley to the other regions in Kattal. That bracelet had come from a tiny, exquisite shop on the seaside in Grace-upon-Alatayle, the largest city in Alosaa, the regional tract to the east. He had laid down nearly a full tidepin for it, with extra quartermarks and fullpins for a pretty, carefully crafted wrapping just to bring the bracelet home for Sarene.

Sentimental, indeed—just another way to say *I'll sell it for all it's worth when you aren't looking.* Assuming she still had it.

He bet every bit of that foolish tidepin that it belonged to someone else now.

Prove me wrong. Please prove me wrong.

Just once he wanted to be wrong in all the right ways, especially when it came to her—or anyone else he fell in love with. Instead, *wrong* seemed to follow him into every relationship and stuck around like a curse to laugh him right on out of them.

Sighing, Mayr pinched the bridge of his nose, his eyes squeezed shut before Haddie called his name.

"Yeah, just… go with Blythe," he said quietly, opening his eyes and returning Haddie's concerned frown. "She's one of mine and Aeley's. Trained with me for the last eight years. She'll escort you to Dreca's office and stay if you want her to. I'll be along shortly, too—I'll come and support your case to Dreca. I just need to do one thing, then I'll be all yours for however long

Dreca takes to sort this." He turned to Blythe. "Short way 'round, please and thanks? I've got... something to see to." Mayr glanced over his shoulder, Sarene's dress a flicker of colour on the edge of his sight. Most of the crowd had dispersed, several onlookers lingering and talking in hushed tones, but Sarene remained under the tree, cheerful and bright, surrounded by soft warmth.

He was asking for trouble—and the most ridiculous part of him loved it all the same. No matter how anxious he was. No matter how hurt. No matter how twisted in knots his sensibilities were. Love always had its own damn mind.

And I'm absolutely doomed.

"Yeah, of course," Blythe said, raking one hand through her close-cropped, black-red hair. Dark eyes narrowed, she glanced in Sarene's direction, lips pursed. Yeah, he knew she knew, and the rest of the Dahe guards would probably know before the end of the day. Why not, considering the day after his breakup with Sarene, the guards had offered him sympathies and their shoulders to cry on, all without him mentioning it to them. Gossip was practically a sport the way the guards played it. If there was anything he hated more than being boxed in by a crowd, it was being the ball kicked around the rumour mill... an entirely different problem that dug up old feelings he had no interest in battling right then. He was supposed to be civil, not moody about a relationship long dead, the brittle skeleton clinging to his ankle, unable to completely let go...

To his relief, Blythe said nothing, just arched a brow in his direction. "Right, let's go, ladies." She gestured to the footpath to their left that curved around a carefully tended village garden and its communal well, leading from the main road to the next road over where Dreca kept his office. With smiled farewells, Haddie and Tiele followed Blythe, leaving Mayr to collect his thoughts.

He should have walked with them. Escaped with what dignity he had left. Not fought every instinct that told him to avoid Sarene. No doubt if Aeley knew what he was doing, she would have sent Pellon down to stop him—or tromped down the road herself just to give him a smack up the head and get him to see reason. For a moment, he almost looked to see if she *had* done that. A best friend's love; one he needed to keep him from making another mistake, because courting Sarene the first time...

A look behind him kicked those thoughts aside.

He was a fool, but a fool that would hear Sarene out, whatever she had to say. Their relationship had failed, and maybe that was for the best, perhaps even necessary for them both, but the hurt was still there. No anger, just a deepening loss; a grief he was never able to shake. That sense that he had ignored the signs and kept going, only to fall onto a sword never meant to protect him to begin with. Always his fault, missing the truth of what was, only to die a little more when that truth finally punched him in the gut.

But the look on her face... it pulled him in, her smile as alluring and warm as the intent in her eyes. When he offered a smile of his own—faint but genuine—Sarene's face brightened, her arms shifting around the small, sky-blue basket she carried.

Run, me. Don't do it. Just don't—

Funny, because for all the thoughts that screamed at him to do just that, Mayr's body had other plans. Before he knew it, he was walking across the road and stopping in front of Sarene.

He swore someone snickered over by Orae's tavern.

"Hey," Mayr said softly. Crossing his arms, then uncrossing them, he bit back a growl at himself, unable to keep still. "You wanted to talk?" He rubbed at his throat, only to wrap his hand around the back of his neck and hold on for lack of something better to do, fingertips digging into the black symbols tattooed around his neck.

Sarene's gaze followed his fingers, a slow, sweet smile playing up the shine in her eyes. "Well, you know..." Her quiet tone drifted into the silence. With a shrug, she met his glance, her smile melting into a sheepish blush of a thing. "I've had time to think. Get some perspective." Sarene reached up to his throat, fingertips grazing his skin, hesitant. Chilling, with all the lightness of a breeze playing with the heat. She tugged on his braid, pulling its length over his shoulder and stroking the tied end. "I miss you," she murmured, "and… I might've been wrong."

Mayr sucked in a breath. Dangerous ground…

"I… It's been a long few weeks." Sarene sighed, her fingers working up his braid to his shoulder. She stepped closer, her basket hitting his knees, the faint scent of her flowery perfume all but yanking images into his head. Her bedroom always smelled of flowers, no matter the time of year, and her bed… waking up to that scent… It toyed with him more than her touch did. "I mean, I *thought* I wanted to break up, but watching you there, settling that scuffle in the road—I remembered *so* many things about us, things I'd…" Chin lowered, she glanced up at him through fluttering eyelashes. A blush crept across her cheeks, giving her pale tan skin a dark pink hue almost the same shade as the powder brushed over her eyelids. "Well… I'd kind of like them back."

Mayr stopped breathing. Stopped hoping.

She could have kicked him in the heart, broken his breast bone, and *still* not come close to the aching blow those words dealt him.

"Sarene…" he managed, but barely, his mouth dry. Two and a half weeks—that was how long they had been apart, their split more than clear.

Forever, she had said. *Forever and ever and beyond never again.*

But now...

"Yeah, I know," Sarene said quietly, caressing his chin. "I think I misspoke '*never*.' Maybe got ahead of myself?" Her fingertips slipped down his throat to settle in the hollow, just above the neckline of his shirt.

Mayr shivered, ready to run. Except that deepening desire was back in her eyes, the one that had kept him in her bed as often as he could spare. That stripped-down and dirty look of want that drew him in, as sly and knowing as the smile she gave him then. Fingers playing down his chest, her touch retraced a path traveled so many times before. She came in close, almost pressing hip to hip, the basket falling to the grass with soft noise.

"I'm sorry," she whispered. The heat of her breath teased his lips, her fingers flattened over his stomach, splayed as she drew them over his ribs. Another tremble surged through him, his breaths hard to keep steady. "I didn't mean it, darling. You need to know that. I mean, how could I just throw away eight months of being together? My relationships don't usually last that long, so I thought maybe you'd... that we'd..." Sarene sighed and pressed against him, her chest to his. "Tash says I was afraid of what we had—that it was so different I didn't know *how* to deal with it, so I ran. And maybe he's right. He knows about these things. Maybe I *was* running from us."

Mayr watched her carefully, the name of her friend not familiar, though Sarene seemed to take comfort from whoever Tash was, a hint of regret in her tone. Was that who he had to thank for getting to see her now? Had Tash intervened and sent her back to Mayr?

Sarene flashed another smile—shy, almost hiding as she lowered her chin. "But seeing you here, handling those men... it just brings back *so* much. Reminds me of what I wanted for us. Things I wanted to try to see if we could be the perfect couple. But silly me, I went and ruined that. And I'm sorry for it, because I didn't really want to hurt you. Didn't mean it, not at all. It just came out that way. It's awful, but it's true."

By the bloody teasing Four—

She was pulling out everything, and believing it was going to break his heart all over again, but...

She was coming back. She wanted *him* back. No one did that. Not ever. Not with him. He was never that lucky. Never that worth it.

Once they're gone, you're nothing. But she's here, and she's looking for something...

If Pellon were there, he would have put words to that something, a bit of logic that made sense and was difficult to refute. Except Pellon was at the estate, filling in for Mayr as his role of second-in-command required, and reason...

Where was reason when Mayr had first approached Sarene nearly nine months ago? When he had hoped to court her and nearly fell on his ass when she said yes, ice and snow taking him down a moment later, leaving her laughing hard enough to bring her down on top of him?

Where was reason whenever he saw something shiny and beautiful and wanted Sarene to have it because she was so brilliant in spirit and full of joy, a light in dark times ever since Aeley's father, Korre, had died; a man Mayr considered a second father and loved deep enough to still feel his death two years later.

Where was reason during midsummer, when he had accompanied Sarene to the Feast of Emeraliss held at the Dahe estate, then skipped the party and fooled around in the barn with her for almost the rest of the night. Their romp in the hay had completely embarrassed the stablehand who came across them and left two of the Dahe guards in giggles for days afterwards... only for Sarene to break up with Mayr two weeks later, an irony not lost on him, considering the Feast of Emeraliss was also a celebration of hearts, dedicated to their Goddess of Love.

Reason would say he was about to step into trouble, and Pellon would say the same. But Pellon had never liked Sarene, so his opinion...

I love you like a brother, but you've got your own girl problems, and me —

He was tired of being alone, of falling in and out. Of watching the door slam on every love he had. He would bend over backwards and work himself into whatever shape he had to if it saved love from locking his heart away forever. One day, giving everything he had to his lover would save him — save them, whoever *them* was, *whoever* they were — and right then, he wanted Sarene to be that someone. She could have him, lead him down, love him however she needed. No argument. No fight. No nothing, because what fight he had…

Mayr swallowed back the memories. He needed to focus on Sarene, on the now. He needed to move on, keep going forward, not squander it.

He slipped his hands around her waist, loving the feel of her against him. Thumbs tucked into the folds of her bright blue sash, he caressed her back, drawing out her own shiver, guiding her closer. "You want to get back together," he said quietly. "A second chance at us?"

"Yes." Sarene looped her arms around his neck, the ends of her blue hair ribbons crushed between them. "I want you back, sweetheart. I want *us* back."

Her kiss came on fast, so sweet on his lips it felt like falling into longing and need. All he could do was hold tightly, scared that she would turn around and walk from his life all over again, leaving him to shadows that were always so cold, so unforgiving. He could do this. *They* could do this—

The kiss deepened, her tongue sweeping over his, stealing his breath as she took command and scrambled everything keeping him in control. A nip at his lip. A lick across his mouth. A moan as she kissed him harder, wetter, messier, searching for the passion they had felt for months, drawing them together and laying them flat whenever they were alone. Such wicked memories caught between sweaty, come-soaked sheets and their floor-scraped knees…

The moment she drew back, Mayr groaned at the loss.

Sarene laughed. "I know, sweetheart. Me, too." Her caress along his nape brought another shiver, one that had her pressing a chaste kiss to his lips. "How about you come over tonight? We can continue… discussing this. Or leave the discussion for the morning," she added with a smirk. "I'll leave the porch door open. Come by when you're finished work and we'll see what happens. I hear make-up sex is one of the best things going. And darling, I want it *hard*."

The slip of her hand down the front of his pants did nothing to soothe the ache in his cock. She played to win, and what she wanted, she would get.

"Tonight," he murmured, his pride smashed into shards and piled at her feet.

"Good." Sarene leaned in close, her lips brushing his ear. "And bring the sexy guard image with you. After the display earlier, I feel like getting arrested... or maybe just a little tied up."

With a giggle, she scooped up the basket from the ground and flounced across the yard, her hips flicking back and forth, skirt swaying as her hair swept from side to side, flattened ribbons bouncing.

Hurling curses at the orange and gold leaves scattered across the ground was all Mayr could do to keep from shutting down before they even began.

Chapter Two

Day three—win, lose, or just spin myself in circles. By the Four, it's like being eighteen all over again...

Mayr sighed and glared at the tankard in his hands, lukewarm water lapping at the dark wood rim as he leaned against the kitchen counter, well away from the still-warm stone ovens to his left. With the fresh, fruity scent of sweet spice bread lingering and the soft, welcoming light streaming in from the row of windows along the wall to his left, he should have felt lighter. Happier. Tempted to sneak away one of the honey-drizzled adlenut pies sitting on the cooling table across the room.

Instead, he might as well have been shackled to a barrel of ale and rolled down the hillside, hitting every stone and shrub along the way. Three days into being back with Sarene and he was already trying to tame his nerves all over again. He was ready to disappear into the training room for the day and have a go at every weapon there until he passed out in some dusty corner, sweaty and collecting grime. Alone. Where he usually belonged, or so the Goddesses seemed to think.

Instead, he forced himself to stay in the open, surrounded by voices and bodies and collective stares in his direction, none of them accompanied by the questions he knew people wanted to ask. Here, in the Guard House at the Dahe estate, he was Head of the Guard always; top of the ladder and not interested in spreading personal details about himself. Thankfully, most of the guards knew to leave well enough alone, save the few who had known him long enough to be genuine friends, even family.

That never stopped them from talking behind his back, however, no matter how much he glowered, growled, or threatened to make their life that much more difficult. One hundred and forty guards tended to be beyond reining in where their mouths were concerned, at least outside of their actual positions. When they were on duty, one look could shut them up plenty, but not any more than that.

Which was why standing in the communal kitchen in the Guard House was one of the worst possible ideas he could have had that afternoon. If he were smart, he would have opted for hiding in the massive main house, probably in Aeley's study. There was always something to talk to her about, considering a Tract Steward's work never ended, not with all of the summons and policies and problems she had to sort on a daily basis. Had she been available, he likely would have sat her down to talk security arrangements while attempting to dodge whatever concerned looks she gave him, dependent on what all she had heard about him and Sarene.

Except she's locked up in meetings with magistrates and Lira, so that leaves me out of luck. Please tell me tonight will go better. Luck, you'd better not have completely sauntered off, you prickly ass.

Staring off into the distance, through the open doorway directly across from him, he was aware of the dining hall with its dozen long brown tables and old wooden chairs, but he focused on nothing in particular and faded into the silence of the kitchen. He was going to try wooing Sarene all over again, their night planned as well as he could manage with hope tucked neatly in each moment. They had stayed together for eight months, the longest a relationship had gone for him in a long time. Most of his prior relationships had ended before two months, so this... It was a rough patch for them—a challenge they needed to overcome together. But if they kept at it, if he tried harder to be what she wanted, it could work out. Then maybe he would finally stop staring at the inevitable lonely end to his life, desperate to hold onto everything that died. Or left. Or was sent away, never to be found again.

Abandonment issues... He snorted. Yeah, he had those, and they were a real bastard to negotiate with. At least with Sarene, he had the chance to fix what had gone wrong the first time.

He prayed their trip to Vasserey Call would curry him favour. As the largest city in the Gailarin tract, Vasserey boasted an assortment of establishments for its thousands of citizens, including a hand's count of popular theatres. Aeley had lent him unrestricted use of the Tract Steward's box at those theatres, his name on their lists of sanctioned officials anytime he wanted to attend one of their plays. Usually his duty to Aeley kept him tied to wherever she was, whether in Dahena or elsewhere. But every now and then, if no one needed him to mind the estate, tavern, or farm, he caught an evening long enough to leave Dahena completely if someone wanted to join him.

For the third time, that someone was Sarene, who had clearly enjoyed the first two times—she had kept him confined to bed the entirety of the day after the performances, using him in at least a dozen ways at her pleasure. Perhaps they could recapture what had been lost by revisiting where they had been; a reminder of the good to temper the grief. He had already sent a messenger ahead to inform the theatre of their attendance and arrange a room in one of the nearby inns. Tomorrow night, they would return to Dahena, their relationship fully on its way to reparation.

If anything, maybe it would do something about that damned guy she kept mentioning—Tash, the former lover who was possibly still in between them, going by all the times Sarene kept bringing up his name. Tash had made an impression on her, for whatever it was worth, but it left Mayr cursing the bastard more than once, especially when they were trying to piece their relationship back together.

And yet, whatever he said sent her back to me. Mayr frowned at the floor. Try as he might, completely hating Tash was unfair. *She left him for me. She sees value in us, more than some fling. He was just a filler — a means to cope. Nothing serious —*

A steady rhythm of knocks on the pantry cupboard to his right startled him.

Mayr rammed back against the counter, almost smacking his head off the cupboards just above him. Water sloshed over the lip of his tankard and spilled down his hand, several drops landing on his formal black tunic and polished black boots.

"Dammit," Mayr spat out, flicking water from his fingers.

"Sorry," a voice said, the tone deep and quiet. "You were busy." Pellon stepped out from the other side of the black-brown pantry, its height and size almost in competition with Pellon. Tall and muscular with short, red hair that could give flames a fight for vividness, Pellon was difficult to miss — except when he crept in from the second doorway on the other side of the kitchen, no doubt disguising his movements by sticking close to the wall just to hide behind the panty cupboard and scare Mayr to attention.

The loveable bastard.

Even when he was dressed in his heavy black leather armour with metal plates and the thickest set of brass and silver bracers he owned, Pellon only appeared more intimidating than he truly was at heart. Right then, though, he looked at ease in a charcoal-grey tunic, loose black pants tucked into his worn, brown knee-high boots, and a lightweight ash-grey vest that was almost the same shade as the stone ovens. There was a slight flush to his dark golden-tan skin, proof that he had been outside for some time, checking on the patrol teams as they walked the estate's perimeter.

"Yeah," Mayr said dryly, "just be thankful I like you, kid."

Pellon laughed, both comforting and familiar. "Said the brat."

Setting his tankard on the counter behind him, Mayr shrugged. "Not my fault you're so old."

"*Ha!* Funny." Pellon snorted and leaned against the pantry doors, arms folded over his broad chest. "Because being ten months older than you *clearly* makes me better. More experienced." He flashed a mischievous smile, his blue-green eyes shining in the sunlight. "Just generally more amazing at everything—*Toddlin*."

Mayr flicked his fingers at Pellon and stuck out his tongue. "Remember, I grew up with you, *Out to Pasture*. Shared the same room, even. Can't fool me now. Besides," he said, smirking as he crossed his arms, "Cook still likes me better."

Pellon rolled his eyes. "Spoiled cheat," he muttered.

The moment Pellon's eyes lost their playful spark, his lips in a grim line, Mayr braced himself. He knew that look—nineteen years worth of it.

Mayr sighed and let his head fall back, folded arms pulled tighter across his chest. "What did I do *now*?"

"You know what you did, and you know better," Pellon said softly. "She's not good for you, brother. You need to walk away and stay there, broken heart or not. Leave her be."

Sarene. *Of course.*

"Look, I know." Mayr raked his fingers through his hair, careful not to undo the black silk tie keeping it all back in a neat tail. "You've said more than enough—"

"Really? Because you tripping off to Vasserey with her seems like it bounced off your damn balls." With an aggravated sigh, Pellon rested his forehead against his fist. "She sent you packing and you've been off since, just like every time this happens. They leave, you get all messy and moody, then I worry about you." Pellon lifted his head and scowled. "I hate watching you go on like this, *especially* going back to her. She was bad for you then and she's bad for you now."

Mayr snorted. "*I* was bad for me. Not paying attention to the signs before things fell apart. Not catching on in time to fix it. Just like Be—"

He bit his tongue. No. Not saying her name was best. *That's in the past, where it needs to—*

"Keep telling yourself that," Pellon murmured as he stepped closer, "because she's using you, and you know it. We *all* know it."

Before Mayr could snap back with sarcasm, Pellon gave a shrill whistle, loud enough to leave Mayr wincing.

Not a breath later, in came the reinforcements, two entering from each doorway.

Groaning inwardly, Mayr glared at Stick, Stuck, Keyer, and Lilia. All of them were tough, none of them known for suffering him without a solid head on their shoulders. Each one of them had enough years to their name in the Dahe Guard to know when he needed his balls kicked in.

"Low blow," Mayr grumbled.

Lilia shrugged, her thin lips pursed, concern thick in her brown eyes. "Someone's got to do it."

And no doubt they figured that sending in one of the oldest guards would do the trick. Lilia was nearly old enough to be his mother, having served Korre Dahe for most of her life. She had spent more than half her career as a main sentry trained by Mayr's predecessor, Lensen, while Mayr had ensured she remained the primary trainer of new sentries. Usually they got along well, but that no-nonsense look on Lilia's face had him biting back more than his tongue.

"What do you want me to say? That I don't care for her? Because I do." Mayr clenched his jaws, fists hidden in the crooks of his arms as he peered at each face, their worry so blatant it dragged irritation through every nerve. "She said she was too quick to cut us off; that she wants this. That I'm the only one she wants."

The look the lot of them shared right then nearly had him cursing them to all the tar-filled pits in the afterlife and walking out.

"Are you even hearing yourself?" Pellon asked with so much sadness it hurt. It dug too deep into Mayr's roughest times, throwing them back in his face. *Ten years ago and it's still stabbing my heart to bits.*

"Yeah, I am." Mayr gritted his teeth. "And again: *what do you want me to say?*" He and Pellon had *had* this conversation a dozen times too many, ever since Mayr had started his relationship with Sarene. There was nothing more to say except *forget you*.

"That you have different intentions," Stick answered, his expression tight, stealing a portion of the undying youth from his face. "That you'll never want the same things." He drew his fingers through his white-blond hair and sighed, his ice-blue gaze once again saying everything he usually kept to himself. "You want commitment and a family; she flirts with anyone with a cock and a pretty face, especially if they've got money—anything that makes them worth a second look the morning after. You want forever; she's looking for something she can stop tomorrow."

"Goddesses know she's flirted with more than half the guards whenever she's around," Lilia muttered, "and half the village lookers, besides." She leaned back against the washbasin counter, her legs crossed at the ankles, the knives strapped to her thighs catching the light. "Always looks like she's at market, that one. And I'm not talking what the farmers haul in."

"But she comes back to me," Mayr argued softly. "At the end of it all, it's been me. My bed, not someone else's. That has to mean something."

Keyer groaned and slapped vir forehead, faint wrinkles noticeable around vir hazel eyes. "*Do not go back to fair-weather exes*, Mayr. That's damned bloody messy. Rule number one around here."

Pellon grunted. "More like fifth. One through four are avoiding certain death."

"It's all looking the same right about now." Keyer shrugged before flicking vir hair over vir shoulder, the thick, dark grey curls a tangled mass that never seemed to play well during any of the fifteen years Mayr had known Keyer. "This isn't like the others, the exes you're still friends with. That's a fine line, but one that's relatively manageable—but only because no one came sniffing around to get anyone else back. You just agreed to part on amicable terms."

The disapproving frown Keyer cast Mayr had all the aged tenderness of one of Korre's scowls, immediately kicking Mayr's anger to the bitter wind.

If Korre were still alive, he would have given that same look, paired with a quiet but pointed talk that would have left Mayr's insides in a twisted, torn pile of emotional disaster needing a breath of fresh air.

But he's not here, and no one's him. Just me and what decisions I've got lying around. Maybe they're right, maybe they're wrong, but Sarene's the only thing that's helped since he died. How do I throw that away and pretend like it doesn't change everything?

"Dammit, Mayr. Look at me." Stuck stomped forward, the high tail of her shoulder-length brown hair swinging back and forth with no less ferocity than what her gaze pinned on him, bright green-gold eyes narrowed. "I'm playing the Other Mother card, and I don't care *what* you think. We want you to be the one who leaves instead of the one that's left. Pick up your courage and *use it.* By the Goddesses, just pick up your bloody heart and hold onto it for a while—save it for someone who actually *wants* it all. Who deserves it." Muscular arms crossed tightly over her chest, she glowered up at him. "No, Mayr. Just say no."

"But—" Mayr started.

"*Just say no.* No, no, no, no, no."

"Stuck—"

"*For your protection, dammit!*" Stuck growled, her golden-brown skin taking on a darkening flush. "Say it, you can't-be-arsed bastard. Save yourself *this once*. Don't be anyone's cute little puppy following them around, waiting to be loved back. Bite this in the balls and rip 'em off."

Mayr cursed under his breath, both of his palms pressed to his forehead. Eyes closed, he caught the impatient tap of Lilia's foot, Keyer's constant fidgeting, and the ragged breaths coming at him from Stuck, who was ready to bury him where no one would ever find him. Only Stick and Pellon stood perfectly quiet, but Pellon was likely plotting his death in the damning silence, which most likely would involve Aeley's assistance. She was as exasperated with him as the rest of them.

As much as he was.

Because living with it was even worse than staring down their disappointment, never living up to who he ought to be. Never being that everything someone needed long enough to see a safe future, one he could be proud to call his with someone he would die for by his side.

There was no argument Pellon loved him as a brother and that the others cared what happened to him. Goddesses knew that Stuck was breathing immortality into her nicknames by just being there, sticking to him as a cause she would fight to the teeth for, and even pulling the Other

Mother act on him, something she usually did with everyone else *but* him. Except he was still going to walk into the fire stoked between him and Sarene because the burn... it hurt when it went out, but while it was in play—when the flames were being fanned up high, searing through passion and need and licking at the possibility of forever...

He was a fool, but the alternative was to settle for being alone. To cry at the darkness and surrender to his greatest fear as it stole the very life from his soul and clawed him to shreds, never to be whole, only slip through the cracks again and again, a fragment of something worth losing. Being lost in that void was torture best avoided, even if he was being played.

"I know, Surie," Mayr murmured, hoping Stick's given name would calm her down, showing that he *was* listening and not being a *complete* ass. "But just... let me have this, all right? And if it all falls apart, you have the explicit order to tell me 'I told you so.'" He drew his hands down his face and sighed into his palms. "Can we at least agree to that?"

Stuck pursed her lips. "I'll be the first one to do it."

Pellon snorted. "You'll have to beat me to him."

"Or just plain ass beat him," Lilia said.

Mayr rolled his eyes towards the ceiling. "And with that settled—"

He left them there to stew in their own frustrations. There would always be more to say, but he had been ambushed enough for one day. If he was going to act against their better judgment, he had best get to it. And if it all crumbled to dust, at least he had the punishment to fall back on.

"Oh, sweetheart, it's not nearly that bad. Stop worrying about it. We're excited, remember?"

Mayr gave Sarene a sheepish smile as he slipped his arm around her shoulders, pulling her closer to his side. They leaned back against the soft black cushions of the carriage, in the centre of the bench that faced the driver's box. Around them, the small, closed carriage rocked back and forth, creaking out of time with the clip-clop of hooves almost as though the driver were purposely hitting every dip and rocky patch in the road.

Though with Sarene cuddled against him, her arm around his waist as she smiled up at him, he supposed he was over-thinking things. Which was ridiculous considering she looked entirely too beautiful to be sitting beside the likes of him, her face lit up with joy and the late-afternoon light. He had opted for simple but formal, content with a tighter, softer tunic than normal, a new pair of pants purchased for that very trip, and his best pair of knee-high boots, complete with knives in the sheaths sewn inside—two for each boot, plus the one on his belt, what with leaving his sword at the estate. His lighter black leather long coat lay on the bench across from them, mostly so he could wear it while walking around the city. He had appearances to keep, ensuring no one bothered them, assuming the tattoos around his neck, his stark black attire, and his usual glare failed to keep trouble at a reasonable distance. All in all, he was comfortable, but still not to be trifled with, eternally on duty.

Sarene, however, was like a tamed image of their goddess Emeraliss—or a kindred spirit, assigned to oversee matters of lust, keeping him wrapped around her fingers like strands of precious shells. Curled and styled carefully, her blonde hair was swept up with brass combs and thin red ribbons with tiny gold bells at the ends— the same ribbons Mayr had purchased for the Feast of Emeraliss. Tight, errant ringlets brushed her neck and bare shoulders just above the neckline of her crimson gown, and while the dress was not as fancy as Aeley's or anyone else's he knew from the Grand Families, the way Sarene wore it paired with her ever-shining confidence was enough to distract anyone from the fact. All people would see was someone they could assume was a prim heiress escorted by the representative of a prominent Tract Steward, not a woodcutter's daughter and the son of farmers who was happier in the field than in the city. For the night, they were whatever they appeared to be, living whatever fantasy they wanted.

A fantasy he was happy to slip into for the short while they had it, but not to run from reality or any sense of shame—just to start over. To make a sharp cut in what grief and sadness there had been and give every possibility to this chance at a new beginning.

If only he could have forgotten the warnings and looks before they had headed out the door.

By the Four, was it so much to ask just to be *happy*?

"Darling," Sarene murmured, lifting her head from his shoulder. "Look at me for a moment?"

"Hmm?" Mayr complied—only for her lips to crush his, a hard kiss he welcomed gladly, one hand slipping around her neck to pull her closer. She moaned as his tongue met hers, playing with the taste of dry summer wine and sweet preserves, licking at every bit of the candied flavour she offered. Fingers crawled across his stomach, slipped over his hip and down his thigh, sneaking close to his belt buckle but never touching. Just that soulful kiss spreading warmth through him from chest to cock, commanding he give more, faster, harder, squeezing tight and stealing his breath.

Without warning, she drew back, leaving him cold and pining for more. "There, that's better," Sarene whispered, her fingertips grazing his freshly shaven cheek. For such a soft touch, it jerked on his insides, wrapping his thoughts around her and no one else. "Thought I was losing you. You looked a bit… distracted."

Before he could reply, Sarene crossed over to the other side of the carriage and slid into the centre of the bench across from him. As she fanned the skirt of her gown across the seat, the soft, delicate fabric a shock of vivid red against the black cushion, Mayr frowned, confusion and disappointment settling in like old friends.

Except her mischievous smile slammed down hard on those feelings—the lewd, cruel smile she gave whenever she was about to take him down all the way, cock and come and all, with no intention of giving up until he screamed her name.

The lift of her leg caught his curiosity, his focus following it to the left as she bent her knee and rested her foot on the cushion next to her, dainty red slipper peeking out from beneath the layers of gown and underskirt. Then there was a gentle tug, a drop of chin, the skirt creeping up her legs—

Bared thighs and the hint of blonde curls between her legs had him reaching for the curtains.

Sarene grabbed his wrist before he could draw the curtains shut. "Don't," she said huskily. "Leave them. I want you to see this—*all* of this. Now sit back, sweetheart."

Swallowing back any foolish reply he could have given, Mayr recoiled from the thick, dark mauve curtains and sat back. He fidgeted as the fabric continued up her waist and pooled around her hips, taut just above her lap, baring everything to him. Lips parted slightly, she opened her legs further, her knee angled towards the back of the carriage, slipper almost coming off as she dug her toe into the cushion. Everything. She was showing it all for him, glistening in the sunlight, her clit ready for the worship if only he could just...

He groaned as her fingers made it to her first, passing through the slickness. Then again, one finger sliding inside her as she lifted her hips towards him. She pushed in once, twice, and again, hips rolling gently before she drew out to rub her clit.

Her moans. Goddesses, her *moans*. He could have listened to them all day. She played herself softly, fingertips teasing her tip and wet folds, inviting him in but not to touch—just to witness. To taste her from across the divide with only memory to fill in the gaps and feed the growing ache of his hardened cock. The thought of her coming for him and screaming loud enough for the driver to blush into eternity left him spiraling into desperation, needing to see it, to watch her revel in every moment, the power to devastate him in her skilled hands. Hands that had roved over him the same slow way they did through her, claiming her, so wet and perfect his heartbeat refused to calm down, only picked up pace with another one of her low, drawn-out moans.

All he wanted was to kiss her, anywhere she wanted. Just a bit of her on the tip of his tongue, the scent of sex and sweets wreaking havoc on everything inside. Just a lick at her swollen clit, a nibble, a piece of time he could savour with her. It was bad enough she worried her bottom lip with her teeth. If anything, he wanted to kiss at that worry, that focus, and draw it in, trading breath for breath.

But her fingers... Looking away meant missing every moment, but watching her touch, that easy slide into herself, the drop of come as it parted from her and fell onto the cushion, marking her place—it took every bit of patience he had to stay put, his own legs opening to give his cock a chance to stop feeling so damned suffocated in his pants. Did she want him to play, too? He could, if she asked. If she took it for herself. If she just said the word.

A quiet laugh kicked his aches into further torment, followed by her lips on his, her kiss hard enough to hurt as he moaned his appreciation.

Slick fingers worked into his mouth, just the tip of one, then two, eased between their lips, their kiss shifting angles as she sought his tongue, hers slipping over her fingers as hungrily as his. Still kissing him, she withdrew her fingers for a moment, only to bring them back, her scent stronger, there for the taking.

Breaking their kiss, Mayr sucked her fingers into his mouth and licked them clean. Her breath played over the shell of his ear, urging him onwards.

A contended sigh was all he heard as he guided her back onto the opposite bench and kneeled before her, her legs opened wide to allow him access. Knees scraping the wooden floor of the jostling carriage, he clutched her thighs and held on tight, his tongue working inside her and over her hard clit, driving deeper just to hear her cry for more.

"Mmm, darling, I missed you," Sarene managed between panted breaths. She whimpered as he slid a finger into her, then curled the tip to stroke inside. Nails dug into his neck, keeping him close. "I missed this... so much... so damned much. Just... yes. Please, *there*. Just *that*." A whine. A rougher grip around his neck. The warmth of come rushing down his tongue and over his lips. "*Yes. There. Keep doing—*"

With a louder cry, Sarene turned everything around and nearly upside down, the carriage rocking and protesting noisily as she pushed him back against his seat and tore at his belt. The clink of buckle hitting the floor barely registered, not with her rushing to get him in her mouth, his pants pulled down his thighs before he could even think of doing anything else. And her lips...

by the Four, her tender lips wrapped around his cock as she took him down, the slide over her tongue and into her throat as damning to his focus as it ever was. The ease with which she took him to the root, fingers caressing his sac, tugging gently… He missed this, too, maybe more than he wanted to admit. Some part of him felt guilty about it. Humiliated.

Growling at the ridiculousness in his bloody rotten mind, Mayr held fast to Sarene's head as she sucked and licked the pre-release from his cock, careful not to disturb her hair any more than was necessary, only to let her go completely for fear of breaking the combs.

Almost as though taking pity on his plight, Sarene released him and kissed her way up his cock before she finally pushed off the floor and straddled him. Her fingers replaced her mouth on his shaft, playing its length between them as she kissed and tongued his lips.

"I don't know what I was thinking, giving this all up," she said, her tone rough, voice gravely. "All this gorgeous body of yours against mine — so many nights missing it, missing you in me, hitting hard and coming fast." Sarene kissed him, deep and long, thumb grazing the tip of his cock as she caught his gasp. "Mmm, love this. And how you're a screamer. *My* screamer. What about that, sweetheart? Screaming for me — here? Just a little. Just for me. Me, coming for you." She gripped him tightly, squeezing another moan from him. "Give in to me, *please*?"

Mayr thumped his head against the carriage, eyes rolled back as he hissed and lifted his hips into her. Whatever she wanted, she would have. They both knew it, just as they knew that *please* would always get her there even faster like it always had. Like she had never left.

With one hand braced on his chest, she drew his cock to her wetness and sank down, taking all of him into her.

Not a moment later, she was off him again and licking at his lips. Her swollen folds teased his cock but she stopped him from slipping inside, sending his focus into a spin. She played instead, merciless as she rolled his sac in her moistened palm.

Heated breaths graced his ear again, her quiet moans adding sweet pressure to everything twisted up inside, caught in the building heat. "I have so many things in mind, truest," Sarene whispered, lips pressed to just below his ear. A shiver raced through him, rushing him closer to release. "So many things I want to try. Things to rekindle us—bring us even closer. Things I wouldn't try with anyone else." She licked the shell of his ear, followed by a bite on his lobe. "Fantasies, truest, ones I want with you. More than the ones we've done already... just a few more. Something new... because I love you."

Mayr groaned as she slid down on him again, hips circling as she worked his cock inside her. Hands on her hips, he followed her rhythm. Nothing else mattered, not even the driver or the open windows, just the constant up and down together.

Sarene kissed him, long and slow. Her light tan skin was flushed as she pulled back, locks of hair slipped out of their pretty restraints. "Have you ever thought of having more than one woman at once?" Her fingers crept between them again, hips lifted just slightly. They gasped together as she stroked his shaft and her clit at the same time, on the edge of coming. "Because I've... mmm... I've wondered what it's like being with two men at once... with someone like you twice over... at the same time... dammit, *yes*."

Kisses blazed a path up his neck. Her tongue found his ear, breath blowing across the moisture and—Goddesses, he was almost there...

"Wish I could have two of you right now." She clutched him tight, hips circling faster. "With me as your prize. Makes me come so hard. Just the thought of you—"

Sarene slamming down on his cock nearly made *him* come, his moan swallowed by a rough kiss.

"What do you say, truest?" she said against his lips. "What if we run with that fantasy, make it ours? You, me, and someone who'll make it all feel so good... this good..."

She was up on her knees the next moment, only the head of his cock inside her. Her hips remained still as she drew her skirt up to her waist, their connection on display. The wetness slicking his cock and thighs glistened along with her fingers, the scent of sex and perfume dulling his senses.

"Consider it, truest? A threesome with me... my choice... Tash..." Sarene asked quietly. "Please? For me? I'll play out your deepest fantasies if you do. Any of them you want." She wiggled her hips, took him just a little further.

He nearly cried out, every reply scattered, lost in meaning and word.

And that name... that damned name was back... right in the middle of bliss. Right there, dropped so quickly. Just *Tash*, as if riding Mayr's cock had anything to do with it, because dammit, he needed her to calm the chaos she had started.

But too long—he waited too long to answer. With a sigh, she started to pull off completely—

Mayr pulled her into a hard kiss and thrust into her, needing her to come with him. They were so close, with her shivering in his arms, almost at her end, every breath an effort, every bit of control being yanked away by the need to let go.

"I'll consider," he murmured, nuzzling her cheek. "I swear I'll consider."

Her wicked smile was too playful to say no to, and so was the way she rode him hard, biting his ear, clawing his shoulders as they came together, her cry in chorus with his.

It took stepping out of the carriage in Vasserey Call to realize what all he had agreed to… and the gnawing, suffocating dread it stirred, with humiliation and regret clinging to its heels, threatening to drag his every step over the sett-paved streets.

Love had the strangest sense of humour and one impressive uppercut. He just wished he knew whether he was supposed to laugh or stab himself in the foot.

Sacrifices. Compromises. There always needed to be something worth giving up for the things that mattered most, and this time, Mayr needed to be ready to give it all up for Sarene. No fear. No excuses. No hiding. Even if it meant destroying what remained of his fractured pride, running headlong into what scared him.

Not that it's anything new, that fear. Or the threat of losing everything. Mayr tossed his worn, brown leather saddle onto the chair in the corner of his horse's cleaned stall, staring at the fresh hay covering the floor. *Some people get wealth and family and everything they could possibly want. And the luckiest get a life they truly need. I'm just lucky enough to be one of the cursed fools who gets to watch everyone else be happy. Thank you, oh, Reverent*

Goddesses, for your soured kindness. You didn't have anything better to do the day I was born, did you?

Grumbling, he swept dirt off his black pants and turned up the sleeves of his black tunic. In the corridor behind him, Hetlan scraped the dark wood floor with one hoof. Mayr spun around to grasp the reins hanging loosely from Hetlan's bridle.

"More like I lost a bet," Mayr crooned, pulling Hetlan's black nose to his. The thick scent of horse overpowered all other smells of the stable, reminiscent of home and childhood, raising the ghost of all those years he had mucked out stalls and cleaned currycombs.

Hetlan stomped the floorboards. His large, black body shifted backwards a half step.

"What? That's something that'd happen to me. You can't honestly tell me it wouldn't." When Hetlan lowered his head with a subtle shake, Mayr frowned. "Yeah, of course you'd say that. Thanks for having my back, friend. Next time I gamble and lose, I won't be looking for sympathy from you. And you can forget the extra helpings of ferat berries. I'm keeping them."

Hetlan raised his head to sniff Mayr's hair, his chin jerking the long strands.

"Yeah, *now* you go for the sympathy." Mayr held Hetlan's head still. "Nice try. You just keep thinking like that, traitor." He caressed Hetlan's forehead. "Don't think I don't know you've been goosing Lira into feeding you sweets. She'll spoil you rotten more than you already are, you pretentious mongrel."

Whinnying, Hetlan stepped back and waited as Mayr picked up the brush from the bench beside the stall. Around them, the other horses made quiet noises, waiting for the stablehands to return and release them into the grassy field and hillside behind the Dahe estate.

Lost in the soothing motions of grooming Hetlan, Mayr thought of the play he had taken Sarene to just two days ago, though it could have been that morning for all the memories piled on his concerns. Then there was the way Sarene had teased and toyed with him all through the performance, stroking him well out of sight of anyone else as they sat in the darkened, lavish box alone, his focus too far gone to remember even half of what the actors said. And how she had kept him in bed the next day, trapped between her thighs for most of it, telling him more of her fantasies, how she wanted to play them out by his side and enjoy everything life had to offer.

But his thoughts were forever caught on a line, stepping one foot then the other on two sides, seeing both the light and the dark. Shadows haunted and danced between them, echoing sentiments and kicking up their own memories.

Like the way she made life cheerful and easy to love, drawing him into her secrets and sharing in the beauty around them. The bright light in her eyes whenever she found an object she desired, sharing her infectious delight with others. The unpredictable times she would launch into a fit of giggles without a care about how ridiculous she sounded to passersby, combating ridicule with confidence...

The agony of his emotionally battered heart being kicked again and again, the finality in her voice when she cast him aside as sincere as any dismissal he had heard.

The sweetest danger in how she said she wanted him back, and the pathetic manner in which he had accepted the offer.

Then his thoughtless agreement to consider sharing her former lover's bed for a night...

This won't end well. Mayr sighed and brushed the dip in Hetlan's back. *But at least we're trying to work it out... doing it together. As a couple. That's worth something, right?*

"I hope," he whispered.

A second chance *was* hope. He was good to love for a day, a month, a year, if even that. But once lust wore away, he was nothing again, knowing he would never be good enough. Not to stay for. And maybe his lovers were right to leave him to that loneliness—maybe he had given everything he had years ago and now there was nothing worth having left over.

His position, his title, the prestige... his lovers always enjoyed them at first, but the glamour wore off with the reality of duty; what it truly meant, and what lengths he would go to best serve Aeley and keep the Dahe family safe, as he had promised Korre years before. The fact that the staunch, tough bearing of duty was just one half of him, not the whole, did him no favours, either.

Nor does it play well in the bedroom. He scowled and gently combed his fingers through the wavy, ink-black strands of Hetlan's coarse mane. Soft. He preferred to be soft in love. Being a guard, particularly head of the lot, was hard, rough, with a need to be stern and harsh when required. But romance, intimacy—he wanted to please. Serve. Touch gently and show the other half of him to someone who deserved it all and more, if not going to the ends of the world to place eternity in their hands. It was a second nature to duty, another side to the spirit of unyielding loyalty. He would protect love to the furthest point of his greatest failings and ensure that whoever loved him back had all they needed, as much as they wanted.

That was one of the most notable contentions where Sarene was concerned, with her dismissing him just as surely as she brushed off his hesitations. What she witnessed when he had stopped the fight between Raine and Vedan... he had his suspicions as to why it reminded her of their relationship. Why she had wanted Mayr to visit her that night with rope and cuffs in hand. She enjoyed the playing of roles and bluster, none of which had settled comfortably with him but he had indulged nonetheless. There was no price too great. No nerve too frayed.

He would damn well keep trying. If she wanted that intimate game, his comfort came second, maybe even third if it was about fulfilling a need. As awkward as the first times had been, at least this last time had felt familiar. That was something. At least he hoped it was. She could leave him just as quickly as she had taken him back, and the thought scared him even more than pretending to be someone else. He owed her his fears as much as anything else.

Whoa, there, a voice nagged from behind his thoughts, resembling his father's scolding tone. *Before you start dancing naked through the streets and throwing flowers to the Goddesses, think about Sarene's proposal. She's come back, sure, but for what? Don't you think her plan to fix things is a little much?*

Mayr studied the brush, resting his other hand on Hetlan's side. His doubts had a fair point. A night together with another man. Someone she had slept with while separated from Mayr and spoken about on several occasions, and with more than a slight fondness. A man he had never met, never seen.

"It'll be good for us, you'll see," Sarene had said the morning after the play. *"It'll be exciting! Something new. We'll have so much fun, and we'll be doing it together, you and me. Isn't that romantic,*

truest? Not everyone can, you know. It'll be special, just like us. And Tash is a real sweetheart. The two of you will get along just fine." She purred contentedly in his ear, her thighs squeezing his hips as her hardened nipples grazed his bare chest, one of her hands caressing his side. *"He likes it filthy dirty, and he likes doing it hard, truest, so you won't be bored. It'll be perfect, you'll see. Don't you worry about a thing."*

But he did worry. Especially if Sarene had left him for Tash to begin with.

And the way she had laid it all out…

Could he ever shake the feeling that he was being put on display? That he was being compared to someone else, shown off for whatever reason? For all he knew, Tash had planned the entire thing with Sarene, or at least goaded her into it, toying with whatever fanciful notions they had passed between them during their time together.

Then again, for all Mayr knew, they were *still* together and he was the toy to be batted about between them until they lost interest. Goddesses knew he had been thoroughly tricked once before, and in an even worse fashion than whatever Sarene and her damned annoying *Tash* could come up with.

"Why am I so ridiculously foolish?" Mayr asked Hetlan. "I mean completely, walk-into-a-wall-until-it-kills-me foolish? You'd think by now I'd have smartened up."

Hetlan stayed silent, gazing out the open doors of the stable.

"Great, you've got nothing, either." Mayr brushed Hetlan's mane. "I still haven't given her an answer. It's ridiculous how no and yes are equally excruciating to say. I choke every time I go to tell her my decision. Do you know how frustrating that is? And for a Head Guard, no less?"

Eye on Mayr, Hetlan turned his head.

"Yeah, guess that's a useless question, for more than one reason." Mayr flicked his hair over his shoulder and tightened the thin tie holding it back. "We can stick you with a dozen mares for half a day and you'd have mated with most of them by sunset without arguments or fits. They just gravitate to you; even the ones I think will kick you. That's it. Next life, I'm a horse."

"Good idea, since you're always talking to Hesalfemmer there like you expect him to talk back," Aeley's voice teased from the other end of the corridor.

Mayr whirled towards her, smiling as she sauntered up to him. Aeley's dark blonde hair cascaded over her shoulders and embroidered green tunic in a lightly tangled mass. "He listens better than most people I know. The fact you still can't remember his name's *Hetlan* says it all."

Aeley punched Mayr's arm, her slender nose and pink, glossy lips scrunched. "I know his *name* just fine. You're not the only one with a sense of humour."

"Oh, is *that* what that was? And here I thought Lira was the funny one." Mayr tilted his head, his grey eyes narrowed. "Wait, did you two attempt to switch personalities and fail horribly?"

"Funny."

"I try." Mayr sighed loudly, drawing it out. "You don't know how many nights I stay up pondering witty, hilarious things to say just so you can—"

Aeley punched his arm again.

"—do that. Exactly. Didn't sleep well, I take it?"

"Slept fine. It's the messenger I could kill." Aeley flexed her fists inside the crooks of her arms, annoyance in her brown eyes. "Nothing like finding out the rest of the Derossa family is showing up at the Feast of Eleia. It's *just* the way I wanted to end the summer."

"Ah. That'd do it." Mayr placed the brush on the bench without a clever retort. He shared Aeley's disappointment about Lira Derossa's family, one of the influential Grand Families in the Republic of Kattal's aristocracy. After Lira's brothers had attacked innocent villagers, then kidnapped and tried to force Aeley into marriage two years before, Mayr's tolerance for the family was low to the point of nonexistent. He could be gracious with forgiveness, but some things were unforgivable. The fact Lira's family treated Lira as though she were an unforgiveable wretch did nothing to woo his respect. Scribe or not, she deserved more than sneers and coercion. She was like another sister, even if Aeley had not fallen in love with her. He would protect Lira from her father and mother as much as he protected Aeley from the dangers of being Tract Steward for their region. They were two of the best friends he could ever have.

"There's still time before the feast comes up," he offered softly. "Maybe they'll change their mind. Everything can change in a day, remember, and there are several left."

"Yes, but it's highly unlikely." Aeley shuffled her feet, staring at her dirty, knee-high boots. "I think they're coming to use us like they did the last time. After what Emon and Ryler did to me and everyone else, their family's even worse off than they used to be. They couldn't be more socially deprived. The sons finally outdid the greed of the father and destroyed their reputations completely." She quirked her lips, then frowned. "Even the entire High Council refuses to step foot in their estate—and there are *twelve* councilmen. *Twelve.* You'd think one of them might try to do something about them, but no one wants anything to do with the Derossas. They're too afraid of what comes next. Asha tried to obliterate my father; his sons took revenge out on innocent villagers just to make me do whatever they want. What comes next? Etalynn poisoning a councilman and blaming another, throwing Kattal into disarray?"

She huffed, her nose crinkled in disgust. "Even if they really *were* coming to check up on us like they said, I don't appreciate it. Lira's the only one who matters and they can go drown themselves. I want nothing from them. Not their money, not their support, not their anything."

Mayr grunted. "Not at all what you said during that marriage contract disaster."

"That was then; this is now. I've been Steward for a couple of years. Got my footing. I've shown the villagers, the Grands, and the High Council I can govern. And that's *without* having my father hold my hand from the other side of death. So what if Asha and Etalynn Derossa withhold their love? Lira and I have more than enough supporters."

"What does she say about it?"

"She's as impressed as I am, so their funeral will be during dessert."

Caught on a dry laugh, Mayr coughed. "Whole guard's invited?"

"Of course. I'm expecting you to bring the roasting forks."

Eyes watering, Mayr cleared his throat. "Great. I'll pass the assignments around to the guards and tell them to savour each morsel like they won't eat ever again. I'll starve them for days beforehand just to make it a glorious feast." He brushed back Aeley's hair. "Though seriously, I'll increase guard presence that night. Make sure it's clear beyond clarity that no one will start anything. If I hear even a whisper of a fight, I can't promise I'll be my usual charming self. And if Etalynn threatens to go off on Lira again, I might just forget all manners and pitch the nuisance into an abandoned well."

Aeley kissed his cheek. "And I'd probably let you, you sweet, sweet man."

So sweet I run off every girl I've ever been with. How is it you're still here, always standing by me?

Mayr forced a sly smile. "Sweet man's just one of my names. Extraordinary lover. A being too sexy and perfect to actually exist. Shame you keep forgetting those." They were not the words he wanted to say and far from what he needed, but they made Aeley laugh, just as she did whenever he spoke highly of himself. Cocky words she took as a joke and overabundant confidence.

Words that were nothing but lies, hiding a painful truth she could never know.

Nor could he reveal what gnawed on his conscience. If there was anyone he should have been able to talk to, it was Aeley, his best friend since childhood. Despite being raised in a Grand Family with a politically important father, Aeley had not overlooked Mayr like others would have. She had sought him out, instead, befriending him when they were eleven years old. Even during the turbulent times of adolescence, rife with ego-wounding scraps, awkward scenarios, and questionable predicaments, she had stood by him. Together they had played innocent games, trained with her father's guards, and gone to battle against her brother. He had bandaged her bloody wounds and broken limbs, and allowed her to patch his invisible injuries, ones that could not bleed. For her alone, he would remain Head of the Guard.

But as much as he wanted to tell Aeley about Sarene and ask for her opinion, he knew better than to involve her in the matters of his love life. He trusted Aeley with his family, his livelihood, and his life, but where lovers were concerned...

I don't need the lecture. Or to have something arranged with some friend of hers. Last time that happened, I was left standing in the rain with wilted flowers, believing said friend when she said I wasn't good enough. I still haven't thanked you for that help, Ae.

Aeley had meant well, but her choice in lovers for him had gone even more poorly than his own attempts. Still, it was not the only reason he kept quiet about Sarene. Aeley's idea of intervention worried him more.

Bitter memories surfaced from where he had crammed them, taunting him as his heartbeat faltered. Try as he might, he would never forget Betta, his wife in all ways but one and mother to a child who haunted him with regret.

What Aeley had done to Betta over that regret could never be repeated with anyone else.

Aeley could inflict substantial damage with her temper, let alone her military training, and Betta had caught the painful end of both, much to his horror. Granted, he had given Aeley more than half a dozen pieces of his mind over the unnecessary confrontation, and forgiving her was still difficult, no matter how much he understood why she had lost control. Since then, Aeley had kept her fists to herself, though her words and opinions were an entirely different matter, now backed by the weight of a title and one of the highest ranks in Kattal.

His girlfriends, however, were not so well-trained or lucky. The last thing he needed was Aeley sticking her nose in where it did not belong and trying to fix everything. It was best to share only the good with her, when his relationships were going blissfully well and all he needed from her was a smile and congratulations. Not telling Aeley about his relationship troubles kept everyone on the safe side of moving on.

Although, knowing Aeley, she's killing herself with all that behaving and taking it out in the training ring.

Mayr grinned and retrieved his sword from the bench, strapping it on as he spoke. "If it makes you feel any better, there's one good thing about the Feast we know for certain."

One of Aeley's golden brows lifted. "Which is?"

"Emon, Ryler, and that shameful thing we call your brother won't be there. *At all.* If they were, they'd have to be executed on the spot."

"True," Aeley agreed. "Warden Rea assures me the three of them are being worked to the full extent the quarry can offer."

"It's funny how things go after you get stuck in prison for the rest of your life," a soft voice added from the open doors behind Mayr. Lira stepped into the stable, the loose curls of her dark brown hair swept back on one side and held by a jeweled comb. Her light blue gown covered most of her pale body except for the gradual dip in her neckline. "Not that I'm complaining. Meeting Allon Dahe once was one time too many. And growing up with Emon and Ryler... I honestly don't mind the rest of the world having them."

Aeley's face brightened as Lira stopped by her side. Without a word, Aeley's lips took to Lira's, both of them surrendering to a kiss that ripped at Mayr's heart like a dagger.

Watching them killed him more each time.

"Afternoon, you," Mayr greeted. "Come to plot your parents' demise? Have a suggestion for what drink pairs best with a funeral rite?"

Lira rolled her eyes. "Why waste a beautiful day on that?" She curled her arm around Aeley's, flashing her ink-stained fingers and the green and white jewels in her gold marriage ring. The ring matched Aeley's, though the pattern of the stones in Aeley's was reversed. "I just came to bring her back to the house. Vant is waiting on us. Again."

Mayr snickered. "You keep making your solicitor wait, Ae, and he's going to start thinking you don't like him. Or he'll die of frustration. Old age is already threatening to get him. Honestly, if he goes, who would we get to keep you out of legal troubles?"

"If our law processes weren't boring and long-winded, maybe I'd enjoy them." Aeley held up her hands. "If they ended in 'jab the pointy end here,' I'd be on it."

"But they don't, and Vant's patience is wearing thin. He also has an appointment with the High Council afterwards, as do I. So let's go." Lira pulled Aeley towards the doors, stroking Hetlan's side as she passed. "We'll see you at dinner, Mayr, assuming we don't get held up."

"Or accidentally tumble into bed without any clothes on and get stuck there," Aeley added, turning the corner and disappearing onto the other side of the stable.

Mayr stared through the open doors to the red and green field, listening to Aeley and Lira giggle. He wanted what they had: a relationship where they could be who they were without apology, punishment, or abandonment. Without waking up every morning, wondering if it was the day the person they loved would leave and never look back. A partnership that overcame obstacles, strengthened over time as if scripted by fate.

With the right person, he could have it all. For a short time, he'd believed he had.

There has to be more than this.

And that was it, his decision made. If Tash was the means to save his heart, so be it. Anything was better than being alone.

"I'm done for," Mayr told Hetlan. "Thirty years old and I still think it'll work out. I've heard miracles can happen; that strange things are actually normal in the world. That the Goddesses really do care what happens to each of us. If that's true, this'll go just fine, right?"

If only the rest of him could believe in such a miracle.

Chapter Three

"You won't be sorry," Sarene insisted, leading Mayr through the packed tavern by the hand. Close together, they bypassed tables of laughing women and burly men talking over the noise in the lantern-lit dining room. Sarene flashed Mayr a sweet smile, all pink-painted lips and eager brilliance. The light dusting of pink powder around her eyes matched her faded pink dress, the ribbon laced through the elegant twists and plaits of her blonde hair an even brighter pink. The delicate fern-green sash around her waist trailed down her back, catching on the slightest breeze.

Bright and cheerful, she was a vision of grace and colour, always in stark contrast to Mayr. Where her sweet-scented skin was unblemished, his brawny body was marked by various scars and a growing collection of tattoos. The dark icons around his neck remained visible and tended to make others wary, and he intended to keep it that way.

If she was the day, he was the night, dark and calm until a storm raged. And if the man Sarene wanted to sleep with did not approve, Mayr hardly cared.

I agreed we'd go through with this, not that I'd change anything about myself. Still, Mayr self-consciously ran his hand through his hair, wishing he had ignored Sarene's suggestion to keep it loose. *Who knew that tying it back actually gives a guy an extra boost of confidence? Ugh. I'm wearing clothes, but I still feel naked. I even left my sword behind, and I have a very special relationship with it. Oh, the things I'm doing for you…*

Like this tryst three days after she had proposed it. *Best get it done sooner than later*, or so he figured. First, they would have a light dinner with Tash, then there would be whatever happened in the room she had booked in the tavern under Mayr's name. *"Because they know you so well,"* she had said.

What she meant was he would pay for it, in more ways than one. Not to mention they would get the best room Orae could offer, given Mayr's title and position—and his close, personal connection to Orae and her family.

A fact confirmed as serving women welcomed Mayr with enthusiasm and insisted the moment he needed something, they would oblige immediately. Despite how busy the tavern was, he would receive their attention above all others. Most days, the special treatment was worth receiving, even if he *still* felt like he should be working for it, hauling crates or clearing away the dishes like he used to.

Tonight, however…

"There he is!" Sarene yanked Mayr's hand and pushed through the crowd of raucous men standing in the middle of the dining area. The room smelled of roasted meat, herb bread, bitter ale, and sweat from the men they passed. Drink splashed the floor near Sarene's feet, but she ignored it and the jeers from the drunken men, her focus on her target. Once on the other side of the tavern, she rushed towards the corner table beside two open windows. A man with broad shoulders and sturdy build sat with his back to the door, the fabric and gold embroidery of his red robe shimmering in the light.

The robe of a priest.

If Mayr could have glared the bastard to ash where he stood, he would have.

Great. Guess you forgot that tiny detail, Sarene. Because sure, let's get into trouble with the Temple of the Four. Or even better: the Goddesses Themselves. I certainly haven't had enough fun with priests in my lifetime. Mayr let out an agitated breath, more than ready to turn around and leave before things got worse. *This one had better be the real thing or I'm skipping the part where we have words and going straight for the throat.*

"Sorry to keep you waiting." Sarene kissed the man's lightly whiskered cheek and pulled Mayr to the other side of the table. With a playful grin, she swished her long skirt. "Mayr, darling, meet Tash, my favourite priest from the Temple. Tash, Mayr."

Scoffing, Tash tucked his shoulder-length brown hair behind one ear and stood. "She always embellishes." He smiled and extended his arm, his palm open.

Hesitant, Mayr clasped Tash's forearm, clenching Tash's dark leather bracer as tightly as Tash gripped his arm. *All right, not what I expected.*

He studied Tash's face carefully, on the search for anything amiss. Tash was older than Mayr anticipated, his wavy hair streaked with blond, matched by the close-cropped beard framing his lips. He was striking, his face softly curved, but his bright blue eyes… they stole Mayr's attention. Intense in hue and gaze, they could have stopped him dead in his tracks any day.

They also shoved every one of Sarene's glances out of his mind.

And while Tash wore dark pants, a loose white shirt, a simple belt with a small coin pouch, and the open red robe of a priest, the clothes emphasized his lean build. Had Mayr not known he was a priest, he might have taken Tash for a bounty hunter or soldier.

Especially given those. Mayr eyed Tash's bracers with suspicion, releasing Tash. *What priest wears armour? They're too busy with worship and doing good deeds and whatever else behind temple doors to need them. And here I left mine at home, thinking they might not be appropriate.*

Tash gestured to the table. "Please, sit." His gaze fixed on Mayr's. "I thought you might appreciate sitting in the corner. A fair vantage point and all."

Sarene frowned and sat in the chair in the corner. "I don't get it."

Of course you wouldn't. You don't need to see everyone or beware of people trying to kill you. Funny thing is he shouldn't know anything about it, either. Please don't tell me I'm being duped again. Please tell me he really is a priest.

"Thanks," Mayr murmured, falling into the chair beside Sarene, across from Tash. An awkward silence fell between them until he cleared his throat. "You need another?" He pointed at the almost empty tankard beside Tash's hand.

Tash's small smile never wavered. "I apologize for starting before you, but sure. It's supposed to be dinner, after all." He waved at one of the serving women.

"Here, let me," Mayr offered, raising his hand. "Sometimes they take a while to—"

"What can I get for you?" A petite, brunette server, Jesa, bounded up to the table with a wide grin and demure dress. She held an empty tray against her hip, batting her lashes at Tash then Mayr. Her glance did not stray to Sarene. "Obviously another drink for you, your priestliness, but I'm guessing food, too. Perhaps a little of everything Cook's got going? This one never seems to know what he wants," she said, nodding at Mayr.

"Thanks, Jes." Mayr snickered. "Any other truths of mine you'd like to spill while we're at it?"

Jesa laughed and hugged him around the shoulders. "Sorry, love. I just haven't seen you in days and days. We miss seeing your face around here." She straightened and tapped the table. "I'll just go and find you something good, then? Bread, meat, cheese. Fresh stew. And I'm pretty sure I saw a *tart*."

Mayr bit his tongue as Jesa pinned her gaze on Sarene with the last word.

Before he could suggest she be nicer, Jesa blew him a kiss. "I'll be right back with your usual drinks." She disappeared into the crowd with a flounce.

"If I wasn't in the corner," Sarene muttered, glaring after Jesa. She recovered quickly and seized Mayr's thigh before sliding her hand towards his groin. "I can't tell you how happy I am that you're finally meeting each other. I just know you're going to get along." Her mischievous smirk rattled something in Mayr's stomach. "I'm going to be a very, *very* lucky woman come morning. And so incredibly happy, I might just ask for seconds."

Mayr choked on his breath. To his relief, Jesa appeared with two full tankards of ale and a goblet of gaffa nectar for Sarene.

"You all right?" Tash asked, pushing one tankard closer to Mayr before accepting another. "Here, drink."

"Fine, thanks." Mayr sipped the ale, Tash's concerned expression not lost on him. Of course Sarene would say something bold. *And of course I'd react like a fool. I have no idea how I'm going to get through this.*

Except that was not completely true, not anymore.

For days, he had expected little of Tash and imagined all manners of appearance, wondering if Sarene's gushing had simply embellished Tash's merits. Mostly he had expected a man much younger than himself, likely blond like Sarene, and a member of one of the Grand Families with a refined carriage and manner. A man he would want nothing to do with. He never expected Tash, whatever he really was.

And he certainly never expected the wave of attraction drawing him in.

In seeing Tash, the idea of sharing a bed with him was *much* more appealing, and Sarene's taste... it had its own merits. Mayr had never been a stranger to the thought of sleeping with a man—Goddesses knew he had considered the possibility a couple dozen times since adolescence, only to tuck the desire away and do his best to ignore it, afraid of the complications it would bring when he had complications enough.

But this…

This was a chance to finally give in rather than settle for admiring from afar and hanging on to the wish of a touch. His thoughts ran rampant, their lust outdone by his hardening cock. To see that body that was hidden under the humble cloth of a priest, to have those blue eyes close to his…

Tash's coy smile chased Mayr's thoughts away. "Have a question? Or do I have something on my forehead? I can never tell with these places. Nor the temple, for that matter. Priests can have a terribly wicked sense of humour. Priestesses are even worse."

Mayr blinked. Had he been staring at Tash the whole time? "No. Maybe. How long have you and Sarene been… you know?"

Sarene slapped Mayr's arm. "Mayr! I told you already. You're so paranoid. We were only together while you and I were taking our little time away. It wasn't anything serious. Just a little harmless fun."

Paranoid… maybe, though harmless… Mayr offered a strained smile. "Isn't that against the rules of the Temple?"

"What? Casual intimacy?" Tash asked. "Or intimacy with someone outside of the priesthood?" He shrugged. "Neither, at least not for Rese-level priests like myself. We're in the middle, with plenty of freedom to roam and experience life. Part of our station is to nurture the Goddesses' values: justice, protection, wisdom, and most certainly love."

He paused with a wink as Jesa returned with several plates and placed them on the table. "Now the Metah-level priests, the novices," Tash continued once Jesa left, "they're allowed intimate activity but only a few times over a span of days. They're expected to pay attention and serve the Temple more than partake in personal pleasure. As for the highest of the order, the Uldana-level priests, they abstain except for the rare occasion and only should they be chosen." Tash glanced at Mayr. "Anything else you'd like to know? Anything, no matter how ridiculous or strange it may be."

Mayr studied the silver ring on the middle finger of Tash's right hand. Long, sharp, and curved, the ring resembled a thick talon wrapped around Tash's finger from knuckle to tip. A thin chain extended from the base of the talon and over the back of Tash's hand, attached to a metal ring on his bracer. The choice of adornment played against Mayr's expectations of a priest. Normally they portrayed a softer, less intimidating demeanor.

If he could ask only one question of Tash, it would be why Tash seemed different, almost to the point of making no sense.

"Anything," Tash repeated softly, moving his right hand closer. He stopped just shy of touching Mayr's fingertips. "Generally it's better if we get to know each other before the first touch."

Or maybe it's better if I know nothing at all. It'll be that much easier to forget. Mayr drank back the other answers that came to mind. *I'm here for Sarene, no one else.*

"Well, if you won't ask, I will." Tash tilted his head, watching Mayr with a hint of amusement. "Have we ever met before, you and me?"

Mayr picked at his food, aware that Sarene ate quicker than usual. "Uh, no...? Pretty sure I would have remembered."

"I know. Me, too. It's just you seem familiar, somehow."

"I hear I have one of those faces everyone knows. Though I've always figured it was because of too many brawls, among other things." Mayr snorted. "Maybe we got drunk and forgot."

"Maybe. Then again, if we had, I'd have remembered. I don't forget the good-looking ones, especially those I'd make love to in a heartbeat."

Mayr swallowed hard. Had he been eating right then, he would have choked on it all and died in mortification.

Tash leaned forward. "You might want to drink that nervousness down," he suggested, loud enough for only Mayr to hear. "And maybe talk about yourself. Help me out. I'll make it easy if you'll let me. Have faith." As Tash sat back, he motioned to Jesa for more drinks. "So, you're Steward Dahe's Head Guard. I'm curious what that means, exactly."

Considering Tash's words, Mayr let a long moment pass before answering. "Mostly I just keep her from getting herself killed." He sighed, the muscles in his back relaxing for the first time since entering the tavern. Something in Tash's smile taunted him with a calming effect, but only if he let it. "I keep the rest of our guards on point and trained. Every politician has people who want them gone. Every estate has its weak points. And every region needs fighters that are ready to take on anything from village riots to disasters to war. I just tell people what to do, where to be, and when."

"*And* you put nasty criminals away and awful murderers," Sarene added, scrunching her nose. "I don't know how you do something so dangerous. I never could." She scowled at Mayr. "You get into too many fights, even during your so-called training. You need to be more careful. Whenever one of your foolish guards bruises you or breaks your nose, you look absolutely horrifying. Considering all you put up with, you don't get paid half as well." Sarene gripped his wrist. "You really should talk Aeley into divvying out the wealth more fairly. You say she loves you like a brother—it's time she proved it. Besides, with her brother gone and her wife so wealthy, there's no reason you shouldn't reap any of that benefit. You only save their scandalous hides."

Mayr clenched his teeth. This was neither the place nor the time. "We've been here before, Sarene."

"Sarene," Tash said, touching her hand, "let us be thankful there are those like Mayr who take on the more difficult paths. It's because they do that you and I are free to live in peace." When Jesa approached the table, he patted Sarene's fingers. "Although I think your stew is getting cold. And you have a fresh drink, see?" He took the drink from Jesa and set it before Sarene. "There. Much better."

Tash faced Mayr and grimaced as though apologizing for Sarene's complaints.

As though he had intentionally deflected her attention.

Thanks, Mayr wanted to say, but kept quiet. The last thing he wanted was for Sarene to take the word as an insult and storm out.

No, it isn't the last thing. Oddly enough, the last thing I want is to leave. Mayr listened quietly as Tash spoke about the tavern and the numerous altercations he had witnessed in the past, some of them humourous more than violent, but all of them usual fare for the establishment and no different than what Mayr had seen since his youth. Except for the occasional interjection, Mayr allowed Tash and Sarene to dominate the conversation.

Although uncertain about his role in the rest of the night, Mayr was surprised by how easy it was to be around Tash. Part of him was convinced he should hate Tash for his involvement with Sarene, but there was a measure of comfort to Tash's presence, one Mayr could neither describe nor understand. Maybe it was because Tash had saved him from Sarene's demands, or maybe it was because Tash seemed to care and understand, even though they had never met before.

Or perhaps it was because Mayr was starting to see why Sarene would like Tash, with his sweet but mysterious smile and subtle control.

The sudden realization threw him off. He rethought every word, glance, gesture, and nuance. Even more, he questioned his decisions. His plan had been to stumble through a quick dinner then rush through what he hoped was an even quicker romp in a dark room—just enough to please Sarene and leave the next morning without regret.

Was that still what he wanted?

At this point, I have no idea. I don't know what I want. It sounded so simple before we sat down, but now...

More than once, he had found another man attractive enough to seriously consider making his interest known, the words on the tip of his tongue, the potential lover there for the asking—and he reasoned himself out of it every time.

Either he would convince himself the attempt would only end in rejection or he reminded himself he had no idea how to be intimate with a man and feared ridicule. Any attempts at pretending he could have anything better would have been disastrous. His relationships with women were difficult enough, so pursuing men, too... that was asking for more trouble, especially after seeing what Pellon and other guards had gone through with their boyfriends.

There's too much ego involved, not to mention the abundance of aggression and suffocating need to establish dominance. Men play games with the best of them, no lie about that. They might be more open about how they mess around, but it's still there.

It was those games he had no desire to wrestle with. He felt used enough, wrung out and forgotten—there was no point in having it rammed through his head even further. The effort demanded too much work for something that would fail faster than what he already had.

But then there's Tash. Curiosity crept through Mayr as numerous unanswered questions played through his mind. Opportunity lay at his feet, open and inviting. He had an idea of what Tash's interests were and how understanding he could be if Mayr proved inept. There was little left to fear. Nothing to lose.

Except for the unnamed something that made Tash unlike all the others, pulling on Mayr's desire to get to know him. Beneath that desire was an even deeper need that rattled Mayr's insides more than the blue eyes he could stare into for days. The burgeoning attraction extended beyond Tash's peaceful, reassuring manner and the way his face lit up from his genuine smile. Or the way he appeared hard and soft at the same time.

If anything, it's almost like he's... familiar.

Of all the things he felt, there was no explaining that one.

Giggles sounded from his left. Sarene moved around the table and slid onto Tash's lap. Both arms wrapped around his neck, she laughed and rocked him while kicking her feet.

"Sarene, perhaps this isn't the time." Tash slipped his arm around her back, catching her as she fell back from an awkward kick at the table leg. "Maybe this is better saved for upstairs, hmm?"

"Oh, you're no fun tonight." Sarene pouted, sparing a glance at Mayr. "If this is about him being here, don't worry about it. He doesn't care. Otherwise he'd never have agreed to this." She kissed Tash's jaw and drew one hand down his chest before smiling slyly at Mayr. "Just showing you how it's done, darling. Besides, you're both here. Does it really matter where we start this?"

Yes, it did. And yes, he did care.

"I need another drink," Mayr mumbled, standing. "I'll just—"

When Sarene kissed Tash full on the mouth, Mayr left the table, grumbling under his breath. What did he expect? Especially with all the warnings in his head from Pellon and Stuck and Keyer and—by the Four, the whole damned guard with Aeley at the helm. The mess he was in with Sarene was the same story as before, just a different girl.

How can I be this desperate? I never used to be like this. It's enough to make me sick, which would be a shame because dinner was really good.

"Another round," Mayr told the bartender, then turned away to watch the other tavern patrons. Most of them were villagers who frequented the tavern, though three were strangers dressed in travel clothes. A quick study of them revealed few weapons, allowing him to lower his guard slightly. Provided they obeyed the laws, he would leave them be.

From the crowd, a man stepped close to him, enough to knock their arms together.

"I'm sorry."

Mayr turned his head, his gaze finding Tash's. Without a table in the way, they stood eye to eye. "For what?"

"Sarene," Tash answered in a lowered voice. "This wasn't part of any plan."

"Well, not yours. Or mine. Hers, however... It's fine."

"It's not, not really." Tash moved closer to murmur in Mayr's ear. "You're apprehensive.

You're not comfortable with this arrangement. You haven't been this entire time."

"No." Mayr stepped back, shivering from the warmth of Tash's breath on his skin. "I'm fine. Just fine." He motioned to the bartender as she placed their drinks on the bar. "I'll just get this last drink and it'll be perfect."

Tash leaned into Mayr again. "We don't have to go through with this. If you need out, if this isn't what you want, we won't do anything. It'll end whenever you say. You can walk out of here and nothing changes."

'Nothing changes.' If only. Mayr debated his options. No one had ever given him the chance to back out of sleeping with them. He had always been the one to say it, giving his lovers every chance to decide how quickly their relationship evolved. On one hand, Tash's offer was kind, considerate. If he'd had no interest in Tash whatsoever, he might have taken the offer.

Fortunately, or unfortunately, the only 'if' here is if he gets any closer, I might just kiss him myself.

On the other hand, Tash's concern reminded him of everything that would change if he backed out. He would *not* renege on his agreement with Sarene. Their relationship was worth nothing if they refused to at least try.

"It's fine," Mayr said. "I'm not changing my mind. It's not like I'm losing a limb or anything, right?" He laughed nervously. "Please tell me I'm not. And if I am, by the Four, take my non-fighting arm, would you? I need everything else."

Tash smiled sadly and grasped Mayr's hand, hiding the gesture between them as he squeezed Mayr's calloused fingers. "I'll take care of you, I swear it," he whispered, his lips pressed to Mayr's ear.

Slow to part from Mayr, Tash grabbed the drinks and walked away.

Ignoring the stares from the patrons around the bar, Mayr looked at his hand. To his disappointment, the sensation of Tash's tender touch was already wearing off, the warmth of his compassion only a memory. Never had Sarene's touch affected him in such a way. Her hands always sought, ventured, and took. But with one touch, with few words, Tash gave him something precious.

Hope.

Rules. Plans. Experience. He liked having all of them. They put him at ease.

From where he stood in the middle of the room, Mayr stared at the door as Sarene slammed it shut, wishing he knew how the night was supposed to play out. There were no rules, no plans, and, according to Sarene, nothing that could not be tried at least once. The three of them were in the best room the tavern could offer, visible in the soft yellow light from a single candle on the low table beside the bed. The cream paint on the walls was chipped in places and the creaking floorboards needed to be replaced. Still, the room was intimate and embellished with two paintings of Dahena Village, dark like the blankets on the bed.

"Now what?" Sarene giggled and peered over her shoulder at Tash. "I think one of you needs to tell me how a girl pleases two guys at the same time, because I *don't* know *what* to do. I'm just *so* innocent." She batted her lashes at Mayr. "So many choices, so little time. Maybe I'll make it *really* easy and you two can sort it." Seductive and serious, she slipped one shoulder of her dress down her arm, exposing her pale breast.

Mayr glimpsed the darkened skin of her hardened nipple as pink fabric teased the tip. Had it been just the two of them, he would have caressed her. In a matter of moments, he would have done away with the dress and tasted her, nipping her from breast to the wetness between her legs.

Not now, not when his attention was divided.

The idea of another man touching her should have angered him, burying him under unbearable jealousy. Instead, anticipation diverted his focus onto Tash. The touch that sparked the demanding ache in his gut had not been Sarene's, but Tash's. What was meant as a reassuring gesture had left an invisible bond between them. Would it be too much—too weak—to clasp Tash's hand in return and be content?

Stepping away from the door, Tash raised his hand. "Please, you two should start." He draped his robe over the chair at the writing desk against the wall. "I'll just make things a bit more comfortable."

Sarene tugged Mayr closer by his belt buckle. "Comfortably naked," she murmured, looping her arms around his neck to bring his face down to hers. The strength of her kiss robbed him of the chance to breathe. She tasted of sweet nectar laced with the slight bitterness of seasoned berries. With one hand, she undid his belt and threw it aside, her lips never leaving his.

When she finally tore her lips away to yank his shirt over his head, Mayr stole a glance at Tash. In the few moments Mayr had been occupied by Sarene, Tash had removed his belt and lit the two white candles on the table near his robe. He crossed the room with the first candle to a fourth positioned on the mantel above the hearth. Shadows danced across the brightened room as Tash moved with little noise.

"You won't be needing these." Sarene laughed and untied Mayr's pants. Eyes shining, she guided the pants to the floor, sinking with them. "But you will be wanting this." On her knees, she kissed his stiff cock, her lips working down his shaft before lapping the head. She drew one fingertip along the underside.

Mayr sucked in a breath, aware of Tash's movements near the bed. If Sarene was not careful, she would end things sooner than she wanted.

What a disappointment that would be.

"Well, you definitely won't be needing this," Mayr said, helping her stand. Careful not to ruin the fabric, he untied the sash and tossed it towards the hearth. Her dress slid easily down her body, exposing her small breasts and willowy form.

Sarene giggled and gazed over her shoulder to Tash. "Mmm, my favourite boys."

Naked except for his bracers, Tash approached them—and Mayr could do nothing more than stare at him. He wanted to touch, caress, his gaze crawling over muscles that were modest but still there, open for the adoration and a good solid lick, assuming Tash allowed him to do that.

Though with the beauty came questions, things that made little sense. Not only did Tash appear fit for a fight, he appeared to have been in one. His skin bore more scars than Mayr's, the depth of the burns and knife marks along his legs and chest suggesting something other than battle. The lines crisscrossed inside his thighs and calves were even more unnerving, pointing to difficult answers and a story all their own.

Stopped behind Sarene, Tash said nothing as she led his hand to the blonde curls between her thighs. Tash kissed Sarene's shoulder and drove his fingers into her, making her gasp then moan.

By the time Sarene recaptured Mayr's lips with a hungry kiss, Mayr was still trying to understand how a priest could bear such damage. How could Tash have withstood what looked more like torture than a fighter's common injuries? The priests and priestesses were peaceful, even the ones who devoted themselves to Hastal and the protection of others. Most of them avoided violence, even when faced with certain death. Their faith was their shield; their carefully chosen words their sword. To attack a devout worshipper of the Goddesses was nonsensical—and lethal, should the Goddesses intervene. Or so the legends warned. Although if Tash had not been attacked while he was a priest, what was he before committing to the Temple? Victim? Felon? Mercenary?

With a touch to his skin, Mayr's thoughts scattered. Fingertips grazed his groin, feather-light as they traveled up to his hip before pulling away.

He held his breath, loosening his grip on Sarene's waist. The caress had not been hers. Both of her hands raked his back as she moved against him, biting his bottom lip before arching into Tash with a low moan. Only Tash could have touched him, stoking the fire lit under Mayr's arousal.

From behind Sarene, Tash lifted his gaze to Mayr's, a silent question in his eyes.

Do it again, Mayr wanted to answer, afraid to mangle the words. *Do something.*

As if understanding, Tash clasped Mayr's hand and led it past Sarene's body to his own, placing Mayr's fingers on his hip.

Mayr was hesitant to clutch, to hold, but when Tash's hand covered his in the same reassuring manner from before, he relaxed. Cupping Sarene's breast in one hand and teasing her nipple with his thumb, he drew his other hand up Tash's side to his waist and down again. Smooth skin welcomed his touch. Tash's small movements into his palm guided him further. As his hand journeyed towards Tash's thigh, Tash took a sharp breath. His fingertips flitted over Tash's cock, rewarded with a murmur of agreement from Tash's parted lips.

Sarene stilled. "The bed." She turned, taking the hands of both Mayr and Tash before leading them to the bed.

Silent, Mayr stole a glimpse at Tash over her head. What they had started appeared to have fueled a lust in them both, given Tash's intense stare back at him.

All part of Sarene's plan, he was sure.

Once Mayr sat back against the pillows arranged along the wooden headboard, Sarene straddled his thighs, facing him, her arms around his neck. Straightened in his tight grip around her hips, she rubbed against him, her swollen folds enticing his with their slick warmth. When Tash kneeled on the bed behind her, she quickened the pace, grinding Mayr's cock harder. The moment Tash placed his hands on her waist, just above Mayr's hands, Sarene whimpered.

Mayr slipped his fingers through her wetness, driving two fingers inside her as his thumb toyed with the most sensitive part of her. She cried out, her body contracting with her release. Nails dug into his shoulder, and she leaned back into Tash, only to shudder as Tash's fingers crept between her legs. They stroked her together, Tash's fingers sliding over Mayr's playfully, pleasing more than just Sarene.

A second release wracked her body. Sarene cried for mercy and thrust her hands down to stop them.

"By the Four," she cursed, removing their hands from her. "I just need... a moment." Sarene maneuvered out from between them. Instead of lying down or cleaning herself as she usually would, she wrapped her arms around Tash's shoulders and positioned herself behind him. Mischief danced over her face as she kissed Tash's cheek and stared at Mayr. "Your turn."

Mayr froze.

"I want you to get to know each other," she said, nuzzling Tash's ear. "Show me how it's done."

Just like that. That's how you wanted it to go—drop it and run? Mayr swallowed back what he could of the fear seizing his confidence. He had been happy with the cautious touches and occasional glance. The slow path. The long journey. All the sudden, he was expected to perform. For her and a man he barely knew. He was at a loss for words, let alone actions.

Cruel, Sarene. I haven't felt like this since I was a kid, fumbling with the ins and outs of what went where and how. And if it didn't work, how fast to get out of it and into something that did without the girl thinking I was completely insufferable. I didn't get to be at least halfway decent in bed these days without enduring that joyful set of experiences.

Time seemed to crawl until Tash neared him with small movements. Mayr prayed it meant Tash was rescuing him from making a fool of himself.

Settled in front of Mayr, Tash hung one of his legs over the side of the bed and bent his other leg, resting it flat on the mattress between Mayr's open legs. He motioned for Mayr to do the same.

Mayr obeyed, mirroring Tash's position. Their bent legs touched, creating a small space between their bodies. He eyed the tightening skin of Tash's erection. How would it feel inside him? What would his feel like inside Tash? And which of the two scenarios was more fulfilling?

Tash took Mayr's hands, one in each of his. While his voice said nothing, the look in Tash's eyes asked everything. In the back of his mind, Mayr heard Tash's voice from their conversation at the bar. First the offer to forgo the evening and then the promise: *"I'll take care of you."*

Of everything said that night, he believed those words most.

With a small nod, Mayr squeezed Tash's hands, trying to ignore Sarene's wide-eyed stare. Even though he would still let her think he was doing it for her, he wanted it more for himself. The exact reason why was still unclear, but the need was real. Focused on Tash's unwavering gaze, Mayr's thoughts tumbled through a dozen expectations.

They were crushed into nothing as Tash caressed the inside of Mayr's wrists with his fingertips. His touch danced lightly across Mayr's skin in slow lines and circular patterns. Several times he withdrew just enough to barely stroke the sensitive skin, drawing one finger down Mayr's wrist to the juncture where wrist met palm.

Mayr could not fight the shivers racing up his arms. Despite the jolt of the nerves in his leg he could not avoid, he fought the urge to pull back. Both sensual and ticklish, the sensation grew deeper, almost unbearable as Tash's touch moved up Mayr's forearms. Each stroke inside his arm forced him to take a sharp breath. Every touch inside his elbow made him whimper. He gripped Tash's bracers, wanting to calm the excitement overtaking him, but it only worsened. Tash's fingertips continued; the pressure varied along the most responsive areas until Mayr wanted to scream. Muscles contracted down his back, the rest of his body demanding equal attention.

The agonizing strokes stopped. Tash grasped Mayr's elbows from beneath and eased Mayr forward. Their lips met gently, the touch as light as Tash's caresses. Lips parted slightly, Tash drew Mayr into him, balancing it with a soft push against Mayr's mouth.

Surprised, Mayr returned the kiss, holding Tash's lips to his. Non-invasive and caring, it was not what he expected. He had anticipated a hard kiss, dominate and claiming. He had expected what women usually demanded from him and gave back until they could barely breathe.

This reminded him of being thirteen years old, kissing someone for the first time. Shy and sweet. Careful. Determined and seeking, but compassionate and generous.

Under his skin, a tingling sensation surged all the way to his toes.

He wanted more. Parting his lips further, Mayr deepened the kiss, encouraged as Tash held him closer. No longer hesitant, Mayr glided his hand up Tash's leg to his back, wanting to taste more than just his lips. From his actions, it was as though Tash understood him; as though he could read Mayr and sense what would alleviate his fears. No lover had ever treated him like that before. They never asked him what he needed. Never inquired if hard, passionate sex, or whatever else they did, was what he actually wanted. He had simply surrendered to them, taking little for himself, even when what he needed was the opposite.

Tash pulled back, lips lingering on Mayr's, his mustache scratchy on Mayr's skin. Beyond the scent of ale, he smelled of fragrant incense and a hint of smoke from a fire. Mayr pressed his forehead to Tash's, soothed by the hands roaming over his back and across his shoulders. They were as close as they could be with their legs still between them.

Gazes locked, they took a breath together, then another. In synch, they breathed deeply, almost as if they were completely alone. No words filled Mayr's mind—just the image of Tash's eyes staring into his, burning into his memory. Tash's breaths teased his lips, accompanied by the steady rise and fall of Tash's chest. He welcomed the massage from Tash's fingers on his shoulder blades. The heat trapped between them made him yearn to be even closer.

For a precious moment, he believed they were where they should be. Something connected them beyond what they could see, hear, or feel. Perfection, wrapped up in peace and partnership. Although he still did not know a great many things, Tash's touch told him it was all right; that he could not fail. Not here, not now. Not with him.

Stroking his thumb along the short hairs covering Tash's chin, Mayr replayed Tash's words through his mind. He could leave anytime he wanted. But he wanted to know what else existed on the other side of Tash's kiss. There would be no leaving. Not from that moment. Not ever.

"Now, boys," Sarene muttered. "I love you playing nice and all, but I *know* you can do more."

Tash squeezed his eyes shut and clenched his jaws, his back tense under Mayr's hand. When he opened his eyes again, his expression softened before he peered over his shoulder. "Sarene, lovely, patience is a blessed virtue. It's good for all things, including the heart, mind, and body. Particularly yours."

Sarene giggled and hugged Tash from behind. "You're always so caring." She rested her chin on his shoulder. "Seriously, though. I'd love to see you go at it, the both of you. Take him, Tash, just like you do me, all passionate and strong. And Mayr, darling, show him how much a man you really are. Be the rutting males I know you can be. I hear it's equally good for the heart, mind, and body."

"No." Tash sat back, pulling his hands from Mayr.

Sarene recoiled. "No? What do you mean no?"

"Precisely that." Without removing his gaze from Mayr, Tash turned his head in Sarene's direction. "I misplaced the oils I need to make it work."

"Can't you just do it without them?" Sarene pouted. "I mean, honestly, they're just oils. It's not like they're necessary—"

"No, Sarene." There was no mistaking the annoyance in Tash's voice. "They don't seem necessary to you but they are for us. I'm not doing anything without them. The pain is hardly sensual."

"But you said—"

Tash cut her off with a raised hand.

Mayr watched their verbal match with disappointment. In addition to shredding the blissful moments where he forgot she was there at all, Sarene had soured the mood. *I'm pretty sure we're also not going any further than this. Great, just when I was ready to—*

A reassuring hand clutched his. Tash's heated glance kicked at Mayr's irritation. "There are other things we can do," Tash said. The slight decline of his head suggested he spoke more to Mayr than Sarene. "Fetch your sash, lovely."

Without wasting time, Sarene hopped off the bed and retrieved her sash.

Tash pressed his cheek to Mayr's and raked his fingers through Mayr's hair. "Trust me," he whispered, his lips warming Mayr's ear.

I already do.

Taking the sash from Sarene, Tash stood and stepped past Mayr. In the instant Tash's back was in his view, Mayr glimpsed a large bird tattooed across Tash's skin in black ink. The wings stretched out across Tash's shoulders, finely detailed like the elaborate crown of feathers and swooped tail curved around his hips. The twisted body covered his spine, its thick talons outstretched on his lower back. Mayr could not identify the bird, only that he recognized it.

Almost as quickly as he spied the tattoo, Tash was behind him, tying the sash around his eyes, plunging Mayr's sight into darkness.

"There." Tash tossed the pillows aside and slipped in behind Mayr. With one leg hanging over the edge of the bed and the other tucked beneath him, he leaned inwards. Still adjusting the blindfold, Tash drew his lips over Mayr's ear, down his jaw, and kissed a path to the thin skin along the back of his neck. Deftly, he swept Mayr's hair aside and ran his hands down Mayr's arms, guiding Mayr back into him. As Tash's hands traversed over Mayr's knuckles, he interlaced their fingers.

Mayr held Tash's hands, following along. Tash's breaths filled his ears, their calming effect interrupted by a quiet hum as Tash pulled Mayr further into him. He could not feel all of Tash's body, but he felt what mattered, including the full erection pressed against his lower back.

Tash's hands moved over Mayr's body, focusing his attention on his own erection. Already aching from the quiet moments with

Tash, his cock strained. Arousal flared from wherever Tash touched. Every time Tash's palms glided down and up his chest, Mayr hoped for more. Desperation led to deep, drawn-out groans whenever Tash teased his nipples or toyed with the patch of dark hair leading to his cock. Every caress across his shoulders and arms, every kiss to his neck, and he was nearly undone. Each tender touch seduced him, their ability to push him towards release heightened by his lack of sight.

So this is where trust in you leads—

Mayr cried out as Tash gripped his cock, fingertips brushing his tightened sac. Hips thrusting, he forced himself deeper into Tash's grasp, lolling his head over Tash's shoulder.

Tash moaned and buried his face in Mayr's neck. "Yes," he murmured, stroking fervently. After fumbling across Mayr's jaw until Mayr turned his face towards him, his lips found Mayr's, taking his mouth gently.

A moment later, they abandoned the soft kiss, overcome by a surge of passion. Deep and full, the kiss stole their breaths in a series of moans that demanded more the longer they held onto each other. Pouring everything he felt against the strength of Tash's lips, Mayr forgot everything except the mounting release ramming against his insides. Behind him, Tash ground against Mayr's back, his need obvious.

If only they could…

Tash's fingertips circled the head of Mayr's cock, driving Mayr to the edge of sanity.

Mayr jerked back, clamping down on Tash's forearms to keep Tash's hands where they were. It was too much to take. He rocked with the rhythm of Tash's hand, rolling his hips. A strange wave of familiarity washed over him. He wished he could drive his cock into Tash and let himself go. Let all of the pain go. The fear. The agony of rejection. Everything. Give it all to a man he knew little about, but felt as if he had known forever.

"Sarene." Tash's voice was quiet but commanding. His free hand moved.

The mattress shifted with Sarene's unsteady weight. Her lips stumbled over his and worked their way down his body, daring him to come. She took his cock into her mouth greedily and guided the swollen head deep into her throat.

One more touch and I'm... I can't...

"Let go," Tash whispered. "Surrender. Let it happen." His lips settled behind Mayr's ear, above the neck where the skin was most sensitive.

The warmth of Tash's pre-release trickled down the small of Mayr's back, sending his mind reeling somewhere else completely. The thought of Tash coming because of him...

Release pounded through Mayr, pulling every muscle. He cried out and clung to Tash. Sarene worked rigorously, sucking back the spurts of release. *If only it were him.* Eyes closed, Mayr imagined Tash's mouth on him, swallowing his cock over and over again.

The rush over, Mayr ripped off the blindfold. Sarene sat back on her legs near the end of the bed, her face flushed and lips glistening.

Tash kissed Mayr's shoulder before he stood. "You should rest," he said, going to Sarene. As she started to wipe her mouth, he shook his head. "Don't. Just leave it."

Kneeling on the side of the bed, Tash pushed Sarene onto her back. She lay across the bed near Mayr's feet, her body visible from the side. Tash positioned himself between her thighs and drew her legs up around his hips. When he slid into her with ease, she groaned and scratched his shoulder. His thrusts were quick, determined, the wet sound of his cock moving in and out of her combating the silence. His tongue flickered across her lips, lapping them dry before kissing her hard.

From where he lay, Mayr watched Tash deliver one hard thrust after another. For a moment, Mayr's glance strayed to Sarene's breasts and hips, but returned to Tash. There was a beauty to the contracted muscles in his arms and back. Mostly it was the way the shaded feathers of Tash's tattoo spread whenever Tash's back pulled taut. The sight of Tash's body, hard and tight from shoulder to leg, left Mayr wanting to come all over again.

Without warning, Sarene cried out and held tight to Tash. He rammed into her and stilled, groaning into her shoulder.

Instantly, Tash looked to Mayr, his gaze filled with a heated want and what looked so much like need...

Goddesses, he was done and ready to go again all at the same time. Mayr bit back a groan and stared back, wishing for... he had no idea. If Mayr's guts could have flipped and danced and strangled him by the balls, they would have. Instead, his twisted emotions stole his thoughts and played with his consciousness, rendering him speechless.

Before Mayr knew it, Tash was crossing the room to the washbowl on the round table beside the hearth, only to bring back both the bowl and clean, folded cloths to the bed. After he placed the bowl on the floor, he offered Sarene one cloth before wetting the other.

Once more, Tash stood behind Mayr. He held the moist cloth to Mayr's neck, cooling the skin before wiping away the evidence of him on Mayr's back. Just as Tash finished and started to wash Mayr's chest and stomach, stopping only to sweep a caress over Mayr's cock with the back of his hand, Tash's gaze caught Mayr's. Contrary to the small smile Tash offered, a strange sadness haunted his eyes. Reluctance peeked out from beneath.

And here we go again, Mayr thought, torn between wanting Tash to say something and being grateful for the silence. *He doesn't make any sense. I don't make any sense. Nothing about this entire situation makes any lick of blessed sense. It'd be all wrong if it didn't feel all right.*

Taking the cloth from Tash, Mayr finished cleaning himself. He silently offered to return the favour, but Tash shook his head and accepted the cloth back, then took Sarene's.

"I'm leaving as it is." Tash tossed the cloths into the bowl and returned it to the table. "I don't like to stay long." He gathered his clothes from the chair and dressed. "Staying too long screams of permanence and attachment—two things I neither want nor need. Besides," he added, gesturing to Sarene before buckling his belt, "this was supposed to be about the two of you. It's best if I leave now and let you revel in your relationship."

Disappointment lashed at Mayr. He was going to be alone with her for the rest of the night? No parting words to put him further at ease. No expectation of reciprocation. Just Mayr and Sarene left to say to each other whatever it was a couple said after sharing their bed with someone else.

Tash donned his robe and dipped his head. "I'll see you both in days to come, I hope. Thank you for inviting me into the sacredness that has bound you. May the Goddesses continue to bless you with good health and fair being." He left the room, adding insult to the invisible wound torn into whatever part of Mayr's existence belonged to Tash.

"Does he always do that?" Mayr asked.

Sarene yawned and curled up beside him, her hands tucked between his chest and hers. "What? Leave?"

"Yeah."

"Sure." She fingered a strand of her disheveled hair. "He's a priest. What can I say? They're never exactly on the same plane as the rest of us. They kind of have to be a little strange to spend all their time as religious servants. And some of them even give up sex. What is with that? Sounds like a sacrifice not worth making, especially if they're just going to grovel all day." Sarene cuddled against him, her head on his shoulder. "He'd be such a waste on it."

Silence followed Sarene's words. Several long moments later, her body relaxed as she fell asleep.

Mayr lay awake, staring at the ceiling as candlelight flickered across the beams. With Sarene in his arms, he should have been thinking about her. About why he was there; why he grappled to hold on to someone like her. About what the next day would bring and whether or not Sarene was happy.

Yet all of his thoughts were preoccupied with Tash.

Tightening his arm around Sarene reminded him of how it felt being in Tash's arms. The kiss he planted on Sarene's forehead dragged up the sensation of the sweet way Tash kissed him, as though Mayr was not accustomed to fighting and arresting criminals. As if he was fragile.

As if Tash cared about him.

Reality hit him hard, suffocating him with a new truth. Sarene might have been the one he was after, but Tash was the one he actually wanted.

Chapter Four

Goddesses, grant me peace.

Tash let out a shaky breath. Rolled his shoulders. Denied the suspicious chill racing down his spine. The cool, still air of the night drew him into its calm, coiling the secrets of the day around its shadows, the whisper of a dare to run with it all and fade into the darkness playing ghost with his conscience. The road to the temple was quiet, only the odd citizen out and about so late, most of them around the village core where light was plentiful. Here, halfway to the temple, only the thin moonlight and single lantern post at the crossroads offered relief from the darkness.

None of it illuminated what was going on inside him, however. No relief to spare for a mind so flustered.

He would have given anything to have held Mayr longer. To have kissed him for all the day to come, words tossed aside, not forgotten, just told to wait. He would have done even more to see Mayr sated and utterly spent for all his life, the bountiful, ever-loving grace of Emeraliss willing.

Instead, he had walked out. Always walking out, never to stay. Never to form that bond any further than what the body allowed. The price was too high to want anything else; to try for anything more. A price he never wanted to pay again.

But this was a different price to pay, leaving Mayr behind, and for the life of him, he had no idea why.

Hands slipped into his pants pockets, Tash kept his gaze on the road as he walked along its grassy edge. The universe worked in such strange ways, taunting and haunting, an ethereal tapestry of connection and oddity, never owing answers, never fully revealing its hand. The Goddesses took pride in understanding that tapestry far greater than any mortal, and They toyed with the threads with all the glee of children tempered with wisdom gleaned from ages far beyond anyone's recollection.

In all his ten years as a priest, he had learned to accept Their meddling, but it would never stop him from asking questions that burned a hole through his curiosity—or praying for some sliver of explanation to put his worries at ease. That included whatever had happened back at Orae's tavern. At best, it was a mixture of all things concerning, and it had him biting back every urge to turn around and crawl back into that warm bed. To have that heated body pressed against him, trusting, falling into his touch and giving in to what could be possible if circumstances were different.

He had no intention of forfeiting his decisions, or throwing aside his devoutness, but Emeraliss save his soul for wanting to be someone else completely. Had his life taken any other path, he would have stayed there, nipping at Mayr's lips and tempting to forget Sarene altogether, at least long enough to attempt to hollow out Mayr's fears a little more. Such beauty shrouded in shadow. Such a need to be loved but a heart so lost. Whatever fate had led them to the same bed also brought vulnerability to the surface; soft, fragile, nothing more than a whisper few could recognize but one that spoke louder than a sobbing cry.

Had Tash been anyone else, he would have offered comfort to ease that pain. Given himself to see that vulnerability guided to a safe place. To see it home.

As it was, he could do nothing to shake the feeling they should have known each other well before now.

For all the sense it made, he felt cheated. Robbed of the time they could have had. He berated himself for not meeting Mayr sooner, for not passing him in a candlelit hallway somewhere, all of that golden light cast across Mayr's face, his cool grey eyes taking on an enticing shine. He lamented not casually bumping into Mayr in the middle of the village market and fumbling with purchases like the fool Tash clearly was.

Like the fool he *most certainly* was, given that Mayr was still back there and Tash was here, on the road, in the dark, alone. And feeling like the worst sort of cur.

"Emeraliss, forgive me," Tash murmured, casting his gaze to the cloudy sky, the moon a hopeful crescent on its way to the fullest of its many faces. His clothes felt wrong, unease clinging to his skin as surely as the scents of sex and sweat did, both of them needing to be washed away once he got into his room at the temple. Or, at least one of them did—he was still fond of the scent and the memory it stirred. Just remembering revived a need for fresh release, and no doubt his hand would take that release into its clutches, all to the memory of Mayr's lips on his...

With a sigh, Tash quickened his pace along the dirt road and gave a halfhearted kick, sending small stones in different directions. His relationship with Sarene was not yet four weeks old. Nothing serious, neither of them looking for anything more than a bit of fun, a fact he had laid bare the first time she approached him for more private, intimate attention—a fact she had accepted happily, saying she was avoiding commitment anyway. It was a narrow middle road they could walk together without one pushing the other into some sort of turmoil they ought to just leave alone.

But Mayr... Tash expected a one-night affair, nothing more. His happiness was best curled up inside the most casual couplings like a content kitten asleep by the fireside. He was safest when he moved from one to another, harmlessly playing, so long as all parties agreed. This was far from being his first single night with anyone, and it certainly would not be his last, but damn him and whatever was aggravating his wants into lusting after another night at Mayr's side. There was no time for it. No place to set for it at the table of what needed to be done. No good could come from entertaining something that would end in disaster—because he felt it coming, that danger that was so busy trying to hide behind the beauty, using the novel and the curious to bait him into walking a line he dared not cross.

He had gotten this far, the line put behind him, fragments carved into him as reminders. There was no need to flirt with it, to test his resolve any more than it was being challenged now.

Strength. He was stronger than this. It had taken years just to get to this point, and no striking, stunning soul could deter him. The Goddesses... he was Theirs, promised and true. Perhaps even bound one day, should They consider him worthy enough to make the journey. Anything else was as destructive as poison, commitment to any one heart even more so.

Blessed Emeraliss, fair of grace, full of comfort, lend me that which I lack. At least get me back home without stumbling over everything I've done and wish I could do.

Tash scowled at the road. Entreat Emeraliss as he might, he had to wonder if She was giggling like Sarene at what all was transpiring. Emeraliss was a kind goddess, loving, gentle like a kiss of breeze on the cheek and tough like any mother trying to keep her children safe. But Emeraliss was also as playful as the birds that filled the sky during mating season, and She delighted in challenge, offering every chance to grow and test murky waters. Was this one of those rippling creeks he needed to find a bridge over or was he wandering too close to a tempest with the ability to shift and twist, raining hail upon him until he ran for cover?

Where Sarene was concerned, it was more like a raging river overwhelming the banks and claiming the earth for its own, spoils afloat on the surface, displaced and headed on a conquest they never asked for.

The disjointed creep of regret unsettled him, the tiny pests of wariness and doubt crawling out from the cracks in memory where he had stuffed them away. His relationship with Sarene had started before she broke up with Mayr, though not with intimacy, only flirting, with that dance of glances and words and sly smiles as if the finality of physical touch was only cleverness come to pass. After overhearing gossip that Sarene was in a committed relationship with Mayr, Tash had told her, explicitly and carefully, that he would not help her cheat on Mayr, if that was her intention.

She appeared to have heard his every word: shortly after, she stumbled into his arms one afternoon in the market, overcome with tears and sniffles, seeking comfort from her breakup with Mayr.

Tash's brow furrowed as he stopped on the road, his gaze on the faint yellow light in the distance from the lantern post at the next set of crossroads. For whatever it was worth, he was sorry to have been the reason Sarene left Mayr. Though it brought into question several things, many of which ate away at him with a growing intensity. Just weeks after she and Tash had started sleeping together, she announced she had reconsidered her relationship with Mayr. That she wanted to try again. Since Tash risked nothing whether she left or stayed, he had let her go, all too happy to move on.

The last thing he expected was for her to come back, saying Mayr wanted a threesome. For fun. That he had promised he would do anything for Sarene—*"anything at all,"* she had said, adding that Mayr had more than agreed, and was *"terribly looking forward to it. I'd hate to disappoint him."* She had pouted ever so sweetly and Tash had given in without much more than a wink and a sneaking suspicion he abruptly quashed.

Except now…

Suspicion came roaring back. Calm as Mayr had been, the false front he put on betrayed more of him than he might have realized. Either that or Tash had been just that in tune with him, able to read him with ease and sympathy. Though if he were truly being honest, the nagging thought of being played boiled just beneath the surface of everything he felt. Sarene had pulled a fast move on them both, him *and* Mayr, or so it seemed.

Or maybe I'm seeing what I want to see. Tash sighed and continued walking, arms crossed over his chest, his fists buried in the crooks of his arms. The realization about Sarene had ruined the mood for him early on, when they were still eating dinner, though he tried to hide it and carried on with whatever the plan had been. Had he not wanted to show Mayr he could be as gentle as Mayr needed and just as passionate in guiding him through uncertainty, Tash would have drawn Sarene aside and told her the scheme was failing—that he had no interest in pushing someone's boundaries when they clearly wanted to be anywhere else but there. He had his own boundaries. Hard limits he would never sever, not for anyone or anything, with his life staked to the appropriate punishment should he even dare.

And yet, despite his misgivings, Mayr had stayed. Touched. Held onto Tash, allowing him taste and find precious moments that belonged to them and them alone.

Still, Tash felt like a complete ass, even if Mayr had consented the whole time. An error in judgment he would have to come to terms with, particularly since the whole time, something about Mayr had been... off. The experience was nothing like it should have been. Nothing like Tash was used to. It sat sweeter than honey on the tongue, but stung so deeply, almost burning to the point of agony. The need to know why stole his breath. Twisted his conviction and stabbed at it with a dozen blunt knives. It even had him turning his head and looking back down the road, towards the village.

All else was dead space in between, ready to pitch him into a void that would swallow him whole if it had the chance.

Goddesses clutch his resolve close because he had choices to make, all of them with tricky thorns best avoided.

Chapter Five

Sarene was out of the bed and bustling around the room before Mayr opened his eyes. The new day was upon them as though nothing had happened the night before, the intensity of the sunlight suggesting it was midmorning.

And I fell asleep at dawn. Mayr silenced a groan and pressed his palms to his heavy eyelids. Plagued by thoughts he wanted to forget, he had lain awake, considering what he should tell Sarene. *Nothing. Tell her nothing. Or tell her it was fine and carry on? Or that it was good and suggest it again? Dammit, I don't know. I don't even know what got into me. For all I know, it was a fluke—it won't ever happen again. Maybe I was imagining it. Or making it into something it wasn't.*

Except doubt feasted on his justifications and threatened to rip them apart. There was still the matter of feeling connected to Tash even without words. Something beyond the tangled bed sheets and sexual desire.

A loud thump and muted clatter beside the bed startled him. Wide-eyed, Mayr sat up to study the bedroom. He looked down to find his black boots lying haphazardly on the floorboards where Sarene had tossed them. The knife he kept in his right boot was on the floor, hidden under the bed, the tip of its black and gold hilt sticking out from under the frame.

Sarene giggled, moving away from the foot of the bed where his boots had originally sat. "You should get up, darling. Things to do. I'm sure Aeley will want you back to work. There's always something, isn't there?" She teased her fingers through her hair and smoothed the blonde strands before twisting and tying them back with her pink ribbon. "Mmm, it's a good morning. I can't believe I didn't do this before. I feel *so* good. It was so invigorating. And he's so amazing."

Sighing wistfully, she slipped into her dress. "I told you he was good. Wasn't he good? Too bad I didn't meet him until a few months ago. We could've had this much fun *well* before now. I wouldn't have had to put up with so many disappointments." Sarene paused and tilted her head, her crinkled sash in her hand. "You know, I never thought about it, but maybe it's a priest thing. Maybe they just know how to please people better. Maybe it's part of their training. There's a love goddess, right? Maybe She has secrets only they know."

Without looking to Mayr for a response, she laughed and tied the sash around her waist. "Or not. Maybe he's just naturally perfect." Hands on her hips, she glanced around the room. "I think that's all I brought. Everything else is yours."

Sarene smiled sweetly, curving her elbows inward and squeezing her waist flirtatiously. "Could you settle the rest of what we owe Orae, sweetheart? I would, but I didn't bring *anything* with me and I really have to get going. My sister just won't wait for me before she starts picking through the market. She's so impatient!"

Before Mayr could ask her to toss him his shirt, she blew him a kiss and flounced towards the door. "Thanks, darling. I'll see you later. I'll come by the estate when I get a chance."

The next moment, she left the room.

Mayr stared at the closed door. *She couldn't have gotten out of here any quicker. Here she was; off she goes. And I'm left settling the fee. As if I didn't see that coming.* Typical Sarene, he reminded himself, getting out of the bed to put on his pants and shirt. She was the same as she was before they broke up, not that he expected her to change. It also was not worth a fight. Worse women existed.

Like the one he had married.

Tried to marry, he corrected. *There's a difference. You keep missing that. It doesn't make it any less true.*

That one lie made every other relationship even more important. The driving force behind why he needed to fix things with Sarene. One day, a relationship would work out and he could stop cursing Betta for her lies. One day, he would stop trying to be perfect enough for someone to stay. One day, he would stop killing himself in the process.

Was it too much to hope for someone to care as much as a complete stranger had?

Mayr pulled on his boots, memories of Tash hijacking his angry thoughts. Whenever Tash had focused on Mayr, it changed everything. He had felt cared for. As though Tash had looked beyond Mayr's title and appearance to tend to the part of him no one could see and few rarely cared about.

Ah, now you're just making things up, my sappy, utterly bitter self. You need to quit that. It'll just get you kicked in the balls or worse: actually marrying someone for real this time. Do you really *need that? In all honesty, why do you care?*

He sighed. Because time was fickle, as was lying in the dark, alone, night after night, deciding what to do with a life he had worked hard to earn. And for what? Himself?

Fully dressed, Mayr bent down to retrieve his knife.

Beside it, barely visible, a thin, dark cord peeked out from under the bed. Once he leaned further, he made out the silhouette of a small pouch.

Curious, he picked up the pouch, surprised to find it resembled Tash's.

Didn't he take it with him? It was hanging on his belt when he left. Mayr's brow furrowed, a memory nudging his attention. *Or maybe it wasn't.* He stared at the bag. There were a couple of ways to find out, the most immediate method within his purview as Head of the Guard and an agent of the law in Kattal. *I'll just make sure it's nothing dangerous before I figure out who it belongs to. Can't be too trusting, not after what Ae's gone through. And the Goddesses know I don't trust Lira's family further than I can poke them.*

After he opened the bag and sorted through the contents, there were no doubts. Along with the handful of bronze and silver coins were Tash's talon-shaped ring and silver chain. There was also a wooden container just small enough to sit inside his curved palm. When he unscrewed the lid, a potent, sweet fragrance wafted through the air. The container was half-filled with oil, and it did funny things to his gut. The scent reminded him of red corina plant mixed with millee nectar. One was used by healers to relax skin and muscles. The other heightened the senses and encouraged arousal—the same effect it had on him the longer he stood there sniffing it, wishing he could press his naked body to Tash's and drown in the sound of low moans.

He capped the container. Why was the pouch under the bed? It should have remained attached to Tash's belt. Unless…

No. He wouldn't lie, would he? Mayr eyed the container, his suspicions telling him what it was for. He had almost forgotten the argument between Sarene and Tash over oil. *'Misplaced,' he said. If that's true, what's this? Far as I can tell, he* had exactly *what he needed.*

Why would Tash lie to Sarene?

Bombarded with more questions than answers, Mayr returned everything to the pouch. He would return it before he went back to the estate. Otherwise, it would taunt him for the rest of the day, worse than his memories already did.

To his relief, no one bothered him as he went downstairs to speak to Orae, the tiny, white-haired woman who owned the tavern. On his way back from visiting Tash, he would settle the account for the room and meal.

She peered up at him with a grin, the wrinkles around her dark eyes deepening. "As if I'd say no? Honestly, Mayr, I thought we were beyond this. Don't make me tell your mother you aren't listening to your elders." Orae wiped the table beside them. "Told you you're welcome anytime and for the price of nothing. Also said you don't ever need to worry about paying right away yet you ignore me and do it anyhow. Just come back whenever, show your face, and we'll call it even." She propped her fists on her hips. "And tell that priest friend of yours he keeps causing a stir in here. Half my girls can't keep their eyes in their head whenever he comes 'round."

She leaned forward, glancing around the empty dining room. "And we need to keep my girls away from your girlfriend," Orae whispered, frowning as she straightened and rubbed her back. "They're not fond of her. At least they aren't now that you're back together. You sure it's a good idea?"

What? That everyone knows my business in this place?

Mayr cleared his throat. "It's fine, Orae. I appreciate the concern, but it's handled." He clasped her shoulder. "I'll be back before midday. Then you can tell me the latest gossip."

Orae's face brightened. "Oh, it's good. Real good. These last few days…" With her fist to her lips, she chuckled. "I tell you, the things I see and hear. A village is never boring. And no one ever pays us tavern folk enough mind." She pushed him away. "But go on. Go. You've made me fall behind. No different than when you were as tall as me, being a scoundrel with the other boys."

"Just because you'd miss it if I didn't." Mayr kissed her cheek. "I'll be back soon." He left the tavern with a quick look back. Orae belonged to a past he found himself missing every few days. As a boy, helping in the tavern had helped him in unforgettable ways. The meagre pay he had earned had restored some of the pride he lost the day he had failed his mother most. If anything, it had assuaged his guilt enough to make each day more bearable.

In many ways, Orae reminded him of Korre Dahe, Aeley's late father, who had given Mayr the chance to be a guard when Mayr had needed it most. Both Orae and Korre had been kind and understanding. They had given Mayr the benefit of the doubt when others scoffed at him for being the gangly son of a farmer. If anyone had been like a second set of parents, it was the two of them.

Preoccupied by the sombre reminder he would eventually lose Orae just as he had Korre, the walk to the Temple of the Four felt longer than Mayr remembered. Located on the outermost edge of the village, the temple shone brightly in the sunlight, nestled in a small wood of blood-red trees dotted with white blooms among the thick leaves. Crafted from pure white marble, the temple stood majestically, separated from the red earth by a dozen wide, white steps leading up to the columns supporting the weight of the temple's front entrance. Exquisite carvings of legendary beasts and heroes adorned the columns from capital to base. Between the columns were small gardens, full of glossy green ferns, feather-like herbs, and white coronni flowers with golden centres as large as his hand. The rest of the temple hid in the shade of the surrounding trees, the other entrances disguised.

Mayr climbed the steps slowly. His mother and father were faithful believers, showing reverence to the Four every morning. The same level of worship had yet to manifest in not just Mayr, but his brother and sister, Loftin and Estara. To them, the four Goddesses were strange mistresses who wanted one thing one day and the opposite the next, only to overthrow the decision the day after that.

At the top of the last step, Mayr paused to study the open doors on the other end of the series of columns. Around the doorway, vines of bright red and pink flowers created an arch. Delicate strands of clear crystals hung from the thick stalks, catching the light and dispersing it across the marble in a vivid array of colour. They swayed gently, making the coloured light dance across the columns.

Continuing forward, Mayr crossed the threshold, greeted by the scent of incense and flowers. The sacred area of worship was spacious and inviting. In the centre of the rounded space was a black stone altar. Four large candles sat in the middle, each with four lit wicks and a flower crown with ribbons of various colours encircling the base. Four large glass goblets and bowls sat on the edge of the table, each filled to the brim with offerings. In the ceiling above the altar was a large pane of circular glass. Clear except for the red pane in the middle, the window spread light on and around the altar space, giving the room a dim red tint. At various positions near the altar were villagers and priests, either kneeling or standing with their heads bowed and open palms held outwards.

To avoid disturbing those gathered, Mayr adjusted the weight of his steps and entered the temple further. He peered up at the statues as he passed between them. Four statues guarded the entrance, two on either side. Chiseled from the same white marble as the temple, the statues of the Four gleamed, their clear glass eyes fixed on everything and nothing. To his left stood Emeraliss, Goddess of Love, and Hastal, Goddess of Protection. To his right, Laytia, Goddess of Wisdom, and Navara, Goddess of Justice. True to every representation of the Four's images found in Kattal, each statue carried two objects, one poised with deliberate meaning in each hand. Both Emeraliss and Laytia carried glass scepters, but where Emeraliss hoisted a grand bird made of silver with a majestic crown and trailing tail of metal feathers, Laytia held out six seeing stones of various hues. Likewise, Hastal and Navara each bore a glass staff, but Hastal carried a golden shield with fine engravings while Navara balanced a pair of bronze scales.

The lifeless gazes of the statues stared after him as he entered the sacred space. Guilt washed over him, followed by sadness and regret. He said a prayer for forgiveness before wishing the feelings away. Just once, he wanted to pass by the statues and not relive the truth of things he had done. Accidents he could have avoided; blood he had shed. Mistakes he could never make right.

Maybe some of his parents' beliefs had rubbed off on him after all.

"May I help you on your path?" a low voice inquired, almost a whisper. A man with short, grey hair approached from the corridor on Mayr's left, shuffling his sandaled feet. Similar to the other priests and priestesses Mayr had encountered, the man was dressed in layers of dark red robes. A glimmering red veil draped over his head and trailed behind him, his aged face fully visible. On his left hand, he wore four silver rings. "Ah, Mayr of the Dahe family. How can I assist?"

"I'm looking for Tash," Mayr answered.

The priest frowned. "Tash?"

Mayr took a deep breath, trying not to show annoyance. *And here's where I find out he's not actually a priest, right? This is just great. I've been had—again. Did he dupe Sarene, too, or was she in on it?* He stole a glance at the statues. *Please, let me be wrong. If there's anything I can ask of You today, it's this. Please tell me Betta's lies haven't completely jaded my life.*

"Yeah." Mayr cleared his throat. "He's my height, hair to here, around the shoulders. Wears bracers. And a ring that's like a talon."

The priest mumbled, repeating the words. His eyes lit with recognition. "You mean Halataldris? Yes, he's here." He turned and motioned to the woman standing beside one of the pillars lining the corridor.

The woman moved towards them. Young and curvaceous with red hair to her lower back, she appeared more of a villager than a priestess, lacking the red robes to which Mayr was accustomed. Instead, she wore a simple, sleeveless white gown with a red sash draped over one shoulder. "Yes, Brother Armamae?"

"Sister Esaline, I need you to fetch Brother Halataldris. With haste, preferably."

Esaline bowed her head to Armamae before she hurried away.

Confused, Mayr watched her disappear into the shadows of the corridor leading past the space of worship, towards the back of the temple. *Halataldris?* He waited silently with Armamae and hoped Esaline didn't return with a complete stranger.

When she reappeared with Tash at her side, Mayr let out the breath he had been unconsciously holding. Tash's smile relieved him even further.

Armamae inclined his head as Tash approached. "I shall leave you to it. Come, Sister Esaline. Let them alone." Taking her arm, Armamae shuffled towards the altar.

"Welcome." Tash tucked his hair behind his ear, revealing a bracer that almost matched the tone of his skin. The bracer was not the only difference from the night before: dark sandals replaced his boots and his red robe was laced closed across his chest. "We should go over here," he suggested, leading Mayr to the corridor.

As they walked down the long hallway, Mayr stayed close to Tash. "You don't look the same."

"Who? Me?"

Mayr gestured to Armamae and Esaline. "None of you. Well, some of you. Sort of. I'm not making much sense, am I?"

Tash hummed. "No, you do. It's the difference in levels that has you confused." He clasped his hands before him. "Those at the Metah level wear only white with a hint of red—they have not yet earned their right to wear only the sacred colour of the Four. Rese priests, such as myself, have earned our first robes. The Uldana priests, however, wear all red and cover their heads in tribute to the Goddesses."

"Oh." Mayr stared at the floor as they passed small rooms, the space of worship no longer in his sight. Muffled voices came from the other side of the doors but the words were undecipherable. He could barely comprehend the words in his head. What was he supposed to say?

He glanced at Tash, one brow raised. "So… Halataldris, is it? Just how many names do you have?" Mayr paused. "And correct me if I'm wrong, but isn't that the name of a bird? Something to do with Emeraliss? Her bird—the one She carries in all the statues—right? He's all white and silver with blue eyes or something?"

A sheepish smile took over Tash's lips. His cheeks coloured as he lowered his chin. "My full name is Halataldris, but I prefer Tash because it's shorter, easier. However, many priests don't believe in short forms. They call me by my full name, not only because it was what I was given, but especially because it *is* the name of Emeraliss's sacred bird, the Father of All Birds." Tash straightened and grinned, a playful expression in his eyes. "I'm impressed, though. You know your legends, then?"

Mayr shrugged. "My parents love the old stories, particularly my mother who swears by the Four each day. I was bound to remember something of them. Though if you asked me to name anything else the statues carry, I probably couldn't."

"Laytia carries the Eseldeer, stones of past, present, and future. Hastal bears Talean the Unbreakable. Navara carries the Onamarre, or Fate's Truth. See? Easy."

"Says the priest." Mayr cocked his head to the side. "Maybe I'll add a new name to your list: Oh-pretentious-one."

Tash's laugh was low and rich. "Sorry to disappoint, but it's already been bestowed." He stopped walking, his expression difficult to decipher. "I'm pleased you came."

An awkward silence fell between them. Mayr tried not to read more into the last words than he suspected they meant but failed. The only thing he could think about was Tash's hand gliding over his skin.

"I, uh, came to give you this back." Mayr cleared his throat and offered the pouch. "Found it under the bed. And I'm sorry, but I had to look inside. I needed to make sure I knew what it was. Find out who it belonged to."

Tash grasped the pouch but did not take it. "And?"

"And maybe I'm searching for something I shouldn't be, but if that's what I think it is in that container, I'm confused. You told Sarene you didn't have anything. So if that *is* what I *think* it is, isn't lying against the rules of being a priest?"

"Sometimes a small, harmless lie is necessary to pursue the greater truth." Tash took the pouch and looped it around his wrist. "Truth is what we're meant to search for and disperse. Besides, I did not lie. I told her I misplaced them, which was true. I placed this bag under the bed while the two of you were occupied. Her interpretation of 'misplaced' was hers alone."

"Meaning what, exactly?"

The expressions on Tash's face morphed before he clasped Mayr's hand and pulled him into a room on their left. Inside, the room was awash with light from clear glass windows above and along the furthest wall. Plants filled the room from floor to ceiling, Mayr realized, as Tash closed the door.

Tash leaned into Mayr, similar to the night before at the bar in the tavern. "I wasn't going to take what you weren't ready to give," he murmured, stirring a familiar sensation in Mayr's gut. "I told you I'd take care of you, and that's how. I didn't care what Sarene wanted. I wasn't going to do it. Your safety—*your* comfort—was paramount, not her selfishness or carnal desires." He gave Mayr a knowing glance. "You know how she is. She was also oblivious to how you felt. She couldn't see the truth. Or wouldn't. So I diverted her scheme."

For me? You purposely ruined her plans for me? Mayr stared at Tash. What could he say to his admission?

Hesitant, Tash touched Mayr's hand. "I need to know: how are you now? Did you find it as uncomfortable as you thought it would be?"

Mayr's face warmed. He knew the answer, but could not say it. Not out loud. Saying it would change things he was not ready to leave behind. Not yet.

"I have to leave," Mayr mumbled, opening the door. "I've got some things to do for Aeley. I just wanted to return your things."

He hurried out of the temple the way he came, thankful Tash did not follow. Had he, Mayr might have stood there, stammering and trying to find something to say.

I'm with Sarene, that's what I'd say. I can't be thinking of anyone else when I'm supposed to be focused on her. I need to pull myself together. It was one night. Strange, mildly enjoyable, but one night. And just for her. Only for her. I can't want anything else because I can't have *anything else. So shut up, rest of me, and stop getting me into trouble. You can't want what you can't have, and that's final.*

"Would you stop giving me indigestion? How's a man supposed to enjoy his breakfast when you keep bringing *them* up?" Mayr forced himself to glower at Aeley and Lira over the dining table. "And stop looking at me like I'm five years old. I happen to *like* breakfast, thank you very much. It's tasty. And Cook isn't trying to kill me. I really appreciate that."

From her seat across from him, Lira tittered, holding her hand to her lips.

Mayr wagged his piece of bread at her. "Yeah, but you just wait until Cook burns those pastries you like so much. Then we'll see who's laughing." To emphasize his point, he chomped dramatically on the bread.

Aeley snorted and shifted in her seat at the head of the long table, with Mayr and Lira on either side of her. "Promises, promises."

Face contorted playfully, Mayr stuck out his tongue at her. Five days had passed since his night with Sarene and Tash. And every day, he tried not to think about it, busying himself with his work. The fact Aeley *still* brought up the issue of Lira's family meant he needed to do more to assure her nothing would happen at the upcoming feast. Any problem or disastrous scenario he could think of would be assigned a plan of action and guards to enforce it. He had been up since before dawn, working on whom he would place where for the greatest effect.

Lira sipped water from her metal goblet. "I digress. You're absolutely right." She offered him an apologetic smile. "Friends again?"

Always.

"I suppose, if I have to." Mayr sighed, flicking his gaze over the dark red wood panels of the walls. "Otherwise these meals of ours will get *plenty* rowdy. I'll say something witty; you'll call me a fool. Aeley will kick me in the shin; I'll throw eggs in her hair. It'll be bedlam. Complete chaos." He settled into the curved back of his wooden chair and skimmed his hands over the table. "Breakfast should be civilized."

Aeley tsked at him. "You shouldn't use words you don't know."

"And you. Should. Eat." Mayr punctuated each word with a push on her clay plate, annoyed by how little she had taken and her even fewer bites. "Don't make me come up with a creative way to get you to, because you know I will."

"Please. It'll end in *you* eating it." Aeley jabbed her food with her spoon. "I'm not hungry. I thought I was, but something lied."

When she glanced at the metal decanters on the wood cart along the furthest wall, Mayr stiffened. The last thing they needed was for her to chase away her irritation with alcohol. They had been there before. Never again, he had promised her.

"Don't you dare." Mayr slapped Aeley's wrist.

Aeley slapped his arm. "I wasn't going to, *mother*." She smirked. "Just thinking of some creative things of my own." The lusty gaze she cast Lira was unmistakable.

Mayr groaned. "Just wait until I'm out of the room this time, all right? Here, I'll grab my things and—"

"Stay put?" Aeley interrupted. "Because that's how *civilized* breakfasts happen."

Pouting, Mayr lowered his head and stared at her over the rim of his goblet. "You're mean. And you smell funny. I should tell the Council."

"That I smell funny?"

"I'll say it's a matter of regional interest."

"And they'll say…?"

Mayr grinned. "That I should be replaced. Then I'll ask for one of their jobs. Ha!" He pointed at Lira. "Then I can solve the problem of your parents *real* quick. *No* problem. None." He waggled his brows. "Council should've made me a councilman a *long* time back. Imagine all of the cleaning up I could've done by now. Especially when I look this good. One of their Council coats would look excellent on me."

"Yes, but then we would miss having you here with us," Lira said. "Who else could make every meal even half as ridiculous?"

"You're so nice." Mayr reached over the platters between them to touch her hand. "Can you be Tract Steward, instead?"

Lira laughed. "Not on your life."

"But you help her do it," he argued, pointing at Aeley.

"Right, and there's a clear difference. You could not bribe me enough to run for election, let alone make Ae lose the position." Lira held up her hands. "I'm happy being a scribe. That's what I wanted to do, and now I have it. Permanently, far as the High Council has decreed. I will happily attend meetings with Aeley for the rest of my life and write until my fingers shrivel up and fall off." She grasped Aeley's hand. "Tract Steward is a special kind of torture I would loathe to endure. Having seen it from this end, I admire my wife for doing it. Especially since half the time, I'd end up saying highly inappropriate things. With one joke, I could start a war."

Mayr watched the loving way Lira caressed Aeley's fingers. They were still happy even after being together for two years, and being married for half of it. They had everything he could wish for them, save a tranquil life. Peace was a luxury Aeley had forfeited after she ran for the election of Tract Steward against her brother.

Since then, her life consisted of governing the tract of Gailarin on behalf of the republic, requiring her constantly divided attention. Whenever Aeley was not involved in the problems of the people, she tended to the requests of the High Council. There was always a meeting with someone, taking up at least half of her time.

Magistrates regularly vied to grab her attention for their villages, demanding improvements to everything in their society, more funds, and special requests on behalf of families and individuals who dared not approach her. Councilmen called upon her almost daily with proclamations, amendments to laws, updates on campaigns and projects that spanned the republic, and enough bureaucracy to drown her.

As long as she was Steward, she would remain wedged between the two groups, one of the official middlemen of Kattal's political hierarchy. The people of Gailarin saw the region's problems as everything; the High Council saw Gailarin as one small part of Kattal. Their demands often conflicted and constantly pulled Aeley between them. When she was not in meetings, she divided her time among visits to villages to gauge their well-being, reviews of guards and soldiers, and Lira. There was little time spent on herself.

And that's where I come in. Not just to make sure no one assassinates her, but making sure she stays sane. Kind of wish I could be on Council, though. I could make things easier for her: for them both. And for Mother and Father. For everybody, actually.

"I know. I was just joking," Mayr told Lira softly. "You know I love you, right?"

Aeley patted his hand. "You'd know if we didn't."

A knock on the wall startled them. Someone cleared their throat.

"Pardon my intrusion," a raspy voice said.

"Morning, Haydin." Mayr faced the elderly steward of the estate. Haydin had lived with the Dahes for most of his life. Before Aeley, Haydin had served Aeley's father and ran the estate while Korre dealt with Gailarin business. To Aeley, Haydin was family, the closest thing to an uncle she had. Somehow, he had managed to outlive even Korre, although his frail form and questionable health concerned them all with each passing year.

"Good morning, Haydin," Aeley greeted, her tone cheerful. "Anything I can help you with?"

Haydin bowed his head, revealing the balding patch in his white hair. "Nothing at the moment, but thank you." His dark eyes turned onto Mayr. "Although you have a visitor. Sarene requests an audience."

Mayr jumped up. Not seeing Sarene for several days had disappointed him. More than once, he'd wondered if she had moved on. "Thanks, Haydin." He looked to Aeley. "Mind if I borrow that dismal abode you call a study? I promise we won't do things on your desk you haven't already done with Lira."

Disgust twisted Aeley's expression. "Don't *do* anything."

"Thanks, Ae." Mayr rushed away without waiting for Haydin.

Sarene stood in the spacious foyer between the main entrance and the wooden staircase leading to the floor above. Her yellow dress and pink shawl brightened the hallway, stealing attention away from the grey and black floor stones set in elaborate, swirled patterns.

"Good morning," Mayr muttered, kissing her before she said a word. He had half a mind to lead her up the stairs to his room. Instead, he grasped her hand. "Let's take this someplace more private."

Their walk through the corridors was quiet. Even as they entered the study, Sarene said nothing. She stopped in the centre of the room, surveying the dark red walls and large stained-glass pane looking out onto green trees. An old desk sat across the room, parchments and rolled scrolls littered across its surface. Except for the beige wood panels on the one wall with a coloured target painted on them and dozens of holes, the study was unremarkable.

"I missed you." Mayr closed the door and turned. "Had I known you were coming by today, I would've—"

"It isn't working."

Mayr froze, his smile extinguished.

Not again.

"What?" He forced the word out of his dry mouth.

Sarene sighed heavily as though his question were an imposition. "It isn't working out how I'd hoped. I thought we could get it right the second time, but it isn't any better. I'm just not feeling like it's any different. So we're breaking up permanently."

"Wait, what? You decided this all on your own? And when?" Mayr demanded. "I did everything you wanted, Sarene. You said you were wrong; that you wanted it to work. I did what you asked me to. Then you don't see me for all this time, but suddenly it's over? No discussion, no nothing?"

"I can't fix what's broken." Sarene shrugged. "Besides, I found someone else; a better match. He's more my type. And I didn't decide it all on my own," she said matter-of-factly. "Tash thinks it's better this way."

Everything Mayr wanted to say disappeared, blown apart by one name. "Tash?"

"We were together last night. I told him about us, and he agreed I should break it off."

Betrayal pummeled Mayr, anger coursing through him in heavy waves. How dare Tash say anything to Sarene; how dare Tash be with Sarene at all. *Is* this *taking care of me? He breaks us up just so he can have her for himself? Nice. So much for respect and all the other things he spewed. I knew it. And here I was tempted to see him and actually give him an answer: to thank him for asking after me because no one ever does. He's just like everyone else, except he got her to do the damage because he couldn't do it to my face.*

"Out." Mayr pointed at the door, unable to look at her. He wanted to hit someone. Repeatedly. *Myself, though it's kind of difficult to land a good punch when your arms are attached.*

"Gladly."

Mayr crossed the room as Sarene passed him without a touch or glance. Stopped beside the desk, he listened to the door close.

He yanked the knife from his belt and threw it at the target on the wall with as much force as he could muster. The knife drove straight into the centre of the target. Lodged in the wood halfway up the blade, it stuck out from the middle of the bright red circle.

Glaring at the hilt, Mayr flexed his fingers. No, he did not know Tash well, but he had believed Tash was more honest than that. He had thought they understood each other in some semblance of the concept, at least enough to possibly forge a friendship. Because whenever they were together, he wanted to stay longer, to know more. He wanted to understand how two utter strangers could seem familiar to one another.

Now he was nothing. Again. And the familiarity was a lie. A trick. An effective manipulation.

With a grimace, Mayr peered at the painting of Aeley's father above the door. "Sorry, Korre. I try not to be a complete disappointment, but I still can't get it right. Even with all your advice. Pretty sure I've got 'patsy' tattooed all over me."

Mayr stared at the target. Knife throwing would not work his anger off quickly enough. He needed more. A better target. To throw his fist at someone hard enough to result in bandaged knuckles.

Maybe I'll haul Pellon off duty. He only has the perimeter shift. I'm sure he'd like sparring with me better than walking circles all afternoon. Goddesses know we've been scrapping since we were fifteen. I'm sure there's something he wouldn't mind whipping me over, some reason I've forgotten. Or we'll make up a whole new reason. Then get drunk. Really, really drunk. Or maybe I should run a surprise training drill. March right into the Guard House and announce it. No, even better; get drunk and then *announce it, just so Pellon and I can watch everyone run around this place like it's on fire. Haven't had one in a while, so maybe…*

His gaze drifted to Korre's portrait again. Regardless of what he did, he could not tell Aeley. The last thing he needed was for her to smash Sarene's head in and kill her.

He could save Aeley in a battle, but not from the laws and punishment of High Council.

Knocks on the door stole his attention. "Mayr? Are you still there?" Haydin's voice carried through the door.

"Yeah." Mayr opened the door. "Sorry, Haydin, I'm just—"

He stepped back, overwhelmed by the urge to punch the man beside Haydin.

"What are *you* doing here?" Mayr stared at Tash, gripping the doorframe to keep from doing something foolish.

Tash took a quick breath. "I wanted to talk to you. I wanted to—"

Mayr threw the door open further, satisfied as it banged the wall. "Fine. Get in here. And you'd better make it good."

Haydin's face paled. Caught between the two of them, he looked from one to the other. "I'll just leave you be." He ambled away and disappeared around a corner.

Once Tash was inside, Mayr slammed the door closed.

Tash did not jump nor did he back away. "I was coming to forewarn you about Sarene breaking things off. I thought I could catch you before she did. But I just passed her on her way out and realized I might be too late." He smiled sadly. "Now I'm here to see how you're taking it."

"How I'm *taking it*?" Mayr thrust his arms up. "Oh, I don't know. The fact I wouldn't mind ripping someone's head off has nothing to do with it. Or kicking you where it hurts most since *you* broke us up. You not only slept with her even though you *knew* she and I were together again, but then you went and helped her out. Sent her here to finish the job you two started. What? I couldn't catch the hint fast enough?" He crossed his arms. "Go on, tell me again how my *safety* and my *comfort* are paramount, because I'm sure you've got more pretty lies where those came from."

"They weren't lies," Tash whispered. "And I didn't sleep with her."

"That's definitely *not* what she said." Mayr snorted. "Sure, break my heart, but you can't even get your stories straight?"

Tash straightened. "I don't know *what* she told you, but I didn't sleep with her. Not after you took her back. And certainly not after the night you and I met. She wanted to, but I couldn't. Not just because she was seeing someone else, but because I honestly couldn't. Not when I was thinking about someone whose moral character makes hers pale in comparison and nearly non-existent."

"Please. Quit with the priestly riddles and spit it out. Stop insulting me."

"Mayr, please, listen. Not just to my words but between them." Tash stepped forward. "Sarene came to me last night. She wanted something she could not have. Instead of leaving, she stayed to talk. I asked about you since I've been worried. That's when she informed me she was leaving you." He took another step. "It wasn't a surprise to me, I'll admit. And yes, I agreed she should leave you."

When Mayr opened his mouth to protest, Tash raised his hand. "No, it was for *you*. It's obvious she was using you. She thought the three of us being together would fix the lack she felt in your relationship, but it changed nothing. She also admitted it didn't go the way she hoped; that the fate of your relationship rested on that one night." Disgust drifted across his face. "She complained that you were inadequate and not what she expected. Her words exactly: *'What's the point of being with the mighty Head of the Guard when he's nothing like that in bed? He's supposed to tell people what to do and act all tough. That's what I wanted him to do with you.'*"

Anger displaced Tash's disgust, his eyes narrowed. "It didn't sit right with me. I believe limits should be respected. You gave what you could, given the circumstances, and I'll defend that to the end, regardless of what anyone else wants. I would do no less if your positions were reversed." He frowned, something without words stirring in his eyes. "I know you cared for her— loved her—but you deserve better than her, so I encouraged her to end it. I then severed ties with her, myself. That's negative energy best left alone."

"And that's supposed to make it better?" Mayr yelled. "You're just plunging the knife further into my back."

"I'm sorry. I take full accountability for my actions, but I promise I didn't want it to go like this. I told you: we priests deal in truth."

"Truth? Right. You couldn't have just spared me with another lie-that-isn't-a-lie?"

Tash's gaze fell to the floor. "No, not over this." He took a deep breath. "But that isn't the only reason why I'm here. I wanted to check on you. You didn't give me an answer the other day and it's bothered me since. Considering you walked out, I took that to mean you weren't all right. Since I'm already apologizing, I equally apologize for offending you and any harm I inflicted. I should have turned Sarene down when she suggested we be together. I never should have stayed." Hands clasped, he lifted his chin. "I've done enough damage for one day. This wasn't part of my plan. I'll leave now—there's nothing else I can say that won't drive this any further down the painful path."

On his way out the door, Tash paused. "I'm sorry."

For a moment, Mayr believed it, watching Tash leave with a twinge of remorse. The longer he stared at the door, the more the truth dug a hole in his anger. He hurt, but not for the reasons Tash seemed to think. While Sarene leaving him was painful, it was not as bad as he anticipated. Although he knew he should feel worse, he was making peace with it quicker than the first time she left him. Shock might have gotten the best of him as she told him they were finished, but it was not the reason for his anger.

No, that honour belonged to Tash, who had swept out of the room with as much ease as he had worked Mayr's affections. A lukewarm withdrawal that only enraged him more, the depth of his feelings rooted in the agony of betrayal, twisting his insides until they ached to bleed out.

Despite feeling as if they had known each other forever, they really did not know each other at all.

Chapter Six

Well, that was two knives short of a finely cooked disaster.

Tash sighed and leaned against the coarse trunk of one of the weeping celorna trees at the edge of the village market. Drawing his hand over his eyes, he bowed his head and tried to ignore the hum of the villagers as they passed by, going about their business while he hid beneath the drooping crimson-gold branches. Usually he was content to stand there and watch life carry on its way, not so much listening but simply witnessing the friendly chatter here, careful negotiations there, and a normalness that would never settle with him again. Those days were over, lost to a youth gone sour, but to see others safe and happy in that normal gave him some peace of mind.

Mayr's rejection of him, however, stung his concern and bruised his consideration.

He could deal with the anger—he was trained to withstand it, despite how emotional he could be. And Mayr was far from being the first to reject Tash for his efforts. That was about as helpful as slipping on an old pair of beloved gloves riddled with holes: they were no good at keeping out the chill but plenty useful at reminding him how good they used to be.

No, Tash had been thrown into the thread and thrum of relationships only to take the fall for his decision to meddle. Had he expected Sarene to act so quickly, he would have done things differently. Chosen different words, given what Sarene had supposedly told Mayr. He would have timed his meeting better if not for Emeraliss casting one of Her more jarring jokes upon them.

Oh, how he loved their goddess to the ends of the universe and beyond, but maybe not so much right then.

Another sigh, another memory, Tash lifted his head to watch villagers mill about the market, some of them wishing him good morning and fair day as they wandered by him with smiles and a quick wave. Most had no idea he was there, his red robe blending well enough behind the cascades of narrow leaves and branches, a gentle breeze occasionally rustling the leaves. He managed a cheerful greeting for those who did notice him, wishing he could solve the problem weighing down his heart with as much ease.

Instead, he focused on the merchants' carts and their abundance of wares, surrounded by the laughter of the villagers as they clutched baskets and caught up on the latest gossip. Metal and glass glinted in the sunlight, the entire village a vision of colour as late summer let autumn quietly edge its way in.

Sarene had not been so gracious, and what she told Mayr only worsened the matter. Whatever her blatant lies, Tash had told Mayr the truth as he knew it. There was no reason to lie, and never as a priest. For ten years he had lived by his oath; would have died by it. He was not about to throw it all away for anyone, not even a lover.

But Sarene seemed to dance with the lies as easily as Tash gave himself to the Four, and that perturbed him as much as their conversation the night before. Nothing she had brought to his door had settled well then, and it certainly roiled with anger now.

Most of all, he was sorry for his part in the mess they were in. Had he not obliged her, they could have avoided the added complexity.

Except he *was* part of the situation and feeling all the worse for it.

Her words—the ones he had repeated verbatim to Mayr—they sat so heavily in his gut, twisted around each other with a loathing he dared not tear into lest memory serve its best revenge. Sarene had said more, her sexual advances as they spoke just as deliberate as her insistence that she wanted Tash and not Mayr. By then, however, he had realized how her game went, like a cogwheel that turned in the correct direction for four revolutions, but never failed to take those steps back on the fifth, sometimes slipping over more than one tooth and getting wedged in between until dislodged. She courted the power of guile, and maybe telling Mayr she had slept with Tash was partly a punishment for turning her away.

Right then, Tash hardly cared what she thought of him. He would leave her to deal with life however she saw fit, happy to leave any feelings about her by the wayside. While he understood what she wanted from her relationship with Mayr and could sympathize with her needs, that understanding stepped aside when compared to the look in Mayr's eyes the night they had bedded down. Mayr, who was so confident when left to be himself in the quiet moments but hesitant to step one foot wrong in love. Tash understood that, too. Empathized with it more deeply than he feared to revisit. Tash had tried to make it easier for Mayr—to make it safer to let his guard down and just *feel*. No demands, no expectations, no judgment.

So much for that—he's on his way to hating me now. Any extra time I wanted with him…

Sabotage taunted him bitterly, kicking jealousy into the mix like a dust cloud swept up over the road, the dirt and grit stinging his eyes as he tried to see a way through. Disappointment was there, too, underlying it all, just as a deepening sadness wrapped around those feelings and held tight. He had hoped for better, not that he expected Mayr to kiss him until their faces all but fell off.

But touch...

Yes, he *had* hoped for that. Even longed for Mayr to look at him with the same interest as he had before, that stunned look on his face and the searching glance—one that slipped through Tash, falling into the cracks just to get at what lay beneath, those haunting eyes searing themselves into his memory. He had wanted that, or at least a taste of it, whether he had to tease it from Mayr or not.

With another heavy sigh, Tash stepped out from beneath the branches and into the light, bringing glances his way. As he raked his hand through his hair, his silver talon ring glided through the thick wavy strands, setting fire to whatever images his lust had thrown at him. Things he had wanted to try with Mayr, options he had wanted to give. A bit of fun they could have had, no one else involved. Just them. Just trust.

If only Mayr would get out of his head—yell himself out of it, even, or walk out of it with more ease than Tash had walked out on him *both* times. It was either that or Mayr needed to disappear from his thoughts completely. That would have been the best way to handle the matter, pretending Mayr had never existed to begin with. If there was ever anything Tash needed more, it was moving on.

Yet Mayr was still there, lingering. Feeding on Tash's desires and twining them around those unsure fingers.

Sometimes it seemed the Goddesses were drunk on humour and looking for company in the misery of the hangover. If everyone's life was simply a tapestry to be appreciated by their beloved goddesses, it seemed They liked jerking on the frayed ends of his tapestry, pulling circumstances tight enough until the consequences snapped.

Or maybe this was something altogether different; something he could not understand from the perspective of a priest, or even a man. Maybe it was a matter of naming whatever simmered in the depths, beneath the hope and the lust. Perhaps he needed to see the world for the essences that lingered in the shadows rather than forcing things into the light.

A frown pulled at Tash's lips as he focused on the group of children playing hop-o'-gain off to the side of the market square, close to the newly repaired porch of a small, modest healing house. One of the children hopped on one foot along a path of squares to circles and back again, retrieving wooden discs along the way without falling, all to smile broadly to their companions at the end and rejoice in their triumph. Innocent. Proud. Playful.

Tash would have loved to feel all of that with Mayr, drawing out the good and keeping the bad at bay. Because that beauty in the stillness, the delicate soul that peered out from beneath the surface of what Mayr showed the world…

It had taken everything Tash had not to kiss Mayr in the study—to take his anger and silence it with gentleness. To wrap the passion in his rejection around an entirely different form of frustration.

But pushing could do more damage. Tear the truth apart more than it's already been.

Glancing along the road out of the market, towards the estate, Tash struggled to contain the emotions demanding release. If he went back, they could very well skip talking and opt for something much more heated, assuming Mayr would let him through the door.

Yet to the temple he would go, alone, despite the thought of Mayr being equally alone killing him. For whatever reason, knowing Mayr's heart was broken and bruised filled Tash with a sadness he had no idea how to ignore, his own heart shattering just to lay down with Mayr's and share the pain. The why eluded him, but damn his soul, he wanted to know it all. Needed to, if only he could be let in that much further.

For now, staring into the distance was the closest he could get, the door no doubt locked tight. Goddesses willing, maybe one day he would find the way to stand by Mayr's side once more, the ruins of what had transpired nothing more than an abandoned thought.

Chapter Seven

Mayr kept his head low. Leaning against the back wall of the ballroom, he kept his arms crossed as he surveyed the guests mingling at the feast. Not just because he mistrusted more than a third of the attendees, but because the last twelve days since the breakup had been long and bitter. He rarely enjoyed socializing at large events to begin with. To then add a shattered heart that was permanently staked to self-induced torture made him far less inclined to be friendly. Surrounded by members of the Grand Families, the councilmen, and other diplomatic guests, he had few kind things to say as it was. At least half of them considered him a servant and nothing more. Their patronizing glances ensured he knew his place.

Given the way he felt, each judgmental glimpse pushed him closer to telling them to shove off, no matter the consequences.

If only he could.

Regardless of his state, he retained what little charm he could for Aeley's sake. She looked happy as lively music filled the air and prompted couples to dance, including her and Lira. Both of them wore gowns embellished with ribbons and jewels, though Aeley was dressed in black while Lira had chosen dark blue. And while Aeley appeared elegant with her blonde hair up, she wore her boots, refusing to don the dainty shoes expected at such a function. If she needed to kick someone out, she had said, she wanted to be comfortable.

With a brief smile at Aeley and Lira's playfulness as they moved, Mayr swept his gaze across the room. From corner to corner of the grey stone walls he observed everything, taking no small space for granted. The dark green banners, orange-red tapestries with autumnal scenes, and cascading arrangements of yellow flowers and bundled chaffs were as suspect as the unlit corners and small spaces beneath the bright green tablecloths. Even with Pellon and their best guards present, there was always something to worry about.

From what he could tell, however, he knew all of the attendees from previous events, and he knew things about each of them. No strangers lurked in the room. Still, he was thankful for the precautions Aeley and he had taken. All weapons had been noted before the feast began and any hint of a blade was monitored. The food was minded with care. He had tasked Stick, Stuck, Lilia, Keyer, Acore, and Legen with the job of supervising the guests even more closely without getting into their faces too much, relying on the expertise of all six like everyone's life depended on it. Considering how long and well that set of guards had served Korre, with all but Stick and Stuck old enough to be Mayr's parents, he knew things would be kept under firm control. In addition to them, extra guards had been assigned to the perimeter of the estate, the inner grounds, and within the house itself.

And if Etalynn rails on Lira, or even so much as grabs her in the wrong way, I have a special cell prepared so she can take a nap. Or a long overdue reflection. She will treat Ae and Lira with respect or she's out.

Mayr glanced at Lira's parents, still in their seats at the dining table, which ran the length of the ballroom. Etalynn, dark-haired and grey-eyed like Lira, sat to her husband's right and observed from beneath lowered lashes. Since their arrival, she had kept her hands to herself and ample space between her and Lira. She watched her daughter from a distance, although the image of her jerking Lira's arm during Aeley and Lira's wedding feast was difficult for Mayr to forget.

Best he could tell, after being ripped away by Aeley and Mayr during that previous display — accompanied by an outcry for decorum from her peers — Etalynn had learned her lesson. From what he could tell, she had spoken little during the current feast and limited her interactions, although not by her design alone. Seated beside the second son of the Laeros family, a Grand

Family in the southern tract of the republic, there was little to say when he avoided Etalynn. Only her husband, Asha, spoke to her.

Even fewer guests spoke to Asha.

An older man with grey hair and blue eyes, Asha resembled the other aristocrats in his long coat, elegantly embroidered tunic, dark pants, and dark gloves. Yet appearance could not save him from long stares and silent snubs. Many of the Dahe family's supporters avoided him at all costs. His transgressions against Korre were unforgivable. Even more since his sons had shown that the poison of the Derossa family still remained.

And that's justice for you. I hope you're enjoying it, you no good piece of—

"Are we having fun yet?" a deep, quiet voice asked from beside Mayr.

Mayr turned his head towards Pellon, taking in Pellon's choice of thin brown leather armour and heavy brass bracers. Anything heavier than leather bracers meant Pellon was in no mood to play around, likely because his lady love, Nesa, was no longer allowed to visit the Dahe estate. After months of Pellon quietly courting her, Nesa's family had declared Pellon was beneath them—mostly because his fathers had found a dozen ways to cut Nesa out of Pellon's life as payback for Pellon messing up their plans. *Family troubles*, Pellon, Mayr, and Aeley called it, though *vicious familial bastards* was far more appropriate.

Just as Mayr spared no love for Lira's parents, he had saved a particular level of loathing for Pellon's fathers and Nesa's family.

That only soured his mood further. Goddesses forbid he ever be left in charge of turning *that* situation inside out and smashing it on its head.

Together, Mayr and Pellon leaned against the wall, both of them brooding silently but trying to pretend otherwise.

"Yeah, well, this is no more fun than staring at a bunch of aristos as they get drunk. Oh, wait—" Mayr slapped his forehead "—that's what we're doing."

Pellon chuckled. "Glad to see your mood has improved some." He feigned a wince. "I'm still hurting from that last beating. You sure you didn't trade your fists for, I don't know, anvils?"

Mayr snorted. "You're one to talk. I have a bruise *this big* on my side still, you massive oaf," he countered, holding his palms one hand's length apart. "I need my ribs, you know, just in case you forgot."

"Ah, well, blame the training." Pellon's toothy grin made Mayr roll his eyes. "Your fault, anyway. If you hadn't gotten so good, I wouldn't have had to keep up."

"Sure, blame the scrawny brat I used to be. That makes my victory even better."

"Heh." Pellon nodded towards the guests. "It's looking quiet. No one's been arrested, kicked out, or received a tart in the face. And no one's been sick on the balcony *or* out in the hallways—I checked, just so you know, so you owe me. From what I can tell, everyone's *actually* on their best behaviour this time. Might be us, might be them, but who cares? All in all, another successful Eleia's Feast, I'd say."

"There's been a couple questionable moments, but sure, let's call it successful." Mayr shrugged and flicked his plaited hair over his shoulder. "Though the night's not over yet."

Pellon elbowed Mayr. "Hey, when am I ever going to see your parents at one of these? It's been, what, eleven years? What about your sister?"

"We've been here before." Mayr stared at the ground, scraping his heel across the floor. "No point in reminding my mother of what she can't do. My father has the harvest to worry about. End of summer, remember? As for Estara: I know why you're asking and I'm telling you, there's no chance for you, not ever. You're on with Nesa and Estara's still married, so that's a rather massively resounding *no*. Even if both of you were single and desperate, I'd *still* never let her near *you*."

Pellon held up his hand, a scowl flitting across his lips with enough sadness to leave Mayr regretting the mention of Nesa. That was a low strike in the already bruised heart. "Hey, I'd never bother Estara. I just like talking to her, that's all. She's nice. Better than *you*."

"I'll remember that the next time I schedule duty roster." Mayr scrunched his nose. "I'll find you someplace really nice. Like cleaning the Guard House for three months."

"Do that and I'll smother you."

"And risk Ae's wrath? Ha! I'd die just to see it. No, really, I would."

Pellon kicked Mayr in the calf. "Fine, snarly wielder of sarcasm, you win. For now."

"Just how I like it." Mayr pushed off the wall. "I'm going for a walk. You have the room. Try not to do anything fun. Be boring. Blend. *Blend*."

On a winding path through the ballroom around the groups of guests, Mayr headed for the doorway, catching snippets of conversation he cared little for. He needed air more than the chance to stretch his legs. The celebration was stuffy and more contrived than usual. No matter how hard he tried, he could not catch a deep enough breath. He just wanted to be left alone.

On his way past the balcony, a flash of red caught his attention.

Tash stood alone inside the open door, staring into the night, dressed as he was in the tavern.

Mayr stopped cold.

So many things to say. So many… I can't… We fought… he left… and I let him.

As though sensing Mayr, Tash turned. A restrained smile flashed across his lips before he approached Mayr and stopped.

They said nothing as they stood still, their gazes locked.

What can I say after calling him a liar multiple times then coming to realize I was the actual liar, not just lying to myself but everyone else, too?

Something. Anything.

Mayr cleared his throat. "Enjoying yourself?"

Tash inclined his head. "I can't complain."

"I'm surprised you're here. How did I not see you earlier?"

"I was late, kept by festivities at the Temple. Then I *may* have purposely hid from your line of sight. But I requested to be here. It's part of what I'm expected to do—bestowing blessings on the hosts and guests and such."

Mayr pointed to the veiled, black-haired priestess sitting at the table. "We already have Priestess Kee. She did the blessings at dinner."

"I know, but the Feast of Eleia the Triumphant is a worthy celebration for a hero. After all, she's considered one of Hastal's most beloved consorts. I wanted to be here."

Really? You came just to celebrate the dead lover of a goddess? Disappointed, Mayr drew his shoulders back. What was he thinking? Why would Tash come to see him after Mayr's spiteful accusations?

Because he made you believe in hope, that's why. He seemed to understand you, even when you didn't say anything. Without the weight of Sarene's expectations on his mind, Mayr had recalled Tash's words several times every day. Tash had asked Mayr to listen between the words, and he had—just not quickly enough. Not when it mattered.

Since then, he had wanted to apologize, but the words failed him, as had his feet. *They're working fine now, though.*

"I'm going for a walk outside." Mayr grimaced. He already knew the answer to his next question would be no, but he needed to ask anyway. "Did you want to come along?"

Tash's eyes widened, his face brightening. "I'd love to."

Everything about Tash's response twisted things inside Mayr he never knew he had, choking him. How could he have said yes?

"Great," Mayr said meekly.

Still processing the acceptance, he led Tash out of the house in silence. *Words. I need words.* As they walked the crude stone pathway around the north side of the house, Mayr reminded himself of the apology he had worked out one night when he felt particularly guilty. The explanation had been good. Polished. Sincere. If he could remember it, he might have the chance to salvage what he had splintered.

Once they reached his favourite spot along the east side of the house, looking out onto the back end of the estate, Mayr stopped to scan the landscape. He often sat where they stood, staring down the long, gradual hill into the wide valley below, a patchwork of fields and a forest that appeared brilliant green in the moonlight. Over the years, he had watched the stars and horizon in the white light of the moon from that spot. Seldom had he shared the space with anyone. Only Aeley and Betta knew how he felt about it.

Almost certain it was where they needed to be right then, Mayr removed his sword belt and laid the weapon down. He pushed aside the vines climbing the grey stone wall and sat with his back against the house. Tash sat beside him. Together they gazed down the hill, their hands resting on their raised knees. Little blue, red, and silver lights flickered in the air like tiny stars. They were diminutive flying creatures Mayr used to catch as a child, with wings as delicate as parchment-thin glass and translucent bodies veined with a multitude of colours.

The silence had to end. He wanted to hear Tash's voice. He wanted to be able to sit in silence without feeling awkward. They could not go on with things left unsaid.

"I'm sorry for everything," Mayr whispered. "I blamed you but it wasn't your fault. Sarene would've left me anyway, with or without your opinion. I already knew our relationship wouldn't change. I knew it the moment she wanted me back. When it was the three of us, I knew it was over, especially with her fawning all over you." He leaned back and glimpsed the stars directly above their heads. "I wanted to believe in more. I wanted to be the lovesick fool I should've been when I'd first met her. But I never was. Not really."

With a sigh, he peered at Tash from the corner of his eyes. "Truth is I wanted to believe I loved her. I wanted to *really* want her that much, but I never did, even if I said the words often enough. I lusted after her, but that's all." Mayr frowned. "I ended up using her, too. Then I lied to myself, convinced she was good for me. I ignored my doubts and the fact I didn't feel much for her, at least nothing all that significant." Mayr grimaced. He was such a fool, having to be pushed this far just to be this honest, his own voice making it sound more pathetic than it did in his head. Goddesses knew what Tash thought of him. "There was nothing real, no deeply felt emotion. Day after day, it was just a string of lies—I just convinced myself they were true, justifying why I should feel them. Then you were involved and I couldn't take it. There was too much truth. I was crushed by the weight of it."

Mayr fingered the grass between them, staring at the ground. "I wanted to see you to say all of this, but I couldn't manage it. Every night, I'd commit myself to going right up to you and laying this all out. But come morning, I felt sick. Afraid."

He waited, not sure what to expect as an answer.

Tash played with the chain of his talon ring. "I really did have your interests at heart," he said quietly. "And since we're being honest: I didn't come tonight just to be a priest. I was hoping to see you. I'd thought of visiting again, but worried it was too soon—that you wouldn't want to see my face again. *I* was afraid you wouldn't trust me or listen to anything I had to say."

Don't we make the pair? Mayr studied Tash's face, tempted to brush Tash's hair over his shoulder to see him better. Maybe there was a chance for them yet.

"One thing you said still confuses me," Mayr admitted. "What did you mean when you said this wasn't part of your plan?"

"It's a priesthood thing. I'm going through for the next level soon, though it's not yet set. I have to do some things before then and complete certain tasks. Prove my worth and how serious I am about committing to it." Tash smiled sadly at Mayr. "That's why I was with Sarene. I was having fun before I have to go through all of that. She offered something that wasn't attachment, just pleasure. Since being an Uldana restricts me from intimacy, I thought it wouldn't hurt."

Tash shook his head. "But I hurt you, and that's not right." He laid one hesitant hand on Mayr's. "I truly am sorry for everything. Sarene made it sound like you were fully into it. Meanwhile, I had the distinct impression you were serious about her even though she was playing you. She's inept and too stuck in her own game to fully comprehend what she had."

Mayr threw blades of grass towards the hill. "You don't need to apologize. You told me I could get out and I didn't. I'm glad I stayed."

And now for the moment of debilitating truth.

"You asked how I was taking it, what we did, and I didn't answer. Because I couldn't." Mayr sucked in a deep breath. "I didn't know *how* to answer you, but I've been working it out. I've had a lot of time to figure out my exact reply."

Rising to his knees, Mayr ignored his doubts. Before he lost his courage, he pressed his lips to Tash's, tugging gently on Tash's bottom lip before offering his mouth fully. It felt right. Good. He should have done it before.

Tonight, he would not shy away. His fear of rejection would have to wait.

As Tash gripped his arm and pulled him closer, Mayr's fears dissipated. When Tash's tongue entered Mayr's mouth, tasting and teasing, it sparked deep emotions Mayr had missed. Sincere desire, transcending the relationships he had accepted as all he could have.

Slowly, Mayr broke the kiss, satisfied with Tash's ardent gaze. "Did I tell you that I'm really, *really* happy you're here?"

Without waiting for Tash's answer, Mayr kissed him hard, wishing Tash could feel what he did. He felt lit up, more than he had in a long time. The relationship with Sarene had become a chore. *And before her, it wasn't any different. I felt the same for the other women as I did her. Just going through the motions, telling myself they could be someone I could stay with for the rest of my life so I wouldn't be alone.* Convinced they would stay and he would be happy, he had given them everything.

All of it had been foolish desperation.

But Tash offered the things missing from most of Mayr's relationships. Joyful intoxication derived from emotion alone. Breathtaking inspiration that made everything else in his life seem lacklustre. The restored hope that someone could consider him enough. Whenever Tash asked about him, his concern sounded genuine. In the smallest action, there was more care and respect than any of Mayr's girlfriends had shown him. The idea of being with Tash was both thrilling and terrifying, but deep down in his tainted core, he needed it.

"I'm hoping that answers your question," Mayr murmured. "Otherwise, it's going to take me a while to convince you, and I still have things to do tonight."

Tash leaned his forehead against Mayr's. "No, you've made it clear. I won't ask again."

"Then I've got a question for you."

"Anything."

"If I said I wanted to see where this could go, what would you say?"

Lips traveled up Mayr's jaw and kissed a path to his brow. Arms encircled his waist, holding

172

him upright against Tash's side. "Yes," Tash whispered against his temple.

The breathy reply wreaked havoc on Mayr's body. A shiver shot through him from the back of his neck to his feet. To feel Tash's interest was one thing; hearing it was another. They were worth every night he had agonized over an apology.

"I have to get back to the feast." Mayr tilted his head. "Do you have a curfew? Do the other priests lock you up if you come home late?"

Tash chuckled. "No. That's only for the Metahs. I'm free to do as I please. Why?"

"If you stay, we could spend time together after the feast is over. Maybe finally get around to knowing each other better?"

"Considering I came here mostly for you… there's no place I'd rather be."

"Also known as yes."

"Yes."

And with one word, hope trounced Mayr's fear into submission.

For the last time that night, Mayr flashed a well-rehearsed, fake smile to a guest as they closed the door to their chambers. Those who needed to stay overnight were finally in their rooms, releasing Mayr from the burden of ensuring they made it safely up the staircases without crushing Haydin with their drunken weight or tumbling down the stairs.

Almost finished for the night, Mayr strolled through the corridors. One last round to determine everyone was where they should be, and then he would retire and allow the night watch to take over. If they valued their legs, he had told the guards, they would not bother him until morning. Unless the estate was on fire, under siege, or someone was being murdered, he was not to be interrupted. They could annoy Pellon with the rest. *He's next in command, anyway. Always says I should give him more to do, so there, I've achieved two things at once.*

The house was on its way to being quiet. Suggestive sounds came from the bedrooms. Household staff cleaned the ballroom with muffled noise. Guards shuffled through the hallways. Torches had been snuffed out selectively, allowing the darkness to seep in. All was peaceful, just as he preferred.

If he could only find Tash, he would find a peace of his own.

He had lost sight of Tash in the ballroom before escorting guests upstairs. Now, Tash was missing. Perplexed, Mayr checked the foyer, dining room, meeting room, study, kitchen, and every open space on the main level. On his way outside, he passed the conservatory and stopped. The doors were ajar when they should have been closed. As he peeked through the narrow opening into the moonlit room, he recognized red cloth.

"So now you're hiding." Mayr slipped inside and locked the doors. "Or were you just making me work for it?"

Tash spun away from the enclosed pool of water that rose up from the centre of the room. "Whichever one you prefer." He gestured to the plants on the ground and up the walls. "I came for the plants, actually. I don't know why, but they've always made me feel calm. Always made me feel… closer."

"To?"

"Everything?" From the way Tash lowered his head, Mayr wondered if a blush coloured Tash's face. "I'd hate to bore you with the rest of that answer. Perhaps we'll just say the Goddesses and leave it at that?"

"Or you don't have to. I understand more than you think." Mayr stepped towards Tash on the white and silvery-blue marbled path, careful to avoid the flowerbeds and vines spilling in his way. He pointed to the glass ceiling and glimpsed the silver moon before it disappeared behind a cloud. "Built by Aeley's ancestor, generations back. Actually, it was the same man who built the first stage of this estate. It used to be just the Guard House out to the west side, but once the family started bringing in more wealth, he expanded and had this house built. Apparently he liked this room, too." Mayr stopped before

Tash, the toes of their boots touching. "But you didn't come here to discuss architecture and history, did you?"

"Not really, no," Tash answered, pulling Mayr in for a long kiss. From his lips flowed a gentle passion; his touch was heavy with desire. With an even, slow breath in, he took them deeper, his fingers creeping up Mayr's neck to slide into his hair and keep him close.

When they parted, Mayr inhaled quickly. Each time they kissed, he wanted to linger and feel each movement of Tash's lips. He wanted to taste Tash, all of him, and drink in every moan, every sigh, every drop of his essence as though everything else tasted like sawdust and Tash the only sweetness. It reminded him of their first kiss, the cautious innocence replaced by confident understanding.

"I have an idea. A game, if you're willing." Tash played with the wisps of hair curled around Mayr's nape. "A way we could learn about one another and enjoy ourselves at the same time. Nothing strenuous."

"And that would be…?"

"Each of us takes turns choosing the topic and posing the question. Both must answer the question, seriously and fully. For every such answer, the other gets to choose a piece of clothing to be removed."

"Until naked, I presume?"

"If you'd like. *Or* we can call a stop partway if you're—"

Mayr pulled Tash against him, hard, and clenched Tash's waist. "No. No partway, no halfway. If you're talking everything, I'm in." He nuzzled Tash's ear, letting a breath slip across his skin. Tash's body tensed in response and drew closer. "I didn't lock the door for nothing."

Tash laughed, easing a small space between them. "I figured you'd say that. Which of us wants to begin?"

"Wants or should?" Mayr tilted his head. "He who came up with the idea ought to start first— unless you want me to delay taking my clothes off?"

"Not in the least." Tash's eyes narrowed. "I didn't come in here for nothing."

"And the truth comes out."

"Be careful what you ask for."

"Oh, no, I know. I'm bracing myself. Do your best, I dare you."

"Are you sure you want to dare a priest? Truly?"

"What? It seems like efficient bait. So go on. Ask your question."

"Fine, I'll meet that challenge." Tash regarded Mayr with a hint of suspicion. "The topic: family. Will you tell me about them?"

Mayr sucked in a breath. *And here I thought he'd ask an easy one.* Why had he not expected it? "They live outside the village, actually, on a farm.

Well, my parents do. The twins live nearby." His glance drifted to the floor. "Renett and Malary—those are my parents. Mother runs the family and Father runs the farm. My sister, Estara, is married and has a couple kids. My brother, Loftin, is also married. His son, we're pretty sure, will be the death of us. Alith's a handful on the good days."

"And where are you in all of that? Older or younger?"

"Hey, that's more than one question," Mayr teased, forcing a smile through his guilt. "I shouldn't answer that. I should get to remove something extra of yours as penalty."

Tash held up his hands. "Sorry, you're right—"

"Older."

"Pardon?"

"I'm the eldest, Loftin's the baby, and Tara reminds him of it every chance she gets." Mayr grinned. "I just wanted to see what you'd say. I don't need the penalty. I can wait this out." He held his arms out at his sides. "What goes first? Don't be shy. Not like you haven't had it in your hands before."

"No, no it isn't." Tash's smug tone made Mayr's cock stiffen, reminded of the attention Tash had lavished upon it. "The belts, if you would. I find sharp weapons... unsettling."

Of course you do. Mayr removed the belt with his scabbard and sword, then the second belt that carried his knife. He laid them beside the path near a bed of bright blue flowers and yellow ferns. "Your turn. Same question, I believe? Those were the rules, right?"

"Yes, they were," Tash murmured, almost as though he regretted his choice of topic. "Parents and an older sister. Parase, Kilienn, and Allaysia. They lived in a village in south Gailarin. Araveena Ford, about half a day from here. Owned the tailor's shop where my mother worked as a seamstress. They're dead, far as I know." Blinking, he appeared to battle tears. A sharp breath later, Tash's expression changed and he straightened. "But now onto the clothes. Your selection?"

"Robe," Mayr replied, but his attention was elsewhere, even as Tash shrugged the robe off and placed it aside. Curiosity pinned his anticipation to his guts and ransacked his thoughts. He wanted to know about Tash's family more than he wanted to see Tash naked. All of them dead? How? When? Most of all, he wanted to hold Tash and let him speak at length of the departed, even if it ended in tears. While there were days Mayr wondered how his own mother could survive, he never wanted to imagine being without his family.

"Your question now."

Mayr struggled to find a question not about Tash's family. "Choice of station," he said. "Why did you become a priest?"

Pain and disgust flitted across Tash's features. When he finally spoke, his voice was low and steady, almost rehearsed. "I got into a lot of things I wasn't proud of. I made bad choices; even worse friends. Getting out of it was the hardest thing I've done, but being a priest felt right. Like where I should be. A fair exchange for leaving those unforgivable days behind." He nodded at Mayr. "Why did you become a guard? Head of the Guard, at that?"

"Needed the pay." Mayr tilted his head, trying to imagine Tash getting into trouble or breaking the law. "My mother couldn't help with the farm anymore and things were difficult. So I asked my father to enlist me with Korre Dahe's guard. We'd met him several times, since part of my father's crop came to the estate. Korre took pity on me and gave me work. I was eleven, then, doing small jobs. Helping guards, carrying stuff, learning some basic training. I moved up to guard when I was sixteen and trained until I nearly killed myself. Aeley helped, of course." He shrugged. "When our Head Guard retired, I was twenty-six and tougher than most of the lot. Determined. Stubborn as Ae and could put up with her foul ass of a brother. Korre trusted me and offered me the position. I couldn't say no—I couldn't disappoint him. So here I am, and you still haven't taken anything off." Shaking his head, he snapped his fingers and pointed. "The belt's got to go."

"Done. Your bracers."

They removed the clothing and tossed them aside.

"Relationships," Tash said. "How many intimate relationships have you been in, including Sarene?"

"By the Four, you're going to make me *count*?" Mayr stared upwards. "Give me a moment."

How many *had* there been? *First, when I was... then her... then her... and that horrible one... Betta... Another, another, another... Tash, you're cruel. And you lied. I count* this *as strenuous.*

"Can I just say enough?" Mayr answered, wincing. "No? That doesn't count as an answer?" When Tash smirked, Mayr sighed and held up his hands. "Fifteen, maybe? And that makes me sound like a—"

"Thirty."

"You... win?" Mayr gawked at Tash. "And haven't you been busy."

"Casual relationships, remember? I haven't been tied to anyone for *years*." Tash tugged on Mayr's black shirt. "And I'd like this to come off. While it looks good on you, I'd rather see *you*." His hands slipped under the shirt. Warm palms slid over the defined contour of Mayr's stomach. "Feel you—"

Mayr yanked his shirt over his head faster than he could think. Fingertips crawled up his skin over the fine, dark hair of his chest. The feather-light weight of Tash's touch sent Mayr's heartbeat tripping on itself, but the moment

Tash's lips delved into the crook of his neck, kneading the skin and biting gently, Mayr's heart raced, pounding harder the longer the touch teased. Was the game supposed to work that way? Did it matter? Exposing more of his neck to the tender touch, he held Tash close, raking one hand through Tash's wavy hair.

"Bracers," Mayr whispered.

"Mmm?"

"Your bracers. The game. They're my next choice."

The questing lips stopped. Tash pushed back, his playful expression gone. "No. Those need to stay on."

"But—"

"I swear everything else is fair game, just not those. Please. *Please*," Tash repeated softly. The piercing fear in Tash's tone matched that in his eyes.

He was begging, not just simply denying.

"All right," Mayr agreed, cupping his palms around Tash's cheeks. "I'm sorry. I'll even things: the shirt."

Tash complied, his desperation to keep his bracers on confusing Mayr. Since the tavern, Mayr had considered the bracers a matter of armour or vanity. Perhaps they were something else altogether. Sentiment? A means to hide something?

The more they bared themselves, the less he knew about Tash. He only had more questions.

Like what Tash's scars were from, he remembered, glimpsing Tash's naked chest. The marks left by blades were disconcerting, but the burns bothered him the most; ugly, dark stains on smooth, enticing skin.

"So." Mayr took a breath. He wanted the sensual Tash back; the one who could not wait to touch him. "Where were we?"

"Your question."

"Right. Hmm. Men or women? Your preference, I mean. For lovers."

"Neither," Tash answered, smiling. "And both."

"Is that *really* an answer?"

"Yes."

"And I think you're trying to get out of this."

"Like you are?"

"Hey, I'm not trying to get out of anything."

"Then answer the question."

Mayr's face warmed. "Women, but that's all I *can* say. I never followed through with men. Not until you." The tips of his ears grew hot, almost burning. Words he had avoided saying had finally slipped out. Did he sound as ridiculous as he thought he did?

Maybe not, he thought as Tash kissed him.

"Thank you. I'll still take care of you." Tash kissed Mayr's cheek. "But the boots have to come off."

"Yours, too."

They tossed their boots aside together, adding to their respective piles.

"Tattoos." Tash traced the lines of the dark tattoos that circled all the way around Mayr's neck. "I'm curious about what they are; what they mean."

"Warnings, protective icons, declarations of justice and peace unless under attack. Basically, I'm harmless until you make me angry. Like waking the Fanged Beast of Adornat—he rips everything out through your guts and *then* tosses the pieces around for good measure. You can see the markings of Hastal and Navara, actually, right here," Mayr said, pointing to the sides of his neck. "And, hold on, shouldn't you know that? You're a priest. You should..." He stopped, seeing Tash's smirk. "Of course you do. What was I thinking?"

"I just wanted to see what you'd say." Tash laughed and held up Mayr's left wrist. "But this, and the ones on your back, I don't understand their significance."

Mayr studied the swirls and curves of the tree tattooed on the inside of his forearm. Memories surfaced, clearer than the scars the tattoo covered. They were no less bittersweet. "Ae's father, after he was elected Tract Steward, wanted a tattoo to remind him of what his position really meant. He chose a tree, on his chest, near his heart. The leaves are the High Council and Tract Stewards; the roots are the people. The trunk is the integrity,

184

trust, honesty, and respect that connect them. 'The Council and Stewards might be bright and can dance to the rhythm of the wind,' he told me, 'but they are grounded by the people. Without the people, they cannot exist.'"

With other memories of Korre in his thoughts, Mayr touched his arm. "He was good to me and my family. After he died, it seemed fitting to do something that reminded me of him. I did this, a copy of his. It's over scars I got defending him." He shook his head. "I was young, naïve. Got into brawls I never should've been near. But this one time, some guys were mouthing off, throwing threats around. They thought it'd be fun to break into the estate in the middle of the night and see what they could do. Me and a few other guards didn't like the topic, so we decided to put them in their place. My friends did; I got my pride shoved down my throat and marks to remember it. I still don't like shattered glass to this day."

"I don't blame you," Tash said. "The markings on your back?"

"They're for my family. Entwined birds for my parents; conjoined bearcat cubs for my brother and sister. The arawolfe for Ae, especially since she's vicious in the morning. And the budding vine for—" Mayr hesitated, unable to say the names. "A couple others." He ran his hands up Tash's back, imagining how the feathers of his tattoo would feel had they been real. "But enough about mine. What about this? It must have taken days to do."

Tash sucked in a breath as Mayr caressed the dip in his lower back. "It did. Days' worth of pain, too. Dare I say what it is? You should already know."

"Say it anyway."

"Halataldris."

"There, that wasn't so hard, was it?" Mayr teased Tash's lower lip with his lips. "Because it wouldn't make *any* sense to get the bird you're named after. Now, how about those pants?"

"Mine for yours."

"Done." Mayr's pants were off before Tash finished with his. Reminded of his aching erection while he waited, Mayr was tempted to glide his hands over Tash's contracting muscles as Tash moved.

When Tash stood unclothed, illuminated by the moonlight, Mayr's gaze drifted down Tash's body. Hard ridges and soft curves whet his desire. His focus wandered over the patch of dark hair leading to Tash's tightening cock strained in his direction, thick and ready for attention. Wearing only bracers and his talon ring, everything about Tash was real. In a blend of contrasts, he was tough and gentle all at once. The longer Mayr stared, the more contradictions fell away, leaving the consuming sense of being connected well beyond their understanding. Nothing could soothe the feeling of familiarity burning him from inside. Touch only fueled the fire.

"Last one. This one's for the ring." Mayr licked his lips, caught between wanting to feel the talon's piercing tip graze his skin and seeing Tash without it. If not for his curiosity, he would have let Tash keep it. It would be another fantasy for another time. "Your scars—what are they from?"

Tash's gaze fell, his expression darkening. Long, silent moments passed.

"Never mind," Mayr said. "You don't have to—"

"Mistakes. Ones I should have never made. Ones I deserved. Just like these reminders. I broke the rules. I didn't do what I was told. I paid the price, taken from my flesh for something as simple as morality. I wouldn't spill blood, so mine was taken in its stead." Tash looked up. "Blood can be remade; death is permanent."

"I'm sorry. I shouldn't have—"

Tash raised his hand. "No, no apologies. Just tell me: your scars, they're battle-born? Brawls, fights, training?"

"Yes."

"Then I'd say the game's finished." Tash unclasped the chain from his bracer, slipped off his ring, and laid it on his discarded garments.

"In case you didn't notice, I don't have any clothes left."

"Ah, but there is one thing I want." Pressed against Mayr, Tash removed the tie from Mayr's braid.

Able to take the hint, Mayr teased the braid apart and shook his hair loose until it hung in waves past his shoulders.

Tash coiled the end of several black strands around his finger. "Beautiful," he whispered, resting his other hand on Mayr's hip. His lips sought Mayr's, and as he tilted his head to claim a deeper kiss, he interlaced his fingers with Mayr's.

Their bodies were almost as one, Mayr realized, moaning against Tash's lips. They shared the same breaths, passion flowing between them as smooth as water. What he poured into their kiss was returned, suggesting, just for the moment, they felt the same for each other. That everything he had thought was only in his head was actually real. Not a figment of his imaginative hopes.

"Come." Tash tugged Mayr's hands, their fingers still locked together.

Without argument, Mayr obeyed. Tash sat on the ground, legs crossed, near the pool but not close enough to touch it. Behind him, the warm water was calm, brightened by the light streaming in from the window above. A broken reflection of the moon filled the spaces between the red and white flowers floating on the surface.

Tash pulled Mayr down to his lap. Mayr straddled Tash's thighs and wrapped his legs around Tash's hips and back. They maneuvered closer together until they were nearly hip-to-hip, their cocks trapped between them. No matter the angle, skin slid along skin, grinding salaciously. Balanced on Tash's legs, Mayr wrapped his arms around Tash's shoulders to keep from leaning back too far.

They sat quietly, focused on each other as Tash's hands explored almost every part of Mayr. Tender fingers massaged Mayr's shoulders and back, relieving a fraction of the tension that plagued him daily. Tash's hands continued to travel over the tattoos and once-torn skin. His fingertips glided gingerly over the bruise on Mayr's left side where Pellon had jabbed him in the ribs. From there, the intimate touch roved over his chest and hardened nipples to his stomach and further below. The journey culminated in pressured strokes along the underside of his cock from root to tip until he groaned and buried his face in Tash's neck.

Touch for touch, Mayr returned the exploration. Satisfaction commanded him as he held Tash's cock firmly and stroked mercilessly. Gasps and moans were not his only reward. A deep, grinding motion accompanied them, which Tash continued even after Mayr removed his hand.

"Is this what you were after?" Mayr murmured, nipping Tash's shoulder.

"Yes." Tash held Mayr still, his hands locked together behind Mayr's neck. "I don't want to rush this." His palm flattened on Mayr's chest, over his heart. "Not all meaningful, beautifully intimate moments require the full act of sex. It can be even more significant when we take the slow path. We can still be one; we can still obtain what we need. That which we pursue patiently can be the most gratifying, especially when our bodies think they dictate everything and leave the spirit to weep in neglect."

"You're talking priest again."

"I'm afraid so." Tash tucked Mayr's hair behind his ears.

Just as Mayr wanted to argue for more talk, Tash's mouth took his, silencing every word with strong lips and a playful tongue. Fingers moved over his cock and balls before slipping beneath to rest in the warm crevice and caress him. Lifting slightly, he granted Tash more access and moaned against Tash's lips as fingertips circled his tight opening. Rarely had he considered how it would feel to have someone inside him. But as one fingertip teased, seeking entry, the thought of Tash thrusting into him made his cock throb. Eager to feel Tash's finger push inside, he ground against Tash's hand.

When Tash retreated instead, Mayr waited in confusion.

Tash cupped both palms around the back of Mayr's neck. "I want to go slow. I don't want to rush, for so many reasons." He kissed Mayr again, the touch as gentle as the first time they had kissed. "I love that you want this, but I want to work up to things. I'm used to this; you aren't. You shouldn't feel pressured, obligated, or taken advantage of. Just know I'm here, willing, and I don't mind being the one you explore with. And forgive me if I'm overly protective at times."

Mayr drew his fingers along Tash's lips, digesting the words. Had it been anyone else, he would have responded with sarcasm or a quip to play off his annoyance at being treated as though he were naïve. Life came with pain, some of it downright unbearable while some offered an equal share of pleasure. He did not need to be coddled or treated like a child. Not when he could break a man's neck with just his hands or shatter ribs in a swift blow.

Despite it all, he savoured Tash's concern and yielded to words he had never realized he needed to hear. Tash saw through him to the breakable parts no one else bothered to look for—not even Mayr.

"Consider yourself forgiven," Mayr said, "if you'll forgive me for being eager. I usually jump into things. I can't help it. Maybe that's been my problem all along." He could count the number of times he had taken a relationship at a crawling pace on one hand, even if half of the fingers were missing. Normally he gave everything from the start and worked to maintain it.

Then when the other person's taken whatever they wanted, I'm left with nothing. Maybe not this time. This time, I'll try something different.

"I'm sure we can find the compromise between us. But there's something else." Tash pressed their foreheads together. "Whatever happens, I don't want you to misunderstand. I want you, but it's better if we keep this from going too far. Let's just keep this casual. Let's not get too involved. We can't fall in love. No matter what, love doesn't factor into this. Otherwise, it's not fair to you. I like you and I want to be the one you try new things with. But I have to focus on being a priest. I can't do love. I just can't."

Love? When had they started discussing that? Mayr dipped his head in agreement, unable to find words that would not have sounded confused or misinterpreted as an insult. *It's not like I'm in love with him. I'm just curious, that's it. Yeah, I feel something, mostly how much I need to come, but it can't possibly be love. Not even close.*

Whatever their feelings were—whatever was budding between them—would die off once they got to know each other. They would spend time together, discover each other's annoying habits, and suck every bit of lust out of their companionship until they were bored. Then they would part ways and continue as though they had never been. If he committed to little from the start, there would be nothing to lose except the pleasure of obtaining release by someone else's means rather than relying on his hand alone. Perhaps a relationship without attachment would be better. He could not lose what he did not expect to have.

I shouldn't be in a relationship anyway, not after Sarene, and Tash doesn't like permanent. I'm only caught up in him because he looks good, feels even better, and I've never been with anyone like him. It's just because he's a man who's paid attention to me in a way I wanted to experience, but was always too scared to ask for. He's answering a question, not changing my life forever.

What he felt was infatuation, just infatuation. And like everything else, infatuation died.

Chapter Eight

Tash hummed quietly, happily. As he drifted through the halls on the way to Overseer Kee's study, the wafting scent of fragrant woodsy incense and spice-infused candles moved along with him. Whatever the stares he received from other priests as he passed, he kept to the medley of sweet ballads he had arranged in his head during his childhood, messing about with a harp while he daydreamed and pretended to know what he was doing. He was near to daydreaming now, the air still warm, the temple awash with sunlight streaming in from every window, the white marble gleaming, and his heart light. It was only slightly past noon, getting ever closer to Mayr's arrival at the temple. They had plans to walk the market for the afternoon and collect items Tash needed, followed by dinner at the tavern and a bit of fun between the sheets until Mayr escorted Tash back to the temple that night.

Thirteen days marked their affair, and what days they had been, worth every moment spent with one another. Granted, they saw each other only a couple days at a time, but that was good enough.

Enough to have Tash smiling his way over the threshold of Kee's study... and losing that joy completely once he stood inside.

Of all the hearts of the gracious Goddesses combined, what had he done to deserve *this*?

Being in Kee's study was usually pleasant, almost a relief, often tempered with the surprise that she had ever paid notice to Tash at all, given his past—one she knew in full, to the ends of the most unnerving details that should have seen him in a prison faster than he could get a word out. The Goddesses knew just how close he had come to that, with the High Council breathing down his neck as angrily as the beasts from the Sinea Grou mountains. But for Kee to have taken him under her tutelage with no less surety than Overseer Callye before her was a shock of gratitude and debt he could never repay adequately, only put his hardest efforts towards and hope they tilted the balance of what he owed.

Which was why the moment he stepped into Kee's study to not only find Armamae standing by her side, but two oracles at her other side—Malise and Radura—a solemn worry seeped around his bones. There was no ignoring how both oracles stared at him as he closed the door and bowed his head.

"Overseer," Tash said softly. "Brother Armamae." He flicked his gaze towards the oracles and added another bow, this time from the waist, his hand flattened over his chest.

"Oracle Malise, Radura, I wish you fair afternoon and fine casting."

Malise and Radura simply nodded and offered him gentle smiles, their hands clasped before them. Like all Uldana priests, they wore long veils and multiple layers of red robes that fell about them gracefully. Over their vestments, however, each wore the regalia of the oracles: a narrow belt crafted from four strips of thin, brown and black leather plaited together, paired with a gold, brass, and silver chain chatelaine. The chatelaines were pinned to their robes, just below the belt, with a glazed, brown wooden brooch, the shape of a tree engraved in the disc. Charms in the shape of trees, nuts, and teardrops decorated the chain of the chatelaine, which draped across their waist and looped over their belt, all to hang heavily with four brass keys, a silver holder containing seeing stones, a simple pocketknife, a small brass case with matches, and a red leather purse of divination coins.

The fact they were there, and two oracles rather than one, could not bode well for him. He had known both of them for nearly as long as he had served the Dahena temple, but knowing them and knowing what they could see were ultimately different things.

"Have a seat, Brother Halataldris," Kee said, gesturing to the furniture to his right, against the wall opposite her desk.

Tash eyed the pristine sky-blue settee and its matching chairs. "If it's all the same to you, Sister, I'd rather stand." The closer he stayed to the door, the faster his exit. A familiar caged feeling crept through him, the instinct to run awakened beneath his skin.

Kee dipped her head and sat in the chair behind her desk, her long black hair a tumbling mass of barely-there waves over both her shoulders, the red of her veil bright against her tan skin. "As you wish." She offered Tash a warm smile, the gleam in her dark eyes playing with the light as much as her robes did. "How are things progressing for you this week? You seem particularly full of life as of late, even more so than usual. Your studies appear to be going just as well."

Her voice was even, the tone rich, notes bright—this was not a reprimand. Was it an extension of his previous lessons with the oracles, instead, studies which all Rese-level priests went through yet few pursued further? His turn at the divinations had not been awful, not as disappointing as some, but had they really been *that* successful? In all honesty, he had worked extra hard with the cards and the discs, having studied their meanings for months, and the prospect of reading bones and spirits held little excitement in his heart, but the coins had fared a bit better than most. Leftovers from his gambling days, he supposed. Or just plain luck.

Either way, a lack of reprimand was enough to let him breathe easier and step away from the door, closer to the settee.

"Yes, Sister, everything has gone very well." Tash's smile wavered as he nodded to Armamae. "We've been catching up on several historical tomes."

Armamae's eyes glinted with a hint of wicked humour, though his grin said it best. "Indeed. It seems our scholar here has a penchant for legends, particularly those caught in the undertow of Utaul Oren and the Ages of the Dissenting. The third era, mostly, before the Fallen Fiend of Ena. We are slowly meandering our way through the shelves, when the books can be bothered to negotiate."

Tash arched one brow, not understanding what about that amused Armamae. There was something to be said about overthrowing dangerous power and clawing across the war-ravaged heartscape to rebuild a new life, one that could benefit all rather than the few. Though perhaps that was the defector in him, trying to keep the past under control but never letting it wander far from the surface. No doubt Armamae would have a hundred things to say about *that* matter.

Kee only laughed, light and soothing, accompanied by a wink. "Very good. We'll be sure to continue that part of your studies, but it will have to wait. We have another matter to attend to." She sobered and cleared her throat, hands clasped on her desk. "The oracles have been busy, reading the signs as they do, and I have seen my own." With the lift of her chin, she straightened her shoulders, a sense of pride about her. "It's time for your Trials, Halataldris, assuming you still want to go through them. It seems the Goddesses are amenable to your offer to serve Them to the fullest of your ability. Your Trials are to begin in a week, according to every one of the castings the oracles have made."

Tash stared, tried to work his lips—to work *anything*.

The Uldana Trials.

A week.

Eight days.

The world could have fallen straight out from beneath his feet and he never would have noticed the difference. Even worse, his breath caught but failed to start again, his heart tripping over itself and screaming at the chaos.

He fell onto the edge of the settee, nearly missing it completely. If sitting was dangerous, he dared not try walking, not when he could barely see through the tears gathering in his eyes.

The timing could not have been any worse.

"I..." Tash swallowed uneasily. "I understand. Thank you, Sister, oracles. And thanks be to the Four in accepting that offer. I'll... do my best... to not let anyone down," he said, dropping his gaze to his hands—hands that were cold, shaking, very much his but not his right then. His fingers moved but they were as numb as his forearms, the ability to feel failing to reach the deepest part of him.

The Trials had found him, and he was coming apart, not a single trial needed to ruin him.

Goddesses, he was a disappointment already, bound to be thrown into the darkest valleys of the Realm of the Dead with *Coward* branded on his forehead. No doubt the noose of *Liar* would be tied around his soul as surely as he was condemned to wander with his regret, lost until the wheel turned anew.

"Halataldris."

He should have obeyed the call of his name, but looking at Kee was more difficult than imagining his rancid, rotting corpse. And his hands... he could not stop staring at his hands, what they had done; the punishment he deserved. Simply stuck on staring, and the blood —

Red filled his sight, robes flowing and falling in shadow and light as warm, calloused hands slipped over his. "Halataldris," Kee said softly. Crouched before him, she squeezed his fingers. "Look at me." Her thumbs caressed the back of his hands. "Have faith, Brother, and raise your eyes."

Tash did as she asked, afraid to disappoint her further.

He was rewarded with Kee's small smile, her eyes offering sympathy. "I know this is frightening, and I know it is a heavy weight to shoulder. But there is no rule that says you mustn't be afraid, only certain. This is not an easy decision, and others before you have felt the same, *especially* those with so much to lose." She cupped his cheek in her palm and gave his jaw the barest shake. "But I promise we have not set you up for failure. If I didn't believe you could succeed, I never would have let you get this far. I would have prolonged your training, restrained you to being a Rese, particularly since it has clearly done you well." Kee smirked, a hint of laughter dancing through her eyes.

The smirk was gone the next moment, both of her hands clasping his tightly. "You can do this," she said quietly. Slowly. "No, you will not come out of it unscathed. I can't do anything about that. But I never would have encouraged you to become an Uldana if you had only half a chance of pulling through it. I have faith in that, Halataldris. Faith in *you*. You've worked hard for this. Your heart is exactly where it needs to be. I agree with the oracles and the Goddesses Themselves: your time has come, and we will stand by that."

If only her words could have crushed his doubt as surely as they warmed his heart.

Still, he had her faith in him, and that was a treasure in itself, a precious gift he never wanted to throw back at her, abused and unloved. The thought of disappointing her or Armamae was as chilling as the prospect of succeeding and making them proud, yet it was that pride he yearned for, that acceptance, and for them to think well of him, always. After years of giving him so much and showing him far more patience than he deserved, the last thing he wanted was to let them down. They were a beacon of hope and second chances, as noble and worthy of his loyalty as Hastal Herself.

He needed to do this, no matter the terror coiled around his insides. He would do it for him, for them. For whatever future the Goddesses would grant a wretched soul once lost among the chaos but now found in the calm.

"Thank you," Tash whispered, giving Kee's hands a light squeeze. "I'll do my best."

"I'll never doubt that." Kee patted his knees and stood, careful not to step on her veil as she fussed with it. "Take the next few days to tie up loose ends and make your peace before the first trial begins. Once the Trials start, you are bound to them, so you may want to settle things quickly."

The pointed look she cast him was as effective as a stab to the gut—one that left the hardest, stickiest lump in his throat and stomach, all but ready to explode and take the rest of him with it.

"Yes, Sister," Tash muttered. He stood slowly, his robe clutched in his fists to steady the tremble in his hands. "Thank you." After a final bow of his head to Kee, then to Armamae, Malise, and Radura, he slipped out of the room.

As composed and collected as he could manage, he journeyed down the main corridor, past the priests conversing in the hallway, and turned right, up the corridor to the kitchen. With his stomach in gnawing, burning knots, the last thing he needed was food—everything would come up, comfort be damned. Even the incense that filled the hallways was coming up sickly sweet, making him want to hurl his stomach against the wall.

He made another right, then a left, and took refuge in the empty corridor to the winter cellar: a short passage that few accessed during the day, unless someone delivered harvested goods or the meads, wines, and ales the temple kept in store. For all he knew, he would be interrupted any moment...

Just a breath. Need to get my head together. Have to...

Tash fell back against the wall, his eyes squeezed shut.

The timing...

Goddesses, *of course* it would happen now, just when he had started something with Mayr.

Groaning, Tash hung his head in his hands. Mayr. So far from being a plaything, but entirely too good to destroy with an abrupt farewell. What would he tell Mayr about the Trials? How could he even begin explaining the why—the *how*?

But then there's the other thing...

Tash scowled and pulled his hands from his face, just as tempted to rip his fingers off and kick them at the wall for all the good they had done. He and Mayr—they were two sides of the same river, truth hidden below the surface, blending into the water's flow and acting more like a mirror than any sort of gateway to enlightenment. With a word, he could draw the truth to shore, expose it, let it dry, and drown it all over again.

With a single name, he could send Mayr into the opposite direction and watch the beautiful warmth in his gaze run cold. And yet for all that chill he feared, its walls up and prospects down...

He needed Mayr. *Now. Right now.*

One deep breath, then two, had him calming down as he played with his hair. After a bit of tousle to the loose, wavy strands, followed by the straightening of his shirt and belt, he was ready.

Tash headed back through the corridors to the main hallway that led to the front of the temple, making sure to smile and greet everyone he encountered, hoping familiarity would ease his aches. As he passed through the herb-scented prayer space in a half-rush, careful to keep his boots from making a sound on the marble, he spared a glance at the white statues near the entrance.

Emeraliss, forgive me. Save me from myself... Laytia, give me the words to get through this without regret... He sucked in a ragged breath, half-formed prayers coming on faster than anything else. *Hastal… protect him where I can't, and Navara, thoughtful and honourable, give me a chance to prove myself to You for good. Failing all else, please grant me that, because all else…*

He moved on before he could finish that thought.

The first step outside brought him close to the tinkle of the spiral wind chimes on either side of the doorway, the nearby marble columns awash with ribbons of rainbow light reflected from the crystals dangling around the doorframe. The next step, however, brought him closer to the top of the stairs, enough to find Mayr already halfway up the staircase.

Without a word, Tash ran down the steps, his nerve roiling with a deep, burning ache.

"Tash—" Mayr stopped and reached out.

With a grab of Mayr's hand and a quick turn to the right, Tash continued down the steps, pulling Mayr along gently. That need to flee was back, all but sprouting wings and whisking him off to somewhere else, no doubt, fear, or regret to be had.

Mayr followed without faltering, not a word falling from his lips, just that unspoken trust to follow wherever Tash took them.

They rushed along the narrow path beside the temple, towards the back entrances, then turned sharply up the grey stone path to the left and ran past half a dozen priests and worshippers, all the while dodging several of the low-hanging tree branches. What was usually a sea of blood-red leaf during the warmest months of the year had finally given way to burnt orange and brown mottled with yellow, the hardy white blooms all but withered and the black-brown nuts ready for harvesting. Just on the other side of the first arc of thick trees, they passed through the carefully crafted, elegantly carved wood gates of the prayer garden, the circles and curves of the gates lending the soft deception of fragility. Inside the garden, a multitude of flowers stole attention the most, their colours vibrant and worth every moment of contemplation.

In addition to the flowers, the white marble and mixed-metal statues also received their fair share of admiration, each depicting a different consort of the Goddesses. Vines encircled the feet of the statues, though some tendrils had ventured further and coiled around some other part of the statues—mostly a sword here or staff there, with the long bow of Ingline the Cunning equally claimed. Even the tip of Dalysha, the ever-filled Drinking Horn of Peace and Plenty, was at the mercy of several tendrils, given how low the horn hung on the belt of the statue dedicated to Parmina the Silenced.

Beautiful as it all was, Tash cut through the prayer garden, along the least meandering path, closest to the line of trees that acted as the garden barrier. Once they passed through the second set of gates, Tash clutched Mayr's hand tighter.

Running felt good, even if he could not flee completely. It had been years since the last time, when he had run until he thought his ribs would snap just to get him to stop...

Guiding Mayr through the next arc of trees and around the short, black metal lantern posts, Tash led them into the private worship garden, a grove used by the priests for solitary pursuits and group ritual. The trees were tall and many, carrying on for a lengthy stretch to the back of the temple's orchard, and the undergrowth was tame, short, concentrated in patches where sunlight hit the hardest. Dried orange petals clung to the grass from the wild flowers, joined by what bright pink and green fruit had fallen with pale yellow nuts scattered all around. The soft trickle of water came from a white fountain to his right, a soothing constant behind the notes of birdsong and the calming scent of fallen leaves. Black cast iron benches sat here and there, all of them the perfect length to stretch out upon and meditate, both of which he had done often enough.

They were also the perfect length to lay a lover flat and find ecstasy in release.

Goddesses save him.

Hands fisted in Mayr's shirt, Tash pushed him against the nearest tree and took Mayr's lips for his own—hard, claiming with every bit of soul he had. He needed everything Mayr could give and loved Mayr's throaty moan as it slipped between their lips, calling on Tash's in return. Fingertips dug into his back, keeping him there as their kiss found a new intensity, a heated passion he was desperate to get lost in.

Nothing inside him played nice, not with all of his feelings caged by fear. He needed to let them go—to scratch and claw his way to finding peace.

Mostly he just needed to hide in the safety of another moment with Mayr. Get lost in the distraction. Maybe even tell his nerve to get its damned self together and do what needed to be done, no matter the cost. No matter the loss.

But the sacrifice...

Tash tore his lips away, cursing the rashness and the questioning look in Mayr's eyes, wondering what had gone wrong. More than likely, Mayr wanted to know why they were there at all, in the open, where Tash wanted to do all sorts of things to him. And take him... Goddesses, Tash wanted it all, with Mayr splayed and slick beneath him, naked and needy, taking Tash and loving what they did. Tash would give him everything if Mayr said he wanted it.

And by the most seductive graces of Emeraliss was Mayr *ever* looking like he would say just that.

"Mayr..." Tash whispered, teasing Mayr's lips with his own. He needed to tell Mayr the truth, lay it all out. *If it were anything but this...*

For all his achievements, he wanted to shrivel up and die. To kneel at Mayr's feet and beg forgiveness for whatever it was that continued to assault his instinct, like a lost memory that took an axe to the walls as its house burned to the ground. A pronouncement like Kee's changed lives, and the path of an Uldana was worth it—it had to be, and it needed to be a thousand times better than where he had been. Otherwise he had nothing left, nothing to show. *And Mayr…*

Mayr, who was caressing his cheek, lips haunting Tash's with the hope of another kiss. A loving soul with tenderness Tash wanted to keep for himself, his smile and husky laugh worth every moment together.

"Whatever you're after, it's yours," Mayr murmured, the heat of his breath dancing over Tash's jaw. "I'm with you in this. I'm not going anywhere." He nipped at Tash's lips as he led Tash's hands to his waist.

Tash's touch fumbled over Mayr's belt, holding fast to where Mayr's sword and knife usually hung but were very much absent—for Tash. He had left them behind for Tash, no different than all the other times they had been alone since their first time in the conservatory.

He remembered. Despite all the things he could have chosen to ignore, Mayr remembered. He took Tash's discomforts into mind. He cared. Enough to melt Tash's heart where he stood, just a fraction of it wondering if the decision to never fall in love was worth giving up just this once…

No.

No.

That was *not* was this was. What it never would be. That was a possibility left firmly in the back of some musty old closet in the middle of nowhere without a single key to the unbreakable lock on the door.

This was hiding from the future. From a cold darkness he feared with every breath of his being but chose to confront nonetheless. *This* was the need to kiss anxiety away and run nervousness into the ground with a wet and messy bout of sexual release. *This* was a matter of confronting everything and nothing before he upended the world he knew for a life he would die to keep. A sacrifice he needed to come to terms with himself before he could tell anyone else.

But there was nothing to stop him from speaking with his hands. His lips. On every part of Mayr. Inside him—

Grabbing Mayr's chin, Tash took to his lips again, his tongue driving deep, thrusting into Mayr's mouth over and over again. The image of making love to him played through Tash's mind, a stunning image that only got clearer, louder, coming out as a moan and the need to lose control as quickly as possible.

It took Mayr little time to unbuckle Tash's belt, and the tie of Tash's pants was far from a challenge. But the touch that crept up Tash's stomach, beneath his shirt, with a stroke of promise Tash wanted around his cock...

Mayr's belt was undone and discarded at their feet almost as fast as Mayr could get Tash's robe off. A nip at Tash's jaw had him groaning, the kiss that followed down his neck a heated attack on his senses. With one knee slipped between both of Mayr's, his hand flat on the rough bark of the tree, Tash dug into Mayr's thigh and gave a tug, bringing Mayr's knee up to his hip without any resistance—just a muttered agreement against his lips as Mayr drew him closer. Bodies grinding together, hardened cocks so close yet so far apart, their clothes were a barrier Tash would have happily burned to tiny piles of ash and buried around the roots beneath their feet. They were far from the first to use the grove as an intimate escape, the land as blessed by ritual as it was by the secrecy of passion and entwined souls, and anything they did there...

Tash broke their kiss and carefully lowered Mayr's leg from his hip. Panted breaths played over his lips, the taste of Mayr lingering on Tash's tongue, sweet as it was bitter: mixed fruit and cream cut through with the bite of spice and tart syrup, almost as intoxicating as the thought of pouring an entire bottle of mead over Mayr's naked body and lapping up every drop—then going back for more until he was drunk and passed out in Mayr's arms. A daydream in itself, one he would never want to wake from if it ever came to pass. If he could offer more than these quiet moments, not caring about anything but Mayr's trust in his hands.

He took Mayr's body in his hands, instead, first raking his fingers through Mayr's hair, the soft black strands loosely tied back with ribbon the way Tash loved most, then grasping Mayr's hand and pulling him to the closest bench. Save for a soft laugh, Mayr followed quietly, his hold tight around Tash's even as Tash drew him down onto the bench and guided him back, laying him flat against the black metal slats, everything about Mayr almost blending into the darkness.

On his knees between Mayr's legs, Tash stole another kiss, leaning down, pressing close, one hand braced on the bench, close to Mayr's hip as he tongued him deeply and groaned. The hand that slipped through his hair urged him on, fisting close to his scalp enough to hurt.

But the moan that came as Tash worked Mayr's pants down his hips; the hiss Mayr let out as cool metal met bare skin—Tash savoured those most, rewarding them with a slow stroke of Mayr's cock, his grip tight around the thickness as Mayr rose into him for another kiss. With another few strokes, pre-release beaded on the tip of Mayr's cock, glistening in the sunlight as Tash pulled back to watch.

Even without a single lick, he could practically taste Mayr already, memories brought raging to the fore. The offer was there, that chance to bring Mayr to release with his mouth once more and swallow him down completely, not wasting a drop.

But there was something else on offer; another pleasure he wanted badly, enough to shuck every bit of clothing and give it all, naked to the elements and stripped raw, crying out his end with Mayr beneath him. A step outside of himself from what troubled him. A step into safety.

Placing a softer kiss on Mayr's lips, Tash caressed the inside of Mayr's thigh, fingers slipping lower to cup Mayr's balls, rolling their weight in his palm as Mayr moaned his appreciation. The fist Mayr held in Tash's hair kept his silent demands for more close to the surface, the raising of his knees against Tash's hips keeping Tash steady as he teased Mayr's entrance. Circling one fingertip over the tight muscle had Mayr's entire body tightening, but adding another fingertip and nudging into Mayr with the barest hint of penetration... that had Mayr scraping his nails down Tash's back and grinding against Tash's hand, biting out curses as pre-release trickled down his cock and wet the hem of his shirt.

Their first time, Mayr's first time with any man—they could do it right there. Moments that could be seared into his memory for life, keeping them alive, anchoring them there, their souls a part of the sacred grove forever even when all else fell apart.

Tender. Mayr needed that. He needed to know he was safe. Cared for. Not used, not overlooked. Not given up for anyone else.

By the Goddesses, Tash wanted to be that man. He could *do* tender every moment of his life if that was what Mayr wanted. He loved it, craved it, needed to give it as much as receive it. Right then, Mayr lay vulnerable beneath him, exposed just enough to let Tash play and send him reeling into a new rush of sensation. They had everything they needed, a vial of oil safe in Tash's robe pocket. He only needed to fetch it and stretch Mayr wide, fingering him until he demanded Tash's cock.

Them. That would be them, riding the crest and falling together, entangled in the grove's essence with beauty all around them, their cries rising up like birdsong. Certainly Mayr's whimpers were something of beauty themselves as Tash slicked his fingers with Mayr's pre-release and worked over Mayr's entrance, rubbing with the tip of one finger but not pushing inside. Just caressing, easing through the motions, barely at a crawl, rushing nothing…

But he was a damned fool, because despite how stunning Mayr looked, trembling and waiting, Tash had no intention of going through with it. Not then. Not there. Not with the truth clinging so close to his head and heart, Mayr could get hurt.

Bastard.

And he most definitely was a bastard, because every desire to make love to Mayr was there, dancing with the shadows, but the bit of him that was busy trying to stop him? *That* was the truth destroying what he wanted all over again, shoving him right up to the edge of the glass before smashing it with his face. If he was reckless, if he took what he wanted, Mayr would pay the price.

No. Not him. Not anyone else ever again, either.

That was a promise, just as solemn as his promise to forsake the kind of love Mayr wanted but could never have from Tash.

If only his want could have shut up and died on its tongue.

Still, that tongue was what he had, and he intended to put it to use.

Tash sank to his knees on the grass and wrapped his hand around Mayr's cock, hoping to distract Mayr from asking questions. With one hard stroke, then another, he held Mayr's attention where he wanted it, his other hand keeping Mayr's fingers in his hair, needing the touch—mostly to keep him grounded, though part of him wanted to weep and fight and weep some more.

Dammit, he was a disaster.

Drawing Mayr's cock into his mouth forced Tash's thoughts into silence, his focus on the salty, bitter taste of pre-release as he licked Mayr's shaft and sucked on the swollen head. Mayr's drawn-out moan kept him there, his hips rising and falling, cock gliding along Tash's tongue and grazing his teeth until Tash swallowed him down completely. Stuck on shallow breaths that only quickened, Mayr wrapped Tash's hair around his fist and held tight, his release close to breaking.

Tash's hand was around his own cock the next moment, stroking hard and fast to Mayr's rhythm. His imagination ran rampant, picturing Mayr's hand around his, fingers stroking his balls, his hot tongue slicking his sac…

Mayr came with a cry, shaking as he came undone. Tash followed not long after, come seeping down his fist as he fought to breathe through the high, licking at Mayr's tip to make him tremble and hiss.

"Damn you," Mayr bit out, only to whimper as Tash drew his come-covered hand down Mayr's softening cock. "Now you're just being cruel, you teasing bastard of priestly proportions."

Before Tash could answer, Mayr pulled Tash into a kiss, his tongue sweeping through Tash's mouth, across his lips, and all but drowning what was left of Tash's senses.

"Remind me," Mayr said, his voice husky, "after dinner. I'll return the favour." He nuzzled Tash's cheek, his stubble meeting Tash's beard. "I'll do it better this time. I just need the practice."

Tash could have wept right then, caught between coming down and wanting to comfort Mayr—to tell him he never needed to doubt what he could do. That his mouth felt good anytime, in any way, on any part of Tash's body, no perfection needed. That he had all the time in the world to learn and do and he *was good at it*.

Yet for all those words rumbling through his head, vying for the speaking, all Tash could muster was a kiss so full of silence it might as well have meant nothing.

Chapter Nine

Was this considered permissible by the rules of their casual relationship or had Mayr overstepped the boundaries?

Over the last fifteen days he and Tash had spent time together, mostly drinking at the tavern, walking around the estate or temple, and meeting for the occasional, understated sexual encounter every couple of nights. Nothing permanent or deeply involved, just two men enjoying each other's company, talking, and having a laugh at no one's expense but their own.

This was different.

Mayr stared down the length of the half-harvested field towards the barn, watching Tash's hands wave erratically as he spoke. Seated on a wooden chair beside Renett, Mayr's mother, Tash appeared immersed in recounting an exciting story, his wide, boyish smile apparent even from where Mayr worked with Estara. At Tash's feet sat three dark-haired children, their small bodies close to Renett's long chair that supported her blanketed, outstretched legs. Efae, Estara's five-year-old son, gaped at Tash, his widened grey eyes threatening to pop from his head onto the yellowed grass. Seeing only the back of Dayla and Alith's heads, Mayr could not tell what they thought, but from the way Alith scooted closer to Tash, he supposed they were just as captivated.

"Well, I'd say he's worth keeping," Estara said, wiping sweat from her forehead. She sighed and readjusted the blue rag tied around her head, keeping her black bangs from falling into her blue-grey eyes as she worked. "Not like this thing. I should've just taken Loftin's handkerchief. It was hanging right there, in his pocket. I could've stolen it."

"Like he wouldn't have noticed you had it." Mayr crouched beside her, pulling on a fistful of leaves with one hand. He used the trowel in his other hand to dig at the red earth, still moist from a light rain. "You're not exactly the fastest thinker around, are you?"

Estara punched his shoulder. "You are so annoying. Can I have a different brother, please? I'd even take a sister."

"Not that she'd like you any better." Mayr yanked the cluster of dark purple and yellow vegetables out of the ground. Most of them were large and round as draysa tubers should be, and none of them were rotten. He tossed the plant onto the pile behind him and wiped his hands on his brown work pants, the rough fabric caked in drying mud. As Estara uprooted another draysa plant, he tightened the tie keeping his hair back. The strands clung to his wet neck and naked back, only one of the hazards of working the farm. Why had he not braided it or had Estara pin it up like she always threatened?

Because Tash likes playing with it. Once more, Mayr cast a glance towards Tash. Caught in a laugh that shook her body, Renett hugged her waist with one hand and swatted Tash's shoulder playfully. Her dark hair had escaped its bun under her straw hat and hung in curls around her softly rounded face.

"Well, would you look at that," Estara muttered, sitting back on her legs. "He's gotten her to laugh. Now he's *really* worth keeping; approved by both children *and* Mother."

But was it too much? Did it resemble a committed relationship more than it should? He had brought Tash to meet the family, partake in dinner and chatter, and accompany Mayr on the carriage ride to and from the farm.

The situation felt wrong, as though he pushed for more, disregarding their agreement.

Mayr peeled his gaze away, redirecting it to the others in the large, mixed field. His father and Teneth, Estara's dark-haired husband, hacked the remainder of the tall, yellow stalks of treelike grass, careful not to cut themselves on the woody, hollow stems. Mayr and Loftin had done the rest earlier that morning, leaving only a small patch, mostly for their father's sake. Malary had refused their offer to do it all, scolding them with his gruff voice and grey glare. Now, while Mayr and

Estara pulled draysa on one side of the field, Loftin and his wife, Orlee, harvested heavy ears of the dark brown kolal plants on the other. Short with a tiny frame, Orlee had to stand on her toes to bring the thick plants down until she could yank the ears off. To Loftin's credit, she rarely had to, not when he cut the plants down before she could try.

Tash had taken on the role of staying with Renett and the children. While Estara's daughter, Dayla, was eight years old and had already assisted with the harvest by collecting herbs, the remaining jobs were beyond her abilities. Everything else was too tall, too heavy, or too dangerous. The same applied to Alith, Loftin's seven-year-old son, who had managed to limit his usually frequent, loud outbursts while helping to tie hay bundles to be stored in the barn over the winter. To Mayr's relief, Alith remained calm rather than making Tash chase after him, something Alith would never have tried if Renett, alone, had been taking care of them.

Instead, Mayr spared his mother the responsibility, trading it for meagre entertainment and social contact. She seldom had visitors besides the wives and sisters of the other farmers and the occasional merchant she knew from the village. Although the farm was not too far from the village, it was difficult for her to get there. Never could she go alone; a caretaker was always required. Given his father was the only one available most days, they did not go often. The farm required as much of Malary's attention as he wanted to give his wife. Since the farm was their livelihood, the farm won nearly every time.

None of it dampened Renett's faith. Even though she would never walk again, she believed the Goddesses would provide for their family and give her the strength to overcome every challenge. Love and concern for her well-being were the initial reasons Mayr had asked Tash to join him at the farm. Rarely did she attend Temple, settling for the well-lit and diligently tended altar at home. Nor did she ask the Temple to send a priest or priestess to the farm, always stating it would be an inconvenience.

With much humility but no regret, he had seized the chance to provide her a portion of what she had missed. Albeit small, it was something. Tash had agreed, his tone never wavering from its comforting gentleness. He had even appeared at the Dahe estate before dawn, just to ensure he was present when Mayr left well after sunrise. Since they arrived, Tash had been every bit the priest Mayr expected, telling stories and offering blessings on everything and everyone. Almost every corner of the house had been blessed, and the scent of cleansing herbs still filled the rooms.

Tash had also charmed at least half the family. What Malary thought of him, Mayr did not know, especially since his father rarely spoke to priests. Though Malary appeared pleased to find Renett enjoying herself, suggesting Tash was a welcome addition. From what he could see, Tash took it in stride, laughing and being his pleasant self.

Except for the hint of concern in Tash's eyes and the glint of trepidation hacking Mayr's doubts. Having stared into those eyes for long moments during their time together, he knew something was coming. The duties of a priest were not the reason, given how experienced Tash was. No, it was something between the two of them. Mayr had seen the same look several times on the faces of his lovers.

Right before they left him.

Was Tash seeing someone else? They had agreed to keep things simple. Their arrangement did not preclude Tash from pursuing a relationship with anyone else. While the idea did not sit well with Mayr, he had never demanded Tash be his alone. They slept together—or, rather played at it, relying on their hands and mouths to please one another before parting for the night—but that was it. Although his infatuation was not yet spent, perhaps Tash's was. Or maybe someone else was better at keeping his attention.

You still haven't been in me, even though I've been willing. You haven't let me inside you, either, always turning down my offers to try. Have you found someone who knows what it's like to take it all the way? Gotten bored with me?

The thought turned Mayr's stomach. He always knew how to sour a good situation.

"Hey." Estara poked Mayr's arm. "Sun getting to you or are you just smitten?"

Mayr blinked, refocusing on her. "What?"

"You're staring a hole into your friend there. Shall I dunk your head in the water trough?"

"Try it and I'll drown you." Mayr shoved her back gently, just enough to tip her before she caught herself on one hand. "Actually, I should do that anyway. I'm sure you owe me for something." He threw a handful of tangled, shriveled roots past her.

"Well *that* was mature."

"You know me, always the model of eldernality."

"I'm certain that's not a word."

"Is now. I managed to say it, didn't I?"

Estara broke ground with her trowel. "Please, don't ever teach my children." She lowered her head, stray strands of black hair peeking out from under the rag. "So thanks, by the way. I'd say you've made Orlee and me some pretty coins. I don't know *what* to spend it on first."

"What are you going on about?" Mayr raised his gloved hands, his calloused skin still raw from earlier. "Wait, don't. Every time you tell something, I want to rip my ears off. And if it's you and Orlee, I *really* don't need to know. If I didn't know better, I'd say *you two* were the twins with the way you carry on."

"Hey, Loftin married her. I can't help it if we get along." Estara wiped her face with the back of her wrist. Except for the dirt smudged on her skin, she resembled their mother almost exactly. "You just won us a bet, is all. Loftin's going to be so mad." With a mischievous laugh, her face reddened more than it already was from the sun. "He bet against his wife. This'll teach him."

Mayr raised one brow. Her tone suggested trouble—at his expense. "Tara, what did you do?"

A sly smile curved her pink lips. "Nice bruise," she cooed, pointing at Mayr's left shoulder.

Just off his collarbone, the bruise was still dark blue. It was a reminder of the night before last when Tash had sucked the skin hard. At the time, Mayr had welcomed it, but the expression on Estara's face made him self-conscious. "It's nothing."

"Next time, tell your *friend* to aim lower. If you don't want us poking in your personal life, don't make it so obvious. Or you *could* just call him what he actually is instead of just saying 'a friend.'"

"I don't know what you're talking about."

Estara snorted. "Right. I'm sure he wouldn't, either." She gestured to Tash with her chin and pulled her white tunic down over her thickset torso. "Because it sure isn't me he's been ogling, even if my breasts are bigger than your ego."

On instinct, Mayr glanced at Tash and froze.

Tash's gaze was fixed on him, his yearning expression suggesting his mind was not on storytelling or the children.

"Look, far be it from me to say anything," Estara continued, "but let's just call a lover a lover. And let's just call Loftin a loser because he wouldn't listen to Orlee and I. We told him there was something between you two."

"Tara," Mayr warned, clenching his teeth, "I don't want to get into it."

"What? He's nice. You're you. It's a good thing. I don't see why you don't just—"

"It's new, all right? Just stay out of it. And don't get attached. He might not be around long."

Estara pouted. "Aw, come on. Don't tell me you're going to get rid of him. You need someone, you know? It's silly, the rest of us having families when you don't." She poked his wrist with the end of her trowel. "If it's still about that bitch Betta, forget her. She's never been worth a moment of thought."

"Thanks for reminding me. I was actually having a good day." To get away from her stare, Mayr whirled towards the pile of uprooted draysa and tore the leaves away before dropping the tubers into a burlap sack. "It isn't about her. He's just not intending to stay, that's all."

"Like the rest of them." Estara sighed.

"Hey, at least he's honest about it; upfront. It's fine. I wouldn't mind not having to plan my life around someone else's. I'd like trying to be my own person."

Estara grunted, resembling their father. "I don't believe you, but there's not much I can say, is there? It's *your* life."

"Yes, it is, and if your cheerful disposition doesn't stop crawling up my backside, I'll just go and muck stalls for the rest of the day, and *you* can pull draysa. All. By. Your. Self."

Peering over his shoulder, Mayr caught Estara sticking out her tongue at him. "I bet he likes your backside," she muttered, almost low enough for him to miss it.

Mayr let the comment slide. He appreciated her concern, but not at that moment. Not when Tash was at the other end of the field, eyeing him as though he wanted Mayr's lips around his cock. As much as Mayr wanted to give that to him—as enjoyable as the act had been the few times Mayr did it, despite not being able to take Tash's cock down further than halfway without gagging— Mayr's attention was on finishing the rest of the harvest. Family first, pleasure second. *Maybe even third, assuming I don't have to bury Tara. What a shame that would be.*

They continued their task in relative silence, competing to see who would finish their row first. When they finished, Mayr gathering his last plant before Estara could dig around hers, they bagged the tubers and joined their mother, Tash, and the children. Orlee followed behind them, tousling her blonde hair as Loftin hauled their load to the barn with Teneth.

"Go on, drink up, all of you," Renett commanded, pointing to the buckets of water beside her chair. "Head back to the trough. Wash yourselves. Dinner's on when everyone's finished."

Mayr dipped his head and headed towards the barn behind Estara and Orlee, whose heads were close together as they giggled.

Tash grasped Mayr's arm, stopping him. He leaned in close, his lips on Mayr's ear. "I like you like this," he murmured, breathing deep as he nuzzled Mayr's neck discreetly. "Sure you don't want an extra hand?"

There were many things Mayr wanted. If they had been the only ones standing there, he might have agreed. But Estara's laughter reminded him of why he had introduced Tash as his friend to begin with. He did not need his family expecting Tash and him to last.

"No, but keep that in mind for later." Mayr pushed away and strode to the trough beside the barn. After washing the dirt and sweat from his skin with a cloth, he swiped his shirt from the post beside the trough, careful not to knock off the other shirts. Fully dressed, he followed Estara and Orlee back.

Renett reached out to take Mayr's hand on his approach. "Thanks for bringing him," she said, beaming as she nodded towards Tash. "We've had a wonderful time. I forgot how nice it was hearing the old tales from someone who wasn't me. And the children behaved to such perfection." When she motioned at him, Mayr leaned down to receive her kiss to his cheek. "You're so good to me."

Not even half as much as you deserve, he wanted to argue. Deciding against it, Mayr squeezed her fingers, his gaze averted from her legs. He barely caught all of the words spoken by Dayla, Efae, and Alith as they told their mothers what they'd heard while everyone else worked. Most of what they said was jammed between high-pitched chatter and a dizzying cycle of "and then." Estara and Orlee patiently allowed the children to exhaust the topic before chatting with Renett.

Tash stood behind the chair he had occupied, having offered it to Estara. His glance drifted from the children and their mothers to Mayr and Renett. Twisted emotions haunted his gaze, his smile weighted with what looked like regret.

The same emotions Mayr felt.

So many lost chances, so many years taken. Betta, why'd you do it? Why'd you break us? He knew why watching the children broke his heart, but why did it affect Tash?

Loftin, Teneth, and Malary appeared, cutting through Mayr's thoughts before he could analyze them. Washed and fully clothed, their arrival prompted the children to burst into a fit of squeals and another round of "guess what Priest Tash said."

A shrill whistle stopped the banter. Everyone turned to Renett.

"Dinner." She pointed to the house, its dark wood sides and red-stained roof a match to the barn. "Last child there gets the lowest seat."

All three children yelled and raced for the house.

Tash stared at Mayr, his expression blank.

"They like kicking their legs while they eat, and it only works if the chair's high enough," Mayr explained, shrugging. "It's a family habit. Apparently it worked for us, too."

"And none of you starved, last I checked." Renett pursed her lips. "Don't start arguing with my methods."

Mayr kissed the top of her head. "Wasn't going to." He bent down and slid his arm behind her. "Come on, let's get you in."

A hand flattened on his back. "Here, let me. You should rest." Tash moved Mayr aside. "After what the lot of you have done all day, it's the least I can do." With one arm around her back and the other under her knees, he lifted Renett as if she weighed nothing.

Renett looped her arms around his neck. "I'm certain this goes beyond your sacred duty, priest. You don't have to. What would the Goddesses say?"

"That being of such service *is* my sacred duty, and you deserve the full extent of it," Tash replied, standing still to let Mayr tuck the thin, blue blanket around Renett's legs. The fact Tash wore his skin-tone bracers and was missing his talon ring did not escape Mayr. Neither did his laced robe, the red fabric vibrant against Renett's faded yellow gown.

The vestments could do nothing to remove the image of Tash's naked body in Mayr's thoughts, a body he would rather not lose the chance to touch. *But it's coming, I know it is. After it's over, I'm sticking to myself for a while. Work out what I actually want and avoid temptation.*

As the rest of the family headed for the house, Mayr followed behind, watching Tash take Renett up the front porch and over the threshold. She laughed again and held onto Tash. Though she laughed often on normal occasions, she sounded even more joyful than usual. If anything, she flourished under Tash's attention, her pale blue eyes sparkling. If miracles had been commonplace and real, Mayr would have expected her to suddenly walk from Tash's embrace. He would have settled for even the slightest kick.

Never going to happen, so stop daydreaming. Waste your optimism on other things.

Like the idea that Tash fit into their family, and not just because he spun tales and gave Renett a chance to socialize with someone who believed as she did. His reserved manner and gentle humour blended with the hodgepodge of personalities that made their family: Malary's quiet seriousness edged with sarcasm; Estara and Loftin's love for life and mischief; Teneth's good-natured but shy demeanor; Orlee's carefree enthusiasm and the children, who were brazen and curious. Renett was an endearing mixture of them all, dependent on the day and the moment.

Now she's welcomed him in. I definitely can't tell her about us. I can't let her think there's a chance he'll be here more often. Mayr trailed behind Loftin. They passed through the kitchen to the dining room, sidestepping the bodies moving in and out of the kitchen. Sweet incense and bitter herbs scented the air, wafting as he maneuvered around the two tables pushed together in the middle of the small room. Renett already sat at the head of the longest table, facing the kitchen, mumbling as Malary fussed over her. She slapped her husband's hand and offered a wide grin before kissing his cheek. Malary snapped his mouth shut and took his seat next to her, around the left corner of the table. In his silence, he snaked his hand towards hers and clasped her fingers.

Mayr averted his gaze from their intimate display. Despite everything, his parents were still in love; perhaps even more than when he was a child, if his memories and interpretation could be trusted. What he would give to have that, or at least feel it again.

"Priest Tash, come sit." Renett tapped the table at the seat to her right. "Here with me, if you would do me the honour."

Tash dipped his head and complied, pulling his chair towards the table. "If you wish."

"Hey, Reny," Teneth called from the kitchen, "all these platters? And the bowls?"

"If you all expect to eat, then yes," Renett answered.

Orlee sashayed out of the kitchen, a wooden board with two loaves of bread in her hands. "Teneth, love, if it's edible, it's going on the table." She set the board in the middle of the main table and looked pointedly at the children. "No touching. Not until everything's ready." Once she received a nod from each child, she returned to the kitchen.

Intending to help, Mayr turned towards the kitchen.

Estara stopped him with a glare, entering the dining room with a large bowl of leafy violet plants and bright pink fruit. "Don't you even dare. There are enough people moving about." As if to prove her point, Loftin and Teneth stepped out from behind her with platters of cold meat, cheese, and herb tarts. They set the food on the table and disappeared into the kitchen.

Dayla giggled from her seat next to Malary. "Mama told you, Uncle Mayr."

"Yeah, I know. I think she got me mixed up with one of you smelly little beasts." Mayr's raised brow drew laughter from her, Alith, and Efae.

"I heard that," Estara yelled from the kitchen. "And they're my smelly little beasts, thanks. Don't make this perfect beast of a big mama beat you for your muddy talk."

Orlee reappeared with bread. "She's got a point there." Hands on her hips, she tilted her head. "Did you want me to get the offering to the Goddesses, Reny?"

Renett nodded, sending Orlee into action. She picked up the silver plate from the gleaming set at the end of the smaller table opposite Renett and filled it with a single helping of each item of food. When the rest of the food was brought in and everyone found their places, Orlee added the last spoonfuls and left the room through the second door behind Renett.

"Here, let me." Mayr took the polished metal decanter of gaffa nectar from Loftin's hands and looked to their sister. "Tara. Ta-ra. *Tara!*" Estara's head lifted. "Hand me the goblet, would you?"

With an annoyed glare, Estara retrieved a glass goblet from the empty place setting dedicated to the Four. "Because clearly you don't have legs."

"Hey, you banished me from that end. Not my idea." Mayr filled the goblet and placed the decanter on the table. On his way out of the room, he passed Orlee in the doorway and winked at her warm smile.

The thick scent of incense and floral extract-infused wax overpowered his senses as he entered the tiny room. Pillows and blankets were arranged in a pile to his left. To his right, the altar glowed under the light of four large candles. Small grey statues stood on a dark wood box in the middle of the altar, each no taller than the length of his boot. Chiseled into the shape of women, two statues wore their hair long while the other two bore it short. Three wore gowns; one wore armour. A short red veil hung over each of their heads, the delicate fabric glimmering in the candlelight. Red and white petals littered the white altar cloth. Placed on the front edge of the altar was the plate Orlee had prepared. The offering would remain there through dinner until someone took it outside to deposit the food at the base of the offering tree, well away from the house.

Mayr set the goblet beside the plate and stared at the flames. Words escaped him. He never knew what to say to the Four. They confused him, more than anything. How his mother, father, and Tash could offer themselves and believe in the Goddesses despite the terrible things in the world, he would never understand. Still, he would offer the Four anything on his mother's behalf.

After bowing his head, he rejoined the others and stopped at his place beside Tash. To his right stood Loftin, Alith, and Orlee, and across the table from them were Estara, Efae, and Teneth. Only Renett remained seated.

"Priest Tash," Renett said, "would you do Mal and me the honour of saying the blessing?"

"I would never refuse." Tash lifted his wooden goblet towards the chair at the other end of the conjoined tables. Except for a quartet of colourful pillows, the chair remained empty, situated before another silver plate and glass goblet with silver utensils. Everyone at the tables mimicked his gesture. "To the Four, goddesses of life, being, and divine understanding, I ask blessing upon the meal before us and all those here, in physical form and spirit. May Your gentle grace be upon us, Your unconditional love uplift us, and Your bountiful gifts be cherished with a full heart. Blessed be the Four."

"Blessed be the Four," everyone repeated before they sipped their drinks and sat.

"Lovely. Thank you." Renett covered Tash's hand with her own. "Perhaps you can teach my children to say it so eloquently." Her gaze shifted to Mayr, a smile playing at her lips. She suspected something, he was certain.

"Now, Mother," Loftin started, handing Mayr a bowl, "it's not about how pretty we sound; it's the sincerity. We could drunkenly slur it out and still be good. Right, priest?"

Tash chuckled and held a platter for Renett as she started to fill her plate. "Depends what day it is. Sometimes Navara prefers everything clear and perfect to the very letter and tone of each word."

Loftin stopped, gripping a platter. "Wait, you're saying I could have my backside thrashed or otherwise booted by the Goddess of Justice because I slurred?"

"Perhaps." Tash passed the platter in his hands to Malary. "She's incredibly temperamental."

Renett laughed as Loftin gawked at Tash in mock horror.

"Kids, do *not* do what I do. That means you, Alith," Loftin instructed, returning to piling food onto his plate. "Last thing I need is your mother shredding me to pieces because I taught you to say the blessing wrong. Or anything wrong, actually."

"*Now* you get that?" Orlee muttered.

"He can't be that insulting," Estara said, passing dishes to Teneth. "He's still here to annoy us."

"Ha, ha. Thanks, *twin*." Loftin made a face at her, his features nearly identical to hers except for the grey eyes and short hair. "My next turn to make a sacrifice, it's you. All you."

Estara beamed and hunched her shoulders. "Love you."

Mayr shook his head and ate slowly. Whenever he visited, it was always the same. They might have added years to their lives, but their candidness remained. They shared much in common with Aeley, only one of the reasons he got along well with her. Being around her was like being home. Whenever Aeley was in the same room with his family, he could not tell where his family's essence ended and hers began.

Hearing Aeley's name stole his attention.

"What?" Mayr asked, clearing his throat.

"Aeley," Renett repeated. "You need to thank her. Priest Tash and I went through all of the things she sent with you. Such beautiful cloaks. Thick, soft cloaks that'll get us through the next couple winters for sure. They're much nicer than the ones I've made. The extra food she sent will go to good use." Her lips drew into a line. "She's much too good to us, just like her father."

"Hear, hear," Estara murmured between mouthfuls.

"Thank her, for me, for sparing you so you could come home." Renett touched Tash's hand. "She could keep him, you know, but she lets him come here at least a couple days a month. Sometimes we're spoiled with more. Just like Korre used to do. They've always sent my boy home."

Mayr's face warmed. "Mother, it's not like they own me. Never have."

"No one will ever own the likes of us," Loftin said loudly, raising his goblet. Teneth and Estara cheered and tapped their goblets to his.

"That's not what I'm saying," Renett continued. "I appreciate we're recognized, that's all. I *appreciate* that she respects us and takes care of you. Even with the ridiculous things the Grands get themselves into, she remembers to send you home. It's not the only thing she's done for us, either. She's no different than you, *still* doing things you don't have to."

Mayr groaned. He knew what she referred to and with the way she eyed Tash, he knew she was going to explain it.

"He's always helped us, you know," Renett told Tash, rubbing his hand as she glanced between him and Mayr. "Even now, half of what he earns comes to us, or so we've been told."

"That's assuming you *keep* it." Mayr glared at his father. "I know what you did with it a few times, you realize that, right? Ae finally told me. You gave it back to her so she'd pass it along to me. She said she tried to disguise it as extra earnings or some other excuse so I'd take it."

Cheeks flushed, Renett lowered her fork. "Aeley told you?"

"She was drunk, Mother. Ae *always* talks when she's drunk." Aware of Tash's inquisitive expression, Mayr leaned back. He would not apologize for what he did. He would continue to give a portion of his earnings to his parents, just as he had when he was younger. There was no reason to stop doing it—at least not a reason that stuck. Without a family of his own, he had more than he needed. Of what he kept, he spent the majority on his girlfriends and things for himself, mostly weapons or things for Hetlan. Everything else was for his family.

"That's a noble act," Tash said softly, his shoulder pressed to Mayr's. Under the table, Tash's hand squeezed Mayr's knee.

"It's not," Mayr muttered, staring at his plate. It was a guilty act: the behaviour of someone who had sold their spirit to regret. Nothing could buy it back, but he could give his parents and siblings what they needed. What he had taken from them.

The conversation about him ended as Efae asked Tash to tell them another story after dinner, his small voice tripping over the words as he rubbed his ear. The subsequent conversations twisted and turned on themselves, punctured by gibes between Estara and Loftin.

When the topic of sleeping arrangements for the night arose, the lack of rooms in question, Mayr cleared his throat. "We'll sleep in the barn."

Malary scowled as though Mayr had cursed. "Pardon?"

"Tash and I. We'll sleep in the barn or set up a tent under the lean-to like I usually do. It's still perfectly nice outside."

Horror accompanied Renett's gape. "Absolutely not! I will *not* have a priest visit my home and sleep outdoors, especially when I have a room to spare. What's wrong with you?" Patting Tash's hand, she smiled apologetically, her expression coloured by a hint of embarrassment. "You'll take the spare room, there was never any doubt."

"Fine." Mayr breathed out. "I'll sleep on the floor."

Estara gasped and coughed. Her face reddened as she coughed harder. She reached for her goblet with a shaky hand. "Sure you will," she managed hoarsely, her eyes watering.

Mayr glared at her. He did not need to be the topic of conversation again, not with his mother's newfound interest in Tash. As though she envisioned Tash and Mayr as a couple. As though her next question would be about their plans for what she hoped was a shared future.

A future they would never have.

"How about we sleep outside?" Teneth suggested, his bright tone catching everyone's attention. He motioned to the children and Loftin. "How about the five of us? We'll set up the tents and make it good."

"Camp out!" Dayla and Alith yelled in unison. They chattered excitedly until shushed by their mothers.

"Fine, it's settled," Renett said. "Priest Tash and Mayr have the bigger room, Estara and Orlee have the smaller, and the rest of you have outside."

The children squealed, rocking back and forth as they bombarded their fathers with suggestions for a bonfire and tent placement. Estara and Orlee cleared the table, laughing on their way to the kitchen. Malary caressed Renett's hand and spoke with her quietly.

Tash excused himself from Renett's grasp and left.

Confused, Mayr watched him disappear on the other side of the kitchen. Leaving silently was unlike him. Even more unusual was his hurried exit.

"I'll be back." Mayr patted his mother's hand as he stood. He cut through the kitchen and padded through the spacious sitting room and narrow corridors. No one. "Plants," he mumbled, pushing open the front door.

Tash sat on the porch steps. Elbows on his knees, he held his head in his hands.

Mayr closed the door and glimpsed Tash's back and shoulders. He was tense, drawn into himself. Nothing like what Mayr knew him to be.

Silent, Mayr sat on the step beside him.

"Sorry," Tash whispered. He turned his face to peek at Mayr, his hands still on his forehead. "I just needed to breathe."

With a slow hand, Mayr rubbed the back of Tash's neck. "Did you want to talk about it?"

"No, but thank you. I just needed some air. I just…" Tash closed his eyes and craned his head back, leaning into Mayr's touch. "I've always found it difficult to withstand the graces of family. I left mine behind, and I can't ever change that. They're gone. The only family I have now are the priests and priestesses, but it's not the same. The jokes, the stories, the familial bond. The sheer joy and security of just *being* a family. I haven't had that in such a long time. It's hard to be reminded of what I lost."

Explaining the look on his face earlier when we were watching the children, Mayr realized. He pulled Tash into his arms. "This is my fault. I'm sorry."

"For what?"

"I shouldn't have brought you. I should've come alone."

Tash pushed away, leaving a small space between them. "No, don't apologize. I'm happy to be here. Your family is good, blessed. It's nice to see, especially when I know how many suffer. It's refreshing to be here. And your mother needed it, I understand that. She's a bright flame I don't mind being around. There's much of her in you, and that's a blessing in itself."

"But I shouldn't have brought you, should I?" Mayr let out a frustrated sigh. "I can be insensitive, I know. I knew you said your family was dead, but I didn't think about it when I asked. And now—all day—I can't help but think…" He waved the rest of the words away. "Never mind. I'm being insensitive again."

"No, you weren't. You were speaking your mind. You know I prefer honesty. 'Can't help but think' what?"

Mayr grimaced. "That this ruins things for us." He flipped his hand towards the door. "Mother's in there looking like she's imagining us married and with a family like Tara and Loftin. You saw that, right? And no, I'm not overreacting. That's the same look she had when Orlee and Teneth were brought into the house those first few times. It's frightening, actually."

"I'm not sure I follow."

"You, me, this thing we're in. Bringing you to see my *parents*. This is too much like an actual relationship, isn't it? I'm not getting this 'casual' concept, am I?"

Tash leaned close, his lips near Mayr's. "What is it you're really asking?"

Yes, Mayr, what are you really *asking? Ruin it for sure, why don't you?* The voice in the back of his mind muddled his thoughts. He swallowed back the discomfort of the internal battle. "Am I running you off? You had this look earlier, like you were going to lea—"

The rest of his words were lost to Tash's kiss. Their tongues slid across one another, the kiss deepening as Tash clasped Mayr's head. It was almost a complete answer, even if it did not explain the expression in Tash's eyes earlier.

When they parted, neither took more than a shallow breath. "You're not running me off." Tash drew his fingers through the loose tail of Mayr's hair. "I swear you're not."

Mayr could hear the silent 'but' hanging in the air, haunting their conversation with words Tash did not say. Either he would not say them or could not. Still, there was something else. Someone else.

"We should get back in," Mayr said, standing. He would not get the truth from Tash right then. The explanation would come soon enough on its own. "We should help get the tents ready for the kids."

Concern and confusion collided in Tash's gaze, but he stood with Mayr. "Just as well. I'm supposed to tell them of Eleia the Triumphant slaying the Winged Brethren of Akovar. The more gruesome, the better, or so Alith's request went."

"Just not too gruesome or Tara will make a gruesome mess of *you*." Mayr held the door open for Tash and followed him in. "I don't need to explain how bad that would be."

Tash raised one of his brows. "Bloodbath?"

"More blood than bath. I figure she's worse than Ae. Well, if she had the chance."

"We'll just have to make sure that doesn't happen." Tash pulled Mayr into him, his hand in the small of Mayr's back. "The only one getting a bath should be you," he said, low and seductive. "And that requires you being naked, which I particularly enjoy… just a thought to hold us over until bed."

Another thought to add to the many.

Chapter Ten

Sunlight woke him, rays slipping through the crack between the dark curtains to warm his eyelids. A crisp breeze swept around the room. Mayr's thoughts tumbled forth, recalling where he was. Still at the farm, in what used to be the bedroom he shared with Loftin. As soon as the rest of the family was awake and dressed, there would be breakfast, imaginative tales from the children, more chores, and a farewell before he returned to the estate that evening. The list of things he needed to do when he returned to the estate reeled through his mind.

The mattress shifted. Blankets dragged across his waist. The faint sound of breaths changed from deep to shallow.

Sweet incense. Smooth skin. Blue, blue eyes…

A commanding ache twisted Mayr's belly as his cock stirred quickly from flaccid to half-hard, reminded of Tash lying in the bed beside him. He remembered falling asleep in Tash's arms, content after a strong fist and warm throat brought him to release, taking all he had until he was dry. He had done the same for Tash before that, and finally discovering the best way to take Tash's readied cock down fully without needing to spit him back out. On his knees, he had devoured the spurts and milky rush, savouring each moan and restrained thrust against his lips. The salty taste of Tash still lingered on Mayr's tongue; the musky scent still clung to his lips. His senses feasted upon them, wanting to take Tash in again.

His own cock continued to stiffen, protesting the boundary posed by his pants. They were the only clothing he wore, in case an unexpected visitor bounded through the door—mostly one of the children. But he was fully awake and given the long day before, he expected everyone else would sleep for some time yet.

There was more than enough time to work with.

Turned onto his side to face Tash's naked back, Mayr rested his hand on Tash's hip. Tash jerked and sucked in a breath but remained where he was. As Mayr's fingers quested down Tash's stomach to his apparent arousal, Tash slid his arm higher towards his pillow, exposing the taut skin over his ribs.

An invitation.

In a slow downwards slide, Mayr shoved the blankets down the bed until they pooled around Tash's knees. His lips took to Tash's hip as he breathed Tash in and nibbled his skin. Above the waist of Tash's pants, he sucked skin between his teeth, wanting to leave Tash with a visible reminder of what they did together. Satisfied with the dark mark forming, Mayr laid a trail of harder kisses up Tash's hip and over his ribs, nipping and stealing small tastes. The scent, flavour, feel—Mayr could get drunk off Tash's body in ways he never expected. Everything about him lured Mayr in, hijacking his sensibilities. Nothing else mattered, not when it was just the two of them.

He glided his hand over Tash's chest, pausing to feel the quick thumps of Tash's heart. Lips roving over the feathers tattooed on Tash's back, Mayr caressed Tash's nipple before tweaking it into a hardened nub. Tash ground against him, reaching behind with one hand to pull Mayr's hips against his. Caught between their bodies, Mayr's cock rubbed against Tash, ready to be inside him. Need danced through Mayr's body, demanding skin. Wet warmth. Tash's throaty groans as he came from Mayr's touch.

He wanted all of it, everything Tash could give.

Humming into the crook of Tash's neck, Mayr slipped his hand into Tash's pants. Tash's breath hitched, overtaken by a moan. Gripped in Mayr's fist, Tash's cock responded with greedy interest, the skin tight as the core pulsed. Each stroke encouraged it further, filling his grasp. He teased the tip, rewarded with the trickle of warm pre-release that soon coated his palm.

In a flurry of motion, Mayr tore the blankets from the bed and pushed Tash onto his back. Just as swiftly, he untied Tash's pants and eased them down, freeing Tash's flushed cock. He tossed the fabric before removing his own pants and throwing them in the same direction. On his hands and knees, he prowled forward and stopped only to take Tash's cock between his lips. Tash's fingers plunged into Mayr's hair, playing with the loosened strands as Mayr drew his tongue up the underside from root to tip, lapping the moist trail of pre-release. The tip of his tongue wandered and traced the tightened form of Tash's ball sac. When Tash groaned and twisted Mayr's hair around his fingers, his hips thrusting upwards, Mayr swallowed Tash's cock deep and chuckled low and long.

Tash gasped and muttered incoherently. On Tash's release, Mayr downed the intoxicating taste, urged by Tash's barely stifled moans. This was what he had missed all those times he resisted pursuing a man: needy, strained flesh that twitched from his touch and the desperate tones of want. All that was needed to cloud a man's mind.

Would he have enjoyed those other men as much as he did Tash?

The question plagued him as he licked Tash's softening cock until it lay sated. Yes, he found other men attractive, but Tash was different. With the others, Mayr had wanted to thrust his tongue down their throats and make them come, maybe even while yelling his name.

With Tash, lust commanded that much be minimal take only. Even his emotions had a list of wants. They pounded his insides and demanded ransom for his heart, which was tangled up and tied down, screaming for attention.

He glanced at Tash's thinly-opened eyelids and veiled gaze. Had they not agreed to a casual relationship, he could have seen himself with Tash more permanently. *Don't get ahead of yourself. It's still just infatuation, you know,* his nagging, internal voice reminded him. *You like sucking his cock, but it doesn't mean you're ready for the rest of him all of the time. And since he's the only man you've had, who's to say you wouldn't like someone else just as much? Besides, you're still recovering from Sarene and the women before that. Don't dig yourself into something you can't get out of.*

Tash's eyes opened and he sat up with a grin. "Your turn." In an instant, he flipped Mayr onto his back and encouraged him to move up the bed. Once Mayr lay against the pillows, Tash spread Mayr's bent legs and ran his palms along Mayr's thighs. On the downwards stroke, he splayed his hands over Mayr's groin, caressed the crevice where leg met hip, and flitted over his cock. Slowly Tash lowered himself onto his stomach. Lips wrapped around Mayr's swollen cock, his tongue guiding the sensitive head towards his throat.

Soon after, Tash drew away, sucking and teasing. He sank lower and pushed Mayr's legs back. A moment later, his tongue sought skin again, tasting Mayr's tightened sac before circling his entrance.

Hot breaths drove waves of pleasure up through Mayr, and his eyes rolled back as he clutched Tash. Although it was not the first time Tash had explored him, it felt even better than the first two times. The moist tip of Tash's tongue worked the tight skin, darting inside as far as it could, soaking him. Pulling his legs back further, Mayr exposed more of himself. Lips pressed against his entrance before fingertips massaged his muscles until they relaxed.

When a finger slipped into him, little by little, Mayr's breath caught. He resisted the urge to contract, to battle the sensation. Instead, he seized the pillows under him and surrendered, pushing onto Tash's finger until knuckles met his skin. A strange sensation filled him, gradually replaced by an even stranger pleasure. They had not done that before.

"That feels all right?" Tash asked, withdrawing his finger to the tip before entering again.

Mayr nodded, the words lost. It was nothing like he expected. Uncomfortable? Slightly. Surprising? Absolutely. Pleasurable? Yes. Especially with the look on Tash's face, which suggested he wanted more than just his finger in Mayr.

Still, the finger persisted, slow as it slid in and out. On one upward stroke, Tash kissed Mayr with a passion that choked them both.

"Mayr..." Tash exhaled, struggling to form words. "I..."

Gripping Tash's head with both hands, Mayr stared him in the eye. "I want you. All of it. Every last bit of you in me. Here. Now."

Hesitant, Tash backed away. "I can't. I mean, I won't. Not yet."

"Tash—"

Tash removed his finger from Mayr completely. "No, and not here, for two reasons. One, I didn't bring anything with me. I still believe easing you into it is the best way." Tash stroked Mayr's cock firmly. "As good as this is, as much as I want to be in you, it'll hurt more than please. I don't want that to be your first time. *Our* first time."

It'll hurt no matter what *you do,* Mayr wanted to argue. He had thought about it, considered the ramifications. There would be no way out of it for him, but he accepted it happily. Surely Tash knew that, considering he had started somewhere, too. Besides, it would be just one time...

"The second reason?" Mayr's breaths quickened as Tash's strokes continued.

"I'd rather be in a more private space, where we're completely alone. Where no one can be unsettled—it's just us." Tash pressed against Mayr, chest to chest, his lips on Mayr's. "I want you to scream my name, but not in your parents' house. They'd overhear more than they should. I want to do it right, in the right place, at the right time. A place where we can be unrestrained."

With another deep kiss and a few hard strokes, Mayr came in Tash's hand, groaning as his milky release coated Tash's fingers and stomach and soaked the sheet beneath them.

"No fair," Mayr argued.

Tash stood and went to the bowl of water on the dressing table against the wall to Mayr's right. He returned with a wet cloth. "Let me take care of you," he said, wiping down Mayr's stomach and cock before washing himself down. After he finished, he hung the cloth over the windowsill between the billowing curtains and returned to the bed. Once he lay prone on the bed between Mayr's legs, Tash rested his head on Mayr's waist and drew a hand along Mayr's arm. Interlocking their fingers, he craned his neck back.

The look was there in Tash's eyes, unsettling Mayr all over again. Sad. Remorseful. There was even a hint of anger. He wished Tash would just say it, whatever it was.

"What?" Mayr asked, dry-mouthed.

"You're always accusing me of saying priestly things."

"And?"

"Right now, I have something incredibly priestly on my mind."

"Which is?"

Tash bit his lip and stared at the wall behind Mayr. "When I kiss you, my thoughts are everywhere and nowhere, and time means nothing. But when I look at you, I want to know everything about you. Every desire, every delight, every heartbreak, every fear. Except much of it can't be shared; so much has to be buried. I know; I'm guilty of the same." His troubled gaze met Mayr's. "I want to tell you mine, all of it, and I don't know why. Last night, I wanted to talk. I said I didn't, but I did. Just not there, ruining your family's dinner."

"Why do I feel like there's a question here somewhere?"

"Tell me about you, and not just the simple stuff," Tash said. "Tell me four of your deepest truths; the ones most people don't know and would never guess." He squeezed Mayr's hand. "And I'll tell you mine. The soul-shattering, truly telling details of my life in exchange for yours. I swear I'll never tell anyone or rub it in your face. I will never use them to guilt you. I will never use them to ensnare you. I just want to know you, outside of the carnal pleasure. I know your skin; I want to know *you*."

Was that the reason for Tash's strange gazes? He wanted them to get to know each other even more? Mayr swallowed back every emotion battling its way through him. *Stomach doing flips… Heart practically pounding a grave in my chest… and you're talking like this. And I like it. I don't want you to stop. But you're asking for something I don't know if I can give… but I want to. It's like you're in my head, putting words to the things I can't. But it's difficult.*

Except it's only four, right? Just four.

"Why do you talk so good?" Mayr whispered.

Tash squeezed their entwined fingers. "Because I can't stop thinking about you."

The simple answer hit Mayr harder than he expected. Some people could say a thousand words, offer a thousand messages, and he would never believe them. With Tash, his faith clung to every word, seeking a deeper meaning and latching onto each subtle message.

Four. That's all he wants. It's not my whole life, just bits of it. He's the only one who's ever cared to ask. He's the only one who'll actually listen. So why can't I just…

"All right." Mayr cleared his throat, praying what followed was as liberating as he wanted it to be. "All right. Guess I could start. Here it is, then: the night we met, I wasn't thinking about Sarene. After you kissed me, that was it. I was done. I'm pretty sure that's when things with Sarene ended for good."

Tash buried his face in Mayr's stomach and chuckled. His body shook, the coarse hair on his face rubbing Mayr's skin lightly enough to be ticklish. "That's good to know, but you're not trying hard enough." He grinned. "I can do that, too. Like when I was a child, I insisted on being called Hat."

"As in 'if you're going outside, wear a'?"

"Hat, yes. My five-year-old sensibilities thought it was clever. I wanted a shorter name and that's the one I liked most. It eventually wore off. Taldris stuck. Then I came up with Tash. People took me more seriously."

Mayr laughed. "I don't know, but we're getting to this deep stuff rather quickly. Are you always this open with your casual lovers, Hat?"

"Not usually. It tends to scare people. Or it's too strange for them. But there's something about you," Tash murmured, eyes narrowed with confusion. "Something that makes me think I can be completely honest." Quieted to a near whisper, his voice cracked as he continued. "And there's something in me, a relentless, curious feeling that I *have* to tell you these things or I'll be completely dishonest. You're so familiar, like I've known you before, from another lifetime; another existence. We're connected. I felt it in the tavern, and it's stronger now." He took Mayr's hands in his and twisted his arms behind his back, holding Mayr's arms around him. "I feel like I've been looking for you. There's something I need to tell you, something incredibly important that my spirit needs to say to yours, but I don't know what. The more I think about it, the more the words slip away. I'm struggling to understand, but I can't."

Rendered speechless, Mayr stiffened. The sentiments defied everything he could comprehend, slammed against impossibility with the force of a battering ram. How could Tash say the words that never should have existed for them, and at that point in time? Words that connected to what he felt, complementing them, filling the gaps of what he could not describe? Their situation was nothing spectacular nor did it warrant feelings deeper than lust.

Except Tash was serious, his confused gaze genuine. *Maybe there is more to it. Maybe it's not just me going off the romantic end.*

Mayr breathed deep. He would meet Tash's request and offer a more serious truth, even if it hurt. "My mother can't walk because of me. That's the second truth, and a whole lifetime of guilt I can't ever escape, no matter how hard I try."

Tash shifted to lean on his side and pin Mayr's leg to the bed. "What happened?"

"I was foolish and selfish. We were in Dahena, at the market with Mother. The twins were running around, getting into things like regular four-year-olds. My mother was busy bartering." Mayr shook his head. "Tara and Loftin were testing her patience. Then they started playing in the square and got in the way of a cart and team of work horses. Mother pushed the twins out of the way." He tore his glance from Tash's. "She twisted her ankle and slipped on some mud; landed face-first. Caught the hooves right in her back and then the wheels, all three of them on the one side. She hasn't been able to walk since."

Tash rubbed Mayr's arms. "I'm sorry."

"And the *really* awful part? All I had to do was watch the twins like she'd asked me to." Mayr snorted. "But no, I was too busy playing with the other boys, hiding in the alleys. I just wanted my own time. I was eight—I figured I deserved it. By the time I realized what happened, it was too late. Heard her scream. Heard the horses and cries for help. I turned around and there she was, everyone around her and calling for a healer. I can't remember much after that. I know I was with Tara and Loftin, but I don't remember anything else except feeling cold."

"The healers couldn't do much, I take it?"

"No, the damage was done. Other healers have tried, but they can't restore feeling from her waist down. All because I wanted to be like the other boys and feel like I belonged. It's not fair." Mayr clenched his teeth. "I can't fix it, and I can't make the guilt go away. She never uses it against me, but I beat myself with it all the time. I can't ever do enough to make up for it."

"You realize it wasn't—"

"Don't. Don't say it. Doesn't matter how many people tell me I'm not responsible, I know I let her down. I could've changed things. I didn't. Those are the only truths I need. I *don't* need people trying to make it better."

"I understand. I do." A grimace twisted Tash's troubled expression. "I really do."

"One of *your* truths, I take it?"

"Yes." Tash exhaled slowly. "Yes."

"And?"

"And…" Tash moved to sit beside Mayr, his legs bent to the side. "I'm not a normal priest. I didn't grow up thinking it's what I should do. I certainly never acted like one, not until they took me in." He closed his eyes. "For ten years, I was in the Shar-denn."

Frozen, Mayr regarded Tash's pained features. Never would he have guessed Tash's past lay in the clutches of a gang. Known for their brutality and violence, disregard for the republic's laws, and sordid involvement in extortion and exploitation, the Shar-denn was terror embodied. They stood for hate, greed, control, and cared for no one but their members. Even then, membership did not stop abuse or mistreatment.

They were the complete opposite of the Temple of the Four.

The opposite of Tash.

"How?" The question came out quieter than Mayr anticipated.

"My *friends*." The venom in Tash's tone made Mayr shudder. "They got into it through the brothers of another friend. Either they didn't realize it was the Shar-denn or they just didn't tell me, but they took to it easily. First it was good, just a matter of business. They did little things.

Getting this; moving that. We were thirteen—it was a great deal, getting paid to do easy things. I thought it was a way to show I was grown up, so I did it, too." He shrugged. "We received orders and did them. Never saw the faces of the guys we were actually working for, just their lackeys. Didn't think anything of it; didn't see what we were moving. We heard a lot of things bantered around by the lackeys and repeated them, thinking we were smart."

"There's a 'but' coming, isn't there?"

"*But*," Tash emphasized, dipping his head, "after a year, one of their faction bosses visited the village. He was surrounded by four guards much bigger than we were. They gathered us up in a room in a tavern that cleared out just for them. I thought we were in trouble. Instead, the boss clapped each of us on the shoulder and thanked us. Said we'd served so well, we deserved a reward. He gave the four of us each a knife—red and gold, with the skull and fist engraved in the blade. He welcomed us into the Shar-denn. Wished us long life and rewarded loyalty." Tash cast Mayr a deadpan stare. "Then he turned and slit the throat of one of his guards."

"Just like that?"

"Just like that. He told the other guards to gut him like the traitor he was. Then he thanked us again. Turns out some of what we'd repeated from the lackeys incriminated the guard. The guard wanted to take their leaders out and replace them. Or turn them in. The boss said that's not loyalty; that's the fool's way to die. But if *we* were loyal—if *we* kept working hard—we'd never have a problem. We'd want for nothing."

"Please tell me you ran out of there." Mayr took a shaky breath. "You didn't, did you?"

"How could we? We couldn't run even if we *hadn't* been in shock. You don't *run* from the Shardenn. If you want out, there's one way, and it ends in dead."

"So then what? You stood there and said…?"

"'Thanks for the knife,'" Tash mumbled. "He laughed, offered us a drink, and told us to burn the dead guard. Said we'd earned ourselves better jobs. He was impressed none of us had been sick or cried out when he killed the guard. We showed potential."

"And none of you told him no."

"Ress, my best friend at the time, asked what would happen if we ever did."

"And he ended up dead."

"No, he got to keep breathing. He got a knife in the knee for it, though. The boss moved fast. I just remember seeing Ress put his tankard down and the next thing I knew, he was on the ground, screaming." Tash rolled his neck. "We were informed that from our first job, we belonged to the Shar-denn. They owned us. If we stayed, we'd be taken care of. Given opportunities, payment, women, men, anything we wanted or needed. Protection for our families. Defence from the

High Council and Tract Stewards. Everything. We just had to do what we were told, that was it. If we left, we'd die. Our families would lose everything. Bad things would befall us."

"Typical Shar-denn fare."

"Yes. He said they had enough to incriminate us, so we should just stay. They could make those crimes go away. Apparently the things we were moving weren't legal, to put it mildly."

"Stolen?"

"And dead." Tash winced. "There were a lot of things, some of which included what used to be people. Or were. We couldn't tell the difference between a drugged girl in a box and a load of weapons. You want to talk foolish? Let's discuss *that*."

"And this was in Gailarin? By the Four," Mayr spat out. "No wonder Korre had headaches."

"You have no idea. No one really knows unless they're part of it. I saw things... Did things..." Tash sighed and drew a hand over his eyes. "I got deep into it, hating everyone and taking things that weren't mine to have. I played the games and kept my mouth shut. I worked my way up to being a guard, protecting the faction boss because I could fight and I was intimidating. They thought I was intelligent and bold, but I witnessed things I wish I could forget. People got hurt because of me. And whenever I didn't comply with orders—" He motioned to the scars on his chest. "I was punished accordingly. I could beat a man in defence of the bosses, but I never liked committing outright murder, and they knew it. So they tested me occasionally. The other guards liked reminding me I'd never truly be one of them."

"That's why you don't like sharp weapons," Mayr muttered.

"For the most part, yes. We've had a complicated relationship."

What else had he misread? Mayr wondered, although one thing bothered him more than the others. "How did you get out?"

"Not easily. I was twenty-three, and I'd drifted from my family. One day, I realized how much I wanted out. I left everything and ran. Told my family to never search for me, to just pretend I was dead. Because I was. If they harboured me, they'd die for sure." Tash let out a breath. "It took days, but I set everything up perfectly. I knew who'd be where and when. I took off in the middle of the night when no one was watching. Didn't take anything with me, just ran until I couldn't feel my legs then ran even further. Took refuge in a temple about a day away. I remember stumbling in and collapsing, but not much else."

"Then you became a priest."

"Not the next day." Tash laughed softly. "I stayed for months, keeping my head low. When we thought it was safe, a priestess smuggled me to another temple in the Alosaa region. They gave me cloth and wax to work with. I made candles and robes, and the priestess' gowns for the holy observances. It gave me a chance to establish some sort of life and independence—but not too much. We had no doubt the Shar-denn was after me."

"And somehow they never found you?"

Tash shook his head. "I stayed covered up or locked away and called myself Tash instead of Taldris. Cut all my hair off. I spent most of the time paranoid and kept coming up with ways to hide or escape. When I finally decided to be a priest, I left and came to this temple to offer my oaths. I've been here since. Ten years, only by the grace of the Four."

"Aren't you worried they'll still get you?"

"All the time."

"But you keep going?"

"What else can I do?"

"I don't know. We could talk to the Council—"

"And have them do what, Mayr? They can't protect me any better than the Temple does, not that they want to. I've confessed to the councilmen. I've given them what names I could and they've dealt with them accordingly, or so I was told. Considering I'm not looking for trouble, I've not asked them what was achieved. We have an agreement: I remain a priest and they leave me alone. I am neither pardoned nor condemned. I'm simply allowed to exist as a sacred servant."

"So that's it?"

"Yes." Tash swept his fingers across Mayr's cheek. "It's not all bad. I found you, and that's worth something."

"This sounds like you trying to change the subject."

"Perhaps. Is it working?"

"I suppose." Nose scrunched, Mayr considered his next words. Tash's fatigued eyes suggested he needed to think of something else. The memories were painful, evident from the shameful, disgusted expression still on Tash's face. If they were not invested in talking, he would have kissed Tash until he could do nothing but smile. "Another truth, then. Something serious, like the fact I keep getting into relationships that I know aren't good for me? The fact that I honestly don't know how to do any better?"

"I don't know if I believe that."

"Oh, you should. My choice in women has been so bad I can't even *begin* to make it up. I don't have *that* much imagination."

The tilt of Tash's head suggested he still disbelieved. "And yet you take it well enough to try again. You've overcome Sarene quicker than I expected."

Well enough? Now there's a laugh. "You have no idea," Mayr muttered. "Guess I might as well admit that's a lie."

"What is?"

"How well I'm taking it. It's a complete lie—just not one I want everyone to know." Jaws clenched, Mayr debated saying more. The truth was dangerous, playing with his vulnerability as if it demanded to be shattered. That was a challenge best left alone.

Tash leaned his head to Mayr's. "I will tell no one, I swear. No one, ever. Trust me like you did before; like you have been. Please don't stop. Not with this."

Trust. The concept sounded simple when Tash said it. Most of Mayr's intimate relationships had never known his full trust. Where his body was concerned, trust was easy: he was flesh and blood, toughened by a guard's life. His physical being had never been the problem. Everything else was, particularly the parts of him that never hardened enough to protect him. Entrusting anyone after Betta had been impossible, and whenever someone left him, they drove another poisoned stake through the festering emotional wounds. To ignore all of that and trust Tash... he wanted to. Deep down, he wanted to tell Tash everything. Even try letting Tash heal him if the wounds could be repaired.

If Tash stayed with him, maybe there was a chance.

Doubt washed over him, insisting he was too lost to offer anyone unguarded faith again. Trust would never be recovered; it would never be tended with care. Not where his heart was involved. Tash would leave him, taking any possible security of trust with him.

A lie. He needed the doubts to be a vicious lie. Especially right then, when the truth mattered.

Please don't throw this back at me. Stay and prove me right.

"Anyone who thinks I'm not affected is wrong. I am. It hurts me just as much as anyone else to hear I'm no good." Mayr raked his hand through Tash's hair. "Confidence is a funny thing: you can fake it just as deeply as you feel it. Say the right thing, act the right way, and people can believe anything. In everything else, I feel it, but with this *one* aspect of my life, I fake it. And I never used to."

"What changed?"

"Someone made me realize how much I care about what people think of me. Or rather, it's the people I love and who I believe love me." Mayr stuck out his tongue to lighten the mood. He hated being serious for too long. "Because I don't care what anyone else thinks. I've earned my life. The people who hate me are usually jealous, breaking the law, or they're an ass anyway, so I can't take that seriously. But when love is involved, that's when the knives are sharp and hurtful words even sharper."

"Meaning?"

"I walk headlong into a blazing fire for the sake of love and piss and moan when I get burned. Then I do it again because I can't stand feeling empty and alone. I'm convinced if I just keep going, it'll work out. I'll find someone who'll take me as I am, and then I won't care about what *anyone* thinks about me ever again. Because I'll have that one person who won't care about how I do in bed, what I look like, if I'm wealthy, or that I *do* want more than just sex because hey, I believe in romance, too. I was under the impression that's what women wanted. Instead, they enjoy it for a little while then the appeal wears off."

"And your other lovers, compared to Sarene?"

"They had different personalities but the same end. There doesn't seem to be much else to it except I'm never what they want. Never enough. There's always someone better. And *still* I get into the same sort of relationship, even when I can see the disastrous end coming. Pathetic, isn't it?"

"No." Tash splayed his hand over Mayr's heart. "You just haven't found the right person yet. In time, that one will come forward, most likely when you're least expecting it. They'll be the one that you can never let go."

"Do you honestly think that? Because I'm having a hard time believing that's how it works." But he wanted to, Mayr almost added. When death came for him, he did not want to be full of bitterness and spite. He certainly did not want to die all alone. Being alone terrified him.

"I do, even though I've also felt the callous sting of love." Looking at his bracers, Tash bit his bottom lip, appearing to struggle with a decision. Finally, he held one arm up. "It's why I wear these."

"I don't understand."

"I don't… deal well… with a broken heart," Tash admitted, blushing as he cleared his throat and lowered his arm. "When I love someone deeply, losing them hurts more than I can handle. So I… use physical pain to distract myself. And remind myself to never repeat the situation." He touched one bracer. "There's a scar on both arms for each of my serious relationships that have failed. They're the real reason I keep only casual relations. Every time I give myself over to someone completely, they hurt me."

If Tash's whispered words shattered Mayr's heart, the fear in Tash's eyes nearly killed him. Tash's dull stare suggested he expected Mayr to walk away and never return.

The thought of Tash hurting himself turned Mayr's stomach and punched his anger. The scars he could live with. He bore enough of his own, testaments to what he endured. It was the self-harm that worried him. To know Tash had hurt enough to need that for comfort struck him hard. "Can I see?"

Tash pulled his forearms to his chest. "I never let anyone see. And the priests have been kind enough to let me cover them."

"All right, fine. Can you at least tell me *why*? Who?"

"You don't mind?"

"What I *mind* is that you do it at all. Go on, tell me."

Tash eyed Mayr warily. "The first was Inesta, my girlfriend when I was with the Shar-denn. We were together for five years, but she hated what I was doing. She gave me an ultimatum: if I didn't leave the Shar-denn, she'd leave me." His plaintive glance avoided Mayr's. "It was an ultimatum I couldn't meet. Not because I didn't love her—I did, so much that when she left, I couldn't breathe. I couldn't think straight for days. But I couldn't just leave—they'd have killed not only me, but her, too. So I let her go. A few nights later, I put a knife to my wrist. It made things easier to bear, distracting me with a new pain I could actually do something about. I did it a second time, thinking it'd help, and it did."

Instead of yelling at Tash over his choices, Mayr subtly grated his teeth. "The second relationship?"

"Boyfriend. Naliss. We were together in Alosaa before I became a priest. He was easy to love."

"But he didn't stay."

"No. He decided I was too much—my *problems* were too much. He resented my paranoia, my fear of being hunted, and hated that we couldn't be completely open." Tash snorted softly. "Said he loved me, but he couldn't really *love* me. Said I pushed him into leaving—that I ran him off. Naliss couldn't stand living in the shadows and left. That's when I fled Alosaa to become a Metah priest here. I couldn't be like that anymore, who I was with him. I needed to be stronger. Less about me and more about others."

Mayr caressed Tash's stubbly jaw. "I'm sorry. That's not fair."

"It's true, though," Tash murmured. "I forced him out just like I did Inesta. I dragged them into a dangerous life. They were constantly in competition with my bad decisions and trying to survive. They deserved better. If anything wasn't fair, it was me." He tilted his head back. "Not as bad as the third. That one… I broke her."

"Tash—"

Tash held his fingers to Mayr's lips. "She killed herself, and that's on me. When it comes to your mother, no amount of 'it wasn't your fault' can alleviate the guilt. With Erithe, it's the same." As Mayr pulled him closer, he accepted the embrace. "I was a Metah, then, and she lived in the village. I thought things between us were good—more than good. She was sweet, funny. Caring. Made me believe in the power of Emeraliss and forgiveness. Still, Erithe had problems of her own; emotional downfalls that hit without warning. She was honest about it, and I helped the best I could."

"But?"

"She told me it was over, that things between us were too intense. Said I was smothering her and demanded too much." Tash sighed. "I was willing to change. Told her I'd do anything. But she wanted space. Days later, someone found her body in the river. She'd left a note saying she couldn't take living anymore. I found out from her sister that Erithe had gotten worse after leaving me and she'd blamed me for it. After that, I was finished with serious relationships."

Mayr glanced at Tash's bracer, trying not to imagine what the scars looked like. "And you're left with those."

"Yes."

"That's not right."

"Right, wrong, fate—pick one. They are what they will be."

"That's not an answer. That sounds like denial."

Tash shook his head. "It's acceptance. It took me years to accept that love and I don't mix. Now sex," he said, drawing his fingers along Mayr's flaccid cock, "we get along perfectly."

Laying one hand on Tash's, Mayr stopped him from teasing further. "And I call it avoidance."

"Maybe it is, but it keeps me alive. Sane."

"And never gets dealt with."

"It freezes misery," Tash argued softly, "and keeps it locked down. Love is the quickest way to kill me and ruin those I care for. That's why they never come back. I push them away and they can't fight it. They stay gone." He shifted again and raised his knees. "But enough of me. You have one last truth."

"So I should make it good, right?" Mayr stared at the curtains and worn wood planks of the dark wall. All the truths he never could have guessed. Tash hid them well, leading everyone to believe he was carefree and peaceful when deep down, he suffered, pinned by regret. No one saw it. No one felt it. There was no one to stop him. Did the priests understand how much he had been through? How much he needed someone? Did the Goddesses realize Tash needed a reprieve?

Take pity on him, would You? Mayr prayed. *Emeraliss, if You're going to continue toying with me, fine, but give him something. Someone. I know my relationships are Your entertainment, but whatever he's gone through—punishment, the wrong end of a divine bet, fate's boredom—it's cruel. It needs to stop. Go ahead and give me another Sarene if it makes any difference.*

Tash tapped Mayr's shoulder. "Are you all right?"

"Yeah, fine. Thinking, that's all."

"We don't have to continue. It wasn't one of my best ideas, I know."

"No, it's fine. I have one more." Mayr laid a finger on Tash's bottom lip, recalling the soft touch of Tash's mouth on his. "I was a father. Now I'm not."

A dark sadness clouded Tash's gaze. "I'm sorry. I'll pray for their spirit. How did your child di—"

"No, it's not like that. At least I don't think it is." Ten years could have changed many things. He could not rule out the possibility that the tiny girl he once held in his arms—his beautiful Iliane—had not died. Panic offset the rhythm of his heart. "By all that is sacred, I hope she's still alive," he whispered, the blood rushing from his face. To think she was dead... That he was not there to protect her...

Tash gripped Mayr's arms. "Mayr, no. I'm sorry. I misunderstood. Please don't let your thoughts stray to the worst. She's alive. Hold onto that hope. Go back to before I interrupted you. Tell me about when things were happy."

Happy? Had his relationship with Betta ever been truly happy? Could Betta have been miserable and he too ignorant to see it?

"I fell in love," Mayr started. "Twelve years ago. Betta was the most beautiful woman I'd ever seen. She said she was the daughter of a miller several villages over, but she ran business in ours. Said she needed to be on her own, away from her family. At the time, I was just a regular guard." Shrugging, he traced the shape of Tash's fingers with his fingertip. "I married her two years later. At least I thought I did. She was everything to me. Several months later, she gave birth to Iliane, this perfect little bundle..." He held his hands apart, recalling how small Iliane had been. "This big. I could cradle her on my forearm. She used to fight going to sleep. She wanted to see everything. So beautiful. I couldn't have been happier."

Mayr dropped his hands. "Four months later, I came home from the estate to find the baby gone. Betta sent her away. Told me she'd tried and tried, but she couldn't handle it. She said that with me working all the time, I didn't understand the struggles of being a mother. She'd accepted we weren't ready to be parents and sent Iliane to live with Betta's aunt."

"Without talking to you?"

"There was more, too." Mayr snorted. "Behind my back, people questioned Iliane's parentage. They'd seen Betta with another man. *I* only found out because one night a group of us were in the tavern, enjoying ourselves. Next thing I know, there's this drunk talking to me about Betta. How she's cunning and asking for trouble, sleeping with his brother and sending his kid off while make-believing our marriage. He *then* tells me the priest who'd conducted our marriage rite wasn't a priest. He was a friend of his brother's, *paid* to pretend to be a priest. It wasn't sanctified in the eyes of the Goddesses and certainly not sacred to Betta. She just wanted to make it *look* like it was so she could use me—my money, my reputation, my influence. She wanted to be able to get out of it even more easily. If we weren't really married, she wouldn't have to do much to break it off completely."

Tash sucked in a breath.

"Yeah, exactly. Not one of the finer moments in life," Mayr mumbled.

"Did you leave her?"

"Didn't have the chance. By the time I got home, she was gone. I walked in and everything was everywhere. A complete mess. Betta grabbed what she could carry, took my horse, and disappeared. A girl at the tavern had overheard us and told Betta she'd been discovered."

"Have you heard from her since?" Tash frowned. "Did you look for her?"

The short laugh Mayr let out was bitter. "Oh, I looked. For Betta *and* Iliane. Couldn't find either. The aunt doesn't seem to exist. There's nothing to say the family she spoke of actually exists, either. Nothing but lies." He crossed his arms. "Aeley found Betta once, though she's never told me how or where. She refuses to. But according to Ae, she broke Betta's nose, blackened both eyes, and threatened to take a knife to her hair. I got a message from Betta a day later. Only one word— 'sorry'—and the ring I gave her when we got married." Mayr scowled. "I don't count it as an apology. Ae beat it out of her, so it's just as fake as everything else. And now there's a little girl I don't know but wish I did. Mine or not, I haven't stopped caring. From the moment Betta told me she was pregnant, a part of my heart belonged to Iliane. It can't be returned."

"And if you saw Betta now?"

"I don't know, but I'd never hurt her. Ae *never* should've done what she did. It's one of the only things we can't agree on. One of the only times

I've yelled at Ae and meant every word, and I still do. I nearly arrested her for it. Korre intervened and dealt with it, though. I wouldn't talk to her for days."

"So you still love Betta."

"A little. Since then, it's been one disappointment after another. It's not that no other woman measures up, but apparently I don't. I'm good to exploit but that's it."

"That's a falsehood," Tash argued.

"No more or less true than you choosing casual relationships because you say love doesn't agree with you."

Tash's narrowed eyes suggested Mayr's words were a poor hit.

"You know I'm right."

"I'd rather not discuss it." Tash raked a hand through his hair. "Besides, I have one last truth and we're done."

Again, Tash avoided discussing what Mayr suspected he needed to. One day, Mayr would refuse him the chance and demand to know. They could both be stubborn. They both could fight for what they wanted. It was a matter of not backing down.

"Go ahead, then," Mayr said. "The last one."

"I'm terrified."

"What?"

"The Uldana Trials—I'm terrified of them." Tash swallowed uneasily. "Only my mentors know. Everyone else thinks I'm looking forward to it, that I'm walking into them with fearless faith. All of them believe I'm ready. More than I do."

Prepared to tell Tash he would be fine, Mayr opened his mouth.

Seeing the look in Tash's eyes, Mayr snapped his mouth shut. Once more, the questionable expression that twisted Mayr's gut filled Tash's gaze. He had thought it was about Tash admitting his past, but the anxious glance suggested there was much more to it.

That's it. I can't take it anymore. He said I'm not running him off, but something is. *He's practically got one foot out the door. But these questions haven't made sense, not if he's leaving. For believing in honesty, he's not getting it right. While he's not lying, I don't see him tripping over himself trying to tell me, either. Just stalling. So we're settling this. Now.*

"What aren't you telling me?" Mayr searched Tash's eyes, part of him praying Tash would just confess. Part of him wanted to hear nothing at all.

"Mayr…"

"You're holding back. You did it all yesterday, and you're doing it now. You said I wasn't running you off, but you never said you *weren't* running. I thought about it, you know, all those ways to interpret things. I realized that's another way to say you're leaving."

And there it was: the truth, shining in Tash's eyes.

Tash picked at the sheets. "I've wanted to tell you the last two days," he murmured, "but I didn't know how. There wasn't a good time. These days with your family—I didn't want to ruin anything."

Mayr studied Tash's face. What could he say? *Because here you are proving me wrong and rewarding my doubts. Why did I follow you down the path of denial when I knew what it was? Of course you'd do this after I told you how I feel after my previous relationships. I've done it again. Of course I did. Even if I knew it wasn't permanent, I was hoping it would last longer. I'm such a fool. Agree to casual, but I can't help but start making it into something more. Even when I knew you were going to leave. Even when I was just in it for sleeping with you.*

"Is it someone else?" He had to know. At least this time, it would not hurt as much. In lust with a casual lover was nothing like being in love.

"No. I haven't even thought of anyone else while we've been together." Tash's face went lax as though he realized the reason for the question. "Mayr, no. *No.* I'm not leaving you for anyone else. It's the Uldana Trials. They're starting in six days." He sighed and flicked his gaze to the ceiling. "The priests announced it was time for me to do them. Fate's decision revealed itself only a couple days ago. Signs from the Four told the oracles and Sister Kee I must take the Trials now. It's my time, so I must make the journey. I'm not permitted to get out of them without a truly good reason."

The pointed stare Tash pinned on Mayr was not lost on him, just ignored. Nothing good could come of it.

"Then that's it." Mayr swept his hand between them. "This is where we have to end?"

"In terms of intimacy, I think it's for the best. I have to prepare for the Trials. Afterwards, should I succeed, I can't have you. Not like this." Tash drew his palms down Mayr's shoulders. "But I don't want us to never talk again. I want us to remain friends. I'd still like to see you and spend time together. I just can't touch you."

"Then what was all that stuff about—" Clamping his mouth shut, Mayr choked back the rest of the argument. After all the talk about taking their relationship slowly, it was pointless. Even though Tash knew he was ending it, he had still acted as if there was a chance they would continue. What other purpose could telling secrets serve if not to build their relationship? Did Tash realize he sounded more contradictory than sensible? That he led Mayr in one direction while speaking of another? Were priests not supposed to be consistent and steadfast in their conviction?

Perhaps Tash would fail his Trials, simply because he could not overcome the contradictions. *If I could be so lucky. Not that he'd come back to me, but still. I could hope. No, forget that. Hope's how I got here to begin with. I need to stuff all that worthless hope into a box and light it on fire. It keeps getting me into trouble.*

For the moment, though, hope would have to wait for its burial. There was a breakup to finish. At least this time, he was neither shocked nor betrayed.

If anything, it saddened him.

"Tell me about them, the Trials." Hands on his raised knees, Mayr held back from touching Tash. He would rather remember the way they were before sharing their secrets. How he yearned for Tash's grip and desire. The safety he felt in Tash's arms, believing Tash understood him. "You said they start in six days. What happens then?"

In an instant, Tash looked crestfallen; miserable like he had the night before on the porch steps.

The next moment, a sad smile claimed his lips. His eyes appeared no happier despite the cheerful tone of his voice. "There are four. The first tests physical stamina in Hastal's honour and protectiveness. It requires a pilgrimage to the Shatterlands. The candidate must go to the sea, then to where the red sands turn into amber and black stone, where the earth shook and split in three long ago. There, a shard of amber glass must be retrieved and brought home."

A trip—it sounded harmless enough. The journey could even be pleasant, if the rumours Mayr had heard about the extraordinary beauty of the Shatterlands were true. "The second?"

"A test of knowledge and commitment under duress, demanding the memorization of a particularly sacred tome passed down from the Four Themselves and a special focus on duties. A tribute to Laytia."

As if you haven't studied enough, already. Mayr bit back a laugh. While he should not make light of the Trials, they sounded less of a challenge than Tash made them seem. "The third?"

Tash drew a quick breath. "Tests faith and emotional strength to serve Navara. It is a confession: an admission. It is the confrontation and release of darkness to take on the weight and blessing of light."

Mayr's brow furrowed at the description. More priest talk. Sometimes he had no idea what Tash meant. But given the nervous look on Tash's face, Mayr did not push the matter. If Tash wanted Mayr to understand, he would say it in clearer terms. Or maybe he could not say it. Priests were not required to explain their ways.

"And the last, the fourth? What happens then?"

"Devotion is judged," Tash answered quietly. "It is a true test of the spirit. A chance to stand face to face with the Four and declare oneself worthy. It requires deep faith, clear mind, and an open heart with love so deep, Emeraliss welcomes us with joy."

All things Tash had, Mayr realized, disappointed. The first two trials sounded easy.

The third was questionable, though how difficult could it truly be?

The fourth was terrifying. To stand before the Goddesses was like a mortifying nightmare chased by a reality of horror.

Still, he did not doubt Tash would pass the Trials, and easily. Mayr would lose him for sure.

"There's just one thing." Mayr licked his lips and pulled further into himself as Tash caressed his knee. "Why are you doing them at all? Why would you want to? From the way you've talked about it, being a Rese-level priest has been a good life. Why give that up?"

Tash fussed with the corners of the pillowcases. "I need to. I can't explain it. Being a Rese *has* been good. I've enjoyed working outside of the Temple, helping people get through their daily lives. I've never minded helping to repair things or raise barns and then bless them. I've never complained about carrying things for the villagers and blessing their homes and places of livelihood. I'll happily work with my hands, attend their meals, cleanse their lives, and do whatever they need."

He stared hard at Mayr, his lips in a thin line. "Being an Uldana is more than that. I'd like to conduct rites—marriages, children's blessings, funerals, all of them. Even do the oracle readings, assuming whatever skill I have with them decides to be kind. I'd like to bear witness to important events." Tash gave a slight frown. "As an Uldana,

I would have more influence over things in Kattal, help make changes. Advise the republic leaders on matters of peace, justice, and moralities to better serve Kattal's people." A small smile took over his lips as a hint of hope flashed in his eyes. "I will also be taken in as a member of the Sacred Assembly, the exalted believers in charge of the temples and spiritual leadership. It is an honour to be accepted by them, respected for my suggestions and other contributions."

"And that's what you want? For them to pat you on the back so you can tell people what to do?"

"It's more than that." A sigh followed. "I *need* to do it. Surely you understand how that feels." Tash grasped Mayr's shoulder but recoiled just as quickly. "I'm sorry for telling you like this, and here. I shouldn't have. I should have waited another day."

Mayr pushed up from the bed. Why should he care? Fair warning had been given.

Then why did it bother him?

"It's fine." Mayr grabbed his pants and put them on. "You said it wouldn't last. It was just supposed to be a bit of fun, right? A matter of curiosity. I'd say I've discovered exactly what I needed to."

Tash swung his legs over the side of the mattress. "Mayr."

"No, it's fine, really." Rummaging through the small black sack stuffed with his clothes and other personal effects, Mayr seized his hairbrush. He yanked the brush through his tangled hair, tugging his scalp. Each painful jerk poked holes in the anger threading together the rest of his emotions. Anger he should not have.

"Give it over." Tash grunted and held out his hand. "I can't stand watching you do that."

With a raised brow and scowl in protest, Mayr surrendered the brush. He spun around the creaky wooden chair at the dressing table and sat, staring into the dusty, smudged mirror. Arms wrapped around the back of the chair, Mayr said nothing as Tash brushed his hair with steady strokes. When Tash's fingertips massaged his scalp, Mayr closed his eyes and gave into the soothing touch.

"I know so many women who'd kill to have hair like yours," Tash murmured. He coiled smoothed strands around his fingers. "One of the things I'll miss." Leaning down, he nuzzled the skin behind Mayr's ear and breathed deep. "It's beautiful, like the rest of you."

Mayr shivered, hoping the warm lips would travel down his neck.

They parted from him instead as Tash started to plait Mayr's hair. Near the end of the braid, Tash stopped and stood still long enough for Mayr to be worried. Cautiously, Mayr opened his eyes.

Tash gazed at Mayr from the reflection of the mirror, his expression undecipherable except for the sadness. Always the sadness.

"If things were different. If I'd never..." Tash sighed and drew a finger down the back of Mayr's neck. "I wish this could be different."

Then just change your mind. Say no to the Trials. It's ridiculous to put you through them anyway. Can't the Goddesses and the priests see you're devout enough? What's getting a piece of rock, reading a book, and telling the truth going to get you? You can do those every day. Nothing has to change—nothing but your mind.

Despite all the words he could have said, "Yeah, I know," was all that left his lips.

Chapter Eleven

As far as trips went, this one was far more pleasant than others combined. A deep breath in, a clasp of the arm, and he was that much closer to being home.

Tash glanced at the signpost staked to the corner of the crossroads, jolting as the carriage rolled gently to a stop. The topmost sign signaled forward to Vasserey Call, the name painted on the dark brown wood in bright yellow letters. Below that were the worn signs for Dahena Village off to the north, and Merth in the south, their faded paint trying its best to gleam in the early morning light.

No matter their state, he was glad to see the signs again, their familiarity a welcome greeting at the main crossroads outside of Dahena. The walking, riding, and scaling across the Shatterlands—it was nearly over, almost in the blink of an eye compared to most of the challenges in his life that had scraped and crawled across time, dragging his sorry existence along. But now he was on his way home in one piece, triumphant with a cloth-wrapped glass shard in the thin metal case tucked into his boot.

Failing all else, he had that. His shard. His first trial. Twelve days that had stretched out with so much unknown in their grasp but were worth every moment… most of the time. He still had no idea what to do with the regret gnawing at him. Or the fact Mayr's voice was still in his head.

Swallowing back a sigh, Tash smiled at Rydele, the elderly librarian from Vasserey Call who had given him a ride to their current stop. "Thank you for your kindness in bringing me here. I appreciate it."

Rydele scoffed and waved one hand. "Bah, thank *you* for putting up with me. The ride's always more pleasant with company—at least the kind that stays awake through my stories and bad manners."

Tash laughed softly. He had gone out of his way to avoid Araveena Ford with as much distance as he could, sticking close to the Gailarin-Alosaa border and nearly adding another entire day to his trip back. A chance meeting on the highway had gifted him with fortune, however, and as far as riding companions went, Rydele was sweet and talkative, easily making Tash forget he had spent the last two days alone and completely on foot.

"Stories are a joy in life, I've always thought, and sharing them is even better." Tash grabbed his traveling pack from beneath his seat and slipped it over his shoulder, the weight of the blanket and thin bedroll attached to it dragging on the floor of the carriage. "May Laytia continue to look favourably upon you and gift you with even more stories to share for years to come." He offered his hand, quick to share a smile as Rydele clasped his arm and gave a good-natured shake.

"And all the luck to you, keeping company with the temple lot." Rydele winked and released Tash's arm. "I've heard all about those goings-on and the trouble you priests get into. Keep your nose out of the troubles and let the troubles get lost in the middle of all things, hmm?"

A quote, one Tash vaguely recalled. Something about a poem, a dance, and what he supposed was a joke played by fate. A piece he had heard long ago, read to him by his sister—

Tash forced a smile and climbed out of the carriage, hitting the ground with a wince. "I'll do my best." He nodded towards Vasserey Call. "All the luck to you on your way back. You're almost there, and the day's a good one." With one hand raised, he backed away from the carriage as it rolled and stopped again, the tawny beige horse pulling it anxious to leave. "Thank you again and fair day."

Rydele waved in return, a sharp click of the tongue setting the horse in motion. A moment later, Tash was alone once more, staring at the back of the small carriage as it headed up the highway, several dull green chests filled with old books in the back.

In the silence that fell around him, all squeaks from the carriage well gone, he stared up the road to Dahena, caught in the stillness. He had gotten this far, alive. Relatively well, save for the aches and strains that came from walking most of the way with little intention to stop for long. He had even visited the temple in Alosaa that had taken him in just after his defection from the Shar-denn; a quick stop to ensure the priests there were well, and to apologize for not visiting them as often as he wanted to. Still, Overseer Loja had been delighted to welcome him to her dinner table and offer him a soft bed for the night.

That had been three days ago, but it might as well have been a week with all the thinking he had done since then. The pilgrimage gave him far too much time with himself. He needed other voices, other thoughts, not memories that attacked him with more than their fair share of gut punches.

Finally letting out the sigh he had been keeping back, Tash started up the road to Dahena. He would reach the temple by sunset, perhaps substantially earlier, assuming his feet kept moving. And his eyes. They were tired and threatening to do him in for pushing through the days longer than he should have. Though between them and what lurked in the open, he knew what side he would always err on.

At least he had succeeded. Well, at getting the shard, anyway. The first trial was over only when he presented the shard to Kee, officially marking the achievement and gaining her approval. Only then would he receive her blessing to carry on to the second trial.

He was ready for it, the shard small but a perfect fit inside his hand. His keepsake of achievement, one he would have for the rest of his life. Would Kee be proud of him? He hoped so. And Armamae, too.

Though if not for the need to return as quickly as he could, he would have stayed in the Shatterlands for two or three days longer instead of just the one. The journey to the southern tip of the Eruelme tract had taken a little more than five days, thanks to the help of two fellow travelers willing to spare him a short ride along the way. The nights had been long, most of them spent in the woods beside a small fire with only a bout of sleep here and there to occupy the time. The best sleep he'd had was in the temple in Alosaa after Loja insisted he rest for a day.

To her disappointment, he had not passed out for the day as she suggested but opted to leave just after sunrise instead, with the promise to return for a proper visit in the robes of an Uldana priest—an oath she had taken with a solemn embrace and his gratitude. He owed her, too, for the time she had spent protecting him from the Shar-denn. He would see that promise kept and her kindness repaid.

Assuming I get that far. Tash frowned and shifted his pack onto his other shoulder. There had been several moments in the Shatterlands when the sobering truths of mortality met him face to face. Surrounded by the glassy black stone and amber landscape with the long-dead beneath his feet, their warped bodies forever encased in the grim stone, he had considered the futures lost, their stories buried. What had those people thought when the earth had trembled and tore itself apart, taking out everything in its path with the same ferocity as the Skinside Terrors during the Battle of Realms, frightening creatures tied to The Forgotten Dark that had terrorized the world before Parmina the Silenced slew their insatiable hunger? Save for the precious few survivors on the outer barrier of the Shatterlands, had there been any chance for anyone to survive the catastrophe of their world stretching its jaws wide, all the way to breaking, as it roared out the boiling hot guts of the earth? Or had they been doomed from the word 'home,' not one safe place to be had? There were stories abound, a relentless need to understand the world as they had seen it then, but nothing could do the reality justice, the fear caught on display forever.

The gently rolling waves of the blue-green sea had been a glimmering reminder of how life ebbed and flowed, fluid and full of memory. Somewhere between the quietness of a thread of smoke rising from a snuffed-out candle and the cruelty of one's home being leveled by the very earth beneath their feet, upheaval came one day and was gone the next before the next change tumbled through.

Among it all lingered the essence of Hastal, Goddess of Protection and the image of survival. Had She stood there back then, watching the flood, listening to the loss? Walked the shore and thrown stones at the waves in grief, each named for one of the lives taken by the amber deluge? She was battle, She was fight. She was the strength of defiance. Had Hastal run with those poor souls, ushering them into death with Navara's help, tending to the broken and mourning as everything they knew betrayed them? He wanted to believe She had eased those pains, the power of fire and earth at her hands with all the warmth of compassion caught between them.

His fate was in Hastal's hands now, as tangible as her unbreakable shield. This was his journey, his quest. He was no soldier, but he fought to survive from one day to the next, determined to come out stronger. If he should be worthy. If Hastal saw his value.

Gripping his pack tight, Tash continued up the edge of the road, head lowered, his gaze on the dull red dirt rather than the dense woods along either side of him. The Shatterlands had been a kick to the ribs in some ways, heartbreaking in others, and stunning beyond words despite it all. An expanse of shore that carried on for as far as he could guess, providing a glimpse of the Alatayle Sea, fair and enduring. Old forests of wide, persistent trees grew around the outermost edges of the amber stone while the mountains of Sinea Grou loomed in the distance, marking Arminloa's territory and keeping Kattal firmly in its corner of the continent.

For all the death, there was life, and the Shatterlands kept secrets buried as much as it lifted beauty from the surface.

If only he could have shared it with someone.

With a groan, Tash stopped and held his face in his hands. His mind was harassing him again, invoking unwelcome opinions that simply showed up, assaulted his morale, and pranced off with his regret. It was like a stew that kept bubbling over, all the bits and pieces burning away, stuck to the bottom of the pot and stinking up the kitchen. No amount of stirring helped, and there was never enough stock to salvage it, but taking it off the fire was right out.

And he *was* right out—of wishes, of choices, of time.

Mayr would be the death of him, Emeraliss mark his words.

This is ridiculous. Teeth grinding, Tash forced himself up the road. He and Mayr were no longer together, but some part of him failed to catch onto that fact. Even if they could have kept their relationship going as it had been, Mayr would still have had to stay home—but that was logic, and Tash's foolishness was just fine with booting logic into the ditch.

Fine, he could have used the company. Being by himself was excruciating. A laugh or two would have been a helping hand away from his loneliest depths.

And yes, he would have done anything to see Mayr's encouragement come out in that charming smile of his, especially when Tash had worried he would never reach the Shatterlands or return.

But that voice. That deep tone that kept him warm on the cool nights, telling him to keep going, to never give up…

That gorgeous bastard was in his head and refused to get out.

The crushing, suffocating feeling when he thought about breaking Mayr's heart was not enough. The weight of Tash's heart as it struggled to hold onto courage and push everything else away was still not enough.

Even so, it would have to *be* enough. He had failed Mayr but he would not fail this, too.

By his soul, he needed the trial. If nothing else, he would succeed or otherwise feel like he was nothing, and there would be no living with that. Goddesses knew he could not live with himself right then, not after he had walked away from someone who made him feel so much…

This came first. And it needs to come last. There's nothing else in between.

Time. He was living on time he never should have had.

Then there was Kee. She was never obligated to give Tash any kind of chance whatsoever—she could have turned him away. Yet she took him in and was there for him every day, no matter what. She offered him compassion. Forgiveness. Hope. A second chance when he should be dead. And Armamae—he was no less Tash's anchor in all things, a mentor he loved deeply. He needed to show them he could stand by their side and be as devout as they were.

Except Mayr...

The sacrifice.

The ghost.

The never again.

I should've left him alone. Never touched. Never kissed. Never...

So many nevers and not one of them fair.

As a cool breeze kicked up, leaves rustling by the dozens, Tash shivered and gripped the strap of his pack tighter, sparing a thought to the light cloak stuffed inside with a second set of clothes, the map and ice pick Kee had given him, what remained of his herb bread and smoked cheese, a pouch of nuts and dried fruits, and a flask of water. For the moment, his heavy blue shirt would do just fine, his pants dusty but otherwise good enough to keep him warm for a while yet. Once the sun reached the noontime position, he had no doubt the chill would subside.

He took another twenty steps. Ten. Five.

Tash slowed, fighting the urge to stop altogether. Another chill raced through him, this time skittering down his spine as the increasing rustle of leaves dragged up a bitter curse.

That feeling, one he had put aside for years... it crept over his skin, spindly, needles on thin patches, poking steadily towards his heart. A feeling that usually came with a nasty sting and a rancid taste, all of its foul corpse-eating truths wrapped up in the terrifying sense of being the monster under someone's bed, waiting to strike. Ready to take life away.

Someone was watching him. From the shadows. In the trees.

Who. How many. Of everything he needed to know right then, only those mattered.

He was afraid of the answer.

Taking a deep breath, then another, Tash clenched his fists. He kept his gait steady, his head low, listening for any hint of what watched. There was no stopping the downpour of despair washing over him: terrible feelings, ones he had sworn to leave behind. Nightmares he had ceased having. Memories he had fought a thousand times and more, sometimes with his fists jabbing at the air in the middle of the night, punching out at the images in his head, screaming for the agony to just *stop*.

Had the Shar-denn finally found him? Or was it someone else wanting their measure of flesh?

The coins from his boot? A bit of fun on a weaponless stranger?

No matter. He was alone, and while the Shardenn had tortured him to within a pinch of his life, they could not take away the instincts he had worked hard to hone.

Hastal, forgive me for how this goes down. I might need to walk along with You for a while, trial or not.

Where he ended up, however... Or maybe, just maybe, if he kept moving and they lost interest...

A glimpse ahead sent his hope tumbling to his stomach. Off in the distance, a faint figure appeared to be walking up the road in his direction. Bright colours in the light, moving, catching on the dancing breeze.

For all he knew, it was nothing but his imagination, but if he took the chance and it turned out to be an unsuspecting citizen... one without any defence...

Hastal, bless me with Your grace and save me from myself.

He veered into the road and dropped his pack, letting it thud behind him. Stopped in the centre of the highway, he lifted his arms, raised out on either side of him in invitation. If they wanted him, they would have to do it on his time. His way.

Closing his eyes, Tash breathed in slow and let it out before taking another, then another, each breath as steady as he could make them.

A whistle sounded. A second call answered. The faint crackle of branches. Twigs snapping.

Footsteps catching on dirt and stones.

Five, four, three, two…

One punch was all he needed.

Chapter Twelve

Aeley's lips twisted. "I hate highwaymen," she reiterated for the fourth time since walking into the training room, her grip firm around the wooden staff in her hand. She tapped the end of the staff on the floor. "I don't like knowing they're still out there, either."

Mayr nodded, holding back a sigh. He was too tired for her rant. Of all the things on his mind, criminal activity was third; maybe even fourth or fifth. Since he had yet to get a decent night's sleep in the last two weeks, it was difficult to keep track of priorities, especially when they changed daily. Except for the first two—they remained the same. His family always haunted the first spot, although Tash held that position as of late.

"I *really* don't like thinking someone's bleeding to death after being attacked by said highwaymen." Aeley scrunched her nose in annoyance. "The witness *swore* they saw someone being beaten by those men. But no one was there, absolutely no one. Footprints and shredded fabric but no victim. No attackers. Where could they have gone that fast? None of the guards I took could find them. Well, I guess if they took the entire day, but even then the tracks ended in all directions."

She spun the staff slowly in both hands. "Guess I could send more guards on a sweep and see if they find anyone lying in the woods or along the road. I'd hate for anyone to die from neglect on my part, especially after everything with—"

Aeley stopped spinning the staff. Her expression darkened, fury playing through her brown gaze.

Yeah, Mayr knew that look—and he knew what she was thinking about.

They had been here before, two years ago, with faceless shadows wreaking havoc on innocent lives. Highwaymen had never been a surprise, nor had they been expected to simply disappear after Aeley took on the role of Tract Steward. Crime on the roads was expected, but most of the time, the perpetrators ended up caught for their efforts, somehow, somewhere, and usually because they made a mistake along the way—exposing their identity more often than not. But when they had help from someone else who liked to keep details hidden at all costs and had the means to ensure no one knew what was going on...

The republic's three known gangs were frequently the culprits, each of them playing their games behind masks and lies, forcing chaos through hard-earned peace. The Shar-denn was the worst of them, taking control by any means, even if it meant driving a dozen exploding stakes through the best of humanity and leaving the shrapnel and guts to ruin whatever they could touch. To the Shar-denn, mercy was a word only, not a deed, and it generally ended in devastation.

Next to them, the Cigils and the Glim Takers were almost tame, smaller entities with a hunger to succeed but not litter the landscape with broken bodies and shattered souls. They made victims of citizens well enough, though they still were forced to take a knee where the Shar-denn was concerned. Not that they would stay that way forever: once they found a way to overthrow the Shar-denn, they most likely would do so. They were no doubt tired of living under a set of rules that saw them always the lesser threat and never the worthy victors.

Years ago, the gangs would have been answer enough where the current incident was concerned. If anything, they would have been the place to start.

Not anymore.

Aeley's brother, Allon, was his own force to be reckoned with. Even from prison he had found a way to torment others, sending his lackeys to do the damage—a painful lesson they had learned the hard way.

From the confines of the quarry where he was serving his life sentence, Allon had successfully gotten people killed and devastated entire villages, a talent he was quickly honing since his father's death. Not only that, Allon had destroyed Lira's family by convincing her brothers to do his dirty work, not that Mayr was about to shed tears over *that* achievement. He only wished that Lira had never been pulled into the matter—that she could have been spared. Mayr admired her ability to continue on despite the disaster, forging a new life that saw the rubbish left in the dust where they belonged.

Still, Allon could have found new grunts to cause trouble, despite being locked down from visitors, save for Aeley and anyone she sent on her behalf. The Four only knew how many misguided souls were willing to do his bidding. Whenever trouble hit, he would always be that other option; that doubt clinging to the foul taste of injustice.

Except they needed less options, not more. No doubt that was what had Aeley frustrated the most. It certainly annoyed the piss out of Mayr.

Lips set in a grim line, Aeley nodded just the once. "Yeah, that's what I'll do. Get our guys to really stretch their legs today. Thanks, Mayr. I'll just head over to the Guard House and grab a few bodies. And I'll go myself. You can stay here, keep an eye on the estate."

"Don't take Pell. I need him." Mayr glanced across the brightly lit room to the opposite corner where Pellon stood before the racks of swords.

"We're teaching the new guys how not to be fools today."

Aeley tossed the staff to him. "Sure. I won't get in your way. Just don't kill any of them, all right?" She stepped closer and leaned towards him, her voice lowered. "In case you haven't noticed, your mood lately hasn't exactly been anything nicer than rotted cheese on a poisoned pie. You still don't want to talk about it, do you?"

Mayr snorted. What was there to talk about? Certainly nothing she could fix, not even as Tract Steward. "Just you mind your own business." He pointed at the open door leading into the dark hallway. "Better get to it if you don't want your victim bleeding out in some hole all day. And take Stuck with you. Stick, too. They can keep your ass out of trouble long enough to see dinner."

"Fine, but if you eventually want to—"

"Go!" Mayr lunged with the staff in both hands, sending her scampering back. Hissing, Aeley turned and hurried for the door, one hand on the short sword at her waist. As she disappeared into the hallway, Mayr stood the staff against the wall and sighed.

Helpful as she thought she was, he did not want to talk. He just wanted to focus on his work. Right then, his attention needed to be on the new recruits standing in a line along the furthest wall. There were six of them, all between the ages of eighteen and twenty. Most of them were cocky and needed to be brought down a notch. Both he and Pellon had learned the same lesson when they were just as young. Confidence was valuable; pride needed to be left in their childhood. The latter could bring them death before their next breath. The current lesson aimed to chase pride from them, in preparation for the rest of the training.

If only his mind were as committed as his duty.

Twelve days had passed since Tash's pilgrimage to the Shatterlands began. Twelve days since the Uldana Trials had started, officially ending his intimate relationship with Tash.

During those twelve days, Mayr's irritability had flared sporadically, although he tried to rein it in. No one deserved verbal punishment over how he felt. To feel that way at all was bad enough. Each day hurt more than the day before.

Though at the moment, concern trumped his annoyance and anger. Aeley had learned of the attack on the main road leading into the village in the midmorning. She had returned from her investigation well before midday. In such a short time, she should have apprehended at least one attacker. At worst, she should have spoken to the victim and ensured they received any necessary healing. Or informed their families of the situation.

For her to return with none of them was unsettling, particularly since Tash would be on his way back. The trek to the Shatterlands took six days on foot, if not more, and just as many to return. But Mayr could not guess where Tash was along his journey. There was no way to send a message to forewarn Tash of the highwaymen, just in case the group decided a priest was worth assaulting. Had he even worn his priest's vestments on the pilgrimage or was he dressed like an average villager? Garments alone could make him a target.

Mayr let out a deep breath and avoided meeting the stares of the recruits. Even though he was no longer with Tash, he could not help but think about him. He remembered things, the images and sounds playing cruel games with his mind. His lust had not died as expected. It roiled his core instead, threatening to boil over. Combined with the funny feeling in the pit of his stomach, it wreaked havoc on his sanity. Some nights, when he felt the loneliest, it took everything for him to stay at the estate. The unusual connection between them had not severed, either, and words lingered in the silence.

This is getting ridiculous, how I'm taking it. What's wrong with me? Let. It. Go. Focus on the task at hand. Move on.

Determined to control himself, Mayr turned sharply on his heel and flexed his hands. "Time to get to work," he announced. "If you're afraid of blood, broken bones, headaches, dislocated joints, torched pride, humiliation, or change, I suggest you rethink your commission."

He strode towards the recruits, crossing over the yellow, red, and white training rings on the floor in the centre of the room. The recruits straightened and stepped away from the grey wall. "If you're here because you think it'll earn you points in life, you're wrong. If you're here because you think you'll be a national hero, adored and lauded, get out. If you're here because you think you can play around and get away with it, take your cocky backside home. This isn't a childhood game. This is a fighter's life, bloody and painful. If you're not willing to lose life and limb, we don't want you."

That got them. Their eyes widened. Whether they were surprised with his bluntness or the reality of what he said, at least he had their attention.

Mayr pointed at Pellon. "Give either of us a reason to throw you out and we will. You treat him with the same respect you give me. He may be your Head Guard someday, so it's best to lay the foundation now. He also enjoys throwing the likes of you small fish to the deadly creatures. And I enjoy letting him."

With a deep laugh that played to Mayr's serious tone, Pellon twirled a knife and eyed the recruits. One stepped back; the others eyed Mayr and Pellon. Mayr could not blame them. Pellon wore armour for the training, adding to the bulk already on his large frame. Of everyone in the room, he was the one the recruits would prefer to avoid lest he break them—one of the reasons Mayr chose Pellon as his training partner.

"Find yourself a place on the outer ring," Mayr commanded. Once the recruits stood on the thick red line of the largest ring, staring at one another across the circle, Mayr walked around them. His gaze flitted over the room, taking in the racks of weapons along each of the four walls and practice armour on the wooden forms erected on one side of the room. They would work their way up to the swords, knives, axes, and staves by the end of the day, but first, they needed to be aware of their bodies without the extra items. "Strip to the waist. Remove any jewelry, armour, or anything that could otherwise get in the way or break."

As the young men followed his orders, Mayr glanced at each face. The youngest, Gorgan, was eighteen, blond, and shorter than the rest. Quiet with an air of uncertainty, he appeared the most taken aback by Mayr's forthright comments.

I'll keep an eye on you, don't worry. You won't break. You might just be surprised at what you can take. Just give it everything you have. The rest will follow. They were words Mayr would keep in mind to tell Gorgan in the future, no different than what Lensen had said when Mayr was a shy new recruit. Right then, though, he was not in the mood to coddle anyone.

The other recruits were more confident. The eldest, Fraen and Dase, were brothers. Dark-haired and green-eyed, they were tall, well-built, and flashed identical grins that drew attention to their egos. The last three recruits were not as overly confident, although they had their moments. Of varying heights and shades of brown hair and dark eyes, Asate, Koah, and Losan were eighteen years old and best friends. Mayr had known their parents since his youth and placed high expectations upon the boys. One of them could be the future Head of the Guard if they took their duties seriously.

"We'll start simple." Mayr entered the training circle and stopped in the middle, inside the smallest white ring. He tossed his sword belt to Pellon. "No weapons except for your fists, feet, and any other body part you have that's good to strike with." He removed his shirt and tossed it aside. "First off, you'll learn how to punch properly, how to disable a threat with only a few shots, and how *not* to get yourself killed in a flesh-to-flesh assault."

Dase elbowed his brother. "Like we don't already know how to do that. Don't know *why* we'd start there. This'll be easy!"

Mayr snapped his head towards Dase. "Great, a volunteer." He beckoned with both hands and assumed a stronger stance. "Come on, give me a shot."

"Sure. I love being first." Dase smiled at Fraen then rushed Mayr. Fist raised, he aimed for Mayr's jaw.

One punch to the throat sent Dase to the floor.

"As you were saying?" Mayr kneeled beside Dase, his hand on Dase's chest as Dase coughed and wheezed. "And that's why we're starting here." He patted Dase. "Take a few deep breaths and stand up slowly. Fraen, help him. We don't ever let camaraderie go, even in training."

Fraen hurried to his brother's side to help him stand. Backing away, Mayr waited patiently, a smirk twitching his lips. There was always at least one like Dase in every training group. They also tended to be the ones who fell hardest.

When Dase was on his feet, still dazed and red-faced, they resumed the training, beginning with the tiny movements that forewarned opponents of their intentions and single strikes that could dismantle a fight before it escalated. With his back to Pellon, Mayr stood on a thick inner yellow ring and coached the three pairs of recruits. For several moments, he watched Gorgan, the most cautious of the group, gauging Gorgan's nerves as Asate sparred with him. Over time and the occasional won match, Gorgan could overcome his worries—

Footsteps hurried towards Mayr from behind. A sharp inhale followed by a rush of air.

Don't do it, you—

Hands gripped Mayr's shoulders and jerked him back.

In swift movements, Mayr jammed his hip against Pellon, wrapped his arm around Pellon's torso, and flipped him before slamming him to the ground.

Pellon's back hit the floor, then his head. "Dammit!" He winced. Slapping his hand to the back of his head, he scowled at Mayr.

"And that's why he's second-in-command, boys." Mayr wiped his lips and glanced at the recruits. They had jumped back, surprise still on their faces. He bent forward and offered Pellon his free hand.

"Yeah, because I'm still ridiculous enough to try sneak attacks." Pellon yanked Mayr's hand, threatening to pull him down. "I'll get you one day, you tortuous pain in my—"

Someone cleared their throat loudly.

Mayr and Pellon froze before turning their heads towards the door. Haydin stood inside the doorway, his gaunt fingers clasped before him. Beside him was a taller man, young with curled, brown hair. The stranger wore a loose white tunic that flowed to the knees of his white pants. A red sash draped over his left shoulder.

Mayr helped Pellon up and straightened, his brow furrowing the longer he stared at the priest. A Metah, if he recalled correctly. Why was he there?

"Sorry to interrupt, Mayr." Haydin gestured beside him. "Priest Isallen requested to see you immediately."

See me? *What could he possibly want?*

"Yeah, sure." Mayr dipped his head as he approached. "What can I do for you?"

Isallen held out his hand. A small piece of torn parchment rested in his palm. "I have a message for you from Brother Halataldris."

But Tash and I are over, he almost said, accepting the parchment. Except…

That meant Tash was home. He had completed his first trial.

Sending a message to Mayr was never part of the plan, however. Their parting had been amicable, but they were to avoid one another during the Trials. They had agreed to spend time together afterwards, assuming Mayr could withstand being friends.

Mayr read the message, comprised of only four words: *Please, come. Help. Tash*

A chill raced down neck and arms, prickling his skin. The words said almost nothing and too much of something all at the same time. An ominous something he wished he could snuff out before he learned what it was.

"I have been instructed to take you back," Isallen said, his glance darting from Mayr to everyone else in the room. "With haste."

The last three words concerned Mayr more. There should have been no reason for Tash to contact him, and certainly not with such a request. What could have happened for Tash to breach their agreement? They both prided themselves on keeping their word.

Not that I'm complaining. Not really.

Mayr accepted his shirt and sword from Pellon. "Continue with the training," Mayr said, "and keep your head up for when Ae gets home. I'll be back as soon as I can."

Pellon dipped his head and turned sharply on his heel, snapping at the recruits until they fell back into their stances. More than one of them had paled, their nervous glances darting between their group and Pellon.

Once Mayr was presentable, he followed Isallen. They did not talk or falter. Even on their way through the temple, Isallen revealed nothing about Tash. All he did was walk briskly, just short of running, and Mayr followed at the same pace.

Isallen stopped midway in one softly lit corridor and motioned to Tash's private chamber. "I must leave you now." He hurried down the corridor and turned a corner.

Mayr stared at the partially open door, catching a glimpse of the inside. In his memory, he could see the wall to his left, hidden behind the door, covered with an elegant tapestry depicting all four goddesses dancing around a silver fountain in white clothes and red veils. He pushed the door further, revealing the simple wood dresser against the opposite wall and the small writing desk in the corner under the window. They were built from dark wood, a contrast to the temple's white stone.

"Enter," a low voice commanded.

Thrown by the familiar voice that was not Tash's, Mayr stepped inside. Armamae stood on the other side of the room, adorned in red. He welcomed Mayr with a sad smile.

"You have arrived. Good." Armamae looked to the person sitting on the bed to the right side of the room. "I will leave if you wish?"

"No," was the croaked reply.

Mayr flicked his gaze to the bed.

His heart stopped. His stomach seemed to flip and dance. It hurt to think. It hurt to see. The small hairs along his arms and neck stood on end.

"Tash?" Unable to look away from the battered face, Mayr took in Tash's injuries. A stitched gash darkened the side of Tash's face, starting at his temple and curving over his scraped cheeks towards his jaw. One of his eyes was swollen shut; the other was half-open. Large bruises darkened them both. His bottom lip was split, though it no longer bled. Long, red scratches marred his throat. Fingerlike marks darkened his neck. Bandages bound his hands, the cloth thickest over his knuckles.

Fists clenched, Mayr's gaze alternated between Armamae and Tash. "What happened?" he demanded, nearing the bed to kneel beside Tash. If his words came out harsh, he did not care. The bruises and cuts overlying the scars on Tash's half-naked body were his only concern. He drew his fingers over the layers of bandages wrapped around Tash's waist and stomach, tightened around his ribs.

"I achieved it. I got the shard," Tash answered, his mouth mostly closed as he struggled to speak around an injured jaw.

Mayr clasped Tash's arm. "That's *not* what I meant and you know it." When Tash winced, he loosened his grip. "Who did this to you? You *never* said this was part of it."

"It's… not." Tash grimaced and pressed his jaw. "On the way back… thieves. On the road. Wore the same colours… as the Shar. I tried to get away without fighting… but couldn't. Hit a few. Then ran and hid. Got back here… fast as I could."

The highwaymen. The missing victim.

"That was *you*? By the gods-awful foolery of the meddling Four!" Mayr cursed. He should have known. He should have gone with Aeley.

Armamae glared at Mayr.

"Sorry," Mayr muttered, "but I'm not particularly pleased with Them right now." Not when Tash could have been killed—over a piece of glass that proved nothing. The priests already knew how deep Tash's devotion went, no shard needed. He cupped the back of Tash's neck. "Next time, I'm going with you."

Tash tilted his head to the side. "There's no next time. It's done." He hissed as Armamae pressed a repugnant-scented poultice to his eye.

"Here, let me." Mayr slipped his fingers under Armamae's and held the poultice in place.

"Brother?" Tash touched Armamae's arm.

Armamae nodded. "I will give you the room. Call if you require my assistance." After a knowing glance at Mayr, he left the room and closed the door.

Mayr inspected Tash's closed eyes, battling the growing rage inside. He wanted to yell at Tash for putting himself in danger. He wanted to tear into the faces of the men who had assaulted him. He wanted to turn back the days and go on the journey with Tash. While Tash had worked as a guard in the Shar-denn, whatever capabilities he'd had were wasted during his time as a priest. No doubt he was lucky to have survived the attack at all.

If only I'd been there. I could've done something. Protected you.

Tash grabbed Mayr's wrist. "You couldn't have stopped it. Don't blame yourself."

"Ae's out looking for you, you know. Well, not *you*, but whoever was in the attack. Someone told her, and she went to stop it." Mayr tried not to stare at the blackened skin under Tash's eyes. If only Aeley had dragged one of the culprits home. He would have gladly spent his night pummeling the man's face in. Maybe even ripped off certain body parts.

"Tell her sorry. I couldn't stay. Had to get here."

"That's ridiculous. You could've died."

"I have faith in the Four."

"Well I *don't*."

A bandaged palm cupped Mayr's cheek. "I have faith in you, too." Tash leaned forward slowly to press their foreheads together. "Would you... stay? Keep me company?"

The question threw Mayr's thoughts into a spin. He blinked, debating his answer. *Yes, yes, yes, yes, yes,* was all he wanted to say.

No, don't even. Leave now! His doubts screeched in disagreement, loud and resounding. They battled to keep his feelings at bay, struggling to contain the desire tearing at his insides, screaming for Tash. *You only think you'd be helping. It'll end badly. Keep to the agreement!*

"Please," Tash whispered, drawing one fingertip along Mayr's lips. "I haven't been through this in years. I don't know if I'm all right to sleep. I'm not... myself. But with you here... I might rest."

There it was again, Tash's begging tone. A plead Mayr could not refuse. He understood the pain and the price of violence. Given Tash's past, what could happen after one brutal attack was unknown. Nightmares and flashbacks could not be predicted. If his recovery went badly, Tash would need someone to help him.

"For you, anything," Mayr murmured. The words surprised him; they had not been what he expected to say. Still, they felt right.

"Thank you." Tash sat back, his head dipping once and then again. Wincing, he sipped shallow breaths. His body contracted. "I need to lie down."

With slow movements, Mayr maneuvered Tash back on the bed. When Tash was settled into the pillows and covered by the thin blankets, Mayr sat on the edge of the bed, his legs stretched out on the mattress. He held Tash's hand in both of his and caressed Tash's bandaged knuckles with his thumb. Focused on Tash's breaths, he was relieved when they became slow, deep, and consistent. Even if Tash did not sleep for long, at least he would have some rest.

He wouldn't have needed anything if he hadn't gone. It wasn't supposed to be like this. A simple trip—that's how he made it sound. It shouldn't have been this dangerous. He's a priest! Where's the Four to smite the people who attacked him? What happened to swift justice for believers?

Mayr leaned his head against the wall. Not only did he distrust the trial, his instinct refused to believe the incident was coincidence. An attack on Tash just as he returned was one thing, but the assailants being dressed as Shar-denn was another. Was that why Tash was terrified of the

Trials? Because he knew dangerous things would happen and they would be on purpose? What else was he hiding?

Peering down at Tash, Mayr gritted his teeth. Trials or no, there were names to get. Not just of the highwaymen, gang members, goddess grunts, or whatever they were. No, he wanted the names of the Shar-denn Tash had associated with. He wanted to know what the High Council had done with the names Tash gave them. Tash might have shied from questioning the High Council, but Mayr had no qualms doing so. He would meet with the Council and their bounty hunters to inquire into the state of those affairs.

It was time for a hunt.

Chapter Thirteen

Thin lips pursed, Severn, Councilman of Public Protection, studied Mayr with a seasoned glare that suggested she considered him a tiny creature meant to be crushed under her boot. Of all the High Council, Severn was the most intimidating. She did not accept failure or compromise lightly, and she commanded respect from the moment she entered a room. If her sarcasm and surly demeanor did not capture attention, her long, black hair and wide, dark eyes usually did. The dark red long coat she always wore added to her sinister appearance.

As she leaned back in the chair behind Aeley's desk, Severn crossed her legs and tapped the chair arms. Black leather boots covered her legs up to the knee, fastened with gold buckles identical to that of the chain belt around her black tunic. "So you want specifics. And you want to be included in the ongoing campaign to apprehend the Shar-denn. This is as I understand it. Correct me if I'm wrong."

Mayr glanced at Aeley. For most of the meeting, Aeley had remained quiet, allowing him to facilitate the discussion. After hearing of Tash's predicament, she agreed Mayr would take point. Finally discovering the victim of the assault fueled her need to find those responsible. If the Shar-denn was involved, she wanted them arrested—or dead.

But did he ask too much, especially as a guard? It had taken several days to secure the private meeting with Severn. It had taken just as long to gather all of the information he could on the individuals who attacked Tash in order to hand it over to the bounty hunters. He could not ruin things now.

Except what he did impacted Tash's safety and his future. For him, Mayr would ask for everything, regardless of what Severn thought.

"Yes," Mayr answered, folding his arms and straightening. "The Shar-denn has plagued our tract long enough, and if this group from the latest assault is part of it, we'd like to know. And we'd like something done about it."

Severn smirked. "Not to mention your personal interest in the matter," she said, her tone low and smooth, "and what I anticipate will be a request for a full pardon from the Council on your *friend's* behalf."

Heat spread across Mayr's face. Was there anyone who did not read further into his relationship with Tash? He had purposely said "Halataldris" and spoke in formal terms to keep his personal feelings out of the discussion. "Yes."

Silence filled the study. Mayr flicked his gaze from Severn to the bounty hunters to her left. They were only two of the many that served the republic. Rathen, tall and quiet with messy blond hair, stood with his arms crossed. The leather of his black long coat and dark clothes stretched over his muscular form. Beside him was Kirra, a short woman with long, honey-coloured hair. Dark shading on her eyelids accented her golden eyes, the coal-like colour a match to her black corset with its leather straps and mismatched buckles.

Silent, Rathen surveyed the room with his head lowered, his weight shifted onto one leg, the multiple knives strapped to his thigh in full view. He meant business.

"Fine, we will cut you in." Severn folded her hands in her lap. "It's no less than Steward Dahe deserves. Knowing the details of our progress will not hamper the Council's work in any way. Perhaps you can add to it, seeing as you are in contact with our informant." She turned her head towards the bounty hunters but kept her prodding stare on Mayr. "Rathen, perhaps you can tell them where we sit on the matter?"

Rathen lifted his head, his features twisted with a smile. "Your man gave us forty names, a few of them high up. Thirty have been hauled in. Most were just the arse cleaners, though; easy catches." He licked his lips and winked. "Some of those aren't with us any more, right, Kirra?"

Kirra grunted and held her arms akimbo. "The price of being dung-licking rubbish. Then again, like the Shar-denn always say—"

"The only way out is dead," Rathen and Kirra said in unison, casting droll stares at Mayr and Aeley.

Severn tented her fingertips together. "So glad we could oblige," she added dryly. "Of the surviving catches, a select few were offered positions as informants. They've been helpful, particularly in providing us with other names and locations of members elsewhere in Kattal. I'd say cleaning things up has been much easier thanks to your man. He gave us just what we needed."

Mayr clenched his jaws. *My 'man' has a name, Severn. You should use it. Try shoving some respect in your voice, too.* "I'll let Priest Halataldris know his effort was of service and is appreciated."

"As for the other matter," Severn continued, "I will take it to the Council when I can. I admit it is time to revisit his case, given how useful his information has been. We've been remiss in letting it go this long. However, I promise nothing more for him. You may hope for a full pardon but end up without it. Perhaps he has gained enough leniency with the rest of Council." She pushed up from the chair. "Our meeting here is concluded. I will have Rathen and Kirra debrief you shortly on the particulars of the arrests, including the outstanding names. They will also follow through on the information you have supplied regarding the priest's assault."

"Sure, because we work great with vague descriptions and hardly any leads." Rathen grunted and rolled his eyes. "I love a make-it-happen wrapped up in this-is-useless."

Kirra elbowed him hard in the ribs. She flashed Mayr a sweet, apologetic smile. "We'll do everything we can. Rathen's just being a grump. Ignore him. I do all the thinking, anyway. He just catches the bad guys."

Rathen only glared at her and grumbled.

Severn was around the desk and almost at the door by the time they finished. Without waiting, she threw open the door and left. On the other side of the doorway, Pellon relaxed from his guard although he remained in the hallway. Rathen and Kirra followed Severn; Kirra rushed while Rathen sauntered.

"That went well," Aeley said, turning towards Mayr.

Mayr drew his hands down his face. "Thanks, I hadn't noticed."

"It could've been worse. She could've said mind your own and left." Aeley punched his arm gently. "She might just like you."

"No, she doesn't. But she doesn't mind *you*."

Aeley shook her head. "When are you going to tell him?" Her eyes sparkling with laughter, she leaned into him. "Because, psst," she whispered, "you had a boy in your bed."

"And you've got a girl in yours!" Mayr held up his hands. She would never let the issue rest, apparent from the amused expression she had whenever referring to Tash. "What does that have to do with *anything*?"

"Nothing." Aeley shrugged, then laughed and smiled wide. "Everything." She tapped his wrist. "You should go tell him. Soon. Now."

"I can't." Mayr's shoulders dropped. He was still waiting to hear from Tash about the results of the second trial. After the assault, Tash had rested for three days until most of the swelling subsided. The second trial began the day after that, against Mayr's protest that Tash was not yet ready.

For five days since then, Mayr had waited to hear from Tash, who had promised to send a note to let Mayr know he was all right. Given the problem with the first trial, Mayr had pressured Tash into telling him about the second trial. He needed to know what would happen and if any unpleasant surprises would arise.

Instead, what I got was an earful of ludicrous. Mayr stared at the floor, his arms crossed. *It's absolutely ridiculous, keeping Tash up for days on end just to read some damn book. But no, not even that: he has to recite it word-for-word, too. All while making him go out and do things with people. And for what? Faith, stamina, and understanding? I can't imagine what depriving him of sleep and running him ragged is supposed to prove.*

"Hey." Aeley clasped his shoulder. "Do you need to talk about it? You don't look so—"

A knock on the door interrupted her. "Mayr. Aeley," Haydin greeted, stepping into the room with someone else. "A visitor's just arrived."

Mayr glimpsed the red sash before anything else. Isallen.

"Hey." Mayr's heart raced as he scanned Isallen's hands for a note and found none. *Please, no bad news…*

"Brother Halataldris has sent for you," Isallen announced, "although I have no letter. He could not manage it." Sheepish, he lowered his chin.

While it was not bad news, it was not good, either. Tash had *sent for* him, breaking his agreement not to see Mayr for a second time. If it was anything like the first time, Tash had to be in pain. There was no other reason to call on him, not that it made the situation any better.

"Lead on." Mayr squeezed Aeley's hand and mouthed, "I'm sorry." Depending on what he found, he might not be back before Rathen and Kirra returned for the debriefing. Aeley and Lira would have to do it on their own. He wanted to see the Shar-denn matter through, but if Tash was hurt…

Mayr followed Isallen, once again silent. Inside the temple, Isallen led him to a darkened corridor in a lower level. Lit by a single torch, it was empty except for the dark figure pacing in the shadows—a man that dragged his heels, circling and shuffling, his erratic patterns moving him closer to Mayr and Isallen. The scuff of feet was accompanied by mumbles and rasped words, none of which made sense except for the occasional name of a goddess. A throaty laugh occasionally interrupted the jumbled words.

When Tash finally entered the light, Isallen ran.

Tash did not respond. He continued to shift his feet. His fingers twisted and bent around one another, almost to the point of breaking. His body shook with every few steps. No longer swollen, his face still carried a hint of bruise. A deeper darkness underneath his eyes attested to how tired he was. In the light, the whites of his eyes appeared red.

"Tash?" Mayr held out one hand.

"Mayr?" The question was barely audible. Tash stopped pacing. He blinked, staring at Mayr blankly. Horror flashed across his face, followed by relief. Fingers trembling, he took Mayr's hand.

He fell the next instant, his body colliding with Mayr's as his knees buckled. "Mayr," Tash whimpered, clinging to Mayr to keep from hitting the ground.

Arms wrapped around Tash's waist, Mayr shifted and balanced Tash's deadening weight. Mayr's heartbeat faltered and tumbled, his heart thumping hard enough to fill his chest with deepening pain. Shallow breaths were all he could manage. Panic tore into him, gnashing and clawing at his every thought.

"Your room," he murmured against Tash's temple. "We need to get to your room."

Tash nodded and Mayr slipped an arm around Tash's back. When Tash curled a weak arm around Mayr's shoulders, Mayr gripped his hand.

"I'm here. I've got you." They shuffled through the corridor. Mayr caressed Tash's hand to reassure them both. "Just keep going. I won't drop you, but you have to keep going."

With slow, agonizing steps and the occasional falter, Mayr guided Tash to his room two floors up. As they passed priests and priestesses, Mayr could not help but sneer and glower. Never had he wanted to attack them with spiteful words, not until that moment. No matter how they rationalized it, pushing Tash into such a state was nothing to be proud of. The Trials were more painful than they should have been—and he hated it. If anything, they were torture. Coerced suffering under the guise of piety. Tash deserved none of it. He had suffered enough. There had to be another way to prove himself.

You wanted to save me from pain. I just want to do the same for you. I want to make it stop, all of it. I never want you to get hurt again, ever.

Mayr eased Tash onto the bed and stripped him, carefully placing the clothes on a chair in the corner nearest the door. The cuts and bruises

Tash received from the attack were either healed or still in the process. Except for the violent shudders and sunken eyes, Tash appeared more like himself than he did before the second trial began.

"Come on, get under there," Mayr said, holding up the blankets and nudging Tash under them.

"Will you stay?" Tash clamped the blankets in his fists.

If it would stop your pain, I'd stay forever.

"Yes." Mayr removed his weapons and laid them on the chair. After he persuaded Tash to move back, Mayr lay on the bed on top of the blankets, one arm under his head and the other around Tash.

Tash curled into him, whimpering. He tucked his fists between their bodies and pressed closer. "It hurts. Everything hurts. My thoughts are killing me. Eyes burning. But I did it. I did. Recited it. Every word."

"Shh, go to sleep."

"I don't want to," Tash argued, his voice wavering. When he peered up, his eyes were wet. "It hurts too much. So tired, but I can't. I just want to be with you. *You*. Not much time left. No time." He buried his face in Mayr's shirt and sobbed. "I need you and there's no time."

I cannot kill the priests. I cannot kill the priests. I cannot kill the priests. Mayr glared at the ceiling, pulling Tash close enough that it hurt. Tash's weak cries hurt him even more. They drove a stake through Mayr's heart, impaling him over and over with each shake of Tash's body.

"Close your eyes," Mayr told him, stroking Tash's back. "Just close your eyes and rest."

Grateful when Tash did not argue, Mayr continued to move his fingers along Tash's skin. The sobs ceased and gave way to a deep sigh. Tash's body grew heavy as his muscles relaxed. He breathed quietly, his chest rising and falling evenly. Every new change suggested he was asleep or near to it.

Just enough for me to get more comfortable. Mayr glanced around the room. Simple and bright, the chamber contained furniture and basic personal effects. Any decoration was like the tapestry: dedicated to the Goddesses, including a small bronze statue of Emeraliss and her bird on the bedside table. Little of Tash could be seen in the room. Devoid of a personal touch, the chamber could have belonged to any priest. For all of his care and consideration, Tash had little to show for it. Only his tribulations were on display, carved into his flesh. *No family, no freedom, nothing but perpetual servitude.* After everything, Tash should have had more. There was more to life than duty. And there was more to love than pain.

Wet fabric strained across Mayr's chest as Tash rolled away. Mayr had said he would stay, but he needed to remove his shirt and boots if he was to stay all night. One small movement at a time, Mayr drew away until he stood awkwardly from the bed. He tugged off his boot.

A hand grabbed his wrist.

"Please, don't go," Tash said groggily, his eyes half-open.

"I'm not. I'm just getting more comfortable."

Tash's eyes widened. His grip tightened. "*Please*. Don't leave me. Don't leave." His terrified plea was childlike, heart-wrenching in its vulnerability. "I can't lose you, too. Stay."

Mayr stared at Tash's bracers. The issue was not leaving the bed, Mayr realized. The problem was leaving *him* like the others had; the people Tash loved, who had offered him choices and made it impossible for him to win, or blamed him for their unwillingness to stay. *Lies and games. They were nothing but cruel lies and terrible games.*

He slipped his hand into Tash's. "I won't. Just let me do this one thing and I'll be yours again."

The response appeared to be acceptable. Tash released Mayr's hand, allowing Mayr to continue undressing. Wearing only pants, Mayr slid under the covers and curled both arms around Tash, pressing their naked skin together in hopes it calmed Tash quickly.

Tash snuggled against Mayr's side, his face buried in the crook of Mayr's neck. He nuzzled the sensitive skin around Mayr's ear. "I wanted to make love to you," he whispered. "To be your first… your only… your everything." After a whimper, Tash slumped into Mayr, lost to unconsciousness.

A breath was all it took for Mayr to realize Tash was finally awake. As bright blue irises peered up at him quizzically, Mayr's heart hammered a quick rhythm of relief.

"How long have I been asleep?" Tash rubbed his eyes and sat up. "And how long have you been sitting here?"

Mayr tossed the parchment from Aeley onto the bedside table. The summary about Rathen and Kirra's debrief would have to wait. He was more interested in the details, anyway, and he would not get them until he returned to the estate.

"You've slept a full day and then some," he replied, raising his knees and rolling his neck. The bed would have been much more comfortable had he stretched out properly instead of sitting on the edge. But after Tash's sprawled body had taken up most of it, he took what he could get.

Tash blinked. "Please tell me you haven't sat there this whole time."

"No. Some of it has been lying down. Some of it I spent with the priests. Some of it was avoiding certain priestesses who think I'm their next project. Or sacrifice. It's hard to tell which one."

"You stayed?"

"You asked me to."

"And you did," Tash muttered, looking away. "I'm sorry. I shouldn't have. I don't even know why I did. I can't even remember doing it." He turned back with a pained glance. "Whatever I said, I'm sorry. I have no doubt I lost control."

The apology stung more than it should have. While Mayr hated seeing Tash broken to the point where he rambled off truths without a second thought, he wanted to hear the words again. To hold Tash close and soothe the pain that struggled to be released.

"It's fine. You got rest, that's all that matters. The priests will be pleased. They were worried about you." Mayr tilted his head, one brow raised. The time he had spent with the priests had been enlightening. He could almost forgive them. "Apparently they tried to help you before I got here, but you refused. You *actually* refused going to sleep, which is completely backwards. Sleep is good. Sleep is our friend, especially when you've been up for five days straight. That's just too ridiculous for my liking."

A dark blush spread across Tash's cheeks before he lowered his head. "Sorry," he mumbled, twisting the blankets between his fingers.

Mayr tucked strands of Tash's hair behind his ear. "Don't be sorry, just don't do it again. The Goddesses might enjoy it, and the priests consider it part of the job, but I don't."

"Mayr, I had to. You know that. It has to happen."

"No, it doesn't. No matter how many times you tell me it's necessary, I still won't believe it. You've scared me twice, Tash. *Twice*." Mayr cupped Tash's face with both hands. "Both times, I've come in to find you in a state I can't stomach easily. Guard or not, it's not something I can accept just because you want me to. Which makes me wonder: what else is coming?"

Tash pulled Mayr's hands away. "Just the last two trials, that's all."

"That's *not* all," Mayr argued quietly to keep his temper from rising. "Tell me about the next one. These first two… they hurt me, too. I can't imagine what the last two are like, but if these are any indication, I'm definitely not looking forward to them. You need to tell me about the next one."

Averting his gaze, Tash stared across the room. "I told you already."

"No, you didn't. You said something about confession, but that was it. So tell me the truth. What is it *really*?"

For a long moment, Tash was silent, still focused on the wall as he hugged his raised knees. Whatever the truth was, he did not want to say it.

All the more reason I need to know. How many other ways can he suffer?

"Navara," Tash said at last. "It's Her trial. It requires a sacred sacrifice in the name of justice."

"Meaning what?"

The immediate reply was a shaky breath and clenched jaws. Quiet words followed. "I have to go to the people I wronged the most and apologize. I must accept whatever punishment or reaction they deem fit. Honesty and humility are the gifts I must offer."

A chill raced through Mayr. The sombre tone fueled his worst thoughts, driving his anger to the surface. He would hate the answer to his next question, he knew it. "And who is that? What's the apology?"

"My village, Araveena. I have to confess my part in the Shar-denn."

Mayr leapt from the bed. "Absolutely not!" He spun around and pointed at Tash. "Do it and they'll kill you! Do you understand that? If you tell them what you told me, they could *kill you*. You haven't been pardoned by Council. You aren't an Uldana priest. You have no immunity. No protection. Tell people you were involved— what you did—and they can do *anything* they want to you as punishment. *Anything*!" Hands up, palms out, he prayed he could make Tash hear him. "Just wait a little longer. Get Council to pardon you *then* confess. You'll be safer."

"No. It's what I have to do, and I have to do it now. Once the Trials start, they cannot be put off, and certainly not so I can be a coward," Tash whispered. "I have to do this for myself. It's been a long time coming, and I *have* to do it. Strength, courage, and honour. And forgiveness. Faith. That's what the last two trials test the most. How much do I believe in the Four? How much do I value my life so They'll value it just as much?"

"And I don't care!" Mayr threw his arms open wide. "No gods are worth that! The Four might as well just come here and stab you a hundred times. That'd do the same damage. Torturing you into such *good graces*," he sneered. "Because isn't that what these trials are *really* for? To beat you into submission?"

Tash's glare froze Mayr where he stood. It was cold, supported by restrained rage. "Stop it. You don't have *any* right to speak of Them or what you do not know, especially not here. Not in our home. Here, you speak with reverence or not at all." He pointed at the door. "If you feel that strongly, you can leave. Insulting Them insults me."

Swallowing hard, Mayr watched Tash's pointed finger. It did not waver. Tash was sure about that much. *Too far, Mayr. Too far.*

"I'm sorry," Mayr apologized, "but I just…" He jammed his palms against his closed eyes and shook his head. What if the confession got the attention of the Shar-denn? What if they lashed out because of it? Had Tash thought of any of that? "It's too dangerous. I can't do this. I can't."

And the request I've made of Severn might as well be thrown out. There's no way she can get him pardoned before the next trial starts. Everything with the Council takes forever. He'll die and she'll just shrug it off and I'll be left here cursing the Goddesses until I die. No village will just pardon him for letting people die and hurting them; destroying lives. They wouldn't forget the things that happened. They won't let him go. They won't thank him for being honest. They'll want revenge. They'll want blood. And they'll get it. They'll prove the only way out is dead.

Unless someone gets in their way.

"I'm going with you." Mayr dropped his hands. "You're not going alone."

"Mayr, you can't just—"

"No, this time I'm coming along. I'll ask Ae for leave. Doesn't matter what you say, I'm coming with you. I wasn't there before, but that ends now." Mayr leaned forward, his eyes level with Tash's. "Besides, if you survive, you'll probably just call for me afterwards. May as well make it easy for both of us and have me right there. Say yes and I'll drop it. You're not the only one who's stubborn."

They remained still in their positions until Mayr's back ached from the awkward angle.

Tash broke the silence with a weary sigh. "I yield, but," he held up his hand, "only if you *don't* interfere. *Do not* get involved. You have to let things go. You have to let me get through this. It is *my* decision. Mine. If the Goddesses want me, They'll have me." A solemn stare pinned Mayr. "*Do not interfere.*"

If only Mayr had as much faith as Tash.

Chapter Fourteen

He was dumping everything on her shoulders in a way he never had before.

Standing beside Aeley in front of the estate, Mayr caressed Hetlan's head absentmindedly and stared at the cart hitched to Hetlan. Two days since his recovery from the second trial, Tash had wasted no time advancing to the third. They would take the cart, Mayr had insisted, to carry their things to Araveena Ford.

He intentionally left out the part that worried he would need it to bring Tash's dead body home.

"You're sure you don't want me to go with you?" Aeley asked for the umpteenth time. "Because I will." She pointed to the house. "Won't take me long to get my things. We could be there and back within the day."

Had it been up to him, he would have accepted her offer. But the decision was Tash's no matter what Mayr thought was best. "Thanks, I know you would." Mayr sighed, disgruntled and irritated. "I'm not the one in charge, though. He wants to do things on his own. It was hard enough to get him to agree to *me* coming. He doesn't want you there. You'll just ruin his big day."

Aeley eyed him with an expression that shouted sarcasm. "Sure I would. I have that effect on people."

An awkward silence fell between them.

"Look, Ae." Mayr exhaled with a grimace. "I'm sorry. I know you granted me leave like you don't mind, but I can't help but think I'm letting you down. First with this Shar-denn business, which I'm not helping you handle like I should, and now I'm running out on you for I don't know how long. There's stuff I'm supposed to do here, but I can't let him do this without me. I can't be in two places at once. I keep spending time taking care of him and not you."

"And yet the days carry on, the sky has yet to fall, and I'm poking fun at you at your expense."

Lips pursed, Mayr tilted his head. "Ae."

She hugged him tightly. "It's all right. You have a life, too. And you need to do this, I understand that." Aeley pulled back to cup his face with both hands. "You do whatever you have to. If it's for someone who makes you happy, even better."

Mayr narrowed his eyes at the smile spreading across her lips.

"Don't bother denying it." She tapped his chest with one gentle finger. "Whenever a woman's left you, I've had to restrain myself from locking them up. It's not been any fun keeping myself from kicking in their faces and lodging their stomachs in their throat. Though I won't lie and say I *haven't* had words with a couple." Aeley's lips twisted as she tilted her head and stared past him. "But this one, every time you mention his name, your voice goes a little softer; your eyes a little brighter. I remember another time when you were like that over the woman I wanted to kill for the damage she did to you."

Stifling a groan, Mayr shifted and pushed Aeley back. *Not the Betta argument. Not now.*

"No, listen," Aeley argued, grasping his arms. "I understand. I have Lira, remember? I wouldn't give her up for anything, and I'd do absolutely anything for her. So I understand this. Not to say I understand *him*, but I kind of do. Maybe. I don't know. But I know you. I know this is more than just a quick grab under the sheets. We haven't talked about what's going on between you two, but we should, because I want you to have someone. I always have."

"So you're not angry at me?"

"You have the worst hearing."

"I know." Mayr drew her into a tight embrace. "Only happens with you." He kissed her cheek. "Thanks."

Aeley shrugged. "You owe me answers when you get back. And I mean *answers*, like which one of you takes it and how hard."

Mayr shoved her back. "And that's where this lovely little moment ends, thank you very much."

"I had to try." Aeley nodded towards the gated edge of the circular carriage path. "He's here."

As he turned to look, Mayr expected to see a red robe. Instead, Tash wore everything but his robe, a single pack slung over his shoulder.

"Morning," Tash greeted. He dropped his pack into the cart and stopped, distanced from Mayr by several paces. The dark circles under his eyes betrayed his lack of sleep. "Steward Dahe. Mayr. Are we ready?"

"I don't know. Are we?" Mayr cringed at the sharp words. Bitter thoughts he could not express seeped into his tone, although not on purpose. Still, the trip would be longer than expected if he continued to snap. If only it were a dream. If only the trial could end before it started.

Tash's brow lifted, but he said nothing. He climbed onto the front seat of the cart.

"Guess we are," Mayr muttered, kissing Aeley's cheek again. "Hopefully we'll be back soon." Without another word, he got into the cart and seized Hetlan's reins. There was no point in delaying the day further. He just wished they could have left on better terms. Tash was still annoyed with Mayr's doubts and insistence; Mayr was still angry with Tash's unquestioning faith. The silence was deafening with all of the words they dared not say.

Their journey south was no better. Regardless of Mayr's attempts to lighten the mood with small jokes and the occasional question, they discussed little. There were no intimate conversations about what they felt. No explanations as to why Tash had called upon Mayr during the Trials when he should have avoided contact with anyone outside the priesthood. Tash's thoughts were elsewhere. Even though he glanced at Mayr, he seemed not to see him.

The moment Araveena Ford came into view, Mayr slid his gaze to Tash, troubled by the way Tash curled into himself. *Just tell me* something. *Any thought, any feeling. Tell me whatever it is you really want to say.* He wanted to say the words out loud, but they would have been useless. At least four times during the trip, he had asked Tash the same thing only to receive a vague reply that amounted to little more than "no."

He wanted the old Tash back. *His* Tash, the sweet, considerate man who set Mayr's lust on fire with the gentlest touch and led Mayr to believe the impossible could be overcome. Not this—the painfully quiet, duty-bound man whose resignation to fate left him with misery and nothing to say.

Damn goddesses. Damn priests. Damn everything. I don't care who's responsible, I just want someone to fix this.

They entered Araveena Ford without incident, tracked by curious stares of villagers going about their business. If anyone recognized Tash, it was difficult to tell. Just as well, Mayr decided. They did not need the extra attention. Maybe it meant

Tash could confess and leave without befalling retribution. Maybe the people would prove Mayr wrong.

Once Mayr stopped Hetlan in the centre of the village, Tash hopped from the cart and strode towards the shops along the edge, searching for the magistrate, Galosa.

With a tired sigh, Mayr jumped down and guided Hetlan through the village by the bridle, watching the villagers. Similar to other villages in Kattal, wood and stone buildings in various states of repair circled the village square and spread outwards towards the fields. Carts and tables buried under wares formed a spacious marketplace to his left. Metal gleamed, colourful fabrics fluttered, and merchants chatted loudly, bragging and teasing each other and their customers, bringing life to the otherwise simple space of dry red dirt, dark wood, and grey stone. The scent of freshly baked bread wafted on the air from the baker's shop to his right, followed by bitter ale and roasted meats from the tavern several steps away. Villagers sauntered through the square, peering at him with amusement. Women grasped their baskets and whispered to one another, their excited stares unsettling him. The way they flipped their dark skirts and straightened to display their partially-revealed chests and tight bodices made him want to leave. His reason for being there was morbid, far from pleasant. The expectation of more wracked his nerves.

Squeals and laughter filled the air, followed by a group of children that ran past him. Four boys in dark, dirt-soiled clothes and a girl in an almost-pristine orange dress charged towards the shops behind him before disappearing into a narrow alley. Mayr smiled, reminded of when he used to be like them. In some ways, neither he nor his siblings had grown out of it. They just played adult games instead, the childlike innocence cast aside.

Still looking behind him, Mayr's smile faded. Beyond the alley, Tash reappeared, walking stiffly beside a tall, lanky man with grey hair. Dressed in a knee-length black tunic with dark pants and a sleeveless black and gold robe, the man's long face was drawn. The bronze chain of a Magistrate dangled from his belt. Half a dozen villagers followed, their glowers trained on Tash.

Some people remember. Mayr's stomach churned, worsened by the growing number of villagers who joined the group. Some bounded up, seeming to inquire about the issue, only to have joy ripped from their faces and replaced with sneers. Others stopped and stared at Tash before they followed Galosa, their expressions dark.

One woman ran up to Tash, stopping him cold. Loose auburn hair trailed down her back, bright against her white dress. Tiny in comparison to him, she stood in a defiant pose, her fists clenched.

She slapped him before he could speak, hard enough for Mayr to hear it despite the distance.

"You should've been rotting by now!" she yelled. "Everything you put us through. You should be dead! That's what you deserve."

As she raised her hand to slap Tash again, a slender man with short, dark hair and a pronounced limp hurried around her, catching her wrists. She struggled to get free, jerking on the man without mercy. When the man yanked her back and wrapped his arms around her, she burst into tears and slumped into him. They dragged their feet as they moved away.

Face flushed, Tash remained still. His saddened gaze followed the couple as he gripped one forearm and grimaced. Only when Galosa grabbed his elbow did Tash continue walking.

Mayr guided Hetlan towards the middle of the village, anticipating Galosa's destination from his deliberate steps. The instant Galosa and Tash stepped onto the red stone dais in the centre of the square, the marketplace quieted. Villagers paused and looked to one another as they gathered. Murmurs of confusion and excitement kept the silence at bay until Galosa raised his hand.

A dozen paces behind the dais, Mayr tied Hetlan's reins to the thick wooden pole bearing the green and gold flag of Kattal. Hesitant, Mayr neared Tash and reached for his hand. "I'm here," he whispered, squeezing Tash's fingers.

Tash squeezed back, the tight touch lingering.

"Listen here, citizens," Galosa called, his booming voice carrying through the square. "We have a matter to tend to, set upon us by the ever-gracious Lady of Justice, Navara. Blessed are we to receive such a gift." Brown eyes narrowed, Galosa regarded Tash with disgust, his lip curled. "A gift that is *long* overdue, I may add. One this village has deserved for a great many years. And here you are, walking in as if Navara led you by the hand. How kind of you to finally acknowledge us and the blood we have shed on your behalf, coward."

Tash paled.

From the back of the assembled group, a young woman with thick blonde curls and a bright red dress raced towards an alley at the furthest end of the market. The villagers grew loud and stared at Tash with frowns of disapproval.

Galosa elbowed Tash in the ribs. "I give it over to you, Taldris. May Navara find your confession bearable and true. I can't say the rest of us will," he said, stepping down from the dais.

"Thanks," Tash muttered. He pushed Mayr back and straightened before taking a deep breath. "In the name of Navara, most virtuous and magnanimous of the Four, I offer you this confession, freely and without restraint." His voice carried across the silent square, wavering despite the confidence he projected. Even if no one else noticed it, Mayr recognized Tash's struggle to remain composed. Muscles strained in Tash's back, and his fingers trembled as he clenched and unclenched his fists. Faith had not ripped fear from his heart and steadied his nerves, no matter how much he said it could.

"Some of you remember me, and I've been counting on that," Tash admitted. "I stand before you as Halataldris, son of Parase and Kilienn. They are your friends, honest citizens, innocents, and law abiders. What I say now cannot be attributed to them; the blame is not their burden. I take that completely upon myself. Navara knows this to be true." He glanced over his shoulder to Mayr before turning back to the crowd. "I hereby confess that I, Halataldris, willingly participated in the Shar-denn as a fully-inducted member and sworn guard. Ten years worth of blood passed through my hands. Only a small portion was my own."

Loud gasps were only one of the responses to his words, scattered and staggered throughout the crowd. Several villagers grunted; disgust apparent on their faces. Retorts and shouts for justice followed.

At the front of the crowd, the woman who had slapped Tash glowered at him. Her nails dug into the arm of the man still holding her. The man's face, slender like the rest of him, was worn and discoloured by a long, puckered scar along his right jaw. Focused on Tash, his dark eyes narrowed with spite. As he shifted his hold around the woman's waist, the man's long sleeve rose to reveal a dark tattoo on his forearm. A skull perched on a fist.

A gang brother.

Mayr gripped his knife and neared Tash. He splayed his other hand over the middle of Tash's back, ignoring Tash's shudder. The confession was problem enough without the presence of gang members and how they might react. *If you so much as step towards him, I'll*—

Tash touched Mayr's thigh and pushed. Not in warning, but reassurance.

Reluctantly, Mayr backed away, his gaze still on the other man's face. How many more Shar-denn members were in the crowd? Would someone take Tash down if he said too much? On instinct, Mayr scanned the square, pausing on the alleyways and shadows before studying the crowd for weapons.

Bright colour moved quickly, blurred in the corner of his eyes. Mayr snapped his attention towards the end of the market. Fingers tight around his knife, he anticipated the need to respond swiftly. The girl in red he saw earlier ran into the square, leading an older, dark-haired woman by the hand. Behind them, a man and another woman who resembled him, their faces flushed as they hurried. They pushed through the crowd on their way to the dais, eliciting more shouts and murmurs. Villagers parted to allow them a spot in front of Tash.

Tash's shoulders slumped. He took a ragged breath but did not exhale. Instead, he reached back and sought Mayr, his desperation and panic painfully obvious. When Mayr grasped his hand, cool fingers clutched back.

The older of the two women stared up at Tash, her blue eyes clouded by tears. Eyes that resembled Tash's, along with the same nose, cheekbones, and curves softened further by femininity.

Tash had said his family was dead, but the woman looked enough like him to be his mother.

The man beside her was Tash's height, with the same brown hair although his blond streaks were greyer. Dressed more finely than many of the villagers, he wore clean, well-made clothes, his hair tied back with a black ribbon. The women with him wore blue dresses of the same quality as his clothes, embellished with elaborate embroidery around the hems and necklines. Both women wore small thimbles on their middle fingers and thumbs, the metal dull in the light. The younger woman's mouth alternated between open and closed, silent as her blank, blue-eyed gaze took Tash in. She snatched her plaited brown hair over her shoulder and toyed with it nervously, dragging her fists down the braid, one over another, her thimbles catching on individual strands.

A shiver crawled under Mayr's skin. They were family. They had to be. The resemblance was too strong.

"I—I wanted to—" Tash started, pulling Mayr closer behind him. "I owe all of you apologies I cannot express deeply enough." He cleared his throat and turned away from the three people before him. "I shamed my family and Araveena Ford. I disgraced Kattal. I put the malicious greed of the Shar-denn and my own selfish desires before the lives of innocent citizens. I took advantage of Araveena, repaying kindness with theft, lies, and bloodshed. Although I won't list my every transgression here today, I will submit to a full legal trial, and a detailed statement should Magistrate Galosa and you request it. Names must be spoken. The dead cannot be forgotten."

His head lowered slightly. "In the name of those who did not deserve my allegiance, I committed atrocious crimes against this village and our neighbours. Together with other misguided individuals, I stole things people needed—valuable items and the necessary means to survive—and sold them to benefit the Shar-denn. I then accepted payment for doing so. I also stole people."

Tash's voice cracked, his breaths laboured. Mayr suspected tears clouded Tash's eyes. "I aided in moving them across borders and into the dark places where terrible things could be done to them. I gave them to the Breakers, men trained to do just that—break. Damage. Shred the spirit and shatter the body. For compliance, for obedience, for constant use by those who would pay a worthy sum for pleasure, over and over. While I did not do these things alone, and I never touched them myself, I didn't liberate them. I allowed innocents to be battered until they wanted nothing more than to die: women and men who had done nothing but exist. I took that existence from them without fighting on their behalf. I should have fought. I knew better. I was raised better," he added, facing the sobbing women before him. The older woman covered her face and cried harder.

The crowd erupted with jeers and demands for punishment, pointing at Tash and shaking their fists.

"Tell them the rest, Taldris," the woman with auburn hair yelled, barely audible above the noise. "Tell them whose blood you wear. Tell them who you sent to the Realm of the Dead."

"Inesta, stop, please," Tash whispered.

Mayr glanced between Tash and Inesta, frozen as he recalled Tash's four truths. *The girl he was with; the first one who left him. The one he cut himself over.*

The admission needed to stop. The pain she caused was too much for Tash to bear. A confrontation with her was not part of the plan.

Mayr gripped Tash's forearm to steady him. "I want to get you out of here," he murmured, his back turned to the villagers. "You've confessed enough. I can't let you—"

"Let him finish!" a voice called from the crowd. Other voices rose in agreement.

Tash's misted gaze caught Mayr's. "I have to finish this. I can't go back, and I can't leave it unsaid. Inesta's right: I have to confess the rest or I'm not being completely honest." He wrenched his arm from Mayr's hold.

"I don't like it." Mayr growled and glared at the villagers, gritting his teeth. He could not attack them. By every one of Kattal's laws, they had the right to hear the full confession. He had little right to intervene, particularly when Tash refused his aid. Aeley was not there, but he remained her agent, sworn to uphold the law even when he hated it. That did not stop him from despising every word Tash spoke or the fact Tash cried silently, betrayed by his tear-stained cheeks.

With a raised hand, Tash quieted the crowd. "I spilled blood, this is the truth. Whenever people attacked my bosses or fellow members or tried to seize our goods, I attacked back, often without mercy. To that end, several men and women died from their injuries, some of them from Araveena, many from other villages. Though I didn't murder innocent people, not directly, I bore witness and helped to subdue them. I'm as guilty as those who made the kills. I was also..." His breath hitched. When he continued, his voice was hoarse. "I was also responsible for the deaths of two young couples, treasured citizens of this village. I haven't named the other dead here, but I shall voice these names: Calaro and Griane, Aketa and Leseth—"

A high-pitched wail broke through the square. A red-haired woman wept loudly and collapsed in the arms of the burly man at her side, his cheeks smudged with ash. One of the mothers, Mayr surmised as the woman fought to stay upright.

Tash flinched. "I did not take their lives, but I did not stop their deaths. Calaro and Leseth were young brothers of this village, sons to her blacksmith. They were sixteen, in love, and ambitious for freedom. After I happened to overhear their plans to flee and the intention to take one of the faction boss's daughters, Griane, with them, I did not keep their secret. I used them to further my status and purchase loyalty from Griane's father. The Shar-denn caught them as they escaped, killing Calaro and Leseth in a gruesome display meant to prove a point to all others like them. Aketa and Griane were killed in the fray." He clasped his hands before him. "Without me, they could have lived. Had I intervened in the chase, I could have saved them. Those boys could have been alive today. But I was a coward. I chose to save myself rather than innocent people. I saw to my end rather than rescuing them from theirs. And for that, I will plead until the end of my days for forgiveness from Navara and Hastal."

Facing Galosa, Tash bowed and held his hands out, palms up. "Magistrate, through you and the Blessed Four, I release these truths. I swear upon all that is sacred that the man I was is not who I am now. No words can undo the past, but I pray you may forgive me one day."

That Tash neglected to mention his priesthood did not escape Mayr. *He doesn't want them influenced,* Mayr reminded himself, struggling to keep quiet. *He wants to be treated like everyone else. That's ridiculous. It's a lie, not telling them, regardless of how many ways he can justify it.*

To the protest of enraged shouts, Galosa stepped onto the dais. "Keep praying." His dark glance moved from Tash to Mayr then back to Tash. "Your confession gives us enough to punish you, though there is more. You ran. For that, *we* incurred harm on your behalf. Good people here were threatened and injured during the Shardenn's pursuit of *you*. They wanted information we could not give, but they insisted we knew where you had gone. More than one person was seriously hurt during those years. A young boy lost his life trying to defend his family against men looking for *you*. You have much to answer for, Taldris. You put all of us at risk."

Galosa raised his arms, silencing the crowd. "We will assemble in the meeting hall. Fetch your neighbours. Bring them to the meeting to discuss what must be done to right these acts. Justice will be done before nightfall. Disperse!"

The crowd broke apart. Villagers fled in every direction.

"You are to remain here, do you understand?" Galosa gripped Tash's wrist. "You do not leave. And your family does not attend, as our laws state." He pointed to the broad-shouldered man behind him in a green tunic and dark pants. Taller and more intimidating than Galosa, the blond man regarded Tash with a sneer. "Olona will remain here. He is a soldier for the Council, so no bright ideas. He will allow you time with your family, but if you run off, he has permission to gut you."

"I understand," Tash said.

With a huff, Galosa left the dais, his black and gold robe trailing as he hurried away. Olona backed towards the edge of the square, his gaze locked on Tash.

"I hope they tear you apart," Inesta hissed at Tash. "I can't believe I was ever with a coward like you. You stole parts of my life, Taldris, and I want them back!"

When she lunged at him, she was caught by the man with the Shar-denn tattoo. "Inesta, enough!" he commanded, hauling her back. His voice was deep. His growl was even deeper, guttural. "Let's just get to the shop and calm down. We've a meeting to go to. Leave the traitor alone. He'll just ruin our lives more."

"As if you ever needed my help, Ress," Tash retorted under his breath. "Besides, I don't see you up here."

Ress stopped. Head lowered, body in an offensive position, he cast Tash an enraged glare. "What was that? Thought I heard you complaining, *traitor*." He dragged a finger across his throat. "That's what I hope you get. Turning us in, running your mouth. Bad enough you ran and stuck everyone else with a knife in the back, but you just *had* to drag us out of there, too." Snorting, he spun Inesta around and led her through the square.

Mayr stepped in front of Tash, shielding him from the villagers' view. "So that was your best friend." *Now an informant for the High Council and in league with the bounty hunters,* he recalled from the list Aeley had shown him.

"Used to be." Tash hung his head and scraped the dais with his boot. "That was a long time ago. After I gave his name to the Council..." Dejection weighted his words, underlying pain surfacing with every crack in his strained voice.

Unable to withstand it, Mayr drew Tash into his arms. "I know. I saw the list," he murmured. "You did what you thought was necessary, just like you did here. But it's done. That part's done. Now we have to wait, but don't lose hope. Maybe they'll insist you go to Council for judgment."

Tash wrapped his arms around Mayr's waist and buried his face in Mayr's neck. "You don't believe that. With the way they were…" His grip tightened. "Don't leave me. Whatever punishment they give, please don't leave."

"I won't. Just don't end up dead." Mayr brushed a kiss along Tash's temple and lingered, taking in his scent and warmth. This moment could not be the last time he held Tash or breathed him in. Together as a couple or not, he needed Tash, more than he could admit. As much as he wanted to tell Tash what he felt, the words would not form. Instead, he drowned in a deep sea of emotions he could not share. He barely understood the longing coiled in tight chains around his heart.

A cleared throat interrupted them, followed by boots scuffing the dirt behind Mayr.

Irritated by the interruption, Mayr released Tash and turned to meet the glances of the women and man who resembled Tash. They were calm, their eyes red from weeping. "Can I help you?"

"Mayr." Tash moved Mayr aside. "Wait."

"Little Bird?" the younger woman asked softly, still clutching her braid. Hesitant, she reached for Tash.

Tash stepped from the dais, his stare latched to hers. After a long moment, he took her fingers into his and pulled her against him. "Ally. Ally, I'm so sorry." He held her tighter as she sobbed against his shoulder, her hands fisted in his shirt. They swayed, even as the older woman wrapped her arms around them both.

"Here, let's get rid of these." Tash pushed back and held her face in both hands, clearing tears from her cheeks with his thumbs. "Mayr." He held out his hand until Mayr joined them. "My sister, Allaysia."

Allaysia wiped her eyes with the back of her hands and smiled weakly. She sniffled as she tried to regain composure.

Tash leaned his forehead against the older woman's. "And this, this is my mother, Parase." He kissed her cheek and hugged her, whispering words only she could hear. They were enough to make her cry anew.

"You can probably tell who I am," the unnamed man finished, nearing Mayr. He offered his arm in greeting. "Kilienn, his father."

Mayr clapped his hand to Kilienn's forearm. Just as they released their grasps, Tash faced his father. They regarded each other, the silence twisted by tension.

Kilienn pulled Tash into an embrace that unsteadied them both. "We've missed you. Prayed for you every day. *Every* day."

"I know. I'm sorry, I really am." Tash fell back to stand beside Mayr. "This isn't how I wanted to see you again, and I can't take it back. I'm sorry for that, too. But I—I couldn't—I just had to—" He looked to Mayr, struggling to finish the words he could not spit out. "There wasn't a way around this. I had to do it."

"I thought you said they were dead," Mayr muttered to Tash, scowling as he turned slightly.

"To me. They were dead to me," Tash whispered. "They had to be so we could all move on. Please don't be angry. Please understand."

"I'm not. I do. Just…" Mayr pressed a hand to Tash's chest to commit the rhythm of his heart to memory. Memories would be all he had left, even if Tash survived the trial. "Tell me about them later."

Tash kissed his cheek. "I will, I swear."

"Halataldris?" Parase clasped Tash's hand, a small smile on her lips. "Little Bird, will you introduce us to your companion?"

Laughing silently at the stunned expression on Tash's face, Mayr bowed his head. "Mayr of the Dahe estate, Head of the Guard for Tract Steward Dahe."

One of Kilienn's brows arched. "A man of the law. Interesting choice, son. Any other drastic changes we might enjoy?"

"I'm a priest now?" Tash lowered his gaze. "Almost fully committed."

Allaysia squealed. "You found something good to do. I knew you could." She threw her arms around Tash. "The Goddesses always loved you, I told you. You never listened to me. And now you found someone special, too. This is the best surprise ever." When she drew back, she slapped his arm. "What's with that confession, you horrible little beast? Tissie came running into the shop to tell us you were back and getting yourself into trouble. Then we see you up there and..." Allaysia slapped his arm again. "Don't you dare do that again, you hear? Don't you *ever* scare us again. Not ever."

Her rant finished, Allaysia embraced Tash tight enough to restrict their breaths.

Kilienn cleared his throat and nodded towards Hetlan. "Your friend looks likes he'd appreciate a softer place to stand and something to eat. Water, too. I know you can't leave this spot, so why don't I take him back to our house? We have an extra stall and food." He tapped his wife's hand. "I'll just leave you here to catch up. I'll be back before the meeting adjourns. You can tell me what I missed later. We've got a lot of talking to do." The pointed stare he cast Tash before walking away was enough to prompt Tash to lower his head.

"He's just not sure how to feel," Parase said, holding both of Tash's hands. "He loves you, Halataldris, so much it breaks his heart. Just like it did when you told us you were leaving. Like it did when you said they'd come after you. None of us got over that. I'm sure you never did, either. When you talk to him, remember that. If he raises his voice, it's not because he doesn't care about you, it's because he does." She held him close. "Just like I do. I never stopped."

"I know," Tash answered. Over her shoulder, he looked at Mayr.

The agony in his gaze seeped into Mayr, yanking on Mayr's need to comfort him. The reunion with his family should have been joyful, but it only added to Tash's pain and sorrow. The reality of the situation did nothing but strangle Mayr's hope. *If he dies during this, that's it. I'm never talking to another priest. I'm never doing anything for any goddess, and I'm never stepping foot into another temple. You hear that? He dies, that's it between me and the four of You. Because if You can't just let him live his life, You're no goddesses of mine.*

The day wore on into late afternoon. The square remained abandoned except for Mayr, Tash, Tash's family, and Olona, who sat on a stool in front of a fruit cart, playing with his knife and watching them. On the ground in front of the dais, Parase sat on one side of Tash while Mayr sat on the other. Allaysia sat between Tash's legs, leaning back into him, content to be in his arms. Kilienn sat across from his daughter, facing all of them. There had been no word from the public meeting. Mayr prayed it meant a lighter sentence.

Though for all the time it took the village to debate Tash's case, there was ample time for him to catch up with his family. They traded stories, listened to Tash's experiences as a priest, discussed matters of the republic and local gossip, and inquired into Mayr's family and life with the Dahes. Allaysia reminded Mayr of Estara and Orlee, and Parase of his own mother. Kilienn was more like Korre than Malary, except for the occasional slip of sarcasm.

With Tash's family before him, Mayr felt guilty. How excruciating had the visit to Mayr's family actually been for Tash, surrounded by a family similar to his own? Even though he could not have known, Mayr swore he would make it up to Tash. Together or not, friends or lovers, he would pay Tash back for the unintentional torture.

"So, how long have you two been together?" Allaysia smiled at Mayr. "Who chased who?"

"Ally," Tash warned, squeezing one arm around her neck, playfully choking her. "Not in front of our parents. Have I taught you nothing?"

Allaysia laughed and tugged on his hair. "It's the other way around, *little* brother." She craned her neck to look at up him and stuck out her tongue. "Besides, I've got a lot of time to catch up on. Perhaps you'd like to discuss the size of your—"

"Ally!" Placing a hard kiss to her head, Tash interrupted her. "You start along that path and we might just end up discussing your secret trysts with a certain boy when you were fifteen. Perhaps how he used to—"

Allaysia threw up her hands. "All right! I give! Mother, make him stop."

"Children," Parase said between laughs, winking at Mayr. "You don't seem terribly concerned. I take it your family is this raucous?"

Mayr stifled his laughter. "Worse, actually."

"I can attest to that." Tash offered him a tender smile. "There are more of them, with three of them still yet to come into their own. Your family makes Ally look normal."

"Hey, I resent that." Allaysia flicked Tash's chin. "When we get home, I'm going to start telling all of your embarrassing stories and—"

Bells cut off the rest of Allaysia's threats. Loud and piercing, the noise resonated around the square, spreading the solemn song of judgment.

Kilienn was first on his feet. "Up, up." He helped Parase to her feet. "We can't be lazing about when they get here." Allaysia took his hands and allowed him to help her up. "And whatever they say…" After steadying Tash as he stood, Kilienn wrapped his hands around the back of Tash's neck and held him close. "Whatever they say, we're with you always. *Always*, Halataldris." Lips pressed to Tash's forehead, he continued. "I can't ever condone what you did, but I love you all the same. I believe in forgiveness. I believe the Goddesses will find you worthy. Blessed be the Four in giving you to us. Never forget it."

Tash nodded, silent as he grasped his father's wrists and kept him close.

"Now prepare yourself." Kilienn eased him back. "The Goddesses are well-versed and gracious in the art of forgiveness, but sometimes we mortals forget what that is. There are a hundred ways this could go, but you already know that," he said, glancing at Mayr. "Let's hope the law does right by Navara today."

Footsteps and voices grew loud in one of the alleys. Galosa turned a corner and entered the square, followed by a procession of stern-faced villagers.

"I love you." Parase hugged Tash. "They won't change that." She watched Galosa warily. "Allaysia, say your goodbyes."

Allaysia threw herself into Tash's arms. "You'll always be my favourite brother," she said, kissing his cheek. At her mother's insistence, she backed away to give plenty of space for Galosa's approach.

Galosa stopped in front of Tash before stepping onto the dais and pulling Tash up with him. Eight armed soldiers stood behind him, dressed in bright green cloaks and dark leather armour etched with the green shield and gold bearcats of the High Council. The villagers assembled in a dense crowd.

Mayr squeezed Tash's hand and backed away several steps, his focus on the soldiers. Where had they been hiding? While it was customary for every village to be home to soldiers—sometimes dozens—they made him uncomfortable. If Tash were being pardoned, there would be no need for them except to keep peace in the crowd. But they stood behind Tash, not around the people.

They were there for a different duty.

"We have come to an agreement," Galosa announced, his hands raised. "A majority vote has been cast and so shall it be. Justice will be done for our people." He turned and nodded.

The soldiers moved quickly, a blur of green lost to noise and grunts as they rushed around Tash and dragged him back. Tash struggled in the grasp of two soldiers, staggering and scraping his heels through the dirt as they hauled him to the flag post. A long rope appeared from one set of hands. The ends were tossed to another set of hands.

Gripping the hilt of his sword, Mayr started towards Tash, growling low. When one soldier whirled around and swiped at him with a drawn blade, Mayr stopped cold, returning the soldier's glare. They were soldiers of Kattal; law enforcers of the republic. Mayr enforced only the region's laws. Given the nature of Tash's crimes, the judgment passed by the village fell under the laws of Kattal, not Gailarin. By decree, he was only permitted to watch the soldiers tie Tash to the pole.

He ached and burned, yearning to save Tash from what was to come. Maybe the judgment would prove fair. Maybe the villagers would prove merciful.

His doubts screamed for him to intervene; to not stand idly by. The villagers could not be trusted. They were mortals, slaves to hunger and fear. They would take everything and leave nothing.

Galosa accepted a rolled parchment from a woman in black robes, her ink-stained fingers indicative of a village scribe. As he read from the parchment, Galosa's loud voice filled the square. "On this day, we the people officially declare Halataldris, son of citizens Parase and Kilienn, to be guilty of the following: theft, possession of stolen goods, selling of stolen goods, trafficking, battery, assault, assault resulting in death, and active accessory to murder in the plural, total number unknown. These crimes are as confessed and acknowledged by the accused, offered freely, without persuasion or force. The admission received publicly bears enough weight to justify the judgment, derived by a majority vote. The crimes in question have also been verified by witnesses, including one Ress, a former acquaintance of the accused. The people have heard sufficient debate and stand at the ready for the judgment."

Mayr held his breath and stole a glimpse of Tash bound with his arms behind his back. *Please let it be merciful. Please give in to love, not your hate. Mercy, please—*

Galosa's face tightened with the hint of a smirk. "It is decided that, in the name of Navara, the punishment to be served by the accused is stoning."

No. No! Mayr's heart hammered to a stop. His chest ached, demanding blood that seemed to have stilled.

Parase's wails filled the silence as she fell to her knees. Kilienn scrambled to console her.

Only Allaysia rushed forward. "Stay of judgment!" she shouted, threatening to punch Galosa. A soldier grabbed her around the waist and pulled her back. "This was unfair; one-sided! Give him a trial! Take it to the Council!" Fists beating the soldier's hands, she kicked his ankles and twisted to get free.

The crowd heckled and shouted for the punishment.

Galosa cleared his throat and continued. "The punishment shall be served as such: each individual who feels aggrieved will have the opportunity to throw up to four stones. So it will be until each aggrieved individual has had their turn," he glanced at Tash, "or the accused dies.

Once the punishment is served, the accused will be released to their next of kin."

Parase screamed. Her agony reverberated through Mayr's thoughts, piercing emotions as it raced through his insides, setting a fire under his skin. His lungs felt heavy, sinking into themselves without air to fill them. The soldiers moved sluggishly towards the crowd as if time itself crawled. The roar of the crowd dulled as his mind blocked out the cries for death.

I'll lose him. Goddesses, I'll lose him. I can't. I just—I—

Memories of his mother's accident berated him, piling emotional debris onto his shattered hope. He was a boy then, unable to do anything. He had turned around too late. He had frozen, unable to understand what had happened.

But he was no longer a child. He was a fighter, trained and at the ready. This time, he could do something before the damage was done.

This time, he would.

"*Don't. You. Dare!*" Mayr roared, stalking forward to stomp onto the dais and purposely knock Galosa off balance. "*No one*—not a single *one* of you—is going to throw *anything* at this man."

Soldiers approached him, swords brandished. He drew his sword and clutched it in his right hand, ready to take on anyone foolish enough to confront him. Cautious, he surveyed the villagers. Several carried grey and red stones in their hands.

All it would take was one shot to the right location to kill Tash. From what he could see, there were more than two dozen men capable enough—and angry enough—to throw that one shot. The stones did not appear small, either. A few were as large as his fist.

"Mayr!" Tash shouted. "This is supposed to happen. Stop interfering! You promised you wouldn't."

Mayr glanced behind him, meeting Tash's glower. "I lied."

Feet shuffled as the soldiers formed a line between Mayr and the villagers. One of the soldiers jerked Galosa from the dais and pushed him to the side, one hand on his chest to keep him back.

"I am Head Guard for your Tract Steward," Mayr announced, his grip tightening. "I serve Aeley Dahe, and I will not stand for this."

The villagers yelled back, their protests a cacophony of words he could not decipher.

A sharp whistle silenced them. Galosa pushed past his guard, his face deep red as he trembled with rage. "Guard, you are out of your jurisdiction!" He jabbed a finger towards Mayr. "It is in our right to punish him, and in this manner. It is *not* prohibited by the High Council. No pardon has been issued in his name. His name has *never* been listed in the Council's letters of exoneration or the Justice Assembly's announcements. There is no ground upon which you may interfere, so back off!" Hissing, he sliced his hand through the air. "If you keep it up, we are going to contact Steward Dahe *and* Councilman Severn *and* Councilman Cota. We will petition them to arrest you and request you be replaced, stripped of rank, and forbidden from any similar position. Think carefully. In no way will it save Taldris from his punishment."

Mayr snorted. "Threatening me won't work. You can forget that." If his life were different, maybe the loss of his rank would have been more important. He loved Aeley, but he could not— *would not*—lose Tash like this. "Look at yourselves! Look at what you're about to do." He turned to the crowd. "How is this *any* better than anything he's ever done? Throw those stones and *you'll* be committing assault. *You'll* be committing murder. Is that how you want to be remembered by the Goddesses? Is *that* how you wish Them to see you? As killers?"

With his free hand, Mayr gestured at Tash. "He's paid a price for his crimes. Ten years worth, with decades to come. His guilt pelts him worse than your stones ever could. Each day is a death, knowing that he lives while others don't. But he's making amends—I've witnessed them. So have the priests in more than one temple and the people he serves every day." He motioned to the villagers' hands. "Killing him won't bring the dead back. It *won't* make you feel better. You'll *always* feel this way. I know. I've been there, foolish enough to believe revenge would help, but it *never did*. You know why? Because retribution and revenge aren't justice. They wear the same pretty things and might speak nicely, but they're rotten to their core. They bring death, not order. Just cold—"

"Mayr. Mayr!" Tash barked. "Dammit, look at me!" As Mayr complied, Tash wriggled under the ropes. Not to get free, Mayr realized, but because he was angry enough to hit something. "*Do. Not. Interfere!* You are throwing this trial into utter chaos, and you need to *stop. This* is the test. *This* is the trial. If the Goddesses want me, I'll pull through. You need to step down and shut up. If you respect me at all, you will let it happen."

Tash's expression wounded Mayr more than his harsh words. Each shout, each command, was accompanied by agony.

Mayr slouched. He had held Tash after the first two trials, sensing his pain and the unyielding desperation to fulfill his commitment to the Four. The Trials meant everything to Tash. Enough for him to give up everything and commit to a lonely life spent serving everyone else but himself. Tash honestly believed he needed to pass the Trials to prove his worth. He needed what waited for him on the other side. He would die to obtain it, whatever it really was.

Swallowing, Mayr studied the crowd and Galosa's pinched expression. He had two choices, neither of them acceptable. He could either abide by Tash's decision or save him from harm.

He looked to Tash. *I'm sworn to protect others.* Mayr looked back to the crowd. *But I'm sworn to uphold justice.* Tears blurred his vision. *I'm caught between worlds. I hate this. I hate all of it. I hate myself. I can't slay them, and I can't take Tash against his will. It's a loss no matter what I choose. Either way, I lose him. I can't. I don't want to.* A tear slipped down his cheek before he could stop it. The more he struggled to decide, his chest burned. Sharp pains squeezed his heart, piercing it deeper and deeper like a vine of thorns.

Focused on Tash, Mayr ignored the shouts of the villagers and Galosa's attempts to get his attention. As much as he wanted to save Tash, Tash would refuse his every attempt. Even if he managed to get Tash out of it, how long would it save his life? Not only would Tash be enraged at Mayr and avoid him, Tash would also find another way to succeed in his punishment.

And he would never tell Mayr.

He's smart. I can't guard him every moment of every day. He'd find a way to go through with it and get himself killed. Goddesses, if You're real, if You care, grant me another option. Something. Anything. Even something that's right up the middle of dead and gone.

Mayr snapped his glance towards the soldiers' armour and stared at the shield positioned between the bearcats. *Middle ground. Suggest a compromise. Save him in a way that fits the purpose of the trial. Speak justice to serve justice. Call to the Four to serve the Four.*

All those times of listening to his parents, the priests, and the old stories would finally be useful.

"Divinity Claim!" Mayr held up his hand. "I call Divinity Claim, just like Taleyra the Righteous did for the Thirteen Wayward Defenders. All but one of the Defenders survived because Navara found them worthy souls despite their terrible actions against the old cities. Only one was rotten to his core and paid the price. Twelve were forgiven and taken to form Navara's guard. They've never proven Her wrong." He sheathed his sword slowly. *Please tell me I got that story right because this could go really, really badly. Maybe I should've paid a bit more attention.*

There was no time to debate the legends. He had to act before Galosa lost all patience.

Mayr held up both hands. "So I officially invite the Four," he announced, "Emeraliss, Laytia, Hastal, and Her Most Divine Judge, Navara, to challenge the mortal measures here. The Divinity Claim must be considered once called or it's a miscarriage of the most supreme justice. We are caretakers of justice only. Navara is Justice embodied. Only She can grant a punishment that is true, pure, and devoid of mortal strife. If punishment is to be done in Her name, make it worthy."

When Galosa grunted and crossed his arms, Mayr shook his head. "No, hear me out, Galosa. I promise I won't stop the judgment, but I propose a different punishment. One that truly tests how much he deserves to live or die." Mayr took a breath. "Keep him tied there for a couple days." The crowd murmured and snickered. "No, wait, just listen. The nights are getting colder. The days are still hot. Leave him to the elements and allow them to decide his fate. The Goddesses can control the elements. If he's to die, the Four will snatch him in death. If Navara finds him worthy of divine mercy, he'll live."

I hope. Mayr peered over his shoulder to Tash. He could withstand it, Mayr was certain. After the Shar-denn, the attack on the road, and the second trial, Tash could handle almost anything.

Clearing his throat, Mayr returned his attention to Galosa. "It's a just punishment, more so than stoning. It doesn't take a goddess to land a stone where it can kill him. *Any* of you could aim well enough to land the killing blow with only one stone, let alone four. In fact, *all* of you could, even your children. I was taught to throw as a boy. Accuracy was drummed into me until I could hit perfectly every time. By the time I was twelve, I could kill a man with one throw. Repeatedly." He pulled his knife and held it up. "No different than throwing this."

Mayr sheathed the knife. "But withstanding exposure isn't easy. Even the most skilled man or the best-trained warrior can be killed by the elements. It's a matter of luck and fate, not just skill. If you want justice, allow the Four to pass judgment. Take up the Divinity Claim and give him to Navara. Your people can keep the blood off their hands and meet the Four with their spirits unsoiled. Give them peaceful final days before their spirits are reborn, fresh and clean without the stench of murder." In hopes submissiveness played in his favour, he hung his head. "The Four are central to everything. They gifted us with breath, choice, and the ability to safeguard justice. If we are to keep these gifts, we must strive to keep them pure, as close to divine as possible. We must do as They would. Don't forget who you serve, Magistrate, and who the Council must serve above all others."

Something appeared to have piqued Galosa's interest. He tapped his lips with his fingers, his pensive gaze on Mayr. "I assume that if we agree, you will no longer plague us with your insolence?"

"If you agree, I swear upon my oath to Gailarin, Aeley Dahe, and her departed father, Korre, who I regarded as a second father, that I'll stand aside and allow punishment to be served." Mayr glimpsed Tash and swallowed back the tears threatening to well in his eyes. *I'm sorry. I'm so sorry. Please don't hate me.*

Galosa lifted his chin. "I will call another meeting to discuss the Divinity Claim. We will also fetch four priestesses from the nearby Temple and consult with them, as the Claim dictates. *If* the people agree, we will keep him here for three days—"

"Two." Mayr ignored Tash's glare.

"Three. That's the final suggestion." Galosa's eyes narrowed. "Or we'll go back to stoning."

Mayr nodded. "Three. Thank you, Magistrate. I have no doubt Navara will find your gracious understanding worthy of many blessings."

With a snort, Galosa turned and gestured for the crowd to follow. As the square emptied, Mayr dared to approach Tash. A soldier stepped between Mayr and Tash.

"Keep your distance," the soldier warned, "and keep your weapons to yourself."

"Get yourself under control while you're at it," Tash added angrily, eyeing Mayr. "Quit ruining this or we're never talking again."

"You call it ruining; I call it saving you from your stubbornness." Mayr crossed his arms. "Go ahead and tell me the Trials aren't supposed to kill you. Tell me again how they're *not* beating you into submission. Then tell me I shouldn't be worried. That's my favourite."

Tash let out a frustrated breath towards the sky. "You can't keep doing this. You shouldn't have interfered. You made a promise, Mayr. You *promised* me you wouldn't. You *swore*—"

"And I broke it. I know. I was *there*. Here. Ther—you know what? I don't care!" Mayr threw open his arms, shouting as he continued. "It's the right thing to do. When you love someone, these things happen!"

A chill danced down Mayr's spine. His words echoed inside his thoughts, one word louder than all the rest. *Did I really just say that?*

Tash snapped his mouth shut, his body rigid. He said nothing but tore his gaze from Mayr's.

Guess I did.

Chapter Fifteen

Ghosts, hacking and slashing, prodding the darkness beneath the surface, yanked from where Tash had buried it—or tried to, at least. Ever the brutish beast shirking its skin, frolicking among the innocence he had thrown away with all the recklessness of the vile bastard he was.

Yeah, he knew what he was, tied to the flag post and begging the elements to hold onto life for him: a monster, a killer, a destroyer of families, a nightmare to be quashed as quickly as daylight could set his skin bursting into blisters.

Damn Mayr for his so-called love. That sense of duty. That motivation to keep Tash alive when he deserved the torture the villagers had rightfully looked forward to. At the very least they needed justice. After all the Shar-denn had taken from them over decades, pummeling the spirit of generations straight into the ground and beyond the grave, the villagers deserved to confront the enemy face to face. To send the filth back to where it belonged, the consequences purely at the mercy of the Goddesses.

But no... *Love* had intervened. Spoken too loudly. Nudged its way into his trial with its self-serving busyness, spinning the trial into the nightmare he had tried to keep Mayr from.

But that bastard... *That bastard. He broke his promise. Broke—*

Everything. Everything was broken. Three days into the punishment, Tash could barely sort real from lie. His thoughts twisted around one another like snarled yarn shredded by a cat's claws with all the serration of a bread knife. And hot—he was burning inside his skin, his mouth too dry to function past a weak moan of protest except for when Ally appeared. When she was around, the words tumbled out, mostly without force, though every now and then...

Come on, Little Bird, fight. Fight for me.

But he had. And he had lost.

Ally held out the stick, the thick red wood battered already after Nimae and Bremary had beaten the stuffing out of each other, pretending to be pirates— Bremary, Queen of the Cold Dark Sea, and Nimae, Seafarer the Great, her archenemy and rival. Both of them had fought over treasure they had buried by the pond, one they had promptly forgotten after Bremary had stomped on Nimae's toes something fierce and sent him tripping down the hill, rolling into a fox den, and breaking his ankle. It had taken both Taldris and Ress to get Nimae up on his good leg while Varen ran through the woods faster than anyone else could, yelling for the nearest parent. Bremary had insisted she help, following close on their heels with big tears rolling down her cheeks and too many apologies to count.

Taldris was seven; still only seven when Nimae and Ress and Varen were already eight, the three of them the closest thing he had to brothers while Bremary was like a cousin, even though she was actually Ress's cousin. But Ally, she was hitting fourteen and keeping an eye on him as their parents sorted out Nimae's injury and comforted Bremary inside Ress's home, the closest of their houses. Ress's eldest sister, Lally, was there somewhere, too, hollering for Varen — "Flutterbloom," she called him — and from the side porch came the bang of the kitchen door, followed by Varen shouting back, "Baby Flutterboom, what?" before he bounded down the stairs. His long blond hair was a mess, the curls all tangled and falling out of their green ribbon while he ran around the back of the house.

"Little Bird?"

Ally's voice brought Taldris back to her, the stick jabbing his arm lightly. "Come on, then. Let's have a go."

"But I don't want to hurt you," Taldris said quietly, sniffling and all the more embarrassed for it. Nimae's pained screams had frightened him, the awkward way the bone jutted out of Nimae's ankle a sight he never wanted to repeat. It was disgusting. And it hurt even when he was just looking at it. And he was mad at Bremary for making it happen even though he knew it was an accident. They were playing. Why did something so fun have to go so bad?

Except now… now Ally was offering him the same stick Bremary had used against Nimae, and the thought of his sister being in that much pain… that scared him even more than breaking his own ankle. Could she not just offer him the stick Nimae had used and keep Bremary's for herself?

Ally shook her head, her wavy hair sweeping over her shoulders in a silky mass, so pretty with her new silver combs. "Silly bird. I'll be fine. You won't hurt me. Ever."

"But—"

"I'm your sister, Little Bird. I trust you." She slapped the stick into his hand and curled his fingers around the warped wood. "Just try. For me? Mama says there's bad men skulking around again. I want to make sure you can take care of yourself."

Taldris stared at the stick, the wood shaking with his hand. "But what about you? What if I can't take care of you?"

Ally's laugh played through him like cool water on a hot summer's day. She pulled him close and kissed his forehead loudly, the smack of it leaving him blushing and wiping it off with a groan. "One thing at a time, baby bird. Let's sort you out and we'll worry about the rest later…"

And worry he had, spending years ensuring no one laid a hand on her. His gang brothers could beat him all they liked, but his sister had been off limits, never to be touched lest the bastards lose a hand or two—a promise, not a threat. He would have gone building a collection had they tested him. Goddesses only knew Nimae and Varen would have joined him and been all too happy to break fingers, while Ress would have worked from somewhere in the background, helping in his own way. They would have avenged any of their family had the Shar-denn gone after them, with Tash leading the pack, ready to spill blood. Because that was what the monsters did, and he had dared to excel at it.

Tash groaned, the memory as grimy as it had always been, even when it was nowhere near fresh. Or maybe it was just the searing ache in his back and shoulders doing the talking, his muscles furious at being forced around the flag post for so long. His headache was no better, wreaking havoc in waves, the bigger the better and increasingly frequent. His eyes were still closed, and not just voluntarily. Keeping them open made everything hurt worse, but at some point, his eyelids had fallen shut on their own accord, trapping him inside the darkness of his consciousness—what little there was of it, anyway. He faded in and out, with delusions that made it too difficult to sort what had been and what was, and his skin... His body seemed to have shrunk several sizes, pulling too tight everywhere, unforgiving every time he moved to get even a fraction of relief.

There would be no relief, not for him. He deserved none—a fact, not a pitiful thought.

Mayr had no idea what Tash was capable of; the violence that had come from his hands. The hurt that still *could* come from his hands. Tash wanted to believe he could change, that being a better person was always an opportunity, never an impossibility. Had he been so brutal and uncaring on the Shar-denn's behalf simply to save himself, or had it been motivated by the threat hanging over his family's head because of him? Had that wayward shadow of himself dealt damage under the gang's banner because of some noble purpose gone wrong or because he was naturally cruel?

Some days it had been too difficult to tell, his rage tipped to full scale, his frustration ready to strike at anyone that could cry out at the injustice of it all.

Now, hallucinations and nightmares were screaming that injustice into his face, at least when his mind shut down enough to let the horrors dance. The memories were no better, exhaustion bringing them to the fore with barbed intent, snagging his conscience on a doomed spiral downward.

Except those memories had tormented him first, ever since the end of the first trial. Nothing in him had been calm since the attack on the road, those half-dozen fists punching into him, demanding what he could not give. He had escaped with his life, but the attack left him with flashes of the past that assaulted him with just as much intensity, waking him, scaring him into a sweat, robbing him of time and focus. Sometimes he could hear the words in his visions clearer than when they had been first spoken, but other times the recollections were too mangled to account for every detail. Fears he had once overcome were alive and kicking him in the heart, stealing parts of him and leaving him breathless.

He still had yet to tell Mayr about it all, not that Mayr had asked. From what Tash could tell, Mayr knew already, or at least suspected. If only he knew the half of it—

Oh, how delicious it was, the Breaker screaming bloody murder, his throat scraped raw, that deep voice rasping between gasps for mercy.

Mercy? For that rotten bastard? Taldris snorted. Hardly.

No, the bastard deserved the beating just as much as the rusty meat hook in his leg, keeping his filthy ass upside down and bleeding out.

One rule. All the guy had to do was obey one single damn rule: don't touch Colare's family or his property. Ever. The boss hated anyone's grubby hands all over his stuff. 'On pain of death' was so much more than just a simple guideline.

Well, that just meant all the more fun for the asses who thought they were so bloody special, thinking the rules failed to apply to them. They broke the rules, fine. But that sent them down to this hole in the dung-infested heap of a cache house, right into the clutches of Colare's private guards.

Such a shame Taldris had to be on shift at the time... witnessing the bastard get his for daring to put his sick fingers on Colare's eldest kid...

Taldris tsked at himself and crossed his arms, smirking as he leaned against the dusty, bloodstained wall, letting Mynkyn whip the life out of the guy with barbed wire. He was enjoying the arsehole's punishment more than he should have—they both were. But the guy had it coming, Taldris believed that much, enough that he would have staked his life on that single fact. He knew what the Breakers did to people—had witnessed it enough as an adolescent, his stomach constantly turning in on itself, threatening to kill him if no one else did. So many innocents destroyed, with their identities turned inside out and backwards, beaten from them. Stolen. Brutally ruined, replaced with frightened souls in empty shells, some of whom never lived longer than their first slave assignment.

Yeah, this bastard had it coming, him and those fingers of his, so accustomed to hitting out and injuring until the victim complied or died in the process. Given the choice between whose side he should be on, Taldris was having a damned hard time feeling sorry for the guy, Shar-denn or not. And although Taldris served Colare... the boss could suck dirt for all he cared. He was there for one reason and one reason only.

To keep his family alive.

The Breaker gurgled. "Please... stop, please... please..." Blood dripped to the floor, spreading the pool of it further over the stones, sinking into the crevices and slipping down the angles where the stones were uneven. Mynkyn hit harder, slashing the Breaker's face. Wails rewarded him, tormented cries echoing off the walls.

Taldris turned away, his glance raking over the open door, wisps of cobwebs holding his focus. He would have to bathe before going home, wash the stench of the house off of him. And the blood... He looked his hands over. He hated the clamminess. Hated that damned disgusting feeling as the blood dried, caking his palms and the back of his hands.

There was no way he would take that home to Inesta. Clean. Only clean hands touched her, or as best as he could manage. And what he did here...

She could never know. Not this. How could he even begin to explain the satisfaction of partaking in such a gruesome flailing without her running away from him? She hated the Shar-denn. Always had. Always wanted him to get out. To leave.

By the Four, he would have if it meant saving their lives. If he could have guaranteed she would have everything she wanted—the future she dreamed of.

Instead, he had this. Only this. The best he could offer was to keep Colare alive while hating the bastard all the while. But it kept Inesta alive. It kept his parents alive. It kept Ally alive.

And condemned Taldris to die as a shadow, wasted and pointless.

Well, at least he could take another bastard down with him. If he was going down in flames in the end of all things, he may as well have company.

Pushing off the wall, Taldris held out his hand. "Hey, Mynk, give it over. I'm ready for another round. Let's really make him sorry for it…"

Tash groaned, screams echoing in his head loud enough they could have very well been his. *Had* he been screaming? His throat hurt enough to say as much, but for all he knew he was back in the valley of hallucination, where as conscious as he thought he was, he most certainly was not. Lucidity was a slippery ditch, and his ass only ended up smacking down in the goopy centre of it anytime he tried to claw his way back to clarity.

Hot… so bloody hot… His skull caged him, forcing him to relive the echoes of life, every dream a merciless trap of judgment with poison for bait. Vile and cruel, regret's jaws clamped around his exhausted body, sinking deep, sucking out the life he had left… giving it over to where it belonged… giving it back… giving it…

Whispers. Whispers, caught on the breeze. Death floating by. Calling…

Goddesses, it was so hard to stay awake.

The darkness was coming.

He felt it. Death, just there, just past the last moment, always waiting. Always calling. Whispering. Bringing him home, holding him down. Choking. All the choking, never breathing past the lie. And the voices. Those damned voices, spinning webs, stitching words, angry, so angry…

Tash forced open one eyelid, a creeping feat unto itself, the dryness an ache all its own. A flash of heat had him closing his eye with a quiet hiss. Sunlight. Awful. Not worth another moment of pain, his headache flaring up with all the force of a sledgehammer to his forehead.

Still, something… there was something just past that pain…

He opened both eyes slowly, barely seeing past his lashes, the world a blur of uncertainty. People milled about the square, faded colours coming into focus enough to put a name to the shade. The smell—so dull, soiled by his own stench. Fresh bread would be there somewhere, and his stomach turned just to see if it still could. The muffled sounds of the market collided together, punctured by the clip-clop of hooves. The clanging of shop bells. Laughter, almost as agonizing as the undying ache in his shoulders.

But there. *There.* Just beyond… just that little bit further, on the other side of the square… so close, so far, and everything else in between—

Navara.

Clarity snapped back, all else blurred but Her. She stood there, watching him, her look unreadable. A goddess among the mortals, not one eye upon Her but his.

Death walked among them and not a single soul noticed.

Silk and sinew. Chainmail and scale. She was the darkness in the light, a walker of worlds, singer of judgement. The bustle of the world passed Her by, all spirits led to Her doorstep.

And yet She lingered there, gaze locked to his, not a glimmer of hope or harm to sweep him away.

No circlet adorned her head. No staff stood in her hand. Just that beautiful white silk on her dark golden-brown skin, the shimmer as vibrant as the shine of the gold chainmail patches keeping her gown in one piece. Short, tight curls framed her face, as black as the night he might never see again. Where She walked, souls followed, with or without the weight of flesh to be dragged around. And his soul… it had been dragged, battered, and quartered for long enough, waiting for the choosing.

Goddess, please be kind… Grant me peace. Lead me to the altar of justice…

Darkness took him, slamming down, bruising with such excruciating intensity. A torment like no other.

His heart squeezed inside his chest, breaths yanked from his lungs—and falling. He was falling into the unknown without so much as a goodbye. Without a thought to landing. With only love on his cracked lips, slipping alone into the void without a prayer of returning…

Chapter Sixteen

Tash was unconscious, his skin blistered from the sun.

The sight twisted everything in Mayr's gut worse than any illness. Guilt berated him for calling Divinity Claim. Had it truly been more merciful than stoning? Three days of being tied to the flag pole without water, food, or coverings had done as much damage to Tash's body as the attack on the road. Even from where he stood at the end of the marketplace, Mayr noted the red burn on Tash's face and his sunken eyes. Earlier that morning, Tash had complained to Allaysia about the ache in his head, claiming his eyesight was dim and blurry. His limbs were numb, and he had wondered if they were still attached or if the guards had lopped things off during one of his dizzy spells. Then he had called Allaysia by her mother's name and insisted he tell her a story that became a chaotic combination of five different tales twisted into nonsense by delirium.

Tash needed water and quickly.

Mayr followed Kilienn and Allaysia through the square. He ignored the stares of the villagers as he led Hetlan and Kilienn's grey horse, Sorna, by the reins, the cart rolling behind them. On the other side of Hetlan and Sorna walked Tissie, the blonde girl who had alerted Tash's family on the day of the confession. Only seventeen, she was an apprentice seamstress and daughter of Allaysia's best friend. Although she found Tash's punishment difficult to stomach, Tissie insisted she help take Tash home to be healed.

Galosa met them at the dais. With a nod, he confirmed the punishment was complete. After the sweep of his hands, the four soldiers guarding Tash left their posts and crossed the square.

"The coward is released to you," Galosa said. "I suggest you stop by the Temple of the Four and thank the priestesses who supported your Claim. They certainly know how to persuade." The corners of his lips twitched as he sneered at Mayr. "You're lucky I believe in following the law. I still think the stoning was more appropriate. However, the majority spoke and, apparently, so has Navara. Remove him from our sight. He smells disgusting." He flicked his wrist and walked away.

Unable to look away from Tash, Mayr neared his still body, daring to touch Tash's dry, gritty skin.

Under his fingers, the muscles in Tash's arm launched into spasms.

Mayr jerked back and lifted Tash's chin to study his chapped lips and closed eyes. *Wake up and look at me, just once,* he begged. *Or say something. Call me an ass. Say you hate me. Just talk to me. Anything's better than this. You haven't said a word since I said I loved...*

He bit his cheek and lowered Tash's head gently before joining Kilienn's struggle to cut the tightly knotted ropes bound around Tash. What was he thinking? For three days, he had visited Tash. Talked to him and waited for a response that never came. The days and nights had crawled by, most of Mayr's time spent watching Tash when not with Tash's family, wishing they could go back to how they were before the trial. *But we won't, will we? If it's not about this damned punishment, it's about what I said when I was ranting at you. Why did I have to say anything at all? Why did my temper have to go and spoil it?*

"Here," a man said, approaching from Mayr's right.

Mayr stiffened at the deep voice. His grip tightened around his knife. He flicked his glance to Ress, eyes narrowed at the weapon in Ress's hand. Hissing, he swiped his knife at Ress, prepared to ram the blade through Ress's worn, brown tunic on the way to his gut.

"Relax." Ress stopped, leaving a foot of space between them, and twirled his serrated knife. "If I wanted to kill him, he'd already be dead." He tapped the tip of the knife to the ropes around Tash's back. "When these come off, he's going to fall hard and fast. Why don't you just focus on catching him, huh?"

Before Mayr could answer, Ress sawed the ropes. Portions of rope snapped and Tash's body sagged forward. Mayr sheathed his knife and motioned for Kilienn to do the same. They grabbed Tash, hands on his shoulders and waist. As the ropes split completely, Tash collapsed. Mayr and Kilienn hoisted his dead weight.

Silent and quick, Ress slipped around Mayr to help Allaysia guide Tash into the cart. The moment Tash's body lay on the pile of hay and blankets, Tissie kneeled over him from where she waited in the corner to cover his face with wet cloths. Attempts to rouse him or get him to swallow water failed. The best they could do was take him home to Parase, who waited with everything they needed to heal him.

The ride to the house was mostly silent, save the noises from squeaking wheels and the horse harnesses. Allaysia, Mayr, and Tissie sat in the back of the cart, arranged carefully around Tash's blanketed body. Kilienn drove with Ress at his side.

Mayr cupped Tash's cheek and frowned at the moist rag beneath his palm. The cloth was hot and seemed to make no difference given the little water Tash's skin took from it. No wonder he had mistook Allaysia for Parase: his body struggled to cope with whatever it had left. *Thanks to me. Because I thought I was smart. Because I thought I was helping. I may as well have thrown a stone at his head for all the good it's done.*

There was no holding back the sigh that dragged Mayr's regret down with it. He had wanted to save Tash from the brutality of a punishment that had long since outstayed its welcome, but people loved to see the worst dead for their crimes, and the Shar-denn was far from deserving anything kinder. He had spoken against the matter before, not that the High Council listened to him. He was not of any particular worth to Council, and Severn preferred having all sorts of options available when it came to justice. She likely would have seen little reason to stop Tash's stoning, even if Mayr begged Aeley into petitioning High Council to outlaw the act completely—which he fully intended to do once he returned home. For all he knew, Severn would punish him for interfering, his rank handed off to Pellon.

So let her. Mayr tucked Tash's hair behind his ear, fingertips lingering along Tash's neck. *You're alive—that matters more. And if we can keep you that way, I'll spend the rest of my life making it up to you.*

Assuming Tash let him.

Mayr bit back another sigh. He had gone back on his word, stuck both feet in his mouth, and rolled his ass down the hill of really bad reactions. Tash's silence had only confirmed as much. What came from that...

He had a lifetime of apologies to make, if only Tash could live long enough to hear them.

They reached the house not long after. Parase met them in the front doorway, a thin, wet towel in her grasp. The home was built in a small lot, resembling the dozen others built closely around it in rows. The single-level house consisted of worn black wood and white stone with bright yellow window shutters and flower boxes filled with orange flowers. Behind the house, in the back of the lot, was a simple two-stall stable where Sorna lived.

Parase ushered them into the house. Kilienn and Mayr carried Tash through the front foyer and brightly lit sitting room to a small room in the back corner of the house—the same room that had been Tash's as a boy. Inside, the bed was made with several blankets and pillows. A lavishly decorated table had been brought in from the sitting room and placed near the bed with bowls of oils, water, and herbs on top. Clean bandages and cloths sat beside them. Two buckets of water sat on the floor beside the table, the handle of a wooden ladle sticking out from one of them.

"Get out." Parase shooed everyone out of the room except for Kilienn, using the white apron over her green dress to emphasize her command. "We'll holler when we need you. Now *out!*"

"Leave his bracers," Mayr called back, staggering into the hallway behind Allaysia, Tissie, and Ress. "Please. Do whatever you want with the rest, but leave those. They're important to—"

The dark door slammed closed. He swallowed hard and hoped they listened to him. The request was the least he could do; the last shred of Tash's dignity he could salvage after destroying the rest. *Forgive me.*

Slowly turning his head, Mayr met Ress's gaze. He had questions.

"Yeah, I know." Ress gestured with his chin behind him. "Let's talk somewhere that's not here." He eyed Allaysia and Tissie, his expression thickened with concern. "We'll give Ally and Tissie some space."

Allaysia waved her hand and tread through the hallway. "It's fine. I'll just be in the kitchen, getting some things, calming my nerves. Trying to justify not kicking Galosa where it hurts most. Play nice," she commanded over her shoulder, her voice weary.

Tissie shrugged. "I need to be getting on anyway. I'll be back later." She followed Allaysia and disappeared into another corridor towards the back door.

"Makes that easy. Come on." Ress limped through the rooms, leading Mayr to the front foyer. His wrinkled, dingy clothes seemed out of place in the prim, elegantly decorated home. "Go on, get it out." He faced Mayr, crossing his arms. As his sleeve rose and revealed his gang mark, he glanced at it with a smirk. "Really riles you, doesn't it? You'd probably like to burn it. My arm, too, I'd wager."

Mayr dug his fists into the crooks of his arms. "Your arm. Your head. Considering I've never been one for hard criminals and killers, I'll take whatever I can get."

"And yet you're sleeping with one." Snorting, Ress looked away. "Nice to know where your standards are."

Teeth grinding, Mayr imagined the numerous ways he could break Ress's bones. Then he imagined the words used to kick him out of the house if they fought. Tash's family considered Ress a friend, not an enemy. No matter his opinion, he could not overstep the boundaries of their hospitality. "You know *nothing* about me. You certainly don't know him, not anymore. You don't get to talk about him. You get to shut up. Or I'll be dragging you back to Aeley in chains. She'd *love* to have one of you begging for mercy."

Ress laughed, his eyes gleaming with amusement. "Aww, come on. You can do better than that. Besides, what's she going to do that Council hasn't already done?" One of his brows arched. "You know they own me, right? I'm a dirty hand they conveniently forget to wash. Mess with me and there's going to be a couple of angry hunters after you." He sobered, his laughter dying between them. "You've got a point, though. I don't know Taldris, not like I used to. We can't go back. I don't even know if we can go forward. We're as good as ghosts."

"Why are you even here?"

"Because I'm gagging on nostalgia." Ress stared at the floor, his fingers curling as he hunched forward, drawing into himself. "I did some talking while he was tied up. Spoke to one of my contacts that also knows you. K said Taldris is an absolute fool for confessing, especially since tiny, little, annoying law birds are saying the Council's considering granting him a full pardon. She also said this is some priest thing. She said it's a big deal. She said *you* said it's a big deal to him, big enough to get himself killed. She doesn't understand it, and neither do I, but it got me thinking." He sighed. "I've got my own scores to settle with the Goddesses, but if They can find a way to forgive him, maybe I can, too. And maybe the Four can forgive *me* for being foolish beyond measure."

Mayr scowled and shifted his feet. "I'm supposed to believe this? You made your opinion of him clear after the confession."

"What? I'm not allowed to change my mind?" Ress motioned to the door behind him. "I was angry. He left us behind—*all* of us, including me, his best friend. We were like family, and he just left." He held his arms out wide. "The next thing I know, several of us are being arrested. Hauled around in cuffs and thrown to our knees, told to *choose* between serving the Council and ragging out everyone we knew in the Shar *or* life imprisonment with no kindness whatsoever. Wasn't long after I found out who gave the hunters our names. I haven't been able to think of Taldris without wanting to rip his spine out through his nose. So I'm not sorry if the thought of tying his intestines around his throat was my initial reaction."

Ress shook his head, huffing. "But I'm not too stubborn to see what's in front of me. I saw how much it killed him to admit to everything. And here's news for you: we weren't happy. None of us were. We gave the Shar-denn our souls and they tore into us until we couldn't recognize ourselves. I know that. I *lived* that. He did what the rest of us were too scared to do. He got away with it, the lucky bastard. He got a new life. I can't help but hate and admire him all at the same time. Can't say I forgive him for stranding us and turning us in, but would I have done the same? Maybe." He pounded his fist on his injured leg. "If it wasn't for this, I could've."

"So now what?" Mayr tilted his head, interested in how Ress's expression changed from disgust to annoyance to what resembled self-loathing.

"I leave and let you deal with him," Ress replied, gripping the door handle. "I don't know where he and I sit. We might talk one day. Maybe." He shrugged and caressed the silver handle. "All I know is that whatever happens, I was *never* here. Inesta would have a fit if she knew. She never got over him breaking her heart."

"Right. From what I understand, he had help getting there."

"Yeah, well…" Opening the door, Ress cast Mayr a knowing glance before stepping outside. "Just take care of him. And don't pass this around. It's bad enough I've been caught for my part in things. Now I have hunters telling me when to swallow and choke." He studied the other houses, lingering on the open spaces between them. "Steer him clear of Inesta. She's out for blood, worse than any boss I've known. She's already taken her fill of mine, straightening me out. He doesn't need that." His gaze slid towards Mayr. "Just get him home. Tell him I said to walk safe, breathe deep, and seize life. The bastard's earned it."

The door pulled shut and clicked. Eyes closed, Mayr tried to drown his thoughts in the soft noise of Allaysia's heels on the kitchen floor. What had Tash really earned? What would the ride home be like? If the last three days were any indication, the future was no better than the punishment.

Mayr pushed off the door and wandered to the kitchen. Allaysia leaned against the table in the middle of the room, staring blankly through the open window above the washbasin, steam rising from the wooden cup in her hands. Silent, Mayr sank into one of the chairs at the table. Laying his head on his folded arms, he teased out the muffled sounds of Parase and Kilienn in Tash's room. He was tired but could not sleep. He hurt inside but could not soothe the pain. Not while Tash lay unconscious, the price for Mayr's foolish attempt to save him. After three days of staying awake to witness Tash's surrender to the elements and the cruelty of mortality, Mayr wanted nothing more than to hear Tash say it was meant to be. That Mayr was forgiven for his interference. That he was forgiven for caring too much. That it changed nothing between them.

Who am I kidding?

"You did him good," Allaysia said, startling Mayr. "You did what we couldn't."

As Mayr lifted his head and considered his response, the door to Tash's bedroom opened and heels clicked across the floor. Parase hustled into the kitchen, wiping her hands on the apron balled in her hands. She tossed the apron into the fire inside the hearth on the other side of the room. Flames devoured the white fabric in an instant, growing high and warm.

Parase snatched a towel from the rack above the hearth and turned towards Allaysia and Mayr. "You two can keep him company; keep bringing his fever down. I've got broth to make, not to mention something for us later." She snapped the towel at them. "Go on! Keep talking to him. That's what the healer said. Give him someone to wake to. Everything you need is in there. Your father will bring more water from the well."

Not to be told again, Allaysia and Mayr hurried to Tash's room, passing Kilienn on the way. In Kilienn's hands was a ragged wicker basket filled with Tash's soiled, torn clothes.

"I'm burning these and finding new ones," Kilienn explained, stopped in the middle of the hallway. "Left his bracers, though, since you asked and I noticed he was protective of them. Figured he didn't want to lose them for whatever reason."

Mayr breathed out as Kilienn continued down the hallway. "Thanks," he said, bombarded by the thick scent of herbs and incense. From the doorway, he gazed at Tash. Stripped and bathed, Tash lay under thin blankets, which were pinned to his sides by his arms. Rope burns crisscrossed down his arms and across the leather of his bracers. His face was still red and dry, though better than it had been. At least he looked more comfortable, though his chest still rose and fell rapidly.

Overcome with the memory of the first trial, Mayr fought the urge to hold Tash. *He probably wouldn't be happy to wake up with me all over him, not this time.* Instead, he sat on the stool on the side of the bed opposite Allaysia, who perched on the edge of a chair, dabbing Tash's forehead and cheeks with a wet cloth. When Mayr rolled his sleeves up, Allaysia offered him another cloth.

"His neck," she told him, pointing. "Shoulders, arms, chest. Whatever you want." Allaysia cupped Tash's cheek. "Anything to help Little Bird fly back home."

"Can I ask you something?" Mayr dipped the cloth into the bucket beside his stool and wrung it out partially. He drew the cool cloth down Tash's cheek and curved it around the back of his neck, disturbed by the intense heat emanating from Tash's skin. "Why 'Little Bird'?"

Allaysia blinked. "Because his name's Halataldris."

"No, I know that. But why the name at all?"

"He hasn't explained it?" Allaysia pursed her lips and laid the cloth over Tash's eyes. "That's a shame. It's one of my favourite stories. He always said it was one of his, too." She smiled, tracing Tash's jaw with her fingertip. "During the time our mother was pregnant with him, she kept hearing a little boy singing. In the morning, in the middle of the day, at night—wherever and whenever, and always without warning. 'Such a sweet voice,' she'd say, 'so high and sweet like a bird; so warming like a lullaby.' Except whenever she looked, no one was ever there."

Allaysia soaked a new cloth in the bucket beside her. "It reminded her of the old stories, of Emeraliss and the first of all birds, who was Emeraliss's protector and guardian just as much as he was her companion. Then when Mother saw how blue her baby's eyes were, she knew it was meant to be. She named him Halataldris, born from love; gifted with freedom. Our little bird." She held the cloth to Tash's cheek, biting her lip. "Of course, we never expected him to…"

She cleared her throat and focused on sweeping the cloth across Tash's face and down his neck.

Mayr wet his cloth again. He had too many things to ask, none of them what Allaysia would want to hear. Still, he needed to ask them. The truth needed to be said. The questions would never be asked if it were left to Tash. Someone had to do it.

"Why did you never look for him?" he asked, laying the sopping cloth above the one already over Tash's eyes and nose.

Her breath caught, and she stilled. "Is that what he thinks? That we just abandoned him like he did us?" Allaysia struggled to look Mayr in the eye. Tears started down her cheeks. "Is that honestly how he feels about us?"

A loud sob escaped her. Her hand hovered above Tash's shoulder. "I looked for him. I *did*. I looked as hard as I could with what we could spare." Allaysia clasped Tash's arm. "He forbade us to search for him, but I did it anyway. He's my little brother. I didn't want to lose him. I couldn't. But—" She inhaled sharply, taking Tash's hand in both of hers. Head bowed, she caressed his fingers. "But when I kept coming up with nothing, we took it as a sign. He'd either meant what he said—that we should never see him—or someone had killed him. I—I couldn't bear the thought of him as a corpse and neither could Mother and Father. We were disappointed, disheartened. My parents commanded me to stop. Father told me to accept our Little Bird had flown the nest completely and forever."

Allaysia leaned into Tash and stroked his hair, still holding his hand. "And you did. You fled, Little Bird, so far, so high, so many worlds away into the storm where we couldn't follow. All alone and so much more fragile than you realize you are."

"No," Mayr murmured, "he realizes it. He just forces his way through it. He has no one to make him stop."

"No one except you."

The words haunted Mayr as he stared at his hands, his fingers wrung together. He wanted Allaysia to be right. There were too many things he wanted to do for Tash—things Tash needed even if he never said as much. Things Tash would not accept without a fight, especially if they went against the ways of the priesthood. Were the Four even worth the trouble? Would Tash's sacrifices amount to anything good? Where was the Goddess of Love when She was needed most?

"There's something else. Things Taldris should know," Allaysia muttered. "The fact we stayed out of his business with the Shar-denn is one of the only things that's saved us. Yes, we were hurt after he left. They attacked us, our house, our shop, and we begged them to leave us alone, but Ress stopped it. He bought us our safety. I don't know how, but he did. We owe our limbs, our faces, our every breath to him," she said softly, a caring warmth seeping into her tone. "After that, the Shar-denn never touched us again, and we've kept to our own. 'Head down, eyes low,' as they say. They attacked the village but left us to him. He's our safe place. Inesta, too. He married her and they've never touched her." She laid her hand on Tash's chest. "Whatever you think of Ress, know he's done what he could. Little Bird needs to know that. His friend never stopped being family." Her brow furrowed with her frown. "Just don't tell him until he's recovered."

Mayr nodded, saying little as they continued to dampen Tash's skin and nurse the fever. Time passed quickly, even with the strained conversations and Allaysia's occasional sniffle. When the door opened and Parase stuck her head into the room to announce dinner, Mayr peered out the window, surprised to find the thin threads of sunset laced across the sky.

"Coming?" Allaysia asked, joining her mother in the doorway.

"I'll be there shortly." Mayr glanced at Tash's face. "I just need to..." The rest of the words lodged in his throat. He needed many things, none of them what he should feel, want, or have.

Parase closed the door. In the silence, Mayr listened to Tash's slowed breaths. Even Tash's heart had found a relaxed pace. His skin looked better.

"I'm sorry I interfered," Mayr said, gliding his fingertips down Tash's cheek. "But I'm not sorry I tried to stop them. You deserve better, even if you don't believe it."

Tash breathed deep. His eyelids fluttered, eyes moving rapidly beneath them. As his lips parted, Tash opened his eyes and fought to focus. Confusion flashed across his face.

Mayr jumped to his feet, knocking over the stool. He wanted to say a hundred things, all of them at the same time. "Stay there. Don't do anything. I'll get your mother. We need to get you to drink—"

"Wai—" Tash caught Mayr's hand. "Why?" he demanded hoarsely, his dry voice cracking. "You. This. Why?"

What can I possibly tell you that won't make this worse? Mayr bit the inside of his cheek, stuck on the words he wanted to say. There was such a thing as too much truth. "It wasn't right or fair," he replied finally. "It certainly wasn't just." He tried to pry his hand from Tash's. "I wasn't going to let any friend of mine go through that."

"No." Tash clutched Mayr's fingers tighter. "*Why* did *you*? Real reason. No lie."

"Because." Mayr righted the stool and sat down. Holding Tash's hand to his chest, he stroked Tash's head, more to comfort himself than anything. He did not doubt Tash's stubbornness, even in his current state. But after Tash ignoring him, being hounded for honesty was a blessing. A gift he would cherish no matter how much it hurt. "Because… I'm in love with you." His gaze locked onto Tash's. "I've had time to think about it. All this time, I thought what I was feeling was just infatuation. I thought it would go away, but it never did. It just got deeper. The thought of you dying… I couldn't let them do it."

Tash stared at Mayr. A single tear slipped from his eye before he turned his face away.

"We'll be home soon," Mayr assured him, wiping away the tear. He could imagine the pain Tash was in, emotionally and physically. The experience was worthy of more than one tear. *Then to hear me saying this—it's a wonder he can stand being awake at all.* "Just a few days then we'll go and you'll be safe. Just a little while longer and I'll take you home. It'll be over soon, as if it never happened."

Chapter Seventeen

For the first time, being in a temple gave Mayr peace and happiness. Mostly because once he left, he would go home, a place where he was wanted and appreciated.

The strained words and lonely silence from Tash were driving him straight into exasperation.

They had stayed with Tash's family for five more days after Tash first woke to give him a chance to heal and make amends. Mayr had lost count of the number of times Tash apologized to his parents and sister. Each time, they embraced him, drawing him further back into their family. By the time he left, Tash promised not to run from them again. He would check on them and they could see him, he said, his promise bound when he swore on the names of the Four. His soft-spoken words had drawn smiles and joyful tears from Parase and Allaysia while Kilienn had struggled to release Tash from a tight hug. Love bound the four of them, and they did nothing to hide it.

Love Mayr wished Tash would show him.

They were still distant and tense, similar to the day they had traveled to Araveena Ford. The trip home to Dahena had been just as awkward, even though Tash no longer ignored Mayr completely.

At least he's talking to me, even if they aren't great conversations. Still, he's trying not to say something. It's the same damn game he was playing at my parents', except this time, he's barely looking at me at all. Would you just own up to it, already? Yell, curse. Fine, you didn't want to look bad in front of your parents. So go ahead, rip into me. Tell me I messed things up. Be honest. Stop making me guess why I'm the bad guy. You're welcome for saving your life, by the way. Guess that makes me a really bad guy, doesn't it? Mayr sighed and leaned against the doorframe of Tash's room. Behind him, priests shuffled through the hallway, immersed in a discussion about evening prayer.

Tash tossed his pack onto his bed. He still wore the light blue shirt and black pants his father had given him. Shoulders hunched, he pushed the short white candles on the bedside table across the tabletop with one finger, slowly and without a pattern, appearing lost in thought.

"Do you miss them already?" Mayr crossed his arms. "They really do love you. That sister of yours—Tara and her could do damage to the world if they were in the same room."

"What?" Tash peered over his shoulder, brows drawn together over his dulled eyes.

"Nothing," Mayr muttered. He straightened and glanced down the hall. "I'm just going to go. Aeley's—"

"Close the door."

"Sorry?"

"Close the door. We need to talk."

And here it is. Mayr entered the room and shut the door behind him. "Yeah, we do. This whole time, you've been acting like it's my fault. Like I'm the one who—"

Tash whirled around, his expression dark. "It's over." A cascade of emotions played across his face, none of them happy. "*We're* over, for good. We can't see each other again. Never again. Never."

A breath caught in Mayr's throat, choking back every other response. His mind reeled, the words hitting him harder than any assault. "What?"

"We can't be near each other ever again." Tash buried his fists in the crooks of his arms then unfurled them before curling them again. He moved back and rocked on his heels. "We can't see each other. We can't be in the same space. We have to end this. Here. Never again, Mayr. I should've never gotten you into this. I should've just left you alone. I should've—" His voice broke. Pain flashed across his face before he turned towards the bedside table and hung his head.

Mayr watched Tash's back. Words failed him. His thoughts spun twisted threads of nonsense. "I don't understand."

"Why?" Tash asked quietly. "Why you? Why now?" He faced Mayr, blinking as though battling tears. "Why not years ago, when I could've done something about it?"

"About *what*? What is this?" Mayr stepped forward, raising one arm angrily. "First we're over, but still friends. *Then* you call me here to make you feel better, which I did. Then you go off, insisting on doing something I think is *completely* ludicrous. And *now* we can't see each other? After everything, after what just happened, you're kicking me out of your life just like that? You were going to *die*, Tash. *Die!* So I stopped them. I couldn't just let you—"

"You think this is about *that*?" With a bitter laugh, Tash knocked against the bedside table. "Meanwhile my world is falling apart." He glared at Mayr. "I told you we couldn't fall for each other. I *told* you we couldn't have anything beyond casual intimacy. But I was a fool. I felt it taunting me, and still..." His jaw quivered as he stared at the bed. "Then you went and said the words, and I... What I feel... I can't want it. We can't carry on. It has to end completely, you and me, right here."

Realization washed over Mayr, anger blazing in on its heels.

His damned feelings—his damned heart. He should have known they would be used against him. Just like they always were.

You bastard.

"So wait, *I* say I love you and *you* decide we can't see each other *at all*? What kind of response is that?" Mayr yelled. "Is this *my* punishment for breaking the rules? It's not easy being on this side of it, you know. I didn't exactly plan it. But, hey, I was going to swallow it down and live with it, willing to be friends because it was better than nothing. Losing you completely was worse. Now I find out you don't really care at all, do you?"

"I *do* care," Tash argued, "and that's why it's a problem. I thought the same, too—that seeing you was better than nothing—but that's how we've ended up here." His gaze remained downcast. "It's unfair to continue. I can't do it. I just can't." He shook his head. "I never should have turned to you, no matter how badly I hurt. I never should have sent for you. I wasn't thinking, just acting on my own desires, and that was wrong. I need to do what I should have done fully: I release you."

Mayr snorted. "There you go, doing what everyone else does. Justifying your actions with lies. You like truth, right? Try this: I gave, you took, and you're getting rid of me because I'm no good. Or is it that I'm not man enough to put up with—"

"It's the truth!" Tash rushed towards Mayr and stopped, a foot of space between them. Tears wet his eyes. "I'd love nothing more than to throw you on Emeraliss's altar and make love to you for days and tell you everything I feel, but I *can't*. The last trial is tomorrow. If I fail, I die. If I succeed, I'm an Uldana and alone. The *only* exception is if I'm chosen as a consort during the Feast of

Emeraliss. That's it. I'm as good as dead as far as our relationship's concerned, no matter what I want for us. No matter how much I want you."

Of all the words, Mayr focused on one alone. He would work out the sentiments later. "What do you mean if you fail, you die?"

Tash looked away. "The trial requires us to be put into a sort of trance. To do that, the priests use poison from the menadet plant. To see the faces of the Four, we must journey to the precipice between life and death. We have to overcome the effects to prove ourselves. We have to fight."

"*Are you all out of your minds?*" Mayr shouted, falling back. "That plant kills half of the people who take it—*at least* half!"

"That's the point. It's a spiritual test."

"So you're going to kill yourself? Nice spiritual test!" Mayr kicked the door. He kicked it again, harder. Tash was willing to commit suicide just to see if he could beat it. To prove whatever he believed it would to goddesses who would not care. For good measure, Mayr kicked the door a third time.

Tash wrapped his arms around Mayr's shoulders. "Shh, Mayr, stop." He buried his face in Mayr's hair. "It's the other reason why I was having only casual relationships. But now I'm in love with you," he whispered, "and it's breaking both of us. I knew I should've pushed you away before the Trials started, but I couldn't stand the thought of letting the days go by without having something with you. I was lying to myself, ignoring the truth. Now we're paying the price."

As Mayr tried to kick the door again, Tash's embrace tightened, and he pressed his cheek against Mayr's shoulder. "I don't deserve you. I don't deserve anyone. Love is precious. Fragile. So is someone who'll stay with me. But I can't have either, not after what I've done. It's just as well I do this—at least I'll have a purpose in being alone. It'll be worth something. I'll be forced to let go. It'll consume my life and keep me from falling into everything else. I need that. I can't keep doing what I've been doing. If I'm an Uldana, I'll be too busy to think about anything else other than being a priest."

"But—"

"Absolution, Mayr." Tash spun Mayr around and grasped his shoulders. "You asked me before why I was going through the Trials, and the answer is absolution. The price of it is not having anyone. The price is you. It's lose-lose for me, but I have to accept it. I have to surrender to faith. It's the only way I'll ever obtain forgiveness for everything I've done. You heard what I did, and it's too much. Too much shame and guilt. Too much remorse. I don't want to put that on your shoulders. This is my path, where I've been going all along." He drew his fingers down Mayr's cheek, smiling sadly. "If I'm going to have a broken heart, at least I can find redemption and be useful, then share it with others who need it."

Tash sighed and stepped back. "I didn't mean to fall for you; I didn't mean to break my own rule. Something about you was trustworthy, strong. Secure. You eased the pain. Made me believe my heart could be safe with you. But I can't do it. Not just because of the Trials, but because I'm pretty sure this is just temporary. It wouldn't last, Mayr, even without the Trials. You'd leave anyway. Everyone leaves me. You'd decide it isn't what you want and find someone who actually deserves you."

"And that's a foolish assumption." Mayr sneered. "Don't you *ever* tell me what I would or wouldn't do. You're the *last* person who should be saying that, not after what we just went through."

Growling, Mayr closed the space between them until he stood close enough to feel Tash's breath on his lips. "You want to talk about selfish desires and thinking only about yourself? Let's discuss your reasons for nearly getting yourself killed. Then let's discuss your obsession with absolution. Because I don't care if you load shame and guilt on me—go ahead, try me. I've dealt with my own long enough to consider them my best friends. So add to it. Go on."

Mayr cupped his hand around the back of Tash's neck. "You want to talk about deserving? *I* deserve the chance to deal with things in my own way without anyone deciding what I can and can't do. And what I *can* do is find a way to alleviate the shame. I *can* bear the load of guilt, mine *and* yours. I stood up for you in Araveena, and I'll always defend you. I've *never* demanded you prove yourself. I'll take you just as you are. You're worth something to me, no matter what anyone thinks of you, including yourself. You have from the first night we met." He flattened his hand on Tash's chest to feel his racing heartbeat. "Tell me what you want more: love or to kill yourself slowly? If you care that much for me, why don't you pull out of the Trials and stay at the Rese level? Or stop being a priest altogether? There's nothing that says you can't do good elsewhere. I'm part of Aeley's family—I can get you anything you want."

"I can't. I promised." Tash backed away. "You know what it's like being obligated by oath. I swore to the Four it's what I'd do if They saved me from what I was—if They'd grant me salvation from the Shar-denn."

When Mayr took a step forward, Tash held his hands before him. "No. I bargained, Mayr. I used to plead and beg, day after day, before anyone woke up. It was just me and our family altar, every morning, after I'd spent my nights elsewhere doing awful things. I swore I'd dedicate my life to the Four if They'd save me. And They did. They granted me freedom. So now I have to see those promises through. I can't walk away. Otherwise it'd be more guilt, and I *can't take anymore*. I've ruined too many lives. I'm only alive by the grace of the Four, I know it, and this is the only way to get out from everything suffocating me. I need this as much as I need you."

With several more steps, Tash backed against the window. Lips parted, his gaze fell to the floor. He turned and leaned against the windowsill. "I can't run from it. If I break these oaths, I'll spiral down and drag you with me. I'll regret it forever. Then I'll resent you. I'll hate myself. All of the good I've managed to do will go bad—and that's assuming I live."

Tash held his head in his hands. "No matter my choice, I lose, either love or myself. The fact you're willing to take it on… I *have* to break us up. This last trial made me realize you might be the one person I'll *never* deserve, no matter what I do. And I'm terrified. I can't have you. You're the right one at the wrong time. I *have* to break your heart. And mine."

"So that's it." Mayr grimaced as his voice cracked. He hated his emotions. He hated feeling this mess. He hated seeing it. And he certainly as anything wanted to stop hearing another damned word. After years of being miserable, there was no reprieve. Just when he thought he had found someone who understood him, who saw past the trappings of his position, reality battered him.

"Yes." Tash continued to stare at his hands, wringing his fingers together.

"Fine. You want me out of your life?" Mayr opened the door and backed into the corridor. "I'm out."

Unable to meet the surprised stares of two young priestesses as they passed him, Mayr forced his legs to move him through the hallway. He battled the urge to punch and kick the walls, the conversation repeating in his mind. *At the end of it, you're just like everyone else. Tell me again you don't want to take me down with you, because that's another big lie. You already have.*

Chapter Eighteen

Someone might as well have given Tash a whole trunk of matches with all the damage he was feeling.

The fire raging inside him… there was no putting it out with water or sand, not when words and honesty fanned the flames higher, bigger, giving them depth and the infinite space to burn. It was ugly and destructive, no less terrifying than an all-devouring beast that threatened to take everything down with it. No mercy. No compassion. Nothing to lose, only take. And Goddesses, he had an entire world available for the taking, vulnerable to the very last breath.

One truth and he had sent it all shattering on the ground, the glass of perfect imagery digging into his skin and tearing him to pieces.

Drawing a shaky hand across his lips, Tash shifted on his knees before sitting on the stone floor completely, his naked back pressed against his bed, a half-empty bottle of wine beside him with the sharpest knife he had. No candlelight touched his room, only dim moonlight, silver-white as it poured across the white marble. White curtains danced in the cool breeze, the draft creeping over his bare feet and up his ankles, the light, silky fabric of his white sleep pants doing nothing to keep him warm.

He was cold, inside and out, as loathing burned so hot he would have given his life just to escape it.

And over there... where it began...

He could barely make himself look at the door; the same door Mayr had stormed out of earlier that day, leaving Tash behind. Angrily. So angrily, the harsh noise of Mayr's heels through the hallway still taunted Tash, counting the moments before agony exploded in his chest and destroyed what remained of him.

His world was falling apart all over again. Crumbled to ashes and dust in one beautiful sentiment the truth just *had* to ruin.

Mayr loved him.

So I broke him.

Hot tears cascaded down his face again, wetting his cheeks for the umpteenth time—the souvenir of doing the right thing.

The trial in Araveena had hurt badly enough, his fear well-founded and thrown back in his face as surely as the villagers had wanted to stone him. The fact he was still alive was all the more shocking: he had expected his body to be given to his family after the trial was completed, his soul wandering into the Realm of the Dead with a great deal of apologies to make.

But Mayr…

Mayr had broken his promise then crushed Tash's heart into a devastated ball of nothingness, too broken to say *I love you* back.

Such beautiful words… such a painful death.

Their relationship had died for him at that moment. Tied to the flag post with Mayr yelling at him, the illusion of what they could never have shriveled to scraped bits in front of him, diminished and stripped down to grief. Hearing him say it again while Tash recovered had been worse than dying alone in the heat. It would have been a kinder fate for Mayr to have stabbed him in the heart a dozen times before walking away, leaving Tash to take the loss with him instead of tearing Mayr's heart to shreds.

Tash had willingly played with that fire, stoked it more than he should have, and flirted with it right up to the very edge of danger. But in the end, both of them suffered, the peace in their love brought to its knees and executed without a proper goodbye.

They needed to move on—*he* needed to move on. To follow through on his promise to the Four.

If only he could.

He was failing. Falling. Dying. After the emptiness he had spent a lifetime trying to do something about had finally gone away. After that unshakeable feeling he had been searching for Mayr forever had taken root and blossomed without him realizing it.

All of it gone, replaced with Mayr's hatred of him.

That called for a drink, running his lover off in record time.

Holding the bottle tight, Tash drank down the wine until he needed to take a breath, the bitterness no replacement for the unforgiving burn of harder alcohol. He wanted to *hurt*. Really, truly hurt. More than he had in a long time.

Manipulation. Games. Lies. He had done them all before and paid the price. But this…

Had he manipulated Mayr? Manipulated their relationship to temper his fears of the Trials? He never should have kept Mayr around.

But his comfort… Tash had needed that gentle support. Whenever the hurt had become too much to handle on his own, Tash had needed Mayr to get through it. And with the knowledge that the last two trials were likely to kill him, Tash had fully intended on suffering through them silently, pushing Mayr to the edge of Tash's life before leaving him completely.

He had never wanted to tell Mayr about the lethal part of the Trials. Tash would have done them alone if not for knowing Mayr or the calm he brought to Tash's soul. He *should* have kept the truth to himself, letting Mayr live in ignorance. Had he, Mayr would have heard about the damage well after the fact and been spared the extra worry. Mayr might have grieved for Tash if death had come to pass, but Mayr would have dealt with it and moved on.

Instead, Tash had dragged Mayr along with him, whatever protection he wanted to offer thrown aside and left to rot.

There was no going back. No way to salvage what had been. There was only one path he could walk, and it meant paying back the Goddesses for the second chance at life They had granted him. He owed Them his promise, and there was nothing brave in walking away from it. If anyone argued otherwise, he would argue right on back and defend his decision to the ends of his being. No one would stop him, not even himself. If anyone got in his way, he would push them aside. They were on his time now, so close to the end of the Trials. The fourth trial was his to go through by right. After surviving the first three trials and the deepening aches they wrought, he would not be deterred. He would not run. He would meet his end face to face, however it came, and damn the rest of the opinions around him. If anyone threatened his chance at redemption, he would fight them for it.

He could do this. *Would* do this. The Goddesses came first—They had to. Without Them, he would have been a corpse long discarded. There was no one else, no other calling but Their will and the duty he owed, paid for by the rest of his days.

Still, there was that awful feeling that roiled in his guts, that sense of finding the rest of himself only to lose everything he had saved from utter destruction. There was no running from it, no reasoning with it, no packing it away and pretending like it never existed. He was broken from heart to soul and back again, with the vast emptiness of a widening void swallowing him whole, pulling him into the abyss.

Tears still flowing, his cheeks burning from the never-ending onslaught, Tash set the wine down, the bottle mostly empty as it fell over and rolled back against the foot of the bed. His fingers snaked towards the hilt of the knife and clasped tight, dragging the blade into a familiar hold. He shivered as a gentle breeze played over his naked arms, the curtains kicked up in the gust, a waving white flag against the night. Their shadows danced in the moonlight, as sinister as the ghosts beckoning him into the loneliest depths of the life he had fought so hard for, only to find out how much like death it actually was.

Cutting Mayr out of him was all he had left. They could never be together. Never. But being without him was worse, and loss… Everywhere there was loss, no matter the choice Tash made. Someone had to lose.

Promises. He had made promises. He needed to live them. He needed… *needed*…

The tip of the blade hurt just as badly as he remembered it, but not nearly as much as crying out Mayr's name into a darkness that would never care.

And for every cut, there was another, just cutting, carving him out. Forcing. Forgetting...

Chapter Nineteen

The dining room looks better this way, all dark and empty and blurry and weird, Mayr decided, pain shooting down his spine as he craned his neck to the side and back to study the ceiling. The silhouettes of the beams wavered, lit by the faint yellow light from a torch in the hallway. He guzzled the last of the spiced ale from the metal decanter and wiped his lips on his sleeve. As he peered inside, he shook the decanter. *Empty.* He tossed the decanter behind him.

The decanter clanged on the floor. A shriek pierced the air, and small clawed feet scurried across the floor. Either the verrapossum hated metal or Mayr had almost taken its furry black head off.

"Sorry, little friend," Mayr apologized, grabbing the next decanter in the line next to him on the dining table. Meant to seat fourteen, the table supported his weight without protest. *Good table. Good choice, Korre. You always knew how to pick them.* He eyed the three chairs on the floor to his left, knocked over from when he had climbed onto the table. *Your chairs are a bit drunk, though.*

He sniffed the decanter. Berry mead from the previous summer's harvest—more Lira's drink than his. *Better than nothing.* Gripping the full decanter with both hands, he drank back the mead until it threatened to come back up with everything else he had consumed. *I hate this stuff.* Mayr thrust the decanter towards the verrapossum—at least where he thought it was. "You want it?"

Silence.

"Yeah, guess not. Doesn't go well with grass. Wait, no." Lips twisting, he stared at the red wall. "Dirt? Fruit? Little tiny wriggly things? Hey, what *do* you eat?" Mayr leaned over the edge of the table, wishing he could see the beady green eyes that could be looking back at him.

The table creaked. The floor swam in his vision. Dizziness nearly forced him over the edge.

He sat back and held out both arms until he steadied. "Never mind. I won't be doing that again. And you're welcome for the bread. It's not exactly stale, and Cook will hate me in the morning, but go ahead. Enjoy it. I would, but I can't taste much else but this filth." He giggled and hugged the decanter. "Can't feel much, either. That's a good thing because that whole feeling thing? Isn't worth it. Paralyzed and numb. Now those, those I can do."

After another swill from the decanter, Mayr slammed it down and lay back, banging his head on the table. Mead sloshed over the rim and coated his fingers. Sharp pain raced from the back of his head to the front. He groaned and slapped his forehead with his dry hand. When the pain subsided, he peeked between his fingers to watch the thin light flicker across the wood ceiling. It was not as entertaining as Orae's tavern, but it would do.

Especially since she had kicked him out.

And I thought she liked me, horrible, mean old woman. Here I need a friend, and she goes and kicks me out. "I mean, what is that? I wasn't doing anything." *No fights. Not even looking. Not even talking.* "She was making good money off me. Lots of money. Lots and lots and lots and lots. But they *knew*. All of them—all—they *knew*. They looked at me, like they knew I was thrown outside… aside… whatever that damn word is. They *knew*." Mayr pointed at the wall with a crooked finger. "But she said—she did—she said I couldn't stay there. Called me drunk and sent me home. Like my mother. But she's not my mother. So I listened to her like she was my mother because she *knows* my mother. Old ladies who know your mother can be mean and—and—and mean. But you still have to listen," he insisted, wagging his finger, "because the next thing you know, your face will end up in the bar and not in a good way."

He curled his arms into his chest. Vague, blurred images of stumbling home with Jesa's help flitted through his thoughts. She had left him at the bottom of the main staircase after he insisted he could get himself upstairs to his room without assistance. Once she was gone, he had glowered up the staircase, convinced his bedroom was full of shadows and invisible monsters he could not fight. He had gone to Orae's straight from the temple on purpose: to avoid the beasts inside his head and his room. The nauseating thought of surrendering to them had driven him to fetch the verrapossum from the garden, yell at the night watch to leave them alone, and hide in the dining room.

"Because I'm not done with you and your friends," Mayr told the decanter, searching for it with one hand. "Because no one else wants me, but you like me. And right now, I like you, so we should get together." He tapped his knuckles on the decanter. "Get it? Get together?" With a deep sigh, he struggled to bring the decanter to his lips without spilling mead over himself. "You have no sense of humour, you know."

Soft squeaks answered back from the floor behind him.

"Hey, I *have* a sense of humour. Don't say I don't." Mayr pointed at the corner where the verrapossum seemed to be, judging by the noises and the scratch of claws on wood. Or was it teeth? "I'm funny. I'm just no good at anything else. At least that's what they say. Always leaving. Always going away. Never happy with what I give. And that hurts, because I give a lot. *A. Lot.* I give and give and they take and take and then they go and go and go."

Because I'm not good enough. Because I'm just getting worse. Wasted it as a kid. Wasted it on her. *And I've wasted what I had left on* him. *Him, who chooses things that aren't even real—goddesses who don't care what silly little mortals do. We're nothing but tiny, little game pieces They move up, down, over and over, crushing who we are just for fun. Because They're bored. Can't be alive forever and not get bored. So, sure, make the tiny people dance. He's being selfish over what we could have. Can't have. Because everyone else matters. Always everyone else.*

"Can't be selfish in a different way, so he just pushed me out. Punched me in the whatever makes us feel this. I never asked for it. I just wanted him to take me, you know? Just ram it in and let me sort out the rest. Because I'd never done it. I've always been the one doing it. Just thought I'd stop being a coward. Because I am. Sometimes. Just when it comes to men I want to rip the pants off. And I did with him. I ripped them off and had him." Mayr touched his lips. Were his fingers actually shaking or was it a trick of the alcohol? "I can still taste him if I try." He sniffed the mead and stuck his tongue out. "He was so much better than this. Whose idea was it to serve this, anyway?"

Could just throw it out, but that'd be a waste. He gulped it back, hoping the faster he drank it, the faster he could move on to the next. *Can't leave until it's gone. Not until I can't open my eyes. Can't go upstairs. Can't go... not where he's been. Not alone.*

Alone. Again. Between him and death, he lost.

He threw the empty decanter at the wall.

"Don't fall for anyone, little furry friend. It doesn't work well. Infatuation's such a liar. Wicked. Lies." Mayr stared at the end of the table. "I really *did* think that's what it was. That it was just being with someone different. A man—*very* different—and a priest, and different kind of pers—pres—presonality. Person. Man. Thing. I figured, hey, it'll go away. Everything does, right? Ha. Right. It didn't. It just got out of control. Went absolutely awful. Took me with it, right down—right to there—right?"

And he said he loved me.

"But it doesn't matter, does it?" he whispered. "Love is easier as a word. Actually doing it... that's the lethal part. The part that kills your soul. Rips it out and spoils it so no one else wants it."

And I don't want it anymore.

Boots scuffed the floor in the hallway outside the dining room.

"Go away!" Mayr shouted. "No one asked you." Misery was one extra friend too many. He did not need anyone else to join in his drunken party or tell him what he should or should not do.

Two bodies entered the doorway. Aeley and Lira, Mayr realized, squinting to distinguish them. Even in the poor light, he saw Aeley's concern, the corners of her mouth pulled down, her brows drawn close together. Beside her, Lira gaped. Their hair was loose and mussed. The opened neckline of Aeley's tunic showed more chest than usual, and she carried knives in her boots. Lira tightened her white dressing robe around her waist to better cover her nightdress.

"What are you doing here, oh, glor-i-ous, foul creatures of ni-i-i-ght," Mayr sang, off-key and loud. In his head, the tune made no sense. He strung notes together without caring what they were. "No one asked you he-re, so go a-way-ay-ay. Unless you bear a gift then I shall lo-o-ove you for-ev-er." The sound of his voice was ridiculous. The song was terrible, wherever it came from. He laughed at the absurdity of it all. The obnoxious nonsense was so painful it helped.

"We heard noises," Lira replied.

Aeley rushed into the room and stopped beside him. The displeasure on her face was obvious. She wanted to beat in his head with something. *Go for it. I'm sure I've got something coming for something. Oh, wait, for being this foolish, falling for him. Yeah, I deserve it.*

"What is this, Mayr?" Aeley glanced around the room. "It's the middle of the night. What are doing on the table?" Horror flashed across her face and then disgust. "And *why* is a furry thing crawling across the floor?"

Mayr peered over the edge of the table. The verrapossum scrambled for the safety of a dark corner, wobbling on its stubby legs instead of turning around and bearing its sharp teeth. He smiled—at least he thought he did, assuming he really could still feel his face. "He's my friend. And it's cold outside. Just because I want to curl up and die doesn't mean he should."

"Lira, can you remove our guest?" Aeley asked sweetly through clenched jaws.

When Lira approached the verrapossum, Mayr stiffened. "Don't hurt him! He didn't do anything wrong!" Yes, his compassion might have been out of control on the way into the estate. Yes, he might have scooped the creature up, convinced it was shivering and appeared too thin to survive the colder nights. And yes, it could still die, but he did not bring it inside to have it killed. Not when he could do something, which was no more or less than what he would do for Hetlan or anything else that breathed. *Tash might like being around plants, but I prefer animals, especially over people. I never told him that. Never will, now.*

"I won't hurt him. I promise." Lira's softened gaze put Mayr at ease only slightly. "I'm just going to find him a safer place." She called to the verrapossum and urged it from its hiding spot. With quick hands, she grabbed it by the scruff of the neck and cradled it to her chest before hurrying from the room.

Aeley slipped her arm around Mayr's back. "Time for *you* to go to a safer place. Come on, with me," she instructed, coaxing him off the table. "That's it. I've got you."

"I thought we were good together." Certain his feet were on the ground, Mayr pushed up and held onto Aeley, one arm around her neck. "I agreed to it, being friends. I knew we couldn't sleep together, but I accepted it. Yeah, I fought with me daily about it, but then he killed it. Just like that. From friends to nothing. Just over." He moved towards the hallway, matching Aeley's steady footsteps with sloppy footfalls that worsened as his knees buckled.

"I'm sorry to hear that," Aeley mumbled, struggling to keep him upright. "But you should've told me, Mayr. You should've come to me. Not done whatever this is. I would've taken care of you."

"I know." Mayr nodded. "I'm a bad friend. Bad, bad friend." He hung his head. "Even worse boyfriend. Good thing you don't like me. Or at least what's in my pants. Because that would be really, really weird." He offered her a smile. "We make good friends, you and me. And it'll always be you and me because I love you. I *love* you. Not like I love anyone else, but I still love you. You're always here." Arm tightened around her neck, he kissed her temple. "Such a good friend."

Aeley coughed and pushed against his hold. "That's great. I'm honoured. Now, could you let me breathe?"

Mayr loosened his grip, his mouth falling open. "Oh! Sorry. Too tight."

"Just a little." Huffing, Aeley pulled on his arm, hoisting him higher before continuing forward. "Keep walking. That's it."

The moment Lira appeared from around the corner at the end of the corridor, Aeley beckoned Lira closer. "Can you—?"

Lira ran to Mayr and wrapped her arm around him, under Aeley's. She curled his arm around her neck and clutched his wrist, following Aeley's lead towards the main staircase. "Your friend is fine, Mayr. The guard's finding him a nice, warm space. No one will hurt him. The guard promises. She said you can ask her about it tomorrow."

"Thank you." Mayr leaned his head against Lira's, breathing her in. She always smelled good. But not like Tash, the one he wanted to be drunk on instead of the alcohol that did uncomfortable things in his stomach. Maybe he should have eaten more. He was going to feel it in the morning.

At least the alcohol can come back up and I'll feel better. He ripped my heart out. There's no getting that back.

"I never should've believed him." Mayr eyed the staircase on their approach. They were going to take him to the last place he wanted to be. But he was too tired to put up a fight. Aeley would take care of him. She would scare the shadows away and exterminate the monsters. "You should've heard what he said. *So. Much*. But he said he'd rather be a priest than be with me. No, no, no, no, no, no. Wait, wait, wait. No, this is even better: he'd rather *die* than be with me. Isn't that sweet? Best compliment I've ever had." He forced a laugh, the croaking sound dying in his throat. "Really, seriously. Best thing I've heard. Ever. Even better than Betta and she didn't say a *word*."

Aeley grunted, guiding him up the stairs. "I don't think he said that. Even if he did, I'm pretty sure he didn't mean it."

Mayr stopped to pull Aeley into him. "Why does everyone leave me? Am I that horrible?"

"You're not. You're only a big pain to me. No one else should be leaving you, not like I should. They just don't know what's good for them." Aeley smiled sadly. "They don't realize what a find you are—that they take you for granted."

"Yeah, they do." Mayr forced his feet to take each step. Bed sounded like a good place after all. His head pounded and every time he swallowed, he tasted the disgusting mead.

Lira tugged him closer despite the awkwardness of dragging him up the stairs. "I'm sorry, Mayr, for whatever happened. I didn't think I'd ever see you like this." She was not subtle with her glance over his head to Aeley. He could imagine the pity on her face. Pity he did not need.

"I have," Aeley said, "over that ungrateful whore, Betta."

"Betta?"

Mayr laughed at Lira's surprise. Maybe he would tell her the story one day. Or maybe he would let Aeley do it since she saw Betta last. Perhaps she would reveal to Lira where Betta was. He had too many things to say to his former not-wife, and he wanted to say them to her face just to see if she showed any sign of regret. "You know, I saved coins for days and days and days to buy the baby something nice. Yeah, Ili-lily couldn't wear the necklace, but it was too pretty, just like her. I still have it, Ili's necklace. Still my... Still... Fickle Betta. Sent her away before I could give it. Mean Betta. Worst wife ever."

"Yeah, I know." At the top of the stairs, Aeley shifted her body and Mayr's, getting a better hold on him. "We're almost there. See? There's your door. Nice and close. Just a little further then you can take a good, long sleep."

"Why are you the only one who sees any worth in me?"

"What is this?" Lira's question was thick with disbelief. "I thought you were always so confident? Too sexy and smart for your own good. You remind us of it constantly."

Mayr choked on a laugh. "You think I actually believe that? *Really*? The best lies I've ever told — and you bought it. Better than when I stole all of

Ae's alcohol after you showed up. Needed to stop her drowning and being a flabberjittering jerk."

"Except it worked," Aeley muttered, "and that's not even a word."

"I think you're lying," Lira added.

"No, seriously, she's right." Mayr nodded. "I make up drunk when I'm words. Plus she was swimming in it and—"

"No, *you*." Lira slapped his hand. "You honestly want us to believe you were lying about yourself the whole time?"

Mayr failed at his attempt to shrug, his muscles strained in the process. "Figured if I said it enough, I'd make truth. I'm a mess."

"That's not true," Lira argued, glaring at him. "Regardless of this disturbing version of sulking and weeping, you're better than a lot of men I know. Strong, dependable, caring, fun to be with—"

"A better brother than ours ever were," Aeley interjected.

Lira snorted. "If things were different, I'd have you myself."

Stopped in front of his bedroom door, Mayr giggled at the idea of him and Lira. "Yeah, but you're married. And you don't do men. If you did, Ae'd kick my head in."

Aeley opened the door. "You and Pell, both. And the rest of the guards." She pulled Mayr into the moonlit room and pushed him towards his bed, still tidy from the morning he had left with

Tash. Once Mayr sat on the bed, she yanked off his boots and tossed them aside. "Stay still." He obeyed as she removed his belts and shirt. "Get under the covers and go to sleep," she commanded, snapping her fingers and pointing at his pillows.

"Going to read me a story, too?" he teased. Still, he obeyed and crawled under the cool blankets. His pillows were more comfortable than he remembered them being. They called to him, offering what he needed most right then.

"Keep being cute and I'll punch you out." Arms folded, Aeley leaned against the wall beside the stained-glass windowpane.

"Wouldn't be the first time." Mayr yawned, stretched, and curled his arms around his pillow. "Won't be the last. We're stuck… you and me…" He closed his eyes and took a deep breath, wishing the images of Tash out of his memories. "Don't need… no one. Just you and…"

The last word never left his lips as the darkness behind his eyelids conquered his thoughts. There would be time to say them a different day—one when he was not broken.

Everything hurt.

No, not everything. Just my head and my pride. And my foot from kicking that damn door. Mayr groaned and covered his face with both hands, hiding his dry eyes from the morning light. Memories of the night before assaulted him. Guilt screamed. His conscience tore into him with the blunt knives of regret. He remembered everything. No amount of alcohol could make him forget what had happened. The entire day had been a disaster, and he was an ass. *What I said… did… It wasn't easy for him, either. I saw it. I felt it. I didn't make it any better. I shouldn't have done anything. I shouldn't have said anything. But I did, and I can't take it back.*

Drawing his fingers down to his cheeks, he opened his eyes and stared at the dark red ceiling. How could he have been that unfair? That selfish? After accusing Tash of the same things, he'd reacted rashly, striking out. He knew the end would come. Was that the real reason he was angry? Because he charged ahead anyway, wanting to believe they could remain friends despite what lay beneath their relationship? Or was it because he was on edge after seeing Tash suffer? The last several days had tested him, forcing him to choke down emotions he could not tolerate. To know the last trial could take Tash's life with little effort made a mockery of everything Mayr did for Tash. What was the point? How could Tash believe it was the only thing he could do? There had to be more to the trial. There had to be more to all of it. Otherwise, none of it made sense.

Mayr tilted his head and gazed across the meagrely decorated room to Lira. Curled into one of the black, cushioned chairs beside the window, she slept with her head propped up on her fist, leaning into the curved back and thick arm. With her other arm, she hugged a mauve pillow that matched the thick curtains. She still wore her dressing robe and nightdress but had wrapped a dark blue shawl around her shoulders, the bottom of which draped over her lap. Her dark hair spilled over both shoulders and hid part of her face, her features relaxed and peaceful.

He frowned. How long had she been there? Why was she there at all? He had been drunk, not wounded. She should have been with Aeley.

Slow and quiet, Mayr slipped out of the bed and crossed the room to the simple, unadorned table at the other end. As he stared down at the bowl of water and clean linens beside it, his last conversation with Tash replayed through his thoughts. Splashing water on his face and cursing the bursting ache behind his eyes, he recalled the whispered words that would have warmed his heart in any other circumstance. He had not expected Tash to say he loved him. *Of all the times to say it, it had to be then.*

But it was said, and that's worth something, he told himself, drying his face and hands, watching the curtains billow around the blue-green windowpane. He had accused Tash of not caring, but it was the opposite. If anything, Tash cared too much. After everything, Tash believed he could not change his mind without punishment. *The saddest part might just be the fact he doesn't think he's worth anything more than what the Four thinks he is, like he's something to be bartered away at market, negotiated over until striking the right price. So he's doing exactly what he's done before — pushing me away, just like he did his family. Out of protection. Out of love. Trying to save us while he tries to save himself.*

Mayr scowled as he removed his pants and put on a fresh pair, hiding behind the open door of the armoire in case Lira awoke and turned around. *I'm not convinced he doesn't have a death wish. And there's that constant sadness nothing ever seems to take away. Is he going through the trial because he's stuck on duty or because he's trying to escape all of those things eating at him? I wasn't joking when I said I understood guilt, and he knows that. I'd tackle guilt at the knees and rip its face off for him. It's all part of whatever's really going on between us.*

With every effort to be noiseless, he finished grooming and braided his hair. As he pulled on the rest of his clothes, he knew what he had to do.

I'm a fighter, and I'm not done. I can't put a beating on what he's going through, but I'm not giving up that easily, even with my pathetic lapse last night. I don't care what he said. I'm not leaving. I'm not Inesta, Naliss, or Erithe. I'm not his family, running out of resources or hope. He should have more than a working life, hiding behind tomes and riddles and an elite, sacred title. After all, Emeraliss, right? Goddess of Love. This is Her business; Her grand idea. Mayr returned to the bed to retrieve his boots and pull them on. *He said he couldn't get out of the Trials without a good reason. He said he needed redemption. He said a lot of things that would fall into Emeraliss's domain. So why—why—would there not be a way to have both? If he was so damn unworthy, nothing about Emeraliss would factor into this. But it does. And I can't believe for a moment She'd want him to die or give up. We're supposed to cherish life and love. Nurture them. Not throw them away. It doesn't make any sense.*

Settled on the edge of the bed, he breathed deep, thinking of what he needed to say. Tash believed the only way to manage their relationship was never to see each other again, but it resolved nothing. The decision was unreasonable. They were bound to see each other, unless one of them left the area, maybe even the region. Mayr would not leave Aeley and Tash wanted to remain a priest. Furthermore, as an Uldana, Tash would attend feasts, gatherings, rites, and tend to other matters of the community. They would be in the same room on more than one occasion because of their occupations.

It's better to meet it head-on. We won't be together, fine, but I refuse to just sit around, never seeing him again. Betta made that choice for me once, and I'm not letting him do the same. Not when he doesn't really want it. Not from the way he was acting. Words are one thing; the way he held me is another. He said he needed me; that I eased his pain. If that's not a cry for help, I don't know what is.

Tash had said his piece. It was time for Mayr to say his.

Intentions and determination roused, Mayr approached Lira with soft steps. He kneeled on the floor and caressed her shoulder.

Lira shivered and opened her eyes. She focused on him, pulling her shawl tight. "Good morning."

"Why aren't you in bed?"

"We were worried about you."

"And as sweet as that is, where's Ae? You should be in your room."

"She had the previous shift." Lira yawned behind her hand. "I sent her to get sleep. She needs to be prepared for the meeting with Council this morning. They wanted to talk to her about the Shar-denn issue."

Mayr grimaced. He should attend the meeting with them. *But Tash, the trial—it won't wait.* "I'm sorry. I didn't mean to wake either of you last night. I shouldn't have been down there." He clasped her hand. "I'll make it up to you."

"It happens." Lira touched his cheek, her gaze sympathetic. "You're allowed to fall apart. Next time, just tell us what you're going through. We hate worrying about you." She eyed his clothes and shaven face. "You're up early, considering."

"I've got something to do."

Lira tossed the pillow into the chair across from her before she stood and accepted Mayr's hand. "Do you want me to join you? I don't have to go with Aeley, not if you need me."

"No, I need to do it by myself. But thank you." Mayr kissed her cheek and hooked his arm around hers. "Let's get you to bed."

"If you insist," Lira said, winking. She leaned her head on his shoulder and followed his lead down the corridor to the room she shared with Aeley. "I meant what I said earlier. I don't know what exactly happened yesterday, but you're a good man. Anyone who doesn't appreciate that— there's no hope for them."

They stopped outside the bedroom. Before Lira could open the door, Mayr embraced her tightly. "Thanks."

"Anytime." Lira kissed his cheek. "Now go on, go fix it. Maybe you both just had a horrible day."

If only, Mayr argued, waiting for Lira to enter the room before he walked away. None of his doubts would deter him. Tash might have given up on them, but Mayr refused to.

He bypassed guards on his way from the estate and told them to continue at their posts before they could ask where he was headed. His walk to the temple was just as quiet and unencumbered; precisely what he needed to work out what he would tell Tash. At the top of his list was his refusal to let Tash poison himself for any reason. *Tradition be damned. It's ludicrous—nothing more than an excuse to torture him or force him out of existence. It doesn't help anyone.*

You realize he won't listen to you, right? The nagging inner voice scolded him from between his angry thoughts. *This is his world, his choice. This is what they do, and it works for them. Besides, who are you to judge? Look at what you've done with your life. Fighting, drawing blood, sending people to rot in prisons for the rest of their lives. Not to mention the verbal whipping your mother would give you for insulting her, your father, and, oh, just about everyone who believes in greater beings.*

None of it mattered, not even as Mayr ascended the white steps to the temple. Nothing would stop him from trying to get Tash to at least *think* about walking away from death, even if it meant he had no love for Mayr afterwards.

He rushed between the columns to the closed doors. Without looking at the vines and crystals, he pushed open the doors and strode into the temple, greeted by thick, incensed air. The group of priests gathered around the altar in the centre of the room whirled around, greeting him with surprise followed by irritation. Anger flashed across the faces of two priestesses.

Paying no attention to the statues and priests, Mayr returned the gaze of only one person standing beside the black altar.

Tash.

Dressed only in white pants tied at his hips, Tash stared at Mayr, his expression blank. From beside him, Priestess Kee and an old priest in red robes stepped forward, hands raised, shielding Tash.

Mayr charged towards the altar, weaving past the half dozen priests reaching for him. He would say what he came to say even if they hated it. "Don't do it," he told Tash. "Please don't do it. If not for you then for me."

As Mayr neared, Tash backed away from the altar. He said nothing but blinked quickly. His eyes were dark and fatigued. His hands shook. With his shoulders slumped and growing panic splashed across his face, he appeared a different man.

"Tash—" Hands grabbed Mayr from behind. Fingertips dug into his shoulders. More hands pulled him back by the arms. Two stern-faced Metah priests stepped in front of Mayr and shoved him. "Would you quit that?" He lunged forward, fighting to get loose.

The grips on him tightened, enough for sharp fingernails to pierce his skin through his shirt. They jerked him back, rough and unyielding.

"Let me go! Tash, do something!" Mayr struggled to escape, considering every defensive tactic he could think of. The mob of priests restrained him too well. They were too strong to overpower without weapons. The two Metah priests who had shoved him seized his arms.

They rammed their shoulders into his chest and moved his legs back with theirs. Forcing him towards the doors, they grunted as they shuffled his weight and matched his fight.

"You must leave, Mayr of the Dahes." Kee's voice carried over the noise of the scuffle, a shout that almost had him pausing. Kee never shouted, and never at him, not to mention that threatening tone… "You are not welcome. You are damaging and have wrought enough chaos. Your temptations have hurt Halataldris enough. We will not allow more bloodshed."

"Bloodshed? What are you talking about?" Mayr shouted, kicking at the feet of the priests. The doorway was right behind him while the glass eyes of the statues seemed to glare at him as the priests drove him further. If he could reach his knife, he could coerce the priests into leaving him alone—then suffer the consequences for having the audacity to attack. "Tash? Tash! What is she—"

He froze, staring at Tash's arms. A chill raced through his body, prickling his skin.

Bracers. He's not wearing his bracers. Because his wrists, they're—no. Tash, you didn't. Tell me you didn't.

The priests steered Mayr over the threshold, but he could not tear his gaze from the bandages around Tash's forearms. They were wound tight, the left bandage bound higher than what Tash's bracers normally covered.

Just as Tash turned his back, a flash of dark red on Tash's left arm made Mayr nauseous.

Blood.

The way Tash's arm hung limply by his side was worse. He moved only his right arm as he lit a candle.

The price of a broken heart.

No. No, no, no...

"Fight it!" Mayr yelled, resisting the priests. He needed to get to Tash before he cut himself again.

Tash did not respond. Beneath the shaded feathers of his tattoo, his back muscles strained with every noise Mayr made. When Kee touched his shoulder, Tash nodded and turned. Without glancing at the doorway, he followed Kee and the other Uldana priest to the corridor. They disappeared past the pillars and into the shadows.

"And so it is the will of the Temple," a priest with a deep, husky voice said in Mayr's ear, "that you be gone."

The priests tossed Mayr to the ground. The moment they were inside the temple again, they slammed the doors shut. The stone beneath his feet rumbled, the sound reverberating through his ears. The crystals around the door danced furiously.

"Forget you, too!" Mayr shouted, pushing himself up and standing. For being peaceful, the priests certainly knew how to express their displeasure. Cautious and pained, he pressed his palm to the door. "Don't do it," he whispered, unable to forget Tash's bandages. If only he had returned the night before. If only he could have gotten there sooner.

He stepped back, bumping into a body behind him. A hand gripped his wrist.

"This way, young man. This way."

Mayr yanked his hand away and spun towards the hooded man. "Would you people—"

You. Armamae.

To Mayr's surprise, Armamae took Mayr's wrist again and pulled. "*This way.*" His hold was much tighter than Mayr expected. Rather than fight, Mayr followed Armamae down the stairs. On the last step, Armamae leaned close. "Come back when the moon is at its highest point," he mumbled. "Come to the side door in the west, under cloak, and be quick. Do not be seen."

"Why?"

Armamae smirked. "If you love him, you already know." The smirk gone, Armamae climbed the stairs, leaving Mayr even more confused.

And something tells me it'll only be worse from here because, honestly, how could it possibly get any better?

He could only pray someone stopped Tash before it was too late.

Chapter Twenty

Mayr followed Armamae's instructions to the last detail. He could not afford to be hauled away and forbidden to return.

Because wouldn't that just make Ae's day? I already skipped out on the meeting with the Council and dinner with her and Lira. Mayr pulled the hood of his black cloak further over his face, slowly ascending the temple steps. Partially to make little noise but mostly because the tall trees and cloud cover made it too dark to see where one step ended and the next began. At the top, he recognized the outline of a door, thankful for the sudden thin glimmer of light that slipped between the tree leaves.

He stared at the door. Was he supposed to knock? Wait? *Thanks for the help, Armamae. You're really good at the—*

The door creaked, opening slightly. Mayr flattened against the wall behind the door.

"Are you there?" a hoarse whisper asked. "Mayr?"

Mayr crept towards the crack. "Yeah."

The door opened to reveal Armamae in a narrow, dimly lit staircase. Silent, he ushered

Mayr inside then closed the door softly. He grabbed Mayr's hand and rushed up the stairs. They continued down a short, dark passageway and rounded a corner to a longer corridor. Halfway up the hallway, Armamae opened a door and pushed Mayr inside. He closed the door just as quickly.

Mayr stopped in the middle of the candlelit room, recognizing the tapestry and furniture. One glance at the bed destroyed his hope.

Tash lay on the mattress, sweating under a thin sheet, his arms still bandaged. He tossed and turned, whimpering between strangled cries. A stream of tears left a telltale path of agony down his face.

Agony Mayr felt with him.

In a fight with his own tears, Mayr forced himself to breathe. Short, shallow breaths were all he could manage. Anything else hurt. His chest burned, seizing as if someone had punched a hole through him and mashed his heart. He was too late. The damage was done.

And not one of the priests had stopped him.

Armamae withdrew the cloak from Mayr's shoulders. "He has been under since we ended our evening prayers," he said, draping the cloak over a chair in the corner. "I do not know how long it will take, but he is pushing through." As he passed the dresser, he picked up a wooden bowl and metal pitcher. "Go on, sit." He gestured to the chair beside the bed with his elbow.

"I don't—"

"*Sit.*"

Mayr obeyed. When Armamae handed him the bowl and filled it with water from the pitcher, Mayr watched tiny purple leaves, yellow seeds, and red granules dance and cling to the white linen at the bottom of the bowl. Spices and bitter herbs scented the air.

"They will help the sickness." Armamae returned the pitcher to the dresser. "Treat it as you would any other."

Still struggling to take a deeper breath, Mayr wiped Tash's face and chest with the moistened cloth, his nose crinkling at the strong scent. Tash was hot to the touch, his skin flushed worse than after the third trial. He shivered and shirked Mayr's touch. Sounds that resembled words passed his lips, but they were incoherent and overcome by mournful cries.

I don't know what else to do. Tell me. Tell me what I have to do. I'll do anything, Mayr pleaded, swallowing the emotional outburst banging on his insides, demanding to be unleashed. The cruel images his imagination conjured of Tash dying were horrible enough, feasting on his fears and wreaking havoc on his nerves. His hands were unsteady. His sanity was crumbling. He was not a healer; he was a guard. Fighting was what he knew. Slashing, stabbing, kicking, punching, biting, slamming a body down—they were what he did to win. *I can't do that with this. It's an invisible enemy. Swords and fists aren't any good. They don't matter. I don't matter. I can't kick this thing where it hurts. I can't defend you. I can't save you. I can't help you.*

Tears slipped from his eye. He squeezed his eyes shut and turned his face away. "Why am I here?"

Armamae moved to Mayr's side. "This is not an easy calling, dedicating one's life to sacred beings," he said, his voice even and clear. "We live by extensive rules. I am happy to abide by those rules—I never wanted anything or anyone else. Still, I understand there is a time for strict rules and a time to let them fall as they may and run towards truth." He cocked his head and watched Tash's face pull and pinch. "Most of the others believe celibacy and the avoidance of romantic entanglements are necessary to those of us pledged as Uldanas. Certainly our forebearers did, prescribing them as absolutes, declaring them required measures to preserve our sacred duty. They explained romantic love gets in the way of serving to our fullest ability, and it is accounted for in detail and a persuasive collection of anecdotes we memorize."

Slowly he sank onto the edge of the bed, holding Mayr's gaze. "*I* do not believe it. Once, as a younger man, I thought it was the way of things. With age, I have gained the wisdom that interpretation, fear, and authority are not only powerful, they can be false, and in that, harmful."

Armamae clasped Tash's hand. "I have seen other priests fight with love, deny it, believing that they must forsake it to fulfill their duty. I have seen those same souls wither because they bided their time serving their goddesses while pining for their loves. They are good priests but their spirits lack life. They lack balance. Instead of celebrating love, they bury it because of a rule. I fully believe Emeraliss would understand love and duty can be equal; they can be partners. They can work from each other, not tear each other down."

Standing, Armamae pointed at Tash. "It is obvious which side he is on. What he seeks in you is worth more than rules; ideals never meant for the likes of him. He is faithful and dedicated, but he needs more than bowing to the Four and serving the people. He needs you." A frown curved his thin lips. "And he needs his bandages changed." He nodded at Mayr and turned. "I will get clean ones while you remove those."

Mayr stilled, staring at Tash's arm. Tash hid the marks on purpose. To see them while he was unconscious was wrong and violated his wishes.

Except you're not all right, and you need to be healed. This needs to be done. Reluctantly, Mayr unwound the bandage from Tash's right arm and then the left. Dark scars marred Tash's skin in a series of horizontal and diagonal lines that started above the wrist and continued along his forearm on all sides. They appeared worse than the ones inside his thighs and calves. Each forearm bore a set of three thick, puckered, horizontal scars on the underside. They crossed over dozens of shorter, shallower marks, some of which were beneath the thicker scars while others lay over them. The first of the three scars spanned his wrists from one side to the other, curved over the edge. Jagged and uneven, they suggested he had hesitated.

The second and third scars were even, showing confidence and skill. They were also bisected at the sides of Tash's arm to create the illusion of a uniform line around his forearm.

Clutching Tash's hands, Mayr studied the fresh wounds. Located above the previous scars, they were not straight across his arm like the others. On his left arm, a long, deep gash traveled from the middle of his forearm to past his elbow at a steep angle, weaving back and forth along the way. Stitches bound the skin, but blood still seeped through.

The cut on his right arm was sloppy, shallow, and broken as though he had started but could not finish.

"He cut too far," Armamae murmured, washing Tash's left arm before bandaging it. "He lost the full use of his arm, though we do not know how long the effect will last. Our healers will keep working to restore what they can. Just know that he may never completely recover feeling or strength."

Because of me. Mayr squeezed Tash's hand, unable to let go even as Armamae bound Tash's arm.

"We found him last night just after he had done it, cradling his arm, covered in blood," Armamae continued, his tone softened with sadness. "I will never forget how stunned he looked, how confused. He just stood there, staring at the knife on the floor where he had dropped it. He said he did not understand what had gone wrong; that he had done it so many times, it should have worked."

"And you let him go through the trial *anyway*? What in the Four's name is wrong with you?" Mayr slid his gaze towards Armamae. "He wasn't in any mind to go through with this. Why didn't you stop him? Shouldn't you be protecting him?" His fury tumbled out, burning in his chest with every word. It took everything he had not to shout and throw something at the wall. "Isn't that part of your priests' code, protecting each other from harm, or did you set that part aside just for him? Do you think this is what he deserves after what he's done? Maybe figured you'd let it finish him off since the villagers didn't?"

Mayr gritted his teeth, the image of Tash tied to the post permanently etched into his memory. *Never again—that* was what Mayr had sworn to Tash during the trials. If anyone were to keep Tash safe going forward, that person would be Mayr, and he would swear that oath over and over again until it stuck. He would have pledged himself to Tash a thousand times if it could have saved Tash from where he lay now, lost, clinging, trapped where Mayr could not follow.

Dammit, Kee, he's your *responsibility. And you think* I'm *the problem?* Mayr glared at the floor, the bedsheets, the bandages—anything that he could hate without feeling bad about it. He and Kee had never had an issue with each other before, but that was quickly becoming mud flung up the side of the highway. Their relationship had always been amicable. Kind. Never aggressive. Never angry.

Oh, but I'm all sorts of angry now, enough that we'll be having words.

Except confronting Kee would get him kicked out for a second time and *that* scared him more than pushing any goddess to rage on his miserable ass. All he had was Armamae and blaming him seemed almost as wrong as the scowl on Armamae's face.

"No, this is not punishment," Armamae started quietly, slowly, his tone even with a hint of something darker, "and as much as you want to blame someone, that accusation is misplaced. We take care of our own. Otherwise, you would not be here. I never would have let you break our rules, nor would I have gone against our Overseer's decision to keep you out." Armamae focused on wrapping the last of the bandages. "As for protecting him: you are not the only one who cares for him. I told him the same as you would have. I would see him live and find peace."

Finished with the bandages, Armamae sat back, his frown deepening. "I suggested he was not ready, but he insisted. I was firm. I told him we would do it a different day, but he refused and got angry. He made it clear if we did not help him do it today, he would do it himself without help from me, or Sister Kee, or any one of us. We could not allow that." He sighed and looked to the ceiling. "He was particularly focused on how he had hurt you. For some time, he babbled on about going to see you, but it did not last. He said he had to do this, justifying it with a dozen statements about how it could not be in vain because he would have hurt you both for no reason." Armamae cast Mayr a doubtful glance. "He believed you would not listen to him or return, so he went through with it. Even after you interrupted the preparation ceremony earlier, he did not believe it was real."

You ass. Mayr clenched his teeth and stared at Tash's face. *If only you were awake. I'd yell at you. Or kiss you. Or kiss you then yell at you, because you completely deserve it. I was right there. You could've said something. You could've tried believing in me.* Mayr cupped Tash's cheek, ignoring the slight tremor in his touch. *But you went and carved yourself up, instead. Over me. While I'm sure someone in the world is twisted enough to find that romantic, I don't. It just makes me want to tie you down and make you stop doing it. I hate what you do to yourself. I hate that it was us that made you do it.* He drew a finger down Tash's cheek. If Tash overcame the poison, they would have to talk. The cutting needed to stop. *We'll find a better way for you to deal with things. If you can't do it on your own, I'll do it with you. I'll be forceful if I have to be.*

Armamae shuffled away. Mayr wet the cloth again and laid it over Tash's forehead. With Tash's hand in both of his, he waited. Time dragged on. Silence fell as Tash quieted. He still trembled, but his breaths were slow in a steady rhythm that matched his calmed heartbeat. Although still warmer than usual, his skin was cooler than before. He no longer wept.

Desperate to do something—anything—Mayr stroked the waves of Tash's hair, his fingertips grazing skin. Tash sighed deeply and nestled against Mayr's touch. *You feel it, but do you know it's me?* Was Tash even getting better? If the trial was going poorly, would Armamae say as much? Buried by questions he had no answers for, Mayr kissed Tash softly.

Tash moaned.

Startled, Mayr pulled back, holding Tash's right hand close to his heart. Tash's fingers twitched in Mayr's grasp. His lashes fluttered. He groaned and coughed, turning his head away. After struggling to catch a calmed breath, Tash shifted his hips and legs before facing Mayr.

Disbelief clouded his blue eyes. Relief immediately softened his gaze. "You... you came back," Tash whispered, struggling to form the almost inaudible words. A faint smile teased his lips as he withdrew his fingers from Mayr's to cup Mayr's cheek. The touch was weak, unstable. His fingers slipped down Mayr's face.

Catching them, Mayr pressed Tash's palm to his jaw, his hand flattened firmly over Tash's. Behind him, Armamae opened the door and slipped out to the corridor.

Tash's smile faded, replaced by sorrow and tears. "I was wrong. I... I—"

Footsteps hustled into the room. Hushed voices spoke excitedly. Tash's eyes widened, his attention stolen by the priests with Armamae. Mayr rolled his eyes and looked at them.

"What are you doing here?" Kee glowered at Mayr, her hands balled on her hips. "No matter," she said, huffing before she brushed her black hair and veil over her shoulder. She gave Tash a sweet smile. "Congratulations, Brother Halataldris. You have passed all of the Uldana Trials. The Four have found you worthy. We'll start preparing your ceremony right away." She gestured with open arms to Armamae and the five other priests. "It will be wonderful, a perfect—"

"No. I refuse."

The priests stiffened. All but Armamae eyed Tash with confusion. Kee's lips moved, but she made no sound. Her glance jumped between Tash and Mayr, her shock laced with a sliver of rage.

"But, but," Kee sputtered, stepping forward. "This is what you wanted. Your fate—your wishes—this is—you can't—I don't understand. *No one* turns it down."

Tash held Mayr's hand tightly, his gaze meeting Mayr's. "I can."

Kee moved closer. "I don't *understand*." Her face turned deep red. "How can you just walk away from this? After all your work, all of our time spent training you to be one of us, you would throw it away? *How? Why?*"

"I saw them. All of them. All four," Tash said, still staring at Mayr. "They were there, watching me, speaking to me. And Emeraliss saw me. Embraced me. I fell, and She picked me up." He laced his fingers through Mayr's. "I belong to Her now, She said so. I'm to do whatever She wills, including break my oaths to be full and whole. She demands I follow my heart to where it truly wants to be: bound to yours."

Eyes brightened, Tash faced Kee. His voice strengthened as he continued to speak, the words coming out with more ease. "Emeraliss told me to inform you She has claimed me as a servant, and Her will cannot be contested. She says there's a message for you on your desk, buried in white and silver feathers. They mark these as Her words and not a false testimony."

The priests ran from the room, almost tripping over their feet and each other. Kee's wide, dark eyes filled with surprise. Her mouth fell open before she gripped her robes and hurried after the others. Only Armamae remained.

"I will leave you two alone." Armamae left the room and closed the door behind him.

"So," Mayr started, letting out a breath, "Goddesses, huh?"

"Yes, and They're absolutely terrifying." Tash pushed himself up with one arm. He faltered as he moved up the bed. Mayr steadied him and fussed with the pillows until they supported Tash's back. "The statues don't do Them justice, not in the slightest."

"Oh." Uncertain of what else to say, Mayr looked at the bed.

Gentle fingers lifted his chin. "There was more to it," Tash said softly. "Things meant for only you to hear."

"Like I'm in trouble and there's a fiery pit of hungry beasts with my name on it in the Realm of the Dead?"

"No. Like the moment I was under, I knew I'd made a mistake." The fingers danced across Mayr's cheek, urging him closer to Tash. "I wasn't happy with the choice I'd made. I hated myself for it. And it only grew. The further I went, the more it consumed me. I fought to get out of the world-between-worlds, but I couldn't. Every new path out slammed me into a wall I couldn't breach. Every door was a snare. I was trapped every step I took. I had to work that much harder to get through. To get back to you."

Tash lowered his hand into his lap, his injured arm moving slightly. "I worried I'd resent you and me if I chose us over my devotion." He squeezed his eyes shut and shook his head. "I had it backwards. My conscious self messed with me. It was selfish and cruel and shackled me to a lie. The whole time, the truth was the other way around. And then when I was there—*there*, with *Them*, awaiting judgment—it all felt wrong. Being a priest wasn't important anymore. It wasn't the right choice." His voice hitched on a sob. "By the time I reached Them, I was an imposter. A liar. My heart wasn't as full as it should've been. And They stared at me. They knew."

He held Mayr's face, his thumb stroking the skin under Mayr's eye. "*That's* why I said no to being an Uldana. It wasn't because Emeraliss told me to. I wanted to forgo it before the Four even appeared. The moment the poison knocked me out, I wanted to give it all up for you."

Mayr tore his gaze from Tash's and swallowed hard. The words wounded him though he could not understand why. Anyone in his position would be overjoyed. To hear the things his heart wished for was difficult. They were even harder to accept without wanting to hold Tash tight and never let him go.

"So now what?" Mayr asked, licking his lips. What did people do with a supposed deity-sanctioned relationship?

"Now I know what to do. I understand it. You weren't the distraction—you were the trial." Tash leaned forward, his mouth close to Mayr's. "I thought I needed to fulfill my oaths to find peace and forgiveness, but I already had them. In you. *That* was the real trial. The absolution. The only answer I needed." Raking his hand through Mayr's hair, he touched their foreheads together. "I'm sorry. I'll spend a lifetime proving that to you because I am; I'm sorry. I thought I was doing the right thing, and I was—the whole time I was with you. I just needed help seeing it."

Before Mayr could respond, Tash kissed him, taking his lips with a soft apology. Despite the bitter taste on Tash's tongue, Mayr returned what Tash gave. With both arms, Mayr pulled Tash against him, groaning as Tash's fingers played over the back of his neck. The sensation of skin on skin ignited the ache in his belly, angrily reminding him of the last time they had touched each other intimately.

When Tash drew back, Mayr loosened his hold but did not let go. He needed to keep Tash close.

"This means everything, you coming back," Tash said quietly. "I thought we'd never have anything. I thought you'd hate me. But you're here."

Mayr nuzzled Tash's ear. "Because when I find someone I believe in, someone I care for, I'll fight for them," he murmured. "Even if they don't think they're worth fighting for. Even if they think everything's lost. You can't get rid of me that easily. Just ask Aeley. She threatens to toss me out all the time."

The throaty laugh Tash gave in response warmed Mayr's heart, making it skip more than one beat. They needed it, that perfect moment.

Tash played with the ends of Mayr's braid. "Since we met in the tavern, there's this thing, this feeling. Do you remember how I said I feel like I've been looking for you, needing to tell you something?"

"How could I forget? It's the most romantic thing anyone's ever said to me."

"Oh… I didn't realize that." Tash breathed out, his gaze alternating between Mayr's eyes and his chest. "I know what it is. I know why. And it's not that I love you—because I do, more than I can say—but it's more than that. Being stuck between life and death, I caught the answer, and it makes perfect sense." He removed the tie from Mayr's braid and teased the plait apart. "We're meant to be. Your spirit completes mine. And I need you, not just to be happy but to find the rest of myself. Without you, there are only holes. You've always seemed familiar because we're connected. We have been for a long time. Our spirits are bound together, and only Emeraliss knows how long."

Mayr gripped Tash's waist. "There you go, talking so good again. Why do you do this to me?"

"Because I need you to know you fill in all the empty spaces." They rubbed noses as Tash smiled. "You remind me I'm more than just what I do for others and I'm not being punished for every bad decision I've made. You tell me I don't have to be alone. I just had to learn what you really were: everything. You are everything. You're not afraid of my past. You take my issues in stride. You didn't leave me even though I broke us."

"You break us; I put us back together…"

Tash kissed his forehead. "There's no one who's loved me enough to do that. I believed no one would ever be willing to help me carry burdens or be there when I needed them most. But here you are," he whispered, "and I heard your voice when I was between worlds. You're the first one who hasn't come up with reasons to leave. You've only ever talked of reasons to stay."

Mayr grunted. "Because I don't *want* to leave. I'm pretty happy being right here, thanks."

"I love that about you. At the end of it all, I just love *you*. And you need someone who'll return everything you offer—someone who respects you and knows what you need. I can do that. I'll give anything just to be that someone. I'd rather have a future at your side than cling to the past. That means being with you, being yours completely." Tash arched his brow. "*Completely*."

The carefully enunciated word caught Mayr by surprise, fueling salacious thoughts. He choked on a breath and coughed. "Please tell me that means what I'm hoping it means," he said hoarsely, "because I'm willing. I'm so *completely* willing, you have no idea."

Again, Tash laughed. "I know, and I'll apologize for that, too." He tucked Mayr's hair behind his ear. "Taking things slowly before—I said it was for your sake, and it was, but it wasn't just you. I needed to go slow for me, too. I wanted what we had so badly. I didn't want to taint it. Doing everything felt like a huge step for us both. I also knew the Trials would come and ruin it all. But I want to give you everything I can." Wrapping his arm around Mayr's neck, he pulled Mayr in for a quick kiss. "If you'll let me," he murmured against Mayr's lips.

A whimper of agreement slipped from Mayr before he could stop it. "I recall you saying something about an altar."

Tash hummed behind his smile. "Emeraliss's altar. I want our first time together to be perfect and ours alone. Once I'm recovered, we can do it right. The first time. Then the second. And the third—"

The rest of Tash's words were lost as Mayr claimed his lips. The number was irrelevant. As long as Tash was his, nothing else mattered.

Chapter Twenty-One

If he kept staring at his feet, maybe the sick, sinking feeling would go away.

Tash struggled to breathe, the weight of whatever pressed down on his chest refusing to let up. The last six weeks had brought a calm to life he sorely needed, the consequences of relinquishing his status as an Uldana not nearly as painful as he feared they would be. An ache lingered, the ghost of failure clinging to the sense of duty he still held onto tightly, but he had yet to lose the people who mattered most in his life and that was everything he needed to keep going.

Except with one of the Keepers of the Sacred Assembly standing right there in the meeting room at the Dahe estate, wanting to speak to him privately, it was more than likely Tash was about to lose at least half of that life. Whatever Kee thought, however supportive Armamae had been, the Sacred Assembly could take his priesthood away with a single word. Kee might have insisted Tash remain as a Rese-level priest at their temple and assured him that he would always be part of their family, but if the Sacred Assembly decided otherwise…

"Hey," Mayr said softly. He slipped his arm around Tash's waist and drew him close. "Do I need to ask them to leave? Isn't this more of an Overseer matter, anyway?" A slight frown pulled at his lips. "Or is this a throwing-over-rank sort of thing?"

Leaning into Mayr, Tash shrugged one shoulder and glanced up the empty hallway. "I don't know." As his gaze wandered back to the sunlit meeting room to their right, he shivered and hugged Mayr. "I've never had to speak to the Keepers alone. I've only ever seen them with the Overseers I've known, and only when they've come to visit the temples. For any of them to come here…"

Granted, the Keepers could have visited the estate at any point, particularly if festivities were involved or if the Tract Steward needed the Sacred Assembly's counsel. But to see him? They could have waited for him to return to the temple that night or the next day. It was not as though he lived at the estate… at least not until Mayr asked him to. If Mayr ever wanted that from him.

A different problem for a completely different day. Tash scowled at the subtle dents in the dark red doorframe, a sigh battling through the anxiety chomping away at his clarity. There was little point in loitering further on either issue: he could not run from the one discussion nor force a future with the other. Forward was what he had, with going backward reserved as an unpalatable option he needed to avoid. The Goddesses had given him Their blessing to live rather than simply survive, and he intended to do so, whatever the sacrifice. If anything, They believed in him, and that was worth any reminder They threw at him—even if it meant losing his vocation.

With a quiet sigh, Tash smoothed down the folds in his loose beige shirt, then his single red robe. After a strained smile at Mayr, he crossed over the threshold of the meeting room, his hands clasped behind his back, dread following on his heels like a mangy pup with diamond spikes for teeth. Priest or not, he could still serve the Goddesses, and he would always be Emeraliss's willing servant, no matter what any Keeper said.

But Mayr... there was no giving up Mayr. There was only loving him as fully as possible, standing by his side—right where Tash knew he belonged, no questions or disbeliefs to be had, not anymore. While Tash could do a hundred things to make good on his promises to the Four, there was only one path to take with Mayr—one that filled the void that had haunted Tash like the loneliest name caught on the tip of his tongue, unable to be spoken until the shattered pieces of soul fell into place.

That thought alone steadied his steps as he ventured further into the room, towards the row of windows that took up the opposite wall, their worn wooden frames hidden beneath heavy green and gold curtains. Against their rich hue, the red robes of Keeper Agera looked all the brighter, shimmering faintly in the autumn light as Agera stared through one set of windows, their back to Tash.

"Keeper Agera," Tash greeted quietly. Stopped at the edge of the long table in the centre of the room, he peered over his shoulder. Behind him, Mayr entered the room but stayed close to the wall next to the door, both hands behind his back as he watched. When Mayr nodded at him, Tash cleared his throat and settled his attention on Keeper Agera once more. "Good afternoon, and welcome to the Dahe estate. I trust your trip was quiet and uneventful?"

Agera turned towards him, a delighted smile at their lips with an equally welcoming warmth in their golden-brown eyes. "Very, and please thank the household steward again for me. He was ever so gracious on my arrival. I'm afraid this is my first time here and it showed." Agera laughed softly as they tucked short strands of their straight, dark hair behind their ear, the brown-black hue almost as deep as their brown skin. After resettling their veil around their shoulders, they clasped their hands before them, the ornate regalia of the Keepers catching the light even more than their robes did. "I'd say the Assembly doesn't send me on errands much, but the truth is I'm out more than I'm in, tromping about the republic more than I see my own bed. It was about time I ended up here, stirring a pinch of trouble."

Tash nodded, his gaze falling to the gold rings and chains adorning Agera's hands. Like all Uldana priests, each of the four Keepers that managed the affairs of the Sacred Assembly wore multiple layers of robes and the trailing veils that marked them as the closest any priest could get to the Goddesses in veneration and duty. But unlike the other Uldana, the role of Keeper came with precious items to be worn always: priceless jewels that represented not only the everlasting beauty of the Goddesses, but also the great weight put upon the Keepers as leaders. They were tokens of craftsmanship, determination, and the artistry of the people, none of which was to be forgotten, only kept on display.

Agera wore the same regalia as the other Keepers, though Agera had only been Keeper for the last three years, not the ten or more years the other three Keepers had served. The thick white gold choker that represented Emeraliss hugged Agera's throat with what appeared to be comfortable tightness, its multitude of white and red diamonds cut in various shapes and sizes. Around Agera's head was the circlet dedicated to Laytia, a piece crafted from intricately twisted strands of white gold decorated with vivid red jewels, most of it concealed by Agera's veil save for the front where the circlet dipped into a slight point.

The rings on Agera's fingers, however, were all forged from yellow gold. There was a ring for every finger, each engraved with the most powerful words of Navara, commanding the Keepers to retain their fairness and just course. A fragile gold chain extended from each ring, all of which attached to a single ring on the back of Agera's hands in a web of links. From there, a lone chain draped over each of Agera's wrists and hooked into the gold bracers they wore. In tribute to Hastal, the bracers were comprised of three narrow cuffs conjoined by tiers of fine gold scales, a shiny, heavy wrapping around Agera's forearms that could cut through fabric as surely as they defended against a knife.

It was enough to have Tash gripping his arm, the leather of his skin-tone bracers soft on his calloused palm. The inside of his forearm barely registered the touch, the recent damage he had done to himself only adding to the permanent damage from all the times before. His left arm would never be the same as it used to be, the nerves injured beyond repair. He still had difficulty lifting heavy objects, adding one more consequence to the fire he had set.

Was that why Agera sought him out? To relieve him of his Rese duties because of what he had done?

Tash swallowed uneasily, his gaze falling to the black and grey stones of the floor. What he had done to Armamae and Kee deserved reprimand. Coercing them into letting him pursue the fourth trial just after hurting himself... It had been far from fair, without a bit of kindness spared for their compassion. They would have protected him if not for his miserable temper flaring up and taking them down with him. They knew what had been at stake and what he was capable of—where he could have ended up. But like the brute he had been in the Shar-denn, he had demanded they comply and cornered them until they did, getting his way and nearly dying for the trouble he caused. For all he knew, he *had* died and no one wanted to tell him so.

No amount of apology could take that regret away. Goddesses knew he had tried, right up to the point where Kee had stopped him with a firm grip on his shoulders and commanded he stop apologizing. Though what she thought of him now... He was afraid to know the truth. Too afraid that the care Kee offered him was little more than a front.

He could have ruined much more than himself during the last trial, and maybe he had after all. He needed Kee and Armamae, not just as mentors but as family. They knew him better than anyone else; cared for him even when he thought himself unlovable. For him to have damaged what he had with either of them because of how hurt he was, how lost...

A tap on his hand tore him from his thoughts.

"Would this be better sitting down?" Agera's voice was gentle, almost a murmur.

Blinking away the darkness prodding at him, Tash shook his head. "Only if you would prefer it, Keeper."

Agera smiled, a glimmer of playfulness in their eyes. "Only if it gets it done faster is more like it, no? Because rare is the person who's ready for one of us to simply drop in and disturb the waters." Agera reached into their robes and pulled out a scroll of parchment sealed shut with the red wax seal of the Sacred Assembly. "This won't take but a short conversation, I promise. All of what you need to know is in this. I'm merely the fancy messenger who volunteered to give it to you."

Tash accepted the parchment, though not without a tremor in his hand. How fast could he throw the message into the nearest fire and walk away?

"You can relax, Brother Halataldris. It's not that kind of missive. You might even want to breathe a little. On my oath as a Keeper, I swear it won't hurt as much as you think." Agera stepped back, their robes sweeping over the floor with quiet sounds as the heels of their boots clicked quietly. "The Sacred Assembly discussed your case at our latest gathering. More specifically, we examined the issue it poses upon our rules and those of the Temple. Your Overseer was in attendance, as was your primary mentor, and they were invited to speak in your favour as well as air any concerns they have."

His *case*? *Goddesses, could you be any vaguer?* The word alone could cover almost everything in his life since he joined the Shar-denn.

"The document you hold details what we discussed and the outcome, including notes on the Assembly's house vote," Agera continued, hands clasped as they rocked on their heels, an unmistakeable shine in their eyes. "It is the opinion of the Assembly and the Keepers that you shall receive the honours of an Uldana priest, with all due respects and expectations bestowed upon you as with every one that's come before you. Just with one small difference." Smirking, Agera glanced in Mayr's direction. "It seems that to have you is to open our home and hearts to someone else by extension, though we're willing to try if you are."

Tash could have fallen flat on his face if anyone dared touch him.

His breath hitched as he clutched the parchment with one hand, his other hand gripping the back of the nearest chair. His heart raced almost as fast as his thoughts, taking any semblance of understanding along for a ride.

Uldana. Agera was announcing him an Uldana. Despite everything. Despite Tash's refusal. Despite—

"The rules," Tash mumbled, the words barely making it out. His mouth was too dry to manage more, not that he trusted his voice.

"Yes, and we discussed them at length." Agera nodded thoughtfully, rogue strands of their shoulder-length hair sweeping across their shoulders. "We heard compelling testimony to warrant revisiting them in both directions. In the end, however, the vote decided you will have both your priesthood and your love, in honour of the Goddesses and Their views on such things." Head tilted, Agera offered Tash a lopsided smile. "We want to do right by Navara, who would no doubt argue that you earned the right to be Uldana, fairly and justly. We also understand the circumstances during your Trials went far beyond what most of our priests encounter, and that the conditions themselves were dangerous from the very beginning, putting you at greater risk of never achieving the end, despite the efforts you put in."

Agera straightened, their knowing smile not dimming. "Even so, we heard how you stood against it all with the will to fight. Your Overseer very much advocated for you, spelling out how your devotion and focus were beyond reproach. Even with all of our rules, it is difficult to ignore that. After all, the Trials are meant to search out such priests so as to reward them for their dedicated service."

"But?" Tash asked weakly, aware of Mayr coming up behind him and lingering close enough to feel the heat off him. Reaching back, Tash sought Mayr's hand and held tight, ensuring he remained upright. All he wanted to do right then was cry out the tears starting to pool in his eyes.

"But it was also argued that the rules apply to all, and that much is true." Agera frowned. "Exceptions are not to be made lightly — otherwise exceptions would be made all the time, and we prefer consistency, particularly where Navara is concerned. However, we are not fools. Emeraliss directly intervened in our affairs, which happens very rarely." With one brow arched, Agera glanced from Tash to Mayr then back to Tash. "The Four usually allow us to operate as we see fit, granting us free will and the choice to decide our fates. They do not interfere, not unless there is a reason to do so. But Emeraliss very clearly did so with a purpose we can't ignore, even if we have no idea what that purpose is."

Tash breathed out. The message. The feathers. True to Her word, Emeraliss had disclosed Her decision about Tash to Kee and the other priests on parchment woven from lustrous silver and gold threads, with Emeraliss's words scribed in amber ink that glowed in both the light and the dark. He had held the note in his hands for all of a moment before it slipped from his grasp, almost too warm to touch. Mostly, he was terrified of the implications. For anyone to argue on his behalf with such conviction, let alone a Goddess... he had no idea what he had done to deserve it, but he prayed that he never proved Emeraliss wrong.

"We will not deny Emeraliss. Her explicitly stated will takes precedence over our rules." Agera clasped Tash's shoulder. "Her charge will be respected where you and your lover are concerned. Your case is not the first of its kind to come to the Assembly in all of its history, but it *is* rare. All such cases have gone through the same challenge, but exceptions can be made when they're warranted. Considering Emeraliss has spoken, and rather loudly, who are we to stand in the way?"

As Agera patted Tash's arm and stepped back, Agera's gaze fell to where Tash held Mayr's hand. A slow smile crept over Agera's lips. "Whatever plans Emeraliss has for you, may they be as fortunate as you both have been." Agera bowed their head. "And with that, I shall leave you to enjoy this good news. Overseer Kee has been informed she can perform your Uldana ceremony anytime she chooses, should you agree to accept the offer. You can turn it down if you so desire, but that would be a terrible shame, if you'll accept my humble opinion."

At that moment, Tash would have accepted anything, the meaning still a jumble of chaos in his head. Even as Mayr kissed his cheek before leading Agera into the hall, Tash was still stuck on what it meant. How it would change things. That he could have everything he needed without giving it all up.

A tear spilled down his cheek, followed by another, then a third before the rest poured out. Happiness—he had almost completely forgotten what it felt like.

He was an exception, not an example to be made. He was free to share his life with his faith and his lover, not choose one over the other. Somewhere along the way, he had made the right decision and joy had finally caught up, along with all else that was waiting to come...

"Thank you," he whispered, the parchment still in his hand, clutched gently. He would have to offer his thanks to Emeraliss in a grander fashion, his words nowhere near enough to fully express his feelings.

But for now...

He was all he wanted to be, no longer trapped in between.

And once Mayr returned after seeing Agera out of the estate, Tash held onto him for dear life, needing to hold on forever without anyone to pry them apart. For all the times he had lost himself, he had been found, and everything to come in their future was just the tangles of love being unraveled, ready for the living.

Chapter Twenty-Two

Kee hid behind the white marble pillar, though Mayr was certain she glowered at him, imagining the ways to get revenge on him for disrupting her plans.

A subtle slap to his arm caught him by surprise. "Stop staring at her," Aeley muttered, shifting her feet and crossing her arms. She uncrossed them and continued to fidget, her arms hanging at her sides. "Besides, you should be staring at your man. He's the reason we're here."

No argument about that. Mayr smiled his agreement at Aeley and cast a glance across the temple to where Tash waited for his ceremony to begin. Standing as part of the inner circle of witnesses, Mayr was dressed in embroidered white pants and shirt as he had promised. In order to see Tash's face during the rite, he stood in the portion of the circle facing the closed doors with Aeley to his left and Lira to his right. Both wore white like him; Lira's gown and bodice simple like Aeley's pants and tunic. Across from them stood Tash's family, also clothed in white. Parase's joyful tears already spilled over her cheeks, and she dabbed them with a cloth.

Mayr's family comprised the rest of the inner circle. The children spoke quietly, occasionally waving and making faces at Mayr until Estara or Orlee stopped them. His mother was the only one who sat, comfortable in a cushioned chair. Malary nodded at Mayr from where he stood beside Renett, a smirk on his lips.

Outside the inner circle was a larger circle formed by priests of the various levels. They spoke among themselves in hushed tones, facing the altar at the centre of the inner circle. Three Uldana priestesses stood at the altar. Soon Tash would be one of them.

Mayr's stomach seemed to flip and flop, his nerve ready to take on anything that could ruin the ceremony for Tash. The rite would be short, according to Armamae, but Mayr prayed it was flawless. In the two months since Tash's fourth trial, Tash had been happier, laughing and smiling without a hint of sadness. Although Tash was still in recovery from his wounds, the stitches had been removed, and he could use his left arm again despite the numbness and weakened grip.

They spent as much time together as they could, mostly at the estate where they could be comfortable to be seen and go about whatever they wanted. Several times, Tash had watched Mayr train and spar with the guards, then followed it with lewd comments intended to bait Mayr's desire. While their sexual activities had not progressed further than before, Mayr expected it to change soon if Tash held true to his word.

Of it all, the news from the Sacred Assembly was what pushed Tash over the edge of ecstasy. Two weeks had passed since Keeper Agera's visit, but with how Tash had acted since, the meeting might as well have been two days ago. The night Agera gave Tash the news, Tash had wept in Mayr's arms, overwhelmed by the judgment. Even now, Mayr knew Tash barely believed the Sacred Assembly's decision was real, despite his Uldana ceremony being moments away.

But there he is, fighting a smile. I know he is. Mayr clasped his hands as Tash and Kee walked out from behind the pillar on the outer edge of the sacred space. Behind Kee, Tash was barefoot and shirtless, dressed only in loose red pants and his bracers. Kee carried his Uldana vestments, the pile of dark red fabric draped over her arms. They crossed gracefully through the circles to the altar. As Kee stopped to the side of the altar, Tash kneeled on the white pillow on the ground, his head bowed to the three priestesses before him.

The shortest of the priestesses stepped forward first, her hair a cascade of tight blonde curls over her shoulders, hanging to her waist. The temple fell silent. "We have gathered in celebration," she began, holding her arms open wide, her gaze sweeping across the room. "It is a blessed day, a joyful day, of life and love; of faith and humility that in all things, the Four reside.

We are together as one, joined in spirit as family, friends, and community. It is as one that we bear witness as the Temple of the Four welcomes Halataldris, brother and devout servant, to the sacred caste of Uldana. His heart is worthy. His intentions pure. So have the Goddesses spoken."

The other two priestesses moved to stand beside the blonde. One was tall with straight, light brown hair while the other was slightly shorter with wavy, black hair to her shoulders. Both carried a symbol of the Four.

"I carry the scepter of our most divine," the tall priestess announced, holding a gleaming silver and glass scepter out with both hands. She looked to Tash, who stared up with a solemn expression. "Through me flows the essence of Emeraliss and Laytia. Benevolent and radiant, They embrace all things. Like water, They connect us all. Like air, They give us being. Through Them, I am Love; I am Wisdom. And so shall you be."

Tash grasped the end of the scepter, his expression unchanged. "In Their grace, I bind myself to Them, in promise and gratitude. I am Love; I am Wisdom. Their will shall be done. As long as I draw breath, I will serve. The hearts and minds of others shall be my light. The essence of Emeraliss and Laytia will guide my soul." He released the scepter to press his hand to his chest.

The black-haired priestess presented an elaborately engraved silver staff. "I carry the staff of our most divine. Through me flows the essence of Navara and Hastal. Compassionate and resplendent, They safeguard all things. Like earth, They sustain us. Like fire, They chase our darkness. Through Them, I am Justice; I am Protection. And so shall you be."

Taking a quick breath, Tash held the staff. "In Their grace, I bind myself to Them, in promise and gratitude. I am Justice; I am Protection. Their will shall be done. As long as I draw breath, I will serve. The spirits and bodies of others shall be my fight. The essence of Navara and Hastal will guide my judgment." Again, he raised his hand to his chest and bowed his head.

Mayr's attention stayed on Tash's face as the priestesses turned towards the altar, their hands moving quickly around the large candles, flower crowns, and glass bowls filled with feathers, water, and earth. They were not as captivating as the relief on Tash's face, or the way he straightened and breathed deep. He appeared trapped between nervousness and excitement, a conflict Mayr found endearing and beautiful.

When his gaze caught Mayr's, Tash beamed. "I love you," he mouthed before returning his attention to the priestesses as they faced him again.

The blonde priestess offered Tash a glass goblet filled with a dark red liquid. "Drink of the sweetness of life and bind your oaths to your body, heart, mind, and spirit. Let the words you have spoken today be heard by the Four and accepted. May your dedication and allegiance please Them for all your days."

Without hesitation, Tash drank deep from the goblet. He offered it back before standing.

Kee stepped forward, arms outstretched. "Pledged and bound, you are Uldana. May all others see you as such, clothed in the colour of the Four." She remained still as each of the three priestesses took a robe from the pile and slipped them over Tash. First was a fully-closed robe, lightweight and loose with straight arms. Next, a heavier robe, laced closed with red cord down his chest and stomach. Last, a flowing, open robe with four gold clasps and flared sleeves to his knuckles.

The glittering, floor-length veil was the final addition, placed upon him by Kee. Gold and white flecks in the fabric reflected the sunlight, but they were not as bright as the blue of his widened eyes.

Turning slightly, Kee accepted a small bell from the blonde priestess. "As you have the attention of the Four on this momentous occasion, do you have anything you would wish of Them?"

"I do," Tash replied. "I am humbled by that which They have bestowed upon me. With great love and a full heart, I ask for their continued blessings and protection upon those I hold dear."

Kee rang the bell.

"For my family, Parase, Kilienn, and Allaysia, I wish joy, safety, and wholeness."

The bell rang again.

"For the priests and priestesses who I have come to cherish and admire, I wish fulfilling lives and great wisdom."

The bell rang once more.

Tash's glance slid to Mayr. "For Mayr, a most sacred gift graciously offered and protected by Emeraliss, so great in worth and depth I cannot repay the kindness, I wish love, peace, and every happiness."

To Kee's credit, she did not huff or sigh as she rang the bell.

"And finally, I wish that Mayr's family, whether it be by blood or by choice, receive blessings as abundantly as they have offered to both him and myself. I see them as my family, strong and loyal. May their lives continue to be graced."

The bell rang for a last time. Kee handed it to the blonde priestess and held out her arms. "The Goddesses hear your words, Brother Halataldris, Uldana priest. Blessings upon you as you walk your path. So shall it be."

"So shall it be," the priests repeated in unison.

"As is tradition, there will be a feast to mark this honour," Kee announced. "Steward Dahe has graciously offered to host it. We will reconvene at her estate early this evening." After the last word, she embraced Tash. The priestesses at the altar hugged him next before others approached to do the same.

Mayr stayed where he was, watching Tash laugh with the priests and accept their welcoming gestures. A twinge of jealousy hit him, but he beat it back. He wished he could have held Tash first and told him how proud he was, but he would do it later when it was just the two of them. Then he could say everything he wanted to say, with and without words.

"That was a nice ceremony," Lira said, smiling as she played with her lace cuff. "It all seems to have worked out."

"Shh, don't say that too loud," Mayr whispered. "The statues have ears. You don't know who has a terrible sense of humour just waiting to strike." He winked. "Oh, wait, that's me. Never mind."

Lira laughed, but Aeley shook her head. "Terrible, yes. Humour? I'm not so sure," Aeley argued dryly.

"That's what I've been saying for *years*," Estara said, nearing them with Dayla, Efae, and Teneth. "No one believes me." She hugged Aeley and Lira before throwing her arms around Mayr's neck. "Good job, though, sticking with him. He's perfect for you. Sweet and fits right in with our bunch. He made Mother cry with his little bit there. She's looking forward to dinner tonight, so don't be late."

"Why would I be late?" Mayr arched his brow, pushing her back. "Loftin's the one with timing issues."

"In more ways than one," Estara muttered.

"Tara! I heard that." Loftin joined them, sneering. "We're at Temple. You're supposed to behave." His face pinched with panic. "Wait. What do you think the chances are I'll get out of here without some kind of spiritual punishment? I'm pretty sure I've got it coming."

Estara rested her forehead in her palm, sighing. "And that's why we never bring you anywhere."

"If you're nice and don't do anything embarrassing, I might just protect you," Aeley told Loftin. "And if you're *really* good, I might just let you stay the night in our home."

Loftin's eyes widened as he gave her a teasing grin. "Really? Oh, Aeley, that's just the *best* news! Can I love you forever and ever and ever?" He embraced her dramatically, pinning her arms and restricting her from hitting him. "Tara, you can shove off. I've got a new sister."

Aeley grunted and swatted his ribs. "Trust me, you don't. Estara, take him back."

"No, that's all right," Estara said. "Thanks for the offer, though."

"You're stuck with me." Loftin giggled and kissed Aeley's cheek. He jumped away before she punched at him.

"Be careful, Loftin, or she might find a special way to get you unstuck," Tash's voice warned. As everyone faced him, he blushed. "Sorry, I thought I'd join the family moment."

Estara hugged him, careful not to remove his veil. "Consider yourself joined. Congratulations! The ceremony was beautiful. You look so happy."

"I am." Tash returned Mayr's gaze and eased away from Estara. "I have much to be happy about."

"It's not over yet." Aeley embraced Tash. "I've got news from the Council you might just enjoy. I'll tell you later when Mayr isn't staring at you like he wants to swallow you whole."

Mayr pursed his lips. "Now you're just being inappropriate, Ae. You and Loftin deserve each other."

Lira made a strangled noise of protest.

"All right, good point. Sorry, Lira." Mayr kissed the top of Lira's head, drawing her into him with one arm. "She deserves *you*. We'll just make Loftin her pet."

Loftin's jaw dropped, his glance raking over Mayr with disbelief.

"And with that—" Tash grasped Mayr's wrist. "I need to steal him away for a little while. There's something important I need to do, and it won't wait." He pulled Mayr against him. "I promise to return him in one piece at dinner."

"Just don't be late!" Estara called as Tash led Mayr away.

Mayr squeezed Tash's hand and fell into step with him. "You know, I have this funny feeling she wants us to be on time."

Tash laughed softly. "She must be reading my mind." His robes swept the floor as he led Mayr through the corridors to his chamber.

"What are we doing? Something inappropriate?" Mayr teased, closing the door as Tash hurried towards his bed.

When Tash turned around holding two dressing robes—one red and one white—Mayr stopped cold.

"No. I'd say it's wholly appropriate." Tash held out the white robe. "Here, put this on."

Knowing better than to argue, Mayr accepted the dressing robe and stripped. Carefully, Tash did the same and draped his pristine robes over a chair. Mayr donned the dressing robe and tied it closed. The belt looped around his waist once to fasten at the hip, similar to Tash's robe. They stopped to stare at each other, Mayr's mind reeling with the possibilities of what was to come. Part of him wanted to ask. The rest of him commanded he not ruin the surprise.

Tash removed his bracers and tossed them onto the bedside table before he held out his hand. "Ready?"

I have been for days, for nights, for the whole time I've known you. And maybe even my whole life. Mayr took Tash's hand. "Yes."

They journeyed through the corridors and down two flights of stairs, bypassing several priests who said nothing, to Mayr's relief. Near the end of a long, dim corridor, Tash led him into a room to their right and closed the door.

While the bright room was not as large as the sacred space above, it was far from small, nearly twice the size of the Dahe estate's dining room. In the centre stood an altar of black and white marbled stone, accompanied by white stone busts attached to the sides of the altar, all of them exquisite carvings of a woman looking outwards with slender eyes, her curled hair expertly detailed. Four white statues kept the altar company, with one statue in each corner of the room, all depicting various likenesses of Emeraliss. All four statues faced the altar, each carrying a scepter in one hand and a silver bird on the other.

Although the statues were beautiful, Mayr was more taken by the soft yellow glow that filled the room. Someone had laid out dozens of white candles, their flames flickering together with shadows dancing on the walls. Several more candles surrounded the altar, just as varied in height and girth as the others, but petals—there were white and red flower petals scattered among them.

Near the opposite wall, two silver candelabrums sat on a dark table with a glass bowl, goblet, a small glass vial, folded cloths, and white flowers on green vines that spilled over the edge and coiled around the table legs. A fragrant scent clung to the air, sweet enough to make

Mayr's mouth water for the taste of honey and mead.

Candles, everywhere candles. And that's probably all I'll remember of this room when we're done. I definitely won't be thinking about the statues watching us because… no.

From behind, Tash wrapped his arm around Mayr's waist, his lips working up Mayr's neck with light kisses. Mayr sucked in a breath only to exhale just as quickly.

"I had Brother Armamae prepare the room," Tash murmured, nuzzling Mayr's jaw and clutching his hip. "He was elated to help." Firm against Mayr, Tash's arousal was obvious, unrestrained by the thin dressing robes. His body taunted Mayr, reeling Mayr in with the promise that once inside him, Tash would be his completely.

Humming quietly at the thought, Mayr curled his arm around Tash's neck and rubbed against him—a slow, seductive grind that had Tash groaning his approval in Mayr's ear, enticing him to press harder. He tugged Tash's hair gently as Tash's lips explored the crook of his neck, the tip of his tongue roving over Mayr's tattoos, licking a path across Mayr's throat that left Mayr shivering. Tash's touch at Mayr's hip was just as ready to play, his fingers creeping over the folds of Mayr's dressing robe and slipping inside the soft fabric, the touch of skin on skin hot and smooth and perfect as fingertips followed the thin patch of coarse hair leading down Mayr's belly to his swollen cock. Mayr moaned as Tash gripped him tenderly and drew his fist along Mayr's length once, twice, and again, the pressure alternating between soft and hard as Tash stroked him.

There in Tash's arms, it was all too easy to surrender, with every bit of his fears thrown at Tash's feet, his wants and needs and hopes laid bare, ready for the taking. He wanted *this*, all of it, and whatever Tash offered in return. If anything, he fully intended to stoke the fury of passion that stormed through him, one with a terrifying depth and insatiable thirst that reached out to Tash; rejoiced in him. Tash had said their spirits were connected; that he needed Mayr. The truth was Mayr needed him, too, the familiarity he felt for Tash giving way to unadulterated joy.

In the end, they needed each other more than words could say, and this hold, this connection, this trust—all of this was theirs. Both of them had been burned, broken, and haunted, but the future was the life they could share. Never again would he allow Tash to run towards danger without him. Nor would he stop taking care of Tash or protecting him. In Tash, there was love; in love, there was life, and he would fight to keep that life, no matter what.

Breaking free from Tash's hold, Mayr turned to face him and untied his robe. The fabric slipped from his shoulders with ease and pooled on the floor behind him. He drew his loose, dark hair over his shoulders and teased the ends, pleased as Tash's longing gaze followed his movements. With a steady grasp, he flattened Tash's hand over his heart. "You have me, Halataldris. Here. You are my first. You will be my only. I want you to be my everything. What I have is yours, and what is yours I will cherish."

Mayr pressed against him, the rise and fall of their chests in tandem. "Love me, Halataldris," he whispered against Tash's lips.

Tash trembled, his shaky breath escaping his lips and dancing across Mayr's, anticipation teasing them both. There was almost an uncertainty, a tiny moment stuck on *what if*, but that look in Tash's eyes—

His mouth took to Mayr's in a heated kiss, crushing doubt and giving into desperate need. Hands running down Mayr's back and hips, Tash pulled Mayr hard against him, their tongues playing fervently as they traded moans and teasing nips. As Mayr fumbled with the tie of Tash's robe, Tash guided them towards the altar. They maneuvered cautiously, sidestepping the candles while soft petals moved beneath their feet, cool to the touch.

By the time they reached the altar, Tash's robe was unfastened and open. Backed against the warm stone, the altar touched the back of Mayr's thighs. At Tash's silent insistence, urged back by a deep, demanding kiss, Mayr sat on the edge of the altar.

He whimpered in disappointment as Tash broke away.

"Stay right here," Tash instructed. His steps were swift as he headed for the table and grabbed the vial, then returned just a quickly to wrap his arms around Mayr's shoulders, standing between his legs. He claimed Mayr's mouth again, sucking on Mayr's bottom lip and inhaling Mayr's weak breaths. Behind Mayr's head, Tash's hands and wrists made small movements. They stilled before Tash withdrew one arm and put the vial into the pocket of his robe.

Still invested in their kiss, Tash drew his hands over Mayr's shoulders, kneading and rubbing. His fingers slid down Mayr's arms and chest with an oily ease, working the skin with lingering strokes. A familiar perfume stole Mayr's attention: millee nectar and red corina plant, a combination that pushed Mayr's arousal further, only adding to the growing ache in his cock. The oils sank into his skin, pleasurable like Tash's touch.

The kiss ended but the massage continued while Tash kneeled, his hands working a path down Mayr's hips to his thighs. When his fingers journeyed between Mayr's legs, they met his mouth as he swallowed Mayr's cock.

Mayr stifled a cry, cursing silently at how well Tash played his body. To make it even worse, Tash hummed as he took Mayr deeper, his lips locking around the base of Mayr's cock just long enough to leave Mayr groaning. On his way back up, Tash tongued the underside of Mayr's cock to the tip and raked the swollen head with his teeth before flashing Mayr a playful smile. His teasing was far from finished as he kissed the inside of Mayr's thigh, his fingers gliding downwards, over the tight skin of Mayr's sac to the entrance beyond.

Goddesses, yes. Mayr leaned back on his elbows, granting Tash a better angle. Fingertips rubbed and teased, gently stretching him open before one of Tash's slicked fingers entered him, cautious but steady. Mayr spread his legs wider and lifted his hips, only to bite back a curse at the awkwardness.

"Wait," Mayr said, sitting up and lifting Tash's chin. He moved across the altar until he lay along its length. The altar was longer than he was tall, with almost a foot length of extra space left on either end. "All right, $n-$"

Before Mayr could finish, Tash was on the altar. Grinning as he crawled between Mayr's raised knees, he pinned Mayr with an arm on either side. The grin gave way to a quick, biting kiss before Tash sat up, his legs bent under him. The vial was in his hands in the next instant. He poured oil into his palm, stopped the vial, and returned it to his pocket. Bent over Mayr on hands and knees, Tash massaged Mayr's entrance again, his finger sliding in readily.

Even though they had only done it once before, Mayr's body remembered it well enough to immediately demand more. From the sensations shooting through his every limb, up every vein, across every nerve, it seemed as though his body drew Tash in and refused to let go, addicted to the pleasure it offered. He groaned as Tash's finger turned and went further, up to the knuckle. Hips rocking in gradual rhythm, Mayr rode Tash's touch as he withdrew, twisted, and pushed in again.

Another moan had Mayr rolling his eyes back. He was hard and entirely too frustrated to take things slow, his cock wanting attention so badly it hurt. Trapped between Tash and Mayr's stomachs, taunted by Tash's own thick, rigid erection, Mayr's cock wanted a fist, a mouth, Tash's body—anything to relieve the building pressure.

Options. He had few of those right then and waiting…

Mayr gripped his cock and stroked hard, brushing his hand along Tash's cock at the same time.

Tash's breath hitched, and he sank lower, grinding into Mayr. The burn of a second finger entering Mayr lasted briefly, lost to the pressure of Tash's lips on his mouth and neck. Around them, Tash's red robe flowed and pooled on the altar, soft to the touch, a whisper of sensuality in how it moved with Tash.

The fabric was no match for what raced through Mayr as Tash bit his shoulder, throwing a dozen fantasies at Mayr and nearly pushing him too close to coming. While Tash licked and sucked as he nursed what would no doubt become a bruise by the end of the night, his fingers drove deep into Mayr, stretching him, bringing a burn and a promise of not stopping this time. Mayr rocked and pushed hard against him, hissing at Tash's third finger as it worked into him, but it was not what he needed. There was only one thing that would do.

"Tash," Mayr managed between groans.

Worry hit him as Tash sat back and withdrew his fingers. *But…*

The vial was out of Tash's pocket and open before Mayr could argue, with more oil being poured into Tash's palm. After the vial was safe in his robe again, Tash stroked his own cock, coating its length with a mix of oil and pre-release. He leaned over Mayr, their gazes locked, a deep, comforting desire passing between them—one he felt to the tips of his toes as Tash kissed him tenderly.

"Our first time," Tash murmured against Mayr's lips, "just as it should be. Just as you deserve."

Mayr wrapped his legs around Tash's waist, the robe pulling taut. "And we're alone, just like you wanted. Make me scream your name." He lifted his hips further in invitation.

Tash wasted no time, the eagerness in his blue gaze as intense as the messy, heated kiss he gave Mayr before entering him, his cock pushing deeper just a bit at once. Mayr's back bowed against the sharp pain, driving him further onto Tash until Tash was inside him completely. They lay still together, their shallow breaths finding a matched pace.

With his arms and legs around Tash, keeping him close, Mayr shifted, Tash's cock settling in him. The pain subsided, but pleasure—that unraveled like a thick, warm thread, weaving through every part of him while something else fed on his need to know Tash inside and out, every bit of him intertwined with Mayr, laced throughout his life from start to finish. He felt full. Grounded. Found. Ready for more.

Playfully, he wiggled his hips, hoping it was enough of a hint...

Tash chuckled and kissed him again before he shifted his hips, moving in and out slowly, only to quicken the rhythm as he continued. The longer he thrust, the harder it all hit Mayr—how Tash had always belonged there, in him, around him, part of him in all ways. While their bodies responded as if they were meant for each other, what attraction Mayr had felt for anyone else was nothing compared to his feelings for Tash. They had never completed him, never like this. Not to his very core.

Desire blazed inside Mayr, and all he could think about was Tash finding his release with him, bringing them to where they both wanted to be together, no interruptions and no holding back. This was their time, whatever they chose to make of it. These were their moments to finally enjoy what they could have for the rest of their lives, fate willing—and he fully intended to make the best of every moment they had.

Taking Tash's dry hand, Mayr entwined their fingers and squeezed. Tash's movements only intensified, driving hard and deep as his lips and tongue darted over Mayr's throat.

Need raged through Mayr's cock again, his shaft pulsing within his grasp, swollen and ready to tip over the edge of too much. Each stroke pushed him further. When Tash's fist joined his, Mayr moaned and thrust into the touch. Together they rubbed and teased, bathing their fingers in his pre-release. At any moment, he would burst through the barrier between sanity and coming.

Tash freed his dry hand to caress the underside of Mayr's forearm.

Mayr's sanity crashed.

His breaths faltered, loud and quick, his heart racing in competition to see what did him in first. Feather-light and unexpected, Tash's fingertips danced up his arm. He wanted to run. He wanted to stay. He wanted to do everything all at once. But the ache, the cock ramming into him, the musky scent of Tash all around him, the touch—

"Halataldris!" Mayr shuddered and contracted, tightening his hold on Tash. His release came hard and fast, shooting across his stomach. Wet and warm, some of it pooled while the rest flowed down his sides. He rocked into Tash's deep thrusts and drew his knees higher into his chest.

Tash curled around Mayr, cradling Mayr's head on his arms. "Mayr," he whimpered, burying his face in Mayr's neck as his body tightened, his hips moving faster, everything about him on the edge until climax took him. He gripped Mayr as he moaned and thrust through his release until he was spent.

Still wrapped around one another, they recovered, breathing together. Once they were calmer, Tash pulled out from Mayr and sat back on his legs. Mayr pushed himself up and guided the red robe down Tash's arms, loving how beautiful it looked on Tash but needing to hold Tash close, nothing between them but skin. There were no words of protest; Tash allowed the robe to drape over the end of the altar behind him before lying beside Mayr. They faced each other, pressed together with their legs entangled and Tash's hand on Mayr's hip.

"I have to wonder what Emeraliss would think of what just happened," Mayr said, "because I'd like to think we did something good."

Tash's fingers glided over Mayr's smooth jaw. "It's one of the greatest offerings that can be made. Those who choose to make such an offering must have purest intentions and love in their hearts." He kissed Mayr's forehead. "And those we have."

Mayr's glance caught on Tash's scarred wrist; the right arm, with the unfinished cut.

Without thinking, Mayr brought Tash's forearm to his lips and kissed the scars. He worked his way up to linger on the most recent wound. "You will never have cause to finish this, ever. I promise. And you know how important promises are."

A small smile crept across Tash's lips. "I will never push you away again. Nor will I ever believe you are unworthy or not good enough. You are more than enough. You're the rest of me I've never had."

By the Four, I love the way you talk. Mayr kissed Tash softly.

As their lips parted, Mayr froze, staring over Tash's shoulder. Out of nowhere, four white feathers had materialized, bursting into existence in the space between the altar and the door. They drifted to the floor, scattered in different directions. When they reached the ground, they emanated a silver glow with a thin, white streak of blinding light at their core.

"Um," Mayr started, blinking. Had he not seen it for himself, he would have thought it was just a tale. After all the years of doubting the Four, questioning Their existence, he was starting to believe. The Uldana Trials had changed their lives completely, even in ways he still could not fathom. "So, Emeraliss... How much is She keeping an eye on us?"

"Why?"

"Well... those feathers are a bit suggestive."

Tash followed Mayr's gaze. He laughed and turned back to Mayr with a wide grin. "I told you we were supposed to be together. Now She's just proven it true. I'll take that as a sign our offering was appreciated. Shall we aim for a second?"

Between Tash's hopeful expression and the feathers from another plane of existence, Mayr could think of no other answer but one: *Yes.*

Epilogue

Torchlight reflected off the silver gilding of the Dahe estate's ballroom, the flames dancing with as much vigour as the guests. White, blood-red, and bright pink flowers cascaded over the grey walls, their long, dark stems woven into wicker lattices hung between the tapestries. The spring tapestries had been replaced with those of summer, the scenes of merriment and romantic notions reflecting the atmosphere of Valaster's Feast in green and yellow threads. Music filled the ballroom with lively notes, drowned out by laughter. Around the long table spanning the length of the room, couples danced and mingled, their clothes creating a sea of colour.

There was only one colour Mayr's attention strayed to every few moments: a deep red that shimmered even in the faintest light, worn by a single person at the feast. The only one for whom his heart stumbled in and out of rhythm with the heated glances reserved for him.

Mayr turned his back to the guests and faced Tash. Standing near the wall, Tash looked every part the Uldana priest, his robes and veil falling gracefully, hiding the seductive body beneath.

Only his talon ring could be considered out of place. One glance at it made Mayr shiver. The ring had grazed and punctured his skin more than a dozen times in the last eight months, leaving an unforgettable trail of pleasurable pain in its wake.

"Are we having fun?" Mayr asked, swallowing the desire pulsing through his body quicker than he could sort the memories dirtying his thoughts. He wanted to strip the pretty fabric away until all that was left was the supple body he held almost every night.

Tash tore his amused gaze away from the dancers. "Of course."

"Really?" Mayr arched a brow. "Even though you're standing here, watching people with me, unable to dance or do anything even remotely fun?"

One step brought Tash close enough to touch their hips together. "Especially since I'm with you. Everything else is irrelevant. Besides, you forget: I used to do this same thing."

Mayr let out a restrained, frustrated breath. The contact did nothing to assuage what was happening in his pants. "So," he started, mouth dry as he studied Tash's lips, wanting more than a simple taste. "Seeing as Emeraliss is your patron goddess, would you say tonight's been acceptable? Or would every deity and Temple be absolutely horrified?"

"Yes, yes they would." Tash laughed, eyes sparkling as he teased. "Because Aeley and you— no sense of propriety at all." He clasped Mayr's hand. "It's perfect; a celebration worthy of Valaster the Unburdened. Any consort would be pleased with the pains you've all taken." He kissed Mayr's knuckles. "Now stop worrying and go back to staring like you want me."

The command left Mayr's thoughts whimpering for so much more than words. Would he always be that easy for Tash to read?

"Since you went there..." Mayr curled his arm around Tash's waist. "I was thinking maybe we should revisit the altar again. Make another offering. After all, it's the first of summer tomorrow. And tonight's a sacred night, especially since I hear Emeraliss particularly enjoyed Valaster in bed. You said earlier it's a time of renewal, rebirth, and new life—and that's what we gave each other," he said. "I've never been as happy as I've been these months with you. Almost ten months of something I'd kill to protect; of knowing I'd do anything for you. And we have so much to celebrate. Us. Your priesthood and everything that comes with it—all those rites and meetings and the traipsing around Kattal that you do now, just like you wanted. The Council pardoning you. The fact the hunters have tracked down more of the Shar-denn members on your list, getting you some more protection." He slipped his hand under Tash's hair, following the curves of Tash's throat to cup the back of his neck. "I want to celebrate. Our way."

Tash did not hesitate. "All right."

"Really?"

"Really."

Recollection of their first time doused Mayr's rational thoughts. Driven by passion, pursued by need, he let his mind and mouth run rampant, taking Tash's lips in a hard kiss. "I'll lead this time, though," he said, breathless as they parted. "Oils, blindfolds, the entire thing. All for you." A twinge of doubt nagged him. "Assuming Emeraliss wouldn't be offended by it?"

"No," Tash replied, smirking. "She'd delight in it. Might just earn you more feathers."

"Good." Mayr nuzzled Tash's unshaven cheek. "Then I'll scream your name, Halataldris, so loud and so often, even Emeraliss's bird will lose track of what's going on."

Tash shivered. "Say it again."

"Halataldris," Mayr whispered against Tash's ear. Beneath his hands, Tash's body weakened and curved into Mayr. Tash clung to him as though Tash's knees were about to buckle.

"Keep this up and I'll haul you to our spot in the conservatory."

"Or maybe I'll take you right here. If I wasn't working, I'd be inside you right now."

Eyes wide, lips parted, Tash eyed Mayr with surprise before it shot to yearning. Mayr could not help but laugh and grind gently against Tash.

"Wait, you're *together* now?" a woman squealed from over his shoulder. "What in the Four is this? It wasn't going *that* well!"

Mayr spun towards Sarene. Dressed in a bright pink gown with her shoulders bared, wearing matching ribbons and small, yellow flowers in the numerous tiny plaits of her blonde hair, she stood with her hands clenched. Her face red, she gaped at Mayr and Tash's entwined fingers.

"Sarene," Mayr greeted from behind his strained smile. He had not seen her since she broke up with him, not even in passing in the village—mostly because he had not cared to look. "How are you? Where's your latest toy?"

Mouth opening and closing without sound, Sarene continued to stare. Her gaze flickered to the floor. "I'm not with anyone. Can't be with anyone when they keep leaving," she added quietly, wringing her fingers in the gauzy top layer of her gown.

"And what a shame that is." Mayr pulled on Tash. "Sorry, but we need to be somewhere."

As they brushed past Sarene, Tash stopped beside her and grasped her bare shoulder. "Thank you, for everything. Truly. Because of you, we finally found each other. Our search is finished. We are indebted to you." He kissed her cheek. "May your own search find such a joyous end. If you ever need someone to talk to, I want you to come see me."

Stunned and tearful, Sarene watched them as they walked away.

"And since you're you, you actually mean it," Mayr muttered, holding Tash to his side with one arm. They moved around the crowds with ease, taking advantage of the courtesy shown to Tash as people cleared a path.

"She deserves to be happy, too." Tash gazed at him lovingly even while scolding him. "She just isn't included in *our* happiness."

"I know." Mayr sighed, guiding them towards the other side of the room. Aeley and Lira were there somewhere. *Probably causing troub—*

"Mayr?" a quiet voice inquired from behind them.

A chill rushed down Mayr's legs from the knee. The unexpected voice belonged to his past, safe in his memories, not at a ball where Aeley could follow through on her promises.

Tash squeezed Mayr's hand. Swallowing back the nausea and anxiety combating his emotions, Mayr faced the owner of the voice. The blood rushed from his face, his body too numb to do anything else but stand rigid. Betta stood before him in a simple, light green gown with layered black lace cuffs, biting her bottom lip and rocking on her heels. While she still wore her wavy, brown hair long and her brown eyes were still haunting, she looked tired and run down, no longer vibrant and youthful. The years had stolen it all away.

"Betta." The name fell from his lips before his mind could fathom it.

She offered him a nervous smile and stepped closer. "Mayr. How are you?"

How could he answer that? How could she *ask* it? "Fine," Mayr replied without thought, "just... confused. Why? Why are you here, of all places, and *now*?" *Your name wasn't on any invitation I saw. Aeley's going to have a fit.*

"I know." Betta lowered her gaze, her clasped hands trembling. "I shouldn't be here. I'll leave right away, I promise. I—I just wanted to—" Tears gathered in her eyes as she sighed. "I just wanted to apologize. In person. I—I've been thinking about you a lot lately. About what I did." Cautious, she neared Mayr and laid a hand on his arm. She immediately snatched her hand back. "I was wrong, Mayr, and I did *you* wrong. I know that, and I'm sorry. I know it doesn't make up for anything. I'm not a fool. What I did—it's unforgivable. Despicable." Betta fingered one of her cuffs, her head lowered. "I wish I could say I didn't know what I was thinking—that it was only because I was young and foolish or someone made me do it—but I'd be lying. I thought I could do better. I don't know why, I just did. But I didn't realize you *were* the better. I didn't appreciate you. I didn't understand."

To put it mildly, Mayr almost said, biting his cheek. "Well, thanks for sharing your newfound understanding. I'm so incredibly touched you'd *finally* think about me. Guess I'll just fall at your feet and kiss it all better." When Tash elbowed him gently in the ribs, Mayr grunted softly. Maybe he was being too harsh. Maybe he was being just harsh enough. Too many responses drifted through his thoughts. For every instinct telling him to hug her and forgive her, a doubt demanded he hold his ground and deny her the absolution of acceptance. She deserved many things—but he was still uncertain as to what they were, particularly when they were surrounded by people who could sense a matter of gossip from across the room.

Betta nodded resignedly. "You're right to hate me, no less than I hate myself. It hasn't been easy." She held up her hands, panic spreading over her face. "I'm not looking for sympathy, especially not from you. Just saying after I left, I learned all the lessons I'd overlooked the hard way. I found out just how difficult things could really be."

"My heart bleeds," Mayr mumbled.

"So did mine, especially when I found out men didn't want me because I was a mother." Betta smirked sadly. "They didn't want a family, and definitely not some other man's child. They just wanted sex. That was it. My child was a scourge. I could have her or them, but not both."

"I could've told you that." Mayr crossed his arms. "Had you just talked to me, *really* talked, I would've listened. I *always* listened. But you didn't trust me, did you? I know you didn't respect me, but you could've at least tried trust."

"I know that now," Betta said. "I also know you were happy to be a father. That's what made me realize how wrong I was. I was chasing after something I thought I wanted, but the whole time I'd had it and ran away. You were providing for us without complaining. You gave us a real home. We never would've been wealthy, but we would've been secure. Loved. Protected. By the time I realized it, it was too late. I couldn't come back. And Aeley, she—" With a nervous glance, Betta surveyed the ballroom. "She made it painfully clear I was *never* to come back." She rubbed her cheek and smiled. "Now I'm married—actually married—and Barin, he's a lot like you. Kind, caring. It took forever to find him. Being with him… I know how much I lost, how foolish I was. How much you deserve better."

All the words he had wanted to hear. All the things his heart had needed. He had waited years for even just the whisper of them. Finally, the moment had arrived, and she laid them at his feet, free for the taking.

He had no idea what to feel.

Sad that she had stomped on his love but paid what sounded like a hefty price; angry that she had left at all. Happy that she had found someone; thankful they could put the issue to rest. Mayr gripped Tash's hand, wishing the confusion away.

"Why now?" Mayr asked. "Why didn't you say any of this before? It's been *ten years*."

"I didn't think you'd listen. Or that you'd even agree to see me." Betta bit her lip. "I expected you'd toss me at Aeley and just walk away." She exhaled deeply. "I almost did come to you, though, when Iliane was sick, almost dying. We needed a new place, extra medicines, but I—I didn't think you'd help. I didn't think you'd want to see us or be involved."

Before he could stop himself, Mayr grasped her arms. The thought of Iliane sick and dying hurt more than listening to Betta grovel or beg. "Of course I would've helped. I'd have done anything for her. Just because you and I were done doesn't mean I stopped caring for her—for either of you."

Betta nodded. "That's what Priest Tash said."

"Tash?" Mayr slid his glance towards Tash.

"He found us, not too long ago. Talked to us. He wanted to know we were all right—if we had what we needed. He was so kind, so thoughtful. Said time had healed old wounds. So I decided to visit and make sure *you* were all right. Happy." Her gaze passed between Mayr and Tash, and she grinned. "Though seeing you together, I'm pretty sure I've got the answer. You look good. Love suits you. It always has." She kissed Mayr's cheek.

And you've been conspiring, Mayr accused Tash silently, pursing his lips. They would talk about *that* matter later.

A flash of memory replayed Betta's words through his mind. He sucked in a breath and gripped Betta's elbow as another chill surged through him. "Iliane. She didn't…?"

Betta shook her head. "Someone took pity on us. Helped her recover." She pointed into the crowd. "Actually, she's here with me and Barin. Did you want to see her?"

The breath Mayr had been holding whooshed out. "Yes."

After several steps through the crowd, Betta waved excitedly.

Tash slipped something warm and metallic into Mayr's hand, discreetly coiling it in his palm. Confused, Mayr opened his fist.

The necklace he had bought Iliane. A chain of white gold dotted with small, red petals formed from tiny jewels. Three larger white jewels dropped from the centre. He had purchased it because he wanted her to have something beautiful; something that was hers alone because she was special to him. At last, he could give it to her.

Fighting tears, he looked at Tash, who did nothing but smile. They would *definitely* have a long talk later.

Moments later, a girl squeezed through the crowd to take Betta's hand. Together they approached Mayr and Tash, their resemblance undeniable. Iliane's dark hair was curled, the thick ringlets framing her cheerful, round face and large brown eyes. She was skinny and short, her height to her mother's bosom. To his relief, she appeared healthy, her tan skin complemented by her blue gown with its puffy sleeves and white ribbons. On each of her fingers, she wore a colourful, woven ring.

"Iliane," Betta started, pushing her closer, "you remember Priest Tash?" When Iliane curtsied, Betta smiled. "And this is Mayr. He's a good friend of ours; yours and mine."

"It's nice to meet you," Iliane greeted, curtsying again. She hugged her mother, watching Tash and Mayr with interest.

Mayr swallowed, remembering how small she had been. How perfectly she had fit in his arms. "It's nice to meet you, too. See you, I mean. It's been a long time." He bit his tongue. Why could he not think of anything better to say?

Betta rubbed Iliane's shoulder. "You wouldn't remember it, but he knew you when you were little. He was there the day you were born and held you when you cried and took your first breaths. He held you *a lot*. I had to practically tear you out of his arms. It was like fighting a bearcat, all growly and snappy and grr."

Iliane laughed as her mother tickled her arm, her nose crinkling as her eyes brightened. In that moment, she looked exactly like her mother used to.

"He took care of both of us," Betta continued. "He treated us like we were goddesses. We had to leave, but it wasn't his fault."

"It's just how things happened," Mayr added. He stared at his fingers clutching the necklace. "But I have something for you, Ili... ane, something that belongs to you." Kneeling, he held the necklace out. "I thought you might like it."

Iliane's widened eyes took in the shining metal and jewels. "It's so pretty. Just like a grown-up's," she said, touching it. "Mama, can I have it?"

"Mayr says it belongs to you, so of course you can." Betta squeezed Iliane's shoulder. "You'll have to be very careful with it, yes?"

After Mayr clasped the necklace around her neck, Iliane nodded. "I will." She cupped the large jewels in her palms, gaping at them. "Thank you, Mayr," she murmured.

Mayr stood back, overwhelmed with emotion. To see it on her—to hear her say his name—it was as much a miracle as anything. "You're welcome, Ili."

Pensive, Iliane's gaze bounced between Mayr and the necklace. She removed one of her rings. "This one's for you," she said, holding out the ring of red, purple, and gold threads tightly bound and knotted in a banded pattern. "I want you to have it. It means we're friends now."

As though he knew Mayr's knees would give way, Tash wrapped his arm around Mayr's back. *Whatever you do, keep it together,* Mayr told himself, grateful for Tash's touch. *Don't cry. Don't make a fool of yourself. Just take the damn ring.*

"I'd be honoured," Mayr said, accepting the ring to slip it on his little finger. It reached the second joint and sat snugly, though he would get a chain made for it later to keep it safe. "Thank you."

Iliane flashed him a bright grin. "You're welcome." She tugged on her mother's sleeve. "I'm going to show Father my new pretty!" Before Betta could argue, Iliane wandered into the crowd, her head bowed over the jewels in her palm.

"Ili!" Betta rolled her eyes. "I'm sorry. I have to go before she gets elbowed in the head or something. She doesn't always look where she's going." She licked her lips. "This is goodbye, but not for good. You can come and see us. You can see her whenever you want. I won't keep her from you. Something you can consider?"

"Yeah." Mayr was breathless, his emotions still reeling. "I'd like that. Thanks, Betta. I mean it."

"I know." After another kiss to his cheek, Betta rushed after Iliane.

Tired of guests watching them with interest in their eyes, Mayr pulled Tash towards the nearest corner. He needed to get out of there, to retreat to a safe space where it was just Tash, him, and every emotion smashing down the walls of his anger and despair. He would have to settle with an empty corner.

"What did you do?" Mayr kept his back to the crowd as he urged Tash into the corner.

Tash drew his fingertips down Mayr's jaw. "I asked around, talked to Aeley, and had some priests I know do some thinking. It took a few months, but someone knew someone else who had seen them in Temple from time to time, making offerings."

"But why?"

"I told you: I'll take care of you. Always."

"Always, hmm?"

"As in forever. You are forever stuck with me," Tash whispered on Mayr's lips. "Not just tonight, tomorrow, or the years to come. Forever, as far as the Goddesses know it."

An offer I can't refuse, Mayr decided, returning Tash's passionate kiss. *You're my Halataldris, my companion, my freedom, my heart. Everything. Always. Forever.*

Fin

Playlist for Four

(Artists and songs are listed in alphabetical order)

Themes:
Freya Ridings — Ultraviolet
Freya Ridings — Ultraviolet (Live at St Pancras Old Church)
Valerie Broussard — From the Ashes

Mayr & Tash themes:
Conjure One — Extraordinary Way (feat. Poe)
Ellie Goulding — Love Me Like You Do
Nickelback — Trying Not to Love You
SOHN — Carry Me Home

Mayr theme:
Lifehouse — Trying

Tash theme:
Florence + the Machine — Long & Lost

Rest of the Playlist!
A Perfect Circle — The Noose
Ahn Trio — All I Want (feat. Susie Suh)
Au/Ra — I'm So Tired… (Secret Session)

Au/Ra — Ultraviolet (Secret Sessions)
Avril Lavigne — Let Me Go (feat. Chad Kroeger)

Bedroom Rockers — Nothing Else Matters
Blue October — Hate Me

Cinephile — Comatose
Cinephile — One
Cinephile — What Becomes of Us
City and Colour — As Much As I Ever Could
City and Colour — Day Old Hate
Conjure One — Sleep (feat. Marie-Claire D'Ubaldo)

Daft Punk — Beyond

Ed Sheeran — I See Fire
Elijah Woods x Jamie Fine — Stone Heart
Enya — Deora Ar Mo Chroi
Evanescence — Missing

Freya Ridings — Ultraviolet (Live acoustic)
Frou Frou — Let Go

Gotye — Hearts A Mess

Hurt — Somnambulist
Hurt — Still

Joseph Trapanese — Convergence (Score Suite from the film, "Insurgent")

Loreena McKennitt — The Old Ways
Loreena McKennitt — The Old Ways (live, Nights from The Alhambra)

Megaherz — Augenblick
Metric — Gold Guns Girls
Metric — Gold Guns Girls (Acoustic)
Moana and the Tribe — Manawa Tahi

OMNIMAR — You Save Me (Restart Version)

Placebo — Running Up That Hill

Skylar Grey — Words

The Weeknd —Tears in the Rain

Underworld — And I Will Kiss (feat. Dame Eve Glennie and the Pandemonium Drummers) (London Olympics 2012)

Woodkid — Never Let You Down (feat. Lykke Li)

Zella Day — Sacrifice

The Republic Continues in
Blood Borne

For Ress, survival is a complicated nightmare. Caught between two masters on different sides of the law, his life is falling apart one bad decision at a time. All he wants is to be is a good person, a loyal family man, and a successful metalsmith—a dream he can never obtain while he works for the Shar-denn, the violent gang that plagues the republic of Kattal.

To make matters worse, he works as an informant for the High Council. He scrapes through both jobs waiting for his last breath. As the Shar-denn motto says: the only way out is dead.

No stranger to living complicated decisions, Adren is caught between worlds of cir own. As the child of a Shar-denn faction boss, cir life is a conflicted tangle of expectation and duty. When cir family is arrested, Adren manages to escape, but nowhere is safe. Desperate and on the run, Adren is determined to punish Ress for turning in cir family. No one who betrays the gang can live. Ress must pay the price, even if Adren has to go against everything ce is.

Author's Note

Hi there, and thanks for giving this story a read! If you're new to *The Republic* series, many warm welcomes, and if this isn't your first time around, welcome back! These books don't go anywhere without folks like you. <3

This story... it has stories of its own. Mostly that it wasn't something I'd thought of doing until Mayr went and took things over. It's what he does: hijacks everything and changes the whole plan, then laughs it off for a few books before he goes annoying me again. (The fact that book #4 even exists is exactly what I mean.)

Anyway, *Four* wasn't planned. I'd actually been plotting something else at the time, which ended up being *Blood Borne* in the end. But during the process, I poked my nose into things a little too far and stumbled across Mayr, who wouldn't get out of my head. Again. He was supposed to make a simple appearance or two and move on. But no, he wasn't done. Instead, he latched onto my thoughts, dumped an entire story on me, and three days later I had everything outlined for this story, top to bottom. He had things to say, a love to find, and wanted to get out into the world, so... that happened.

But I'm glad it happened, because Mayr and Tash have become so very dear to me as characters. The more I've worked with them, the more I've seen how complicated they are as people and a couple, as well as how complex the world is around them. They've also been the gateway to opening the entire series up to new aspects and directions, mostly the gang element, but also that deeper understanding of their religion and spirituality, both of which have been inspired by real-world Paganism and goddesses. (Plus that touch of inspiration from sex magic near the end.)

In any event, Mayr and Tash changed everything about this series, from how it was being written to where it's going, and their story is far from finished. Their romance is a three-part tale, though they'll appear throughout the series. The second Mayr-Tash book is *Soulbound*, #4 in the series, while the very last book of the series will also be their last installment (that's a rather long time away!).

This book also did something else, though: it kicked off what's actually a trilogy inside the larger series. The next two books complete that trilogy, which ends up really throwing things for a spin where all of the characters and players are concerned. Things are going to get a bit darker and bumpier from here, some of which *Four* already touched on where Tash's past is concerned. Beware the angst. And the grime. And the descent into the darker parts of humanity.

And for anyone who's read both the first edition and this new one: thanks for coming back to it! I hope you've enjoyed this edition with the new scenes and other details woven in. I wanted to freshen up things in the beginning and introduce more of Mayr's world (and the Dahe guards), but I also wanted to add some things from Tash's perspective, just not too much. I still wanted Tash to keep his mystery while filling in blanks at the same time. Not only is he a complicated character, he's also one of the main characters in the series who constantly struggles with mental health issues (complex PTSS/PTSD and depression). I wanted to highlight them a little more in this edition and better connect it to what happens in the rest of the series. Hopefully it's given some valuable insight into Tash's side of things.

Before I sign off, some big buckets of thanks need to go around! This project couldn't have gotten anywhere without help from a wonderful team of folks who helped bring the first edition alive.

First, all my love and deepest thanks to Less Than Three Press for not only giving this story its first home, but also for the continued support after publication. Megan, Sam, and Sasha, you were amazing to work with and I'll always miss that. Thank you for all of your confidence and help! In all honestly, this series happened because of you, so going forward, *The Republic* still belongs to Less Than Three in spirit. I guess you could say that now, it might be a bit like one long love letter written in a dozen parts. Either way, thank you from the bottom of my heart. <3 <3 <3

Next, my heartfelt thank yous to Michelle Kelley for editing the first edition and to Raelynn Marie for the most beautiful map I was finally able to include! Many more thanks go to Natasha Snow for this OMG-IT'S-SO-GORGEOUS cover that still makes me want to cry really squishy, happy tears. It's just so perfect and I'll love it forever and ever. Thank you for making a dream cover come true!!

Special thanks also to my partner for sticking through this with me! It's been up, it's been down, and things can get weird, but thanks for being here in my corner. Love you! xoxoxo

And finally, but never least, *so many* thanks to you, readers! Thanks for picking this up and giving it a go, whether you're new to my work or a return reader. It's such a blessing to have you here, taking the time. <3

For more about what's coming in the series or about my other projects, stop by my website or find me on social media! (My links are on the very last page.) I love hearing from folks, so come on by and say hi.

Blessings and peace to you all,

Archer

Also by Archer Kay Leah

THE REPUBLIC SERIES
A Question of Counsel (The Republic, book 1)
Four (The Republic, book 2)
Blood Borne (The Republic, book 3)
Soulbound (The Republic, book 4)

NOVELS
For the Clan

NOVELLAS
Heart, Lace, and Soul
Of Kindred and Stardust

About The Republic Series

Welcome to *The Republic*, high fantasy romances for across the LGBTQA+ spectrum, where love, fight, and hope are at the very core, entwined with the lives of romantic partners, friends, and families... and maybe a few lifelong enemies, too. Come step into their world where games linger and foul play is afoot!

• • •

Democracy. Family. Loyalty. Honour.
The perfect system.

Freedom. Belonging. Unity.
The perfect illusion.

With the right people and the right price, the Republic of Kattal can be brought to its knees.

Peace and security are never a guarantee when greed and lies threaten the balance. Fear and control know no bounds; and sacred tenets don't keep the monsters away. The right to choose can be a nightmare.

But for every line crossed, someone waits on the other side, ready to push back.

In justice, there is wisdom. In wisdom, there is protection. In it all, there is love. Maybe it means saving a village; maybe it means saving someone you can't live without. Sometimes it's just about doing the right thing and learning to love yourself.

Magic may lurk in the shadows.
Crime may never sleep.
But love doesn't back down.

About the Author

Archer Kay Leah was raised in Canada, growing up in a port town at a time when it was starting to become more diverse, both visibly and vocally. Combined with the variety of interests found in Archer's family and the never-ending need to be creative, this diversity inspired a love for toying with characters and their relationships, exploring new experiences and difficult situations.

Archer most enjoys writing speculative fiction and is engaged in a very particular love affair with fantasy, especially when it is dark and emotionally charged. When not reading and writing for work or play, Archer is a geek with too many hobbies and keeps busy with other creative endeavors, a music addiction, and whatever else comes along. Archer lives in London, Ontario with a non-binary partner who loves video games, composing music, and all things out there in the vast space of the universe.

Website: archerkayleah.wordpress.com
Goodreads: goodreads.com/ArcherKayLeah
Facebook: facebook.com/ArcherKayLeah
Twitter: twitter.com/archerkayleah